SPICE

SPICE

SERESSIA GLASS

HEAT | NEW YORK

THE BERKLEY PUBLISHING GROUP
Published by the Penguin Group
Penguin Group (USA) LLC
375 Hudson Street, New York, New York 10014

USA • Canada • UK • Ireland • Australia • New Zealand • India • South Africa • China

penguin.com

A Penguin Random House Company

This book is an original publication of The Berkley Publishing Group.

Library of Congress Cataloging-in-Publication

Glass, Seressia.
Spice / Seressia Glass. — Heat trade paperback edition.
p. cm.
ISBN 978-0-425-27509-2 (paperback)
1. Confectioners—Fiction. 2. College teachers—Fiction. I. Title.
PS3557.L345S65 2014
813'.54—dc23
2014012892

PUBLISHING HISTORY
Heat trade paperback edition / November 2014

PRINTED IN THE UNITED STATES OF AMERICA

10 9 8 7 6 5 4 3 2 1

Cover photograph by Regina Wamba / Ninestock.com.
Text design by Kelly Lipovich.

To my husband, Larry, for your love and inspiration and support. I couldn't do it without you. Thanks for being a part of my life.

ACKNOWLEDGMENTS

I have so many wonderful people to thank for helping me with this story from genesis to completion. My agent, Jenny Bent, and everyone at the Bent Agency—you are all amazing to this neurotic writer. To my editor, Cindy Hwang, and the staff at Berkley—thanks for making my story even better. I'd also like to thank the Friday Night Writes crew and the ladies of the Mastermind Writers Group—I'm grateful to be connected to such a wonderful group of supportive and inspiring people.

Finally, to anyone suffering through addiction: If you're ready, there is help out there. You don't have to endure it alone.

ONE

"Girlfriend's working a new 'do, I see," Audie slyly observed as Nadia joined her friends at the café table. "Anything we should know?"

The other two women—Vanessa Longfellow and Nadia's business partner, Siobhan Malloy—looked at her in expectation. "I felt like a change, is all," Nadia told them, one hand reaching for her hair. She'd paid the stylist more money than she felt comfortable spending post-Hollywood, but couldn't deny the results. Her no-nonsense ponytail was gone, replaced by a shoulder-length layered cut with streaks of burgundy and copper highlighting the dark brown.

"Uh-huh," Siobhan said. "You suddenly felt like a change. Anything to do with that anniversary we just celebrated?"

"Thanks, Siobhan." Nadia rolled her eyes. Yeah, she'd just celebrated her fourth "birthday"—four years being drug free—but she was also staring thirty in the face like a deer caught in headlights. These women made it bearable: Siobhan "Sugar" Malloy, the best business partner a girl could want, and Audie and Vanessa, two women she hadn't known six months ago. She'd met them for the first time when she and Siobhan had decided to keep the café open late on Tuesday nights as a meeting place for a variety of support groups. It didn't matter what the person had survived—burnout, divorce, abusive relationships, or, in Siobhan's and Nadia's case, drug addiction—all were welcome. It quickly became a necessary component of their week, a guaranteed time to decompress and talk about anything.

"I just think it's time," she finally said. "Time for a fresh start, a fresh look."

"Which can only mean one thing!" Vanessa exclaimed. "Our girl's ready to wade into the dating pool again."

"About time you decide to put yourself out there." Siobhan sipped her tea, her blue-gray eyes sparkling. "You're too young to be a nun."

"So are you, partner," Nadia shot back. "Especially with all those studs at your burlesque shows standing around with their tongues hanging out like a pack of dogs fighting over a juicy steak."

"Yeah." Siobhan snorted. "A thirty-five-year-old steak."

"Like they care when they see that smoking-hot bod you've got." Nadia shook her head. "Anyway, I don't think there was anything wrong with being married to the job for a little while. We had to focus on getting Sugar and Spice off the ground. It was worth all the time, blood, sweat, and tears we put into it."

"Damn right, it was." Audie waved her peanut butter and bacon muffin. "This is the best damn thing I've ever eaten, and it doesn't even have chocolate in it!"

"No one's saying it wasn't," Siobhan said. "We did what we had to do to make this place a success. I think it's okay to ease up a little bit now. And I definitely think it's time for you to have a relationship."

"No! No." Nadia waved her hands. "Sex, yes. Relationship, no. I want the feels without all the drama. Like a male escort."

Vanessa, the proper one of the bunch, narrowed her eyes. "You do know that's illegal, right?"

"Geesh, guys, I'm not stupid. I'm not looking for danger, but I'm not looking for true love either. I don't even believe it exists. I just think it's time for me, for all of us, to think about what makes us happy on multiple levels and take some time to pursue it. If we get a little something-something in the meantime, that's just gravy."

"You've obviously been thinking about this a lot," Siobhan remarked. "So spill the secrets you saw in the tea leaves."

Nadia ignored the sarcasm. "Yeah, I have been thinking. My track record with relationships sucks. The best one I've ever had was with my therapist, and all I did was talk his ear off for an hour every week. How messed up is that?"

She sighed. "So, no to relationships. But sex? Bring it on. The wilder the better."

A wicked glint lit Audie's eyes. At twenty-five, she was the youngest and most sexually liberated of them, sometimes overly so, which was why she'd joined their Tuesday night group. "So you want to let your freak flag fly? I betcha you can find a couple of college boys who'll step up for fun sexy-times. I could hook you up."

"No!" Siobhan and Vanessa said together. Vanessa put a hand on Audie's forearm. "No offense, *chica*, but your taste in men needs an upgrade. Nadia doesn't need a douche bag for this."

Nadia laughed at Audie's outraged expression. "No boys, no

matter the stamina," she clarified. "I want a man. A man who's into more than vanilla sex. A man who will bend me over the sofa a time or two."

"Go on, girl." They leaned in closer.

Nadia's voice rose. "I want a man who knows that *The Perfumed Garden* isn't a boutique in the mall."

"Preach it!"

"I want a man with a cock that should be classified as a weapon of mass seduction."

"I know that's right!"

"I want a man who doesn't freak out when you successfully hit the male version of the G-spot while sucking him dry."

"Okay already! We got it. God." Vanessa swallowed some of her iced tea, then peered into the glass. "I think I need some Long Island in this tea now."

"Sorry, Nessa." Nadia smiled at the group. "You know I've just had my imagination and my B.O.B. for the last few years, and there's only so much the battery-operated boyfriend can do. I'm ready for more. I'm going to get my happy on, dammit. And right now, being happy means no more goody-two-shoes."

"Here's to no more goody-two-shoes." Siobhan raised her glass. "At least when it comes to sex."

The others raised their cups and mugs and echoed her. "At least when it comes to sex!"

"Okay, I have a question," Audie said as she set her mug down. "What's this *Perfumed Garden* stuff? I mean, it really does sound like a store in the mall."

"It's not." Nadia pushed her bangs back. "It's basically an Arabic erotic text from the sixteenth century or so. Kinda like the *Kama Sutra*."

"So, Nadia." Vanessa's smile was completely predatory as the other women sipped their drinks. "Got anyone in particular on your radar?"

"At the moment, no one." Nadia cut her eyes at Vanessa, wondering at the sly grin that curved her lips. "I just made my mind up to jump into this. You know that."

"All righty, then." Vanessa rubbed her hands together. "I'll make a suggestion."

"It's not somebody Audie's dated, is it?"

"I don't think so. What about the professor over there?" Vanessa tossed her chin toward the front windows, where they had several plush chairs and side tables set aside for those who liked to linger. A dark-haired man sat in one of the chairs, a tablet in one hand. He came in often, becoming a regular over the last few weeks, always ordering a matcha tea latte and a sticky bun.

"He's a professor?" Nadia asked Vanessa, who also taught at Herscher University, the research institution that the town of Crimson Bay had been built around.

"He is. Dr. Kaname Sullivan is his name. I think he more than meets your requirements, based on what I've heard."

They all leaned closer to Vanessa. "What have you heard?" Siobhan asked.

Vanessa blotted at her lips with a delicate pat of her napkin. How the bronze-skinned woman managed to eat and drink without marring her plum lipstick was a skill Nadia admired and envied. "He teaches human sexuality, and his classes are always packed. Almost all the students—the female ones, at least—call him Professor Sex. Apparently he practices what he teaches."

"Really." Audie's voice had a purr to it, like a lazy cat deciding it was time to go hunting.

Vanessa shot Audie a quelling glance. "Sheathe your claws, missy," she ordered, before turning back to Nadia. "He became a household name after consulting on a high-profile sexual predator case down in Los Angeles. He's written a couple of successful nonfiction books and consulted with the FBI on some of their more twisted cases."

"Wow." Nadia sat back. "Sounds impressive." *And way out of my league.*

Vanessa grinned. "More than that, I think he's interested in you."

"What?" Nadia spluttered into her iced latte. "I don't know what you're talking about."

"I think you do," Vanessa said in that cultured voice of hers. "He's been in here every day we have. In the same spot. And he hasn't taken a bite of that sticky bun in two minutes. That's suspicious enough right there."

Nadia refrained from looking at the man in question again. She remembered the first day he'd come into the café. He'd been upset about something—his tie partially undone, his thick hair mussed as if he'd ran his fingers through it repeatedly. She'd pointed him at a chair then brought him the sweet bun and green tea latte without asking him for his preference. He'd taken it, tasted it, and instantly transformed his mood. The smile he'd given her as he'd thanked her had elevated him from nice-looking to handsome, but that had been as far as she'd allowed herself to go back then. Now, though, was a different story.

Maybe the professor had earned his nickname. Still, there was a vast difference in being an expert *on* sex and an expert *at* sex. She darted a quick glance at the man in question, currently pretending to thumb through his tablet. Good-looking in a geeky sort of way, he seemed to be a mix of Asian and European with thick, swept-back dark hair and a goatee framing his angular face, his eyes hidden behind wire-rimmed glasses. Dressed in a navy blazer, pale blue shirt, and khakis, he was definitely not her usual type, though lately she hadn't had a type at all.

She shook her head. "I don't know."

Audie bit into her muffin, suppressing a moan of pleasure. "Come on, Nadia. You just declared your sexual reawakening. You can't chicken out now. Especially if you can get with Professor Sex."

"I'm not chickening out. I just . . ." Her voice faded as she looked at the professor again. This time he looked back. She blinked. *Whoa.*

The intensity of his gaze stifled her breath and pulled her in. Everything else fell away as their gazes locked and held. She could read challenge and command in his midnight eyes even though his glasses partially concealed them. He'd gone from geeky to gawddamn in five seconds, and her body instinctively responded, her nipples pebbling, her core clenching. Damn, it had been too long since she'd gotten laid, and she was ready, so very ready. If Professor Sex offered, she'd have to take him up on it.

He raised an eyebrow, and her breath shortened. Then he smiled, and it was so sensual, so full of promise, that she had to shift in her chair. Oh yeah, he was definitely offering. And she was definitely going to accept.

"Earth to Nadia. Come in, Nadia."

Siobhan waved a hand in front of her eyes, breaking the mesmerizing hold Sullivan had on her. She blinked, surprised to find her friends all staring at her with matching grins. "What?"

"You know what." Her partner laughed as she pushed Nadia out of her chair. "Professor Sex is waiting on you to check him out. Go get him."

———

Busted.

Kane flipped through files on his tablet to cover his chagrin. The muffin-lover had nailed him perfectly. He'd been biding his time, studying his target, playing on his unobtrusiveness while waiting for the right moment to make his move. Thanks to the redhead, he had to make his move now. At least the afternoon crowd had thinned out, limiting the witnesses to Nadia's friends.

Nadia Spiceland. He'd wanted her ever since he'd entered the café angry over something or someone he couldn't remember. She'd pointed him to a quiet corner then brought over a pastry of some sort and a cup of tea, a strong, bitter matcha that had reminded him of his mother. That, combined with the scent of baked goods and premium coffee, had calmed him down almost instantly, and one bite into the pastry had made him a goner. Nadia's heart-shaped face, the ready smile on her full lips, and the way she remembered all the regulars had completely won him over. The sweet curve of her hips and high, full breasts only added to her allure. He wanted her for all that she was and for all the things she wasn't: a student, faculty, shy, or married.

He wanted her because the look in her eyes challenged him, dared him to try to please her. He'd gone hard hearing her sexual declaration, need gripping him at the image of handling her smooth curves, bending her over a couch and fucking her until they were both too tired to stand. He wanted to feel her gripping him, milking him until he was empty. He just wanted her, period.

He gathered his things, then stood with resolve. So, sweet Nadia

Spiceland was free and on the prowl. And most importantly, didn't want vanilla sex. Good to know. He didn't do vanilla either.

"Hi, Professor Sullivan." Nadia gave him her best professional smile as she met him at the counter. She'd always called him "sir" before, and he'd seen no reason to correct that. "Did you enjoy the bun?"

"I think by now you can call me Kaname, or Kane," he said, trying not to stare at her T-shirt. It looked to be a size or two too small considering the way it hugged her more-than-a-handful breasts and allowed her belly button to peek from beneath the hem. It bore the café's strategically placed logo, two pin-up style female chefs sitting on the name Sugar and Spice, with the tag line, "Everything nice!"

He gave her a smile as he handed over a twenty. "I always enjoy your buns."

"Ah, oh." She grew flustered as she worked the register. "Well, I guess that's why you're a repeat customer, right?"

"It's one of the reasons." He nodded, then grinned with true appreciation. "No matter what mood I'm in, you seem to have just what I need."

She dropped his change on the floor. He smiled as he heard her friends giggling at the table behind him.

He leaned over the counter, staring at the line of her back beneath the chocolate-colored T-shirt, the luscious curve of her butt emphasized by the tight low-rise jeans. Damn, he wanted to get his palms on that ass, lick every indentation of her spine. "By the way, I don't like vanilla either."

She straightened with a snap, her cinnamon brown eyes deer-in-the-headlights wide. "What?"

"I heard you say that you don't like vanilla. Neither do I."

Her mouth worked silently for a moment. "You . . . don't?"

"Don't get me wrong, vanilla done well can be extremely satisfying. But there's nothing wrong with a little spice, some variety, extra flavor on the tongue. Don't you think?"

She had his change in a death grip, her head down. When she looked at him again, a wicked, challenging light shone in her gaze. He was in trouble.

"I definitely believe in variety being the spice of life, Professor," she said, her voice low and husky. "It's why I make sure I offer a little something extra for every taste."

Let's see how far she'll go, he thought. He leaned forward, dropping his voice to match hers. "I'd like to sample more of what you have to offer."

Her nipples pebbled as he watched. He reflexively licked his lips, his hands curling against the edge of the counter in an effort to resist touching her. He had to remind himself that he was civilized, educated, a world traveler, cultured. One did not throw a woman over one's shoulder to find the nearest flat surface in a public place. But he wanted to. Oh, how he wanted to.

He forced his gaze back to her face, just in time to see a dimple sprout on her left cheek. "Are you serious?"

"Absolutely. Would you be willing to set up a taste test?"

Her gaze roamed over him, then her lips pursed in what he steadfastly believed was approval. "Are we still talking about desserts?"

"Absolutely not."

The table behind him was silent as a grave. He saw her eyes dart to her friends, then back to him.

"A taste test, huh?" She arched a brow. "I suppose you're going to try to convince me that you have a sophisticated tongue, capable of handling whatever I decide to offer up for this test?"

He reached out, his hand covering hers. "I think my tongue and I can handle whatever you're willing to dish out."

Her dark eyes widened with surprise, then darkened with pleasure. "All right then. How about tonight?" She handed over his change. "I can meet you at Pascal's, and we can see what happens."

He took his time taking the money, fingers stroking her palm. "I'll meet you there at seven. Should I bring my copy?"

"Your copy of what?"

"*The Perfumed Garden.* It's more than archaic descriptions and colorful language, you know."

She blinked at him. "Are you for real?"

"You'll find out soon enough, right? See you later."

As Sullivan strolled out of the café, he heard one of the women mutter, "Damn. Anybody got some tequila?"

TWO

"I'm so freakin' nervous!"

Nadia stood in the center of her bedroom in the two-story condo she owned above the café. It had seemed like a great idea at the time, since she had basically lived and breathed her job for the last three years, getting up early to prepare baked goods for the breakfast rush. Now she wondered about the logistics of having a lover over for sexy-times while her employees worked below.

Of course, she had to get to the sexy-times part first.

Five minutes after Sullivan had left the café, Nadia's friends had taken her in hand, determined to get her ready for her date. Other than her new haircut, Nadia hadn't done much beyond the basics with her appearance—when you spent every day elbow-deep in dough, manicures were an unnecessary extravagance. It was also woefully apparent that, besides a few outfits she cycled through when hanging out with her friends, she had nothing to wear on a date and certainly nothing she could wear to upscale Pascal's. Siobhan had sprung into action, taking charge and smoothing the way as she had since the day they'd met in rehab. At thirty-five, Siobhan had the body of a buxom twenty-five-year-old, and her golden blonde hair, creamy fair skin, and cornflower blue eyes made students and businessmen alike stop dead in their tracks when she worked the front of the café. Her looks also made her extremely popular when she performed as "Sugar" Malloy with her burlesque troupe. She was truly the sugar to Nadia's brunette, brown-eyed, peachy-skinned spice.

"You have a right to be nervous," Siobhan told her, laying three different dresses out on the bed. "It's your first date in more than four years. Take it from me, though. I don't think you have anything to worry about with Professor Sex, except for deciding which dress to wear."

Nadia surveyed her choices, all borrowed from Siobhan and Vanessa. Nothing in her closet was even close to their impeccable taste since she'd jettisoned or sold off everything related to her time in LA in the equivalent of a bridge burning to ensure no ties remained to her previous life. The first option was a retro red polka dot sundress with a sweetheart neckline and a full skirt possessing a definite rockabilly vibe, totally Siobhan's style. The second dress was a sleeveless, formfitting knee-skimming number in black sure to emphasize every curve and roll from her boobs to her butt but perfectly suited for Vanessa's svelte figure. The third dress was a teal number with thin braided straps and a plunging neckline that led to a fitted waist before softly draping into a just-above-the-knee skirt. It was simple but pretty, and was sure to complement the warm golden tones of her skin. Nadia liked it the best, but she was afraid it would make her look like she was going to prom instead of on a feeler date for a lover.

Then again, the combination of innocent dress and salacious

intent seemed appropriate. "The red would be great if we were going to see one of your burlesque shows, so I'm crossing that one off the list," Nadia said, thinking out loud. "And the black is just too intimidating. I'm a little too soft in the middle to do it justice and I'm not putting on Spanx when there's a possibility of getting some tonight."

"The teal it is, then." Siobhan slipped it off the hanger, then helped Nadia into it. After adjusting the choker-style collar, Siobhan stood back and observed her. "The good professor is going to lose his mind."

Nadia stared at her reflection and had to agree. The dress was slightly loose in the bodice but actually emphasized the curve of her bust and made her waist seem smaller. Siobhan had done some makeup magic on her too, making Nadia's eyes dark and smoky. She looked confident, sexy, ready for anything.

"I owe you big-time, Sugar. If this goes well, I might even let you take me shopping."

"I get to drag you shopping?" Her partner grinned. "The professor better deliver or we're going to have words. Got condoms?"

Nadia picked up her clutch. "Yep."

"Got cash and credit?"

"That too."

"Got your phone and driver's license in case the sex is so good you forget your name and where you live?"

Nadia laughed. "If all goes well, we're coming back here. The good professor already knows where I live and work, and besides, there's nothing like home-field advantage. I'm in control here." She'd need that control too. At least until Professor Sex proved he was worth losing control to.

———

Nadia handed her MINI Cooper off to the valet then headed up the steps to Pascal's entrance, trying to quell the nervous fluttering in her stomach. She'd picked the nouveau cuisine eatery to meet the professor because she'd heard it had a live band, good tapas, and better cocktails, and the only college-age people were the wait-staff. If this initial sortie with the professor went well, she wouldn't want to fill up on dinner. And if it didn't go well, a chocolate martini beat a pint of rocky road ice cream any day.

She still had her doubts about Professor Kaname Sullivan being the one she needed. The double entendres had been fun, but could the man follow through? Would he even show up?

The restaurant's glass door swung open. She thanked the hostess, and then looked up, stopping dead in the doorway.

Damn. The professor sure cleaned up well. Gleaming dress shoes, loose black trousers and jacket, and a cobalt blue dress shirt showed off his lanky physique and golden skin to perfection. The ambient light caused strands of his dark hair to gleam, making her want to thrust her hands deep into the thick waves. The glasses gave him a Superman double whammy of geeky-sexy but did nothing to blunt the heat in his gaze. Tonight the goatee made him devilish, or maybe that had more to do with the knowing, sensual twist of his lips.

This was not the professor. This was a dangerous man.

"Nadia." He took her hand then kissed her cheek in greeting as if they were old friends and not potential lovers. Then he stepped back, and the toe-to-head perusal left no doubt in Nadia's mind that he liked what he saw. "You look amazing."

She smoothed a hand down the silk skirt. She'd lived in jeans and sneakers for years getting the café off the ground, and being in a dress this nice after so long was hard. Seeing Sullivan's reaction made her glad she'd gone through the effort of prettying up and slipping into something a little more upscale.

And with the right incentive, she could slip right out of it too.

"You're a beautiful woman, Nadia," he said after a long moment. "In this dress or those fantastic jeans you were in earlier."

She felt her brow wrinkle. "You thought my jeans were better than this dress?"

"Don't get me wrong. You're breathtaking in that dress. But those jeans . . . When you bent over to pick up my change, I just about lost my mind. Lucky for me, my jacket covered most of my reaction."

"Thank you. That's good to know since my wardrobe is just about all jeans." *Most of his reaction?* She'd wanted to check out his junk back at the café, but couldn't figure out a way to do it that wouldn't have been obvious.

His grin told her that he knew exactly what she was thinking. "You live in a town sitting by the ocean. You can't tell me you don't own a swimsuit or two."

She laughed. "That's a requirement of living here, isn't it? Beachwear, boards, and blonde highlights?"

He gestured to his dark waves. "Two out of three ain't bad."

The hostess smiled at them. "Your table's ready. If you'll follow me, please?"

"Shall we?" Kane's hand settled on the small of her back then froze as he realized there was nothing but bare skin beneath his fingers. His fingertips did a slow glide down her spine before settling just above her waist, leaving a trail of heat in their wake. Her girly parts went all giddy from the contact, her breath catching at the stroke of his thumb along her spine. A good girl would have pulled away. She pressed into his hand instead.

The hostess guided them to an intimate table tucked into a quiet corner of the restaurant away from the jazz ensemble. Kane seated her like a proper gentleman, and then took his time taking his chair. *Don't look, girl, don't look—okay, maybe just a peek.* She brushed an imaginary wisp of hair out of her eyes as she surreptitiously scoped out his package. Damn loose-fitting slacks.

"Do I pass inspection?" he asked, shooting another grin her way.

"So far, so good." She looked around the restaurant, needing a distraction from his mesmerizing gaze. Pascal's had an Old World vibe, wine-colored brocade and dark wood, tiny jewel-toned oil lamps on the tables, rich burgundy tablecloths. "Do you get out to the beach often?"

"Not as much as I'd like to, but my condo has a decent view of the bay. With the right incentive—say, seeing a certain brunette playing volleyball in a bikini—I'd make more of an effort."

Nadia laughed, relaxing. "If you're challenging me to a game of volleyball, I accept."

Their waiter arrived and recited the night's specials. Nadia ordered a pomegranate martini, Sullivan a glass of red wine. As the waiter left, Sullivan raised an eyebrow at her. "So if I win our game of volleyball, what do I get?"

Nadia held up a hand. "Slow your roll, Professor. It's still too cool out on the bay for volleyball on the beach, especially if you want me to play in a bikini. Besides, I'd have an unfair advantage over you, since you'd be too busy staring at my high beams to hit the ball."

He laughed, the sound rich and warm. "True enough, especially considering the heavenly nature of said high beams." He reached over, clasped her hand. "Do you think you can dispense with the *professor* stuff? I'm not at work and you're not a student. Do you want me to call you Spiceland? Or Chef?"

Visions of *South Park* danced in her head. "God, no."

His thumb stroked over her knuckles. "I could call you Spice, if you like. It fits you."

His smile needed to be registered as a lethal weapon. "I'd rather you call me Nadia."

"Nadia." He said her name as if he tasted a fine wine, rolling it around in his mouth. "Is that from the Russian?"

"Yes. It means *hope*. Daddy Vic's mother was from Russia, and she'd hoped for a loving, happy life for my parents and me."

His brow furrowed. "You call your father Daddy Vic?"

"I have two fathers, Nicholas and Victor Spiceland. They had me and my two older brothers through a surrogate. They're about to celebrate forty years together."

"It sounds like your grandmother's wish came true then." He cupped his wine, warming it in his hand. "You can call me Kane, which is short for Kaname."

"Kane." It suited him, strong, a bite of a word. "Kaname is Japanese, right?"

He nodded. "It means *vital point*. My mother is Japanese."

"And Sullivan?"

"My dad is Irish. He's a foot taller than my mom is, but there's no doubt she rules that relationship. They met in Singapore, had me in Hong Kong, and now live outside of Seattle."

"Wow, you're a veritable international male. How did you end up in Crimson Bay?"

"I love Seattle, but I also like sunshine. Outside of lecturing, I do on-demand profiling work with law enforcement agencies up and down the coast, and Crimson Bay is centrally located and laid back enough to suit my tastes and inspire me to write. Besides, Herscher University has a renowned Human Sexualities Studies program. Are you from here?"

Nadia drew a slow breath, captivated by the way he stroked her hand and focused on her as if no one else surrounded them. "I grew up in Sacramento and San Francisco until I decided to go to culinary school. Then I studied with pastry chefs in Paris, chocolatiers in Belgium, and finally landed a gig in Los Angeles."

Their drinks arrived. Kane asked the waiter to return in a few minutes, and then focused on her again. "So why move here from Los Angeles?"

She fiddled with the stem of her glass, and then gave him a direct stare. "After getting out of rehab a few years ago, Siobhan and I decided we needed out of LA. She has family not far from here, and my folks are less than a two-hour car ride away. So we came here, sank all our money into the café, and finally we're doing all right."

He stared at her a long moment. She stared back, daring him to stay, daring him to get up and walk out. She wasn't ashamed of her past, not really. If anything, she was ashamed of how long it took to get help and all the people she'd hurt before getting that help.

He squeezed her hand. "And now you're wondering if I'm going to cut and run or ply you with questions you don't want to answer."

She blew out a breath. "Something like that, yeah."

"I won't. I just have one question."

She sat back. "Go ahead."

"It wasn't alcohol, was it?" He canted his head toward her martini.

"No. Painkillers and sleeping pills, sometimes harder stuff."

"All right then." He released her hand long enough to take a sip of his wine, giving her an opportunity to taste her martini. She hadn't had alcohol since they'd celebrated the opening of the café, and she needed to pace herself. Besides, Kane was doing a good job of making her light-headed and intoxicated on his own.

"Kane. Are you sure you want to do this?"

"Have drinks with a beautiful woman? Of course."

"Thank you, but that wasn't what I meant." She waved a hand between them. "I mean this. Are you sure you want to take me on?"

"Very sure. Why wouldn't I be?"

"Because of my story." She leaned forward, watching his eyes as his gaze dropped to her breasts, then back up to her face without apology. "I gave you the highlight reel, but everything you need to know about me, good or bad, you can uncover with a good Google search. Probably more than my therapist knows."

He raised his gaze to hers. "Call me old-fashioned, but I prefer to get to know my partners by actually talking to them. Face-to-face. I don't believe everything I read on the Internet, and people tend to be less evasive when they're one-on-one."

Nadia shook her head. "So you're saying I shouldn't search for you online either?"

"It depends on whether you're curious about my professional reputation or my sexual one." He leaned closer. "I'm perfectly aware of my nickname. I'm sure your friends and part-timers have talked your ear off about Professor Sex."

Her brows lifted. "Are you saying you didn't earn it?"

"No." He gave her a slow smile that liquefied her insides. "I lecture on sex. I write about sex. I create profiles for law enforcement based on sex. And I'm not ashamed to admit that I like having sex. A lot of sex, a lot of different ways." One finger tapped the table-cloth. "But I don't have sex with my students, despite the number of blogs to the contrary."

She sighed. She couldn't help it. The man knew what he was doing with all that allure and confidence. "Just so you know, I didn't do a Web search on you. I didn't have to. Not with the friends I have. They were so eager to tell me all about Professor Sex, despite my every attempt to deflect them."

"Why deflect them?"

"I want to make up my own mind about you. They're not your potential bed buddies, I am." She raised a brow. "You haven't slept with any of them, have you?"

"No." His smiled widened.

"Why are you grinning like that?"

"Because you called yourself my potential bed buddy. That's a step in the right direction. Means I'm doing something right."

"I'd say you are. Maybe it's time to step it up." She reached into her clutch.

"Oh?"

"I have something for you," she said, then slid her hand across the table. Kane's hand wrapped around hers, large and warm with a pulse of pure masculine energy that snaked up her arm and then raced right to her ovaries. He slipped the device from her fingers. His eyebrows rose as he recognized the wireless remote for a vibrator, the business end of which she'd tucked into her thong. A slow, sexy smile curved his lips.

"Nadia Spiceland, you are full of surprises," he murmured. "Shall I tell you what this means?"

The deep tenor of his voice, combined with the knowing way he held the remote, caused her pussy to cream in anticipation. "Yes, please do."

"Giving me this is a test. Actually, a challenge," he said as he leaned forward. "You said you're not into vanilla anymore, so this means you're willing to give up control—control of your pleasure, your body, your orgasms."

He thumbed the dial, sending a quick pulse of sensation to her clit before turning it off again with an efficient flick of his thumb. "But you don't want to surrender to just anyone, do you? You want to make sure that the other person is worth it. Worth you, worth receiving what you have to give."

"Damn ri—" Her voice cut off as he thumbed the dial again, increasing the intensity of the vibrations to its strongest setting. She gripped the edge of the table, trying to resist the urge to squirm as the pleasure built. Quickly.

He turned the remote off, then set it down, precisely lining it up with his dinner knife. "You're topping from the bottom," he observed, watching her with those deep, dark eyes. "I like it."

"Are you sure?" she questioned. She wanted to cede control, needed to in this one thing. From her teens, she'd rigorously managed her actions and choices. Having discipline gave her the chance to hone her skills with some great but demanding pastry chefs in Europe and bring that knowledge home. Losing control had cost her a career and a very comfortable lifestyle.

Yes, regaining control had gotten her to the level of comfort and success she currently enjoyed. Sometimes though, sometimes she just really wanted someone else to make decisions for her, to take her out of her head, at least in this one area of her life. Finding the right guy she could trust enough to surrender to sexually was a fantasy she hadn't thought she'd allow to come true.

Yet here she was with Kaname Sullivan, the professor and author known as Professor Sex, offering to give her what she wanted, the way she wanted it. If she wanted it enough.

Again that smile, the one that transformed him from professor to predator. No wonder his students were ninety percent female. "I said I like it, not that I'd allow it to continue."

She flared at that, but subsided as soon as he put a finger on the remote. "As soon as I pass your test, and I have every intention of passing it, you will surrender to me. When you do, I will make sure that you experience all the pleasure you can handle, whether it's acting out scenes from *The Perfumed Garden* or anything else we decide on."

She sat back, vacillating between curiosity and caution. "You're that confident of your talents?"

"I'm confident of wanting you. I'm confident that you're curious enough to dare, and daring enough to put your pleasure in my hands."

The boldness of his words and the frank desire in his gaze heated her insides. She almost asked him to turn on the remote, but the waiter chose that moment to return for their food order. "What do you say to just ordering tapas?"

"I think that's a good idea. No worries about overindulging, at least in food. Allow me?" He thumbed on the controller to its lowest setting.

She bit her lip to keep from moaning as Kane calmly consulted with the waiter then ordered a variety of little plates, all the while discreetly working the mini controller. From the lightest of touches to full out, he had her pussy juicing, her blood rushing, her breath catching. Yet he somehow seemed to know when one second more would push her over the edge, and stopped the vibration altogether.

"You're playing dirty!" she gasped as the waiter left after giving her a curious look.

"Have to level the playing field somehow." He smiled, placing the controller beside his wineglass.

"What do you mean, 'level the playing field'? Seems like you're the one with the advantage here."

"You think so?" He thumbed the dial to a medium setting. She blew out a breath and shifted on her chair as a soft vibration thrummed between her thighs. "I can do this and you can get through it without attracting too much attention. But I have no relief in sight. Everyone's going to know that I have a problem as soon as I stand up."

"Does that bother you?" she gasped.

"Hell, no." He thumbed the setting off. "With you looking as hot as you do, I'm sure there are several other men here in the same predicament."

"Thanks." She fought to keep from squirming again. Damn, she was majorly horny. Would she be able to convince him to progress from talk to action?

He turned on the stimulator's remote control again, snagging her attention. She took a deep breath, and his eyes immediately dropped to her cleavage. Something close to a curse slipped softly from his lips as he turned the power off. "The way your lips parted has me thinking of things best not shared in a crowded restaurant," he admitted ruefully. "I need a distraction. So, *The Perfumed Garden of Sensual Delights*. How did you get interested in an Arabic sex manual from the Middle Ages? I would have thought the *Kama Sutra* or the *Joy of Sex* would be more to your liking."

"I like those too, but I discovered *The Perfumed Garden* during a world literature course in college." She sipped her drink, growing more heated by watching the way he watched her lips. "I like the name, and I find it amusing how the Burton translation is so much more over the top than the original. But I still like the feelings of sensual mystery and discovery it evokes."

"Sensual mystery and discovery." His voice dropped to a low, sensual rumble that made her sex clench. "Like tonight."

"Yes." Hmm, maybe she wouldn't have to try too hard after all. "So, I'm guessing you know a lot about *The Perfumed Garden*?"

He stared at her over the top of the remote. "I do indeed, among other things. It takes material from other sexual treatises that were available during the time, most notably from India, and adds stories as illustrations on some of the methods and treatments it recommends. Do you have a favorite part?"

She held her breath, but he didn't turn the vibrator on. Bastard. "Being a college coed, of course I was focused on chapter six, 'Concerning Everything That Is Favorable to the Act of Coition,' and I thought it would be fun to actually try out those positions. I'm too modern a woman to do more than shake my head at some of the descriptions."

"Oh, you mean like the qualities of a perfect woman?" Capturing and holding her gaze, he thumbed the remote to a low setting. "The sheik said, 'Then the Almighty has plunged woman into a sea of splendours, of voluptuousness, and of delights, and covered her with precious vestments, with brilliant girdles and provoking smiles. So let us praise and exalt him who has created woman and her beauties, with her appetizing flesh; who has given her hails, a beautiful figure, a bosom with breasts which are swelling, and amorous ways, which awaken desires.' You are definitely appetizing, Nadia Spiceland."

He cut the device off then smiled at her, just smiled, and she was ready to take him to the floor. Or grab him and leave. She opened her mouth to suggest it but the waiter chose that moment to arrive with their appetizers. Who knew tapas could be prepared that fast? She tried not to glare daggers at the poor waiter. It wasn't his fault that she'd given control of her clit to a professor with a sadistic streak. She reached for her water as the waiter placed everything then quickly retreated.

"You are an evil man."

His dark eyes twinkled. "Only in the best of ways. And you're enjoying every moment of it."

She was, she realized. Being away from the café, all dressed up, with a man so different from her usual type was making for a most excellent evening. Still, it wouldn't do for Kane to be too confident. She needed to turn the tables, even the score.

She reached for one of the appetizers, something with a bit of sautéed shrimp on top. Biting into it, she let out a moan as the flavors exploded on her tongue, her eyes sliding shut to enhance the tastes. "Oh, that is so good!"

"Nadia."

Her eyes popped open. Kane stared at her, his jaw clenched, his eyes burning. "Are you okay?"

"No." He shook his head. "I'm not okay. I just realized sitting here watching you eat is self-inflicted torture. How are you with desserts?"

"Eating them? Damn good. I'm even better at making them." She smiled as she forked up a bite of another appetizer. His gaze focused on her lips, and she slowly withdrew the fork from her mouth, teasing him. "I test and taste every recipe I create, and if I don't like it, I don't make it. What about you? I bet you've got wide-ranging tastes."

"The more I learn about the world, the more I learn about myself. So yes, my tastes are all over the board. Some people couldn't handle it. Do you think you can?" He turned on the controller again, his thumb working the intensity level from soft to full out, over and over.

She closed her eyes and gripped the edge of the table as her pussy juiced. "I sure as hell want to find out." Just a little longer . . .

The vibrator stopped. Her eyes popped open. Kane gave her an unapologetic smile. "Not yet. You need to eat, to keep your strength up for later."

She gritted her teeth. "Clit teaser."

"Sorry," he said in a tone that said he clearly wasn't. "I just want my cock in you and not a vibrator when I see you come for the first time. Is that wrong of me?"

His directness left her breathless. "N-no, but if you think we're going there without condoms . . ."

"I believe in being safe," he told her, "and that means no jumping without a parachute. I'm not a man-ho by any definition, but I do get tested regularly. I'm clean."

"I'm not a ho either," she said, trying not to sputter out her martini over the way he'd said *man-ho*. "After getting out of rehab, I got tested six ways to Sunday to prove that I was clean on multiple levels. I still get tested every year on my anniversary date of being clean, which was a week ago. I'll show you my papers if you show me yours."

"You haven't been with anyone since you moved here?"

"Getting the café off the ground was more important," she said.

"I've just now decided I can make the time to have a fling. But it's hard when I'm in the café all the time and all my customers are college students."

He leaned forward. "You're not in the café right now."

"No, I'm not."

"And, might I add, I'm not a college student."

She gave him a long look, liking what she saw and wanting to see more of it. "No, you most definitely are not."

They stared at each other for a long, silent moment.

"What are you thinking about?" he wondered.

"Whether you're circumcised or not. What about you?"

"What you sound like when you come."

She carefully returned her napkin to the table. "I think it's time to satisfy our curiosity, don't you?"

"Absolutely." He stood, pulled out his wallet and tossed several bills onto the table. "Your place or mine?"

"I have both floors above the café," Nadia said. "No one's there at night, and I have a nice bit of soundproofing between my place and the café."

"And it's closer than my place." He grabbed the remote with one hand, her wrist with the other, and then pulled her toward the entrance. "Did you drive over?"

"Yes."

"Would you do me the honor of letting me take you home anyway?"

"Absolutely."

THREE

They left the restaurant quickly, then made their way to the adjacent parking lot. Kane approached a dark sedan and disarmed the alarm. He reached for the passenger door, then stopped. "I need to know something."

"Something like what?" she asked, trying not to hop from foot to foot with impatience.

"This." In a smooth move, he snagged an arm about her waist, pulled her close, then kissed her. His mouth slanted over hers, sure, expert, causing her toes to curl in response. She thrust her hands into his gorgeous thick hair as she kissed him back with fervor and frustration and bone-deep need. His hands tightened at her waist, pulling her closer. The feel of his arousal made her groan.

Settling his hands at her waist, he turned her until her back was against the car. In her heels, she was eye level with his throat, and a wild energy filled her, making her want to unbutton his shirt enough for her to set her teeth to his collarbone.

"You've got that look again, Nadia," he said, his voice a low warning.

"What look is that?"

"The look that makes me want to do things right here and right now that will get us both arrested."

Her blood sang. "Maybe we should kiss some more instead."

"Hell yes, we should." He pressed against her, letting her feel the ridge of his arousal. Her mouth went dry at the sensation, the tantalizing promise that he offered. Then he cupped her cheeks in his palms, fingers splaying against the back of her neck, into her hair. His right thumb swept along the curve of her lower lip, almost as if he was readying her mouth for his. Her lips parted in anticipation, her breath light and quick as she waited for him to make his move.

Move he did, slanting his mouth over hers, his lips soft but firm. Her knees went weak as he took full command of the kiss, drawing a fevered response from her. She wrapped her arms around his waist to draw him closer, to anchor herself, to better connect with him. A moan broke from her involuntarily and he took advantage, tracing the bow of her lips with the tip of his tongue, coaxing his way inside. Another moan as their tongues slid together, tasting, teasing, meeting, parting, meeting again.

His hands dropped to her waist then skimmed up her sides, his thumbs brushing the undersides of her breasts. Electric pulses shot through her at his touch, his mouth on hers. The man knew what he was doing all right, his kisses soft then hard, yielding then demanding. She could kiss him forever, lost in the taste of him, the stroke of his tongue along her lips, her tongue.

His left hand moved up into the deep vee of her bodice, cupping her breast through the shelf bra, his fingers expertly plucking her nipple to full and painful hardness through the material. One of them groaned, or both, she wasn't sure. She pressed herself into his hand even as she surrendered to his kiss, his touch. This was what she'd hoped for when she'd made her sexual declaration earlier that day. Someone who knew what to do with a woman's body, who knew how to offer and receive pleasure, who knew the right buttons to push and pushed them with precision.

Her legs threatened to buckle, but Kane thrust his knee between hers, pressing against her, friction holding them up. The weight of his erection, even through the layers of their clothing, branded her. Her hips thrust forward, needing more contact with him. The stimulator in her panties wasn't enough, would never be enough. She wanted him, wanted his cock inside her, as deep as she could take it, as much as he would give. She'd go crazy if she couldn't have him.

She licked along his lips, the hairs of his goatee tickling her with surprising softness, then drew his bottom lip between her teeth, lightly biting down. He growled, one hand cupping her ass, bringing her even closer to his hardened length. His other hand continued to plunder her breasts, sending lightning bolts of sensation through her.

The kiss intensified as they ground together. She forgot that they were in a parking lot. Forgot that she'd wanted to reenact *The Perfumed Garden*. All she could think about was getting naked with him, being taken by him. At that point, he could have bent her over the hood of his car, lifted her skirt, and surged into her and she would have enjoyed every moment of it.

A horn honked, followed by ribald laughter and the standard call of "Get a room." Only then did they break apart, a good foot of space separating them. Nadia gulped for air, her nipples painfully tight, her panties damp, her pussy so very ready, senses shattered.

Kane leaned away from her then lifted his hands from her slowly, as if glue held his fingers to her skin. He took a breath, his erection pressing against her through their clothes, close, so very close. He sucked in another breath, the sound loud and harsh between them, then stepped back as if forced.

"Nadia. Damn." He stepped back again, raking a hand through his hair. "I'm usually better than this."

A pained laugh escaped her lips. "If you were any better, I'd be coming from just your kiss." Laughter died as she focused on his face, the sensual edge of his mouth, the need shining darkly in his eyes, the ridge of his erection behind his zipper. "We need to go, Kane."

"Yes." Kane opened her door for her. He couldn't resist sliding his hand down her back, the swell of her hip as he helped her into the car. Her skin was silky and smooth, sending tingles through his fingertips. Nadia Spiceland was true to her name: spicy, tasty, a delectable morsel he hoped like hell he would soon sink his teeth into. He wanted her legs wrapped around his waist, her nipples in his mouth, her cries of satisfaction in his ears.

He made his way around the car, managing to slip inside with a decent amount of grace. Nadia was so damn hot in that dress that called attention to her luscious curves. Seeing her in the restaurant for the first time, he'd wanted to immediately grab her hand and take her home—his home, her home, the café—hell, any flat surface. He'd thought her beautiful and alluring in her jeans and tight tees. In that dress, seeing her long shapely legs, hot pink painted toes in strappy black stilettos, he'd been struck dumb, even as his body filled with a nearly crushing hunger. It took several heartbeats before he remembered that he was there to win her, to claim her for his own. So he set about playing his cards, seducing her with touches, with words, with single-minded focus.

He'd meant it when he said that her stint in drug rehab didn't bother him. What she was then was not what she was now. What he needed to know of Nadia had started two months ago when he'd first walked into the café and she'd immediately soothed him, then intrigued him with the knowing gleam in her eye and the sauciness of her smile.

Then, just when he thought he'd made a most excellent and commanding impression, she'd slid the vibrator controller to him. He'd gotten so hard at that moment it hurt. Again, the animalistic urge to throw her down and rip enough clothing away to make her his had ridden him, ridden him hard. No other woman he'd been with had been so upfront in her desires, her need, her challenge to him. She'd presented him with a gift by offering him control of her pleasure, and he'd do anything and everything to be worthy of it.

"Take your panties off."

His voice was a loud growl in the confines of the car. He could sense her surprise as she turned her head to look at him. "What?"

"Take your panties off."

She shifted on the seat. "I'm really wet, Kane," she said simply, causing him to groan. "I don't want to ruin your leather."

"You won't," he promised, not that he cared if she did. He wanted her bare. It would be one less thing he had to worry about when they reached her place. Besides, he felt a need to reassert control. He'd felt out of it from the moment she'd handed him that remote.

"Take your panties off, sweet Nadia. I want to know how spicy you are."

Silence. Then she lifted her hips, reaching beneath her skirt. He forgot to breathe as she executed a set of perfect shimmies that fired his blood even more. He could almost sense her challenging grin as she draped the tiny scrap of black lace over the gearshift. "Well?"

Kane inhaled deeply. The scent of her arousal hit him deep in the hindbrain. His grip tightened on the steering wheel. How the fuck long did a red light last in this damn town? Nadia lived two blocks away, but it might as well have been two hundred miles, it was taking so long to get there. "Thank you," he said, keeping his voice level, even amused, with an effort. "Now, spread your knees. Keep your skirt up."

She did, then had the audacity to ease the seat back so that she could put her feet up on the dash. "Would you like for me to touch myself too?"

He wasn't going to survive the night. "Don't be cheeky," he admonished her. "Your orgasms belong to me, remember?"

"The controller—"

"Is unnecessary at this point," he interrupted. "I don't want to give the impression that I need props to give you what you want."

Another fucking light, one more block. Damn downtown Crimson Bay at night. "Tonight is about introducing our bodies to each other. Seeing how we fit. If we suit, we can start the reenactments from the book tomorrow. Is that acceptable?"

"Yes." She drew in a shuddering breath. "I don't think I have the patience or the focus for the book tonight."

"Good." They pulled into the parking deck that serviced the mixed-use development that housed Nadia's café and condo. She gave him the code, then directed him to her guest parking space. Biting back his impatience, he walked around to hand her out of the car, his gaze fastened to her legs as she swung out and to her feet. When she reached for her thong, he said, "Leave it. I want physical proof that tonight actually happened."

Her eyes glittered as they walked to the elevator. "It does seem surreal, doesn't it? I feel like I'm going to jump out of my skin if I have to wait much longer for you to kiss me again." She pushed the elevator button.

The doors immediately opened and he breathed a silent prayer of thanks. "You don't have to wait." He cupped her cheeks as they all but fell into the elevator. He kissed her like a man suffocating and she the purest oxygen, devouring her mouth, taking her taste, her air, the sweetness of her lips. Her arms went around his neck as she pressed herself against him, rubbing against his cock as if she couldn't help it.

"Poor thing." Wrapping one hand around her waist, he slipped the other beneath her skirt to find her core. He caught her moan as his fingers brushed her damp mound, the slick engorged bud of her clit. He probed lower, then thrust his finger into her slit, groaning himself as he encountered the heat of her channel for the first time. "Ride my hand until the door opens," he murmured against her mouth. "Take the edge off."

Without hesitation she did, grinding against his hand as he continued to take her mouth, breathless moans dotting her lips as he kept away from her clit. He wanted that sweet pussy gripping his cock when she came for him for the first time. And the second. And maybe even the third.

He didn't remember much about getting from the elevator to Nadia's door. He did remember standing behind her, pressing kisses along her shoulders and the back of her neck as she fumbled with unlocking the door. "I can't wait to make you come," he whispered in her ear just before his teeth closed on her earlobe.

She squealed, dropping the keys. "Dammit!"

"I'll get them." He bent down to retrieve them, getting a good look at the length of her legs, the strappy black sandals, the bright pink of her toes. "I want you to leave these on," he told her roughly, skimming his fingers up her ankle to her thigh as he regained his feet. "Only these."

Nadia could only nod as he unlocked her door, then stepped back for her to enter. She managed to deactivate the alarm, then tossed her keys and clutch onto the hall table. Turning to face him, she reached for the straps holding her dress up, loosened them, then let the garment fall to the floor, her bra following soon after. Her entire body vibrated with the need to be taken.

"You're so damn beautiful." A gleam of hunger lit the depths of his eyes as his gaze raked her from head to toe. "Or as the ancient Egyptians said, 'She is one girl, there is no one like her. She is more beautiful than any other. Look, she is like a star goddess arising at the beginning of a happy new year.'"

God. Who knew quoting erotic poetry would do it for her? She held out her arms. "I need you, Kane."

"You have me."

The poor man didn't have a chance. She launched herself at him, plastering his face with kisses, hands going for his belt as he worked the buttons of his shirt. It took too damn long, but then again, he had to wear the clothes back home. Then they switched, Kane reaching for his wallet before kicking his trousers away as Nadia pushed his shirt from his shoulders. He extracted a couple of foil packets then threw the wallet toward the door.

Her eyes slid shut at the first touch of bare skin on bare skin. His hand cupped her breast, thumb brushing across the hardened tip. A purr of pleasure escaped her throat as she shoved her hands into his hair, guiding his mouth to her other breast. He obliged her silent request, laving the tight bud with his tongue. The purr grew to a moan as he sucked her nipple into the warmth of his mouth. "Kane."

He scooped her up, walking deeper into the main room. She wrapped her legs around his waist, kissing him for all she was worth, pressing herself against him, needing him inside her.

Still devouring her mouth, he balanced her on the back of the sofa. "Can't go slow right now," he muttered against her mouth as he tore open a condom.

"You've been working me up all night," she shot back. "I don't need slow right now. I just need you to fuck me."

"Then turn around," he growled. "Bend over the couch."

With a little mewl of approval she did, widening her stance, waiting and ready. A thrill of anticipation gripped her as she waited for him to slip on the condom.

"Nadia." He slid a hand slowly down her back, stopping at her waist. "You're so beautiful. Every part of you. Especially this part."

The blunt head of his cock slipped between her thighs. She was so slick, so ready for him, that it didn't take much coaxing to breach her. That first full stretching moment of penetration had her groaning loudly at the oh-my-God fullness. "God, Kane, that feels so good."

"Better than good. Better than great." His voice was a guttural grumble as he withdrew then thrust forward again, sliding fully home. He rocked against her, hands gripping her waist to hold her in place for each sensual slap of his body against hers. Rocking, rocking, rocking, then pleasure so fine she couldn't even cry out. Her hands dug into the sofa cushions as her inner muscles tightened around him, squeezing him.

"Nadia." One hand slipped around her hip, fingers unerringly finding the center of her pleasure. The other hand gripped her shoulder for purchase as he increased the pace and force of his thrusts, driving into her in the relentless pursuit of ecstasy. His voice, low and breathless and hypnotic, wrapped around her, telling her how good she felt, how tight she was, how close to the edge she made him. She could only moan her agreement as she fell deeper and deeper beneath his sensual spell.

With multiple waves of pleasure rolling through every part of her body, she danced a razor's edge between being in the moment and being catapulted out of it. So close, so close . . .

"Oh God. *Kane.* Oh God, oh God, oh God . . ." The orgasm hit her like a sucker punch low in the gut. She threw back her head with a guttural cry, arching her back and grinding her buttocks against his groin to wring out every bit of sensation.

Kane gripped her shoulders as he pistoned into her in a maddening pace, the slapping of their bodies loud in the open living room. With her orgasm still shredding her senses, her inner muscles continued to spasm around his thickness. "God, Nadia," he breathed. "Want to last . . . longer. But can't. Can't. Have to, have to . . ."

His hands dug into her collarbone as he slammed into her one final time, the force of it moving the couch several inches. With a deep rumbling groan he came, pulsing deep inside her and touching off another ripple of bliss.

Spent, overwhelmed, she collapsed against the back of the sofa, dimly aware of Kane easing out of her. Struggling to catch her breath and gather her shattered senses, Nadia could only think one thing: Professor Kaname Sullivan had definitely made the grade.

FOUR

Nadia put the last pan of Wide-Eyed muffins into the oven, dancing as her tablet shuffled through her "shake and bake" baking music mix. She and her assistant Jas always started their very early day with upbeat music because she didn't want to bake while in a bad mood, believing it transferred to her pastries. A silly superstition, perhaps, but she'd learned that from her grandmother and no one argued with Nana Elena. No one ever left the café in a bad mood either.

She joined Bruno Mars singing about sex and paradise as she began to cut the dough for organic fruit turnovers. Jas entered the kitchen, grinning at her as he pulled on his apron then tucked his black bangs beneath a hairnet. "Morning, boss! I guess I don't have to ask you how well it went last night, huh?"

"How do you know about that?" she demanded, not really angry. "You weren't even here yesterday!"

"Two local celebrities hooking up is big news in a small town, even a small college town like Crimson Bay," her assistant said, turning on the faucet at the wash-up sink. "More than a few people saw you guys at Pascal's last night."

"I'm not a celebrity," Nadia argued, feeling her stomach tighten. She didn't want to be the town's entertainment. Been there, done that, bore the scars.

Jas stared at her in surprise. "Of course you are. You're the goddess of goodies, the queen of croissants, the princess of pastries, the star of *Spice of Life*. And the professor, well, you know what his fans call him."

The Spice of Life with Nadia Spiceland. Her very own show, with cooking segments interspersed with trawling the party scene most twenty-somethings in Los Angeles gravitated to, was her prize for winning a reality television cooking competition that had catapulted her younger, stupider self to a level of fame she'd been ill-prepared for. "That was a long time ago, Jas," she said, trying to keep her voice light. "I'm not that person anymore. I'm just a café owner now."

Jas rolled his eyes. "If you're looking at me to blow your skirt up with compliments, I guess I will. Even if you weren't a reality show graduate, you'll never be 'just a café owner.' You've got way too much skill for that. I hope to be half as good as you when I grow up. Am I done kissing ass now?"

Nadia laughed and swatted at him with her hand towel. "You are *so* done. Now get to work on your brizzas." The breakfast pizzas had become a big hit for cash-strapped college kids who needed a healthy, inexpensive option to start their mornings off right.

Successfully dodging questions she wasn't ready to answer, Nadia threw herself into the routine of prepping, baking, and staging. Just before opening for business she pulled out her phone, took a picture of the Wide-Eyed muffins, then sent the photo to her father Victor, with the message: These turned out great! Thanks for the name. See you soon. Smooches!

Less than a minute later, Victor replied. Told you so. :p Can't wait for the next one. Smooches back at you.

Smiling, Nadia slipped her phone back into her pocket and went out to open the café. Daddy Vic had always experimented in the kitchen, with Nadia at his side as soon as she could hold a spoon. As she and Siobhan had planned the menu at the café, she'd sent photos and ingredient lists to both her fathers. It had been as much to solicit their suggestions as to prove that she and Siobhan were handling the pressures of starting their own business. They'd always worry—and God knew she'd given them plenty to worry about—but at least they didn't hover or do random drive-bys from two hours away.

At eight o'clock, just when the first rush slowed down, Siobhan entered the café. "You've got until the time it takes me to make a cup of coffee, and then you're going to spill," her partner said as she rounded the counter.

Nadia rolled her eyes. "Good morning. How are you? I'm fine, thanks for asking."

"I don't need to ask how you're doing. Everyone who comes in the store is blinded by that glow you've got."

"Oh God." Mortified, Nadia examined her reflection in the chrome surface of the espresso machine. "Is it that obvious?"

"Only to everyone who knows you had a hot date last night," her partner teased. "So, you going to spill or what?"

No, she wasn't. Not if she could help it. "I don't know about you, but I have a café to run. Don't you have some soup to make and bread bowls to bake?"

"What, you think I can't listen and cook at the same time?" Siobhan sighed as she took her first sip of caffeine. "Rosie will be here in thirty minutes to relieve you at the register. Come to the kitchen when she does. Audie and Vanessa want me to call them so you can fill us in on all the dirty details at the same time."

Groaning, but knowing her friends wouldn't let her off the hook, Nadia agreed, then went back to helping customers while Jas kept the cases stocked and the beverages coming. Thirty minutes passed by much too quickly, and she nearly bit poor Rosie's head off when the perky student greeted her. After fixing herself a chai latte, Nadia headed for the kitchen. Delaying would only make Siobhan come and get her. The last thing she wanted was to recap her evening in front of their staff and customers.

As usual, stepping into their kitchen made her sigh with satisfaction as the scents of baking bread, simmering soups, and cooking cakes tantalized her. Getting to this point had been a long, hard road for both her and Siobhan, and they both took pride in the results of their efforts.

"Stop daydreaming and get your ass in here," Siobhan ordered as she stirred a vat of the soup of the day. As usual, she had her platinum blonde locks artfully piled atop her head beneath a bright teal bandana, her pink Sugar and Spice T-shirt tucked into turquoise capris. White ankle socks and turquoise sneakers completed the look. On anyone else, the outfit would have been just shy of ridiculous. But Siobhan's hourglass figure and retro-chic style made the look work for her. Siobhan could even make an apron look like high fashion.

"You keep snarking on me and I'm not going to tell you anything," Nadia complained as she headed to the sink to wash her hands. She had cakes and pies to make to complement Siobhan's lunch menu. Jas had already created and decorated batches of cupcakes, and multiple loaves of bread were cooling on the racks.

"Come on, Nadia, you know you want to dish. Besides, why would you deny your best friend the opportunity to live vicariously through you?"

"Because my best friend should be out getting her own."

Siobhan waved her hand in dismissal. "Whatever. Today is about you." She waggled her perfectly arched brows. "So how good was it? Did Professor Sex live up to his name?"

Nadia took a quick look around the kitchen, but they miraculously had it to themselves. She moved closer to her partner and gave in to the grin that she'd suppressed all morning. "Hell yeah, he did. At one point, I think I heard angels singing!"

Siobhan squealed like a teen spotting her boy band crush. "Ooh, let me call the girls!"

Within moments they had Audie and Vanessa on a conference call. "About damn time," Audie exclaimed. "I stayed up past my bedtime to hear this news!"

"How was your date, Nadia?" Vanessa asked, the voice of reason and decorum as always.

Nadia couldn't contain herself any longer. These were her friends, and they'd bonded over sharing their laundry, dirty or otherwise. She couldn't hold out on them. "Guys, it was the most amazing time," she gushed as she gave them the PG-13 version of her night. "It was so good that I'm wondering if it was really that good or is it just because I broke my drought?"

Audie laughed. "Sounds to me like you need another round to

be sure. Maybe three or four. That's how I make up my mind about whether or not I like a guy."

Siobhan shook her head. "Audie, are you at home?"

The silence was answer enough. Nadia sighed. "Audie, remember how you promised to decide that you like the guy *before* you sleep with him?"

"I do not recall making that promise."

"There were witnesses," Vanessa said. "And it was at last Tuesday's Bitch Talk."

"Well . . ."

Nadia leaned closer to the phone. "Do you remember saying that if you broke your promise, I could withhold your dessert?"

An audible intake of breath. "You wouldn't."

"Consider yourself cut off, babe." Siobhan's no-nonsense mother voice cut off any argument. They'd long ago decided that they'd have each other's backs and keep each other on the mostly straight and narrow, and that meant breaking out the tough-love bitch slap whenever necessary. Audie had a problem with falling into bed first and asking questions later. No matter how safe she was, Nadia and the others still worried about where Audie was headed if she didn't get to the root of her sex issues.

"As for you," Siobhan added, turning back to Nadia, "it's been one date. One toe-curling date, which means it's way the hell too early to worry about anything. Just take it one step at a time."

One step at a time. She could do that. That was how she'd been living her life for the last few years. One day at a time, always moving forward and away from the ugliness of the past. Kane had heard her sexual declaration the day before. He knew she wanted no pressure, no entanglements, and definitely no drama.

"Speaking of which," Vanessa said, "when's the next step?"

"Don't know," Nadia answered. "We haven't talked about when yet."

Jas pushed open the door leading back to the main retail area. "Uhm, Nadia? We need you out here, please."

"I'd better go see what's going on out there. I'll talk to you guys later." Nadia disconnected, then handed the phone back to Siobhan. "I'm worried about Audie."

"Me too." Siobhan pocketed her phone. "She's the youngest of us. All we can do is be there for her and support her when she's ready to deal with her issues. Let's go see what fire's burning out on the floor."

Curious, Nadia pushed open the door and stepped into the café counter area, wondering what sort of problem had occurred that Jas couldn't handle. Siobhan followed her. Most days at ten a.m., the shop entered the slow portion of the morning before the run-up to lunch, and today was no exception. The courier holding a gigantic bouquet of mixed flowers was different.

"Nadia Spiceland?" asked the twenty-something blond-haired surfer-looking guy in a navy blue courier company T-shirt and bike shorts. He glanced between Nadia and Siobhan then did a double-take at Siobhan, as most men did.

"That's me."

"Special delivery. Please sign here. . . ." He thrust his smartphone in her general direction, but his gaze was firmly locked on Siobhan, who ignored him.

Amused, Nadia used her forefinger to sign the screen, then relieved the courier of the bouquet so that he could stare at her partner unencumbered. "Thank you. Her name's Siobhan, by the way."

Nadia took the bouquet over to what their staffers called "the bosses' table." She had no idea what the different blooms were, but she didn't recognize anything that looked like roses. She hadn't had flowers since her stint in the hospital prior to rehab, but those arrangements had nothing on the exquisite assortment in the ruby red vase she held now, a collection of flowers that made her wonder if Kane had chosen each one himself.

Siobhan joined her after sending the dazed courier off with a sandwich and several cupcakes. "Looks like you're not the only one who had a great night."

Embarrassment and heat spread through Nadia as she breathed in the heady fragrance that reminded her of spices and sweetness and sex. "Maybe, but it also looks like that courier couldn't take his eyes off you."

Siobhan shrugged, the action elegant on her. "Couldn't take his eyes off the girls, you mean." She splayed her right hand across her cleavage. "He's probably my daughter's age. Besides, we're not talking about my love life or lack thereof. We're talking about yours. See what the card says."

Nadia reached into the colorful stems to extract the card held by a clear plastic pitchfork. Opening the envelope, she pulled out the heavy card. Bold handwriting in black ink was scrawled across the heavy ivory paper. *To an amazing woman. Thank you for an amazing night. Until later. Kane.*

Nadia couldn't help the grin that spread across her face any more than she could help the giddiness that bubbled through her like champagne on New Year's Eve. Kane had hit all her buttons. Most importantly, he knew what those buttons were and how to push them.

She held out her arm. "I think I need you to pinch me."

Siobhan obligingly pinched her inner elbow. "You're not dreaming, girl. You're positively glowing."

She pulled out her phone, handed it to Siobhan. "Would you mind taking a picture of me and the flowers, so I can send it to him?"

Siobhan obliged, and Nadia sent the image to Kane along with a text. Thank you. The flowers are beautiful.

She received a quick reply. Not as beautiful as you.

It was a cheesy line, but it still made her grin like an idiot. Very smooth, Professor.

I have my moments. How are you today?

There was only one word she could use. Amazing.

Are you ready for more?

Was she? Absolutely.

It seemed like an eternity before she received his reply. I'll be at your place by five with dinner. Be ready for me.

They were just words on her phone screen, but they caused her stomach to clench in anticipation. She could easily imagine the sensual command in his tone and the sinful light in his eyes as he'd typed out his response, could imagine it so clearly that her nipples tightened. Yes, sir.

Naughty. Now I have to lecture my class sporting a boner. Think about how you'll pay for that while I figure out a way to speed up time. See you soon.

"You should see your face right now," Siobhan teased. "You're blushing. Whatever he's doing for you, he'd better keep doing it or he'll have to answer to me."

"I'll tell him that." Nadia sighed as she slipped her phone into her back pocket then met Siobhan's knowing grin with one of her own. "When I see him tonight. We're meeting at five."

Siobhan swatted her. "No wonder you're grinning like the Cheshire Cat. If you're that excited to see him again, I'd say the fireworks have nothing to do with a sex drought and everything to do with the sparks you two throw off."

Nadia raised a brow. "How do you know we throw off sparks?"

"Girl, please." Siobhan rolled her eyes. "I may be an old mother hen, but my eyes work just fine. A person would have to be in a coma to miss the sexual tension you two gave off yesterday. Or how you're reacting to his texts today."

The blonde woman placed a hand on Nadia's shoulder. "I'm happy for you, Nadia. I'm proud of you too. You've come a long way from the day I met you, working hard and staying clean, making sure I do the same. You're doing great and you deserve some fun. You deserve this. Let yourself enjoy it."

Moved, Nadia mirrored Siobhan's gesture, resting her forehead against the other woman's bright bangs. They'd been through so much together since they'd met in rehab in Los Angeles. To Nadia, the older woman was more than her partner. Siobhan was her best friend, the sister she'd never had. Siobhan had her back like family did, or in Siobhan's opinion, better than family, and Nadia trusted her implicitly.

"Thanks, Sugar," Nadia said, giving the other woman a hug. "I promise to enjoy myself."

"Good." Siobhan stepped back, giving her a watery smile. "Speaking of Sugar, you should tell Kane about the show and invite him to come with you this Friday."

Nadia stared. "Invite Kane. To your burlesque show. On a date?"

"Yes, a date. You know, like the one you went on last night."

"That was different!"

Siobhan frowned. "How is that different?"

"That was me with him at dinner. This is your show. All of our friends will be there!"

"Are you saying that Kane's not your friend? With some very spectacular benefits?"

"No, I'm not saying that, but—"

"Are you ashamed of our friends?"

"Of course not!"

"Then I don't get it. What's the problem?"

Nadia blew out a breath. She couldn't explain it without sounding silly. Siobhan performed as Sugar Malloy with a burlesque troupe known as the Crimson Bay Bombshells. Show nights were an excuse to dress up and hang out with their expanded circle of friends. It was their prime opportunity to let loose and have fun before diving back into the workweek.

To invite Kane into the raucous madness that was Friday night mayhem invited a level of intimacy that Nadia wasn't sure she was ready for. That was the silly part. She'd left her thong on the man's gearshift, rode his hand while in an elevator, and had him bend her over a sofa. They were intimate up to their eyeballs. But Nadia's life worked because she kept it compartmentalized, and she didn't see a reason not to compartmentalize the sex. She'd already crossed a mental line by accepting a date from a customer. To take that customer-turned-lover and drop him into the den of iniquity that was her friends? She didn't think she could do that to the guy.

"Turn our friends loose on Kane?" she asked with a laugh. "You want to end this thing before it has a chance to get started?"

"It won't be that bad. Besides, I have a feeling your professor can hold his own with our group."

Her professor. Nadia wasn't sure if she was ready to claim him as hers or not. One date and multiple orgasms didn't mean she had any rights to him, did it? Maybe it did, but her stint in LA and in rehab had skewed her perspective on what normal people did when it came to sex and relationships. One night and this was already more complicated than she'd expected or wanted it to be.

Siobhan flicked her ear. "Ow! What was that for?"

Her partner was unapologetic. "You promised to have fun and enjoy yourself with the professor, remember?"

"All right! We'll see how things go. If it works out, I'll ask him about Friday. I make no promises, though."

Nadia decided to place the flowers in a prominent but safe spot near the register until she left for the day, liking the way the arrangement brightened the area. This didn't have to be complicated. All she had to do was make her mind follow her body and remain focused on the sexual fireworks. Complicated always led to trouble, and trouble led to a crash and burn. She definitely didn't need another episode like that in her life.

FIVE

"Sullivan. May I have a word?"

Kane smothered a groan. No, he didn't have time, but no one refused a request from Dr. Theodore Marshall, the department head. So he pasted on a professional smile and followed the older man into his spacious and cluttered office instead of heading toward the exit as he wanted.

Once inside, he cut to the chase. "What can I do for you, Dr. Marshall?"

Marshall glanced at him over his silver-framed glasses as only a department head could do. Through Herscher University was on the forefront as a progressive liberal arts college, it was also a top-notch research institution that thrived on grants from the government and private think tanks alike. More than likely, Dr. Marshall wanted to talk to him about money, which meant entertaining alumni with deep pockets.

"Have a seat, Professor Sullivan," Marshall said, gesturing to one of the overstuffed oxblood chairs that fronted his ornate desk. "Let's have a little chat."

Great. Kane hid a grimace as he took a seat. Marshall saw himself as the benevolent despot and the chats as a way to come off as being engaged with faculty instead of bossy or nosy. He also liked to hear himself talk.

This was going to take time, time Kane didn't have. Nadia was waiting for him, waiting for more of the explosive pleasure they'd had the night before, and he was determined to give it to her. That meant cutting through Marshall's bullshit as quickly as possible and getting the hell out of Prentiss Hall.

The department head was pushing seventy and two hundred and eighty pounds. Evidence remained that his girth had been mostly muscle at one time, but those days were long gone. His shock of silver hair had been brown at one time, if you took the twin caterpillars over his pale gray eyes as indication. Dr. Marshall had the appearance and temperament of a constipated shih tzu.

"I'll get down to brass tacks, Professor," the department head said. "I'm sure you're aware that you have a certain moniker as well as a less than savory reputation among the student body."

This again. Kane hid his anger by taking his time adjusting his glasses. "I'm sure you're aware that I neither condone nor encourage either."

"Yet rumors persist."

"I wonder why," Kane murmured. "I also wonder who manages the care and feeding of those rumors, when I certainly do not." Marshall didn't talk to students if he could help it. He dealt with the faculty. Kane believed someone on staff kept circulating baseless tales about him. He even had two good candidates in mind, neither of whom would weep tears over his departure.

Watery eyes regarded him. "While your expertise and fame garners a great deal of positive attention for our school as a whole and this department in particular, your on-campus reputation is becoming a deterrent."

Kane exhaled slowly, keeping his expression impassive with an effort. He was the maligned party, but Marshall would take any display of anger as a sign of weakness. "I'll remind you that I've never once encouraged the attention of any of my students outside of the classroom. I keep my door open when I counsel students and have one of the graduate assistants sit in on some of the more fraught sessions. I even inform students that they're being recorded. All of these are measures that you yourself signed off on."

He wasn't stupid, and all it would take was one questionable photo posted to a social media site to torpedo his campus career. So he went to extremes and did everything possible to protect himself and still be available for his students and leave his detractors without ammunition.

If there was any sort of black mark against him, it was the six-month relationship he'd had with an adjunct professor in Continuing Studies. That had ended a year ago, not well, but it hadn't been a scandal either. Now he had a new relationship he wanted to focus on, if only Dr. Marshall would *get to the fucking point.*

"You asked to speak to me, yet you've only rehashed old issues that I thought long handled." Kane sat back in the chair, his posture displaying a relaxation he didn't feel. "Am I to assume you have some sage advice you wish to impart? Our normal chat isn't scheduled until next week." And I really hope I'm called for a consulting case then.

"Indeed I do." Marshall sat forward, some of the harshness leaving his expression. "Listen, son, I know this isn't easy for you, just as I know it isn't fair. I do think, however, that your looks combined with your charm and your continued bachelorhood means that you will always be a prize that the student body will want to claim."

Kane blinked, thrown by the change in demeanor as much as by Marshall's words. Maybe the department head really was concerned with more than listening to himself speak. Kane knew that his persistent single state didn't help to staunch the rumors or advance his quest for tenure, but he didn't think Marshall was concerned one way or the other.

"Are you saying that you want me to get married?" He should have been surprised, but he wasn't. At thirty-seven, he'd never been married, a fact that sent his mother into wails of despair. His focus on his career had dominated his life since college, leaving little time for more than casual relationships.

Truth be told, he hadn't found anyone who had made him think long term, and he was okay with that even if most people weren't. Marriage was still the preferred default state for adults in the United States. Who cared that wedded bliss had a fifty percent success rate? If you weren't married, engaged, or in the process of ending a marriage, people thought something was wrong with you.

"I'm saying that you need to take more concrete steps to protect your career," Marshall said, his tone and expression kind. "Right now you're like forbidden fruit, and sometimes our students display a decided lack of self-control. You need to do something to make that fruit less attractive."

Kane barked out a laugh. The situation, the conversation, all of it, was just too ludicrous to be believed. "So in order to keep my job as a professor here at Herscher, I need to get married. Is that what you're advising me to do, Dr. Marshall? I want to make sure I understand where the department head stands on this."

"Professor Sullivan!" Marshall boomed out, his jowls actually trembling with righteous indignation and the volume of his words. When Kane just stared silently at him, the older man blew out a breath and settled back into his chair. "Professor Sullivan," he said again, "I'm not issuing a directive for you to get married. That violates all manner of rules, and as I never saw fit to enter the state of matrimony myself, I can't say that I recommend it. However, whether you believe me or not, I do have your best interests at heart."

"And the best interests of the department," Kane pointed out.

Marshall didn't bother to deny it. "Yes, the success and reputation of our department are important to me. So is its future. I want to make sure it's in good hands when I'm gone."

Ah, the dangling of the tenure carrot. "Of course," Kane said, because it was the only appropriate thing he could say.

"The dean appreciates the exposure your skills and expertise have given to Herscher," Marshall continued. "Your journal papers and books have made the national spotlight. We know how much of an asset you are to the college."

But . . . Kane mentally prodded.

"You wouldn't want any hint of impropriety, no matter how unfounded, to come to the dean's attention. There is a code of conduct we must all adhere to, and I would hate for the president of the board of regents to believe your potential liabilities outweigh the benefits of having you on staff here."

"I understand." He did. Despite all he'd done for the school, all the positive attention and donations, the seminars and conferences and influx of students, it was not good enough. His position was still tenuous and dependent on things beyond his control, and he fucking hated it.

He rose. "If that will be all, I have somewhere I need to be."

"Just one more thing, Sullivan." The corpulent department head rose from his chair like a ship breaking a wave. "The department meet and greet for our benefactors is coming up soon. The president and members of the board will be attending. If you could bring a date with you, not only would that be a refreshing change, but it would be sure to alleviate some of the negative speculation that's aimed your way."

The department meet and greet. Part of the political posturing that was a necessary evil of teaching at the university level. Most of the time he didn't attend, using his consulting work as the perfect excuse not to participate in the song and dance. He doubted if Marshall or Dean Lansing would accept an excuse this time around.

Kane nodded at Marshall. "I'll see what I can do. Have a good evening, sir."

He left Marshall's office, then quickly made his way out of Prentiss Hall and into the crisp pre-spring air. Breathing deeply several times, he pushed away the anger that had bubbled up while he'd been pressured by the department head like a middle-school student called to the principal's office.

Shoving his hands into his pants pockets, he made his way across the quad to the faculty parking lot. As much as he disliked the cronyism and pandering necessary for being part of college-level faculty, he loved teaching and his chosen field of study. It gave him a great deal of pleasure to engage and challenge his students, to expand their worldviews and their attitudes while exposing them to other social constructs and points of view. He thought he was making a difference in his own small way, but if the dean and president didn't think so, he had to consider other options.

He made his way to his car and put Herscher in his rearview, his mind whirling with possibilities. He could quit teaching altogether and go full-time as a consultant, hiring his skills and expertise out to law enforcement on a local and federal level. It was important work but some of the cases he'd worked on took their toll, leaving him mentally and emotionally drained and unfit for company. Being exposed to the ugly side of sexual deviancy wasn't something he enjoyed no matter how necessary it was, and he admired the men and women in law enforcement who saw it as their daily duty. If things went south at Herscher, he'd have to consider it.

He could also write full-time. With three nonfiction works to his name and the seeds to a fictional crime series sketched out, it was a definite possibility. He also had a decent nest egg that would enable him to take the time to do it right. The thought of leaving the college didn't sit well with him, though. He enjoyed the school, the students, and the eclectic little town that surrounded them. He didn't want to leave it.

Yet if he gave any credence to Marshall, and he had no reason not to, his only option for staying and gaining tenure was to make the traditionalists happy and his students miserable by becoming very obviously and publicly off-limits.

Nadia's beautiful face surfaced in his thoughts. He rejected the idea before it could form. There was no way in hell he'd marry

Nadia, or anyone else for that matter, just to stay on at the college. She'd laugh him out of the café for even broaching the subject, *after* she kicked him in the gonads.

A few miles north of the college, he turned his car onto Bay View Terrace. The sun had begun its downward slant into the bay in a spectacular show of color that had given the town its name. His spacious condo had a commanding view of the bay, and he wondered what it would be like to have Nadia standing on the balcony wrapped in nothing but the light of the setting sun like a fire goddess.

Nadia. Just thinking about her lightened his mood and made him hard. She consumed his thoughts, fractured his concentration, occupied his mind, and filled his memory, taking up permanent residence in his psyche. Their night had more than lived up to his expectations. The pic she'd sent of her with the flowers was now the unlocked background on his phone. He knew he was acting like a horny teen with his first crush, but after one explosive night, he was hooked and ready for more.

He'd already thought of her as sexy and sweet. He'd had a couple of weeks of watching her interact with customers, employees, and friends. Her sarcastic wit, ready laugh, and obvious compassion had won him over just as surely as her sticky buns had.

After parking, he quickly made his way up to his condo. Marshall's lecture had put him behind schedule. He didn't know the ins and outs of running a bakery, but he figured Nadia had to get up early, way before sunrise. The last thing he wanted to do was inconvenience her or make her think she couldn't fit him into her life.

He rushed through a shower, then pulled on loose-fitting gray trousers and a black sweater. Before heading out, he stopped in his office, the three-dimensional representation of his brain, the room he retired to in order to write, to think, to dive deep into the criminal mind to create psychological profiles. He grinned as he spotted his copies of *The Perfumed Garden*, the early French, the Kama Shastra Society's translation, and a later, more accurate English translation. He was looking forward to trying out all the positions with Nadia, discovering her favorites. Discovering her.

He'd pushed a bit when he'd ordered that she be ready for him, but he'd sensed she'd be receptive, especially given the way she'd responded to his demands the night before. That *yes, sir* text she'd sent in response had made him rock hard and desperate to be inside her. Need burned through him, and all he could think about was getting to her as soon as possible. If she thought the night before was good, he'd make sure round two was even better.

SIX

The end of the day couldn't come fast enough as far as Nadia was concerned. She zipped through her prep work for the next morning, waved good-bye to Siobhan and the rest of the staff, then gathered her flowers before heading for the door. Anticipation zipped through her as she stepped out into the bright but chilly late afternoon sunlight before quickly making her way up to the building's residential entrance.

Humming, feeling like dancing, she entered her two-story condo, flushing as she caught sight of her couch. Remembering how Kane had bent her over the back caused a spark of need to flare deep inside her. God, the man was good. So good that she hadn't thought twice when they'd made their way to her bedroom and he had her ride him to an explosive finish. She'd actually passed out for a while, only to awaken to a mouth on her breast and his fingers skillfully stroking her clit.

That third time, with Kane rising above her and dominating her with stroke after masterful stroke, had shown her that he was capable of being everything she could want in a lover. More than that, she thought there was a chance he could be everything she needed.

Her mind whirled as she placed the bouquet in a spot of honor on the granite bar, then set the main floor to rights. That Kane could read her so well should have unnerved her, but she couldn't decide if it bothered her or not. Maybe he was just good at what he did; he was a professor of human sexuality and psychology after all. He'd made a successful career out of studying people and their attitudes toward sex and sexual exploration. Given their mini-flirt at the café and their verbal foreplay at the restaurant, she realized Kane had probably systematically formulated a plan of ultimate seduction and enacted the steps needed to achieve his desired result. And that result was her spread beneath him.

That sounded so clinical, but Kane was anything but, she thought as she made her way upstairs to strip and redress the bed. There had been nothing clinical about the heat in his dark gaze or the way he'd touched her. Calculating, maybe. But so what? She'd been calculating too from the moment she'd handed him the remote control for her vibrator. She'd tested him and he'd turned the tables on her to orgasmic results. She'd wanted an expert and that was exactly what she'd gotten.

Their time together had been smoking hot. The man himself was a closeted sex god masquerading as a geeky professor. That part didn't bother her, Nadia reminded herself as she dumped the soiled linens in the laundry room then headed for the master bath. Calculating or not, the sex was incredible. And she'd get to experience it again very, very soon.

Desire hummed in her veins. That was the part that bothered

her. One night, just one night of very, extremely, powerfully hot sex, and all she could think about was the moment she'd get to have it again. She craved the sensations, the pleasure, the release, craved it so much it was like a hunger.

She'd experienced cravings like that before. Needing pills to get her going in the morning. Pills to numb the pain so she could get through a grueling day of cooking, filming, partying, being on for the camera, for the people who depended on her for their bread and butter. Another set of pills so she could sleep deeply and then start the cycle all over again. She'd slipped into a spiraling whirlpool, an undertow of chemical abuse she couldn't break free of until it was nearly too late.

Like it had been too late for some.

She couldn't let that happen again. She could do this. Have sex with Kane, enjoy herself, and make damn sure she didn't go so far that she lost herself in the process.

Blowing away her negative ruminations with a cleansing breath, Nadia dumped the soiled linens in the laundry room then headed for the master bath. In the shower, she closed her eyes as the steaming water sluiced down her body. By herself, alone with her thoughts, she gave in to the wonder of the last twenty-four hours. "Kaname," she whispered, enjoying the way each syllable felt in her mouth. *Kane* was a strong name, perfect for dealing with the college, teaching students, consulting with law enforcement. *Kaname . . .* that was a name to be said on a breathy moan just before you were rocketed up into orgasmic pleasure.

She lathered her bath sponge with a jasmine-vanilla-scented soap then ran it over her heated body, lingering on her breasts. Hunger that couldn't be satisfied with food welled up inside her. She wanted him. Wanted his hands cupping her breasts, teasing her nipples. His mouth gliding over her body, heightening her senses. His tongue circling her clit as his fingers pumped inside her folds. His possession taking her higher and higher until she came when he ordered her to.

"Good grief," she breathed, pulling her hand away from her needy pussy. Just thinking about the man made her thoughts turn to sex and her body prime itself for orgasm. Her hand slid down her body again, and again she pulled it away. She could hold out for a little while until Kane arrived. Besides, she remembered with a thrill, she'd promised her orgasms to him. The reward would be all the more delicious for waiting. And she'd make sure he knew just how much of a good girl she'd been.

Her phone rang as she got out of the shower. Her stomach did a little flip of excitement as she saw Kane's name on the screen. Wrapping a towel around herself, she grabbed the phone. "Kane."

"Nadia." Even through the phone, the low and husky timbre of his voice skated over her senses, making her shiver. "I've been thinking about you all day. Do you realize how inconvenient it is to lecture while sporting an erection?"

Since she knew just how impressive an erection it was, she could guess how inconvenient it was. She leaned against the counter, her breath coming fast. "Am I supposed to apologize for that? I came close to burning several dozen cupcakes after I got your flowers and card."

"Good."

"Good? How is that good?"

"It means that I'm not alone in this, whatever this is. That it's as satisfying for you as it is for me. That you want more of what I can give you."

"Kaname," she breathed, wondering if she had any defenses that could withstand this man.

He released a harsh breath. "I like the way you say my name, sweet Nadia. I want to hear you say it just like that when I'm inside you later."

Her nipples pearled. "So you don't think last night was just a fluke? Or the result of martinis and vibrators?"

He chuckled. "There's only one way to find out, isn't there?" he asked, his voice husky with intent. "Are you ready for me, Nadia?"

"Almost. I just got out of the shower, so I'm only in a towel right now."

"Are you?" His voice dropped lower. "Tell me, you didn't take care of yourself while you were in the shower, did you?"

"I wanted to, but I didn't," she confessed. "How did you know?"

"Because I thought about doing the same thing when I had my shower. I'm glad you didn't, though. Your orgasms belong to me."

She automatically opened her mouth to protest, but what came out was a moan instead of a denial. Somehow, Kane was able to throw that switch in her brain, the switch that made her surrender and say that yes, of course her orgasms belonged to him, especially since he was so good at wringing them out of her.

"I remember," she told him, her voice less than a whisper. She cleared her throat, spoke louder. "I think I deserve a reward for my restraint."

His low laughter made her stomach clench. "Just what sort of reward do you think you deserve?"

She gripped her phone tightly. "Your orgasms. I want your orgasms to belong to me."

Silence on the other end, and she wondered if she'd pushed too far in their sexy game. Then, "Do you, now?"

Her eyes slid closed as the dangerous softness of his voice sent tingles of awareness shooting through her. "Yes." She took a deep breath. "Yes, sir."

Another lengthy pause. "I'm coming to you, Nadia. I'm going to have you for dessert, then I'm cooking you dinner, and then we'll enter the *Garden*. Wear something simple so I don't have to rip it off you. Do you understand?"

She swallowed a whimper of need. "Yes, sir."

"Excellent. Now how do you feel about seafood?"

"I see food, I eat it," she answered. "Everything except oysters. Feel free to surprise me."

"I think I'm the one who's surprised. Pleasantly so. I'll be there in fifteen minutes. Be ready for me." He disconnected.

"Oh my God." Nadia released the breath she held as she put down her phone and picked up her hair dryer. Thank goodness she was already leaning against the counter, because her knees were so weak she nearly slid to the floor. As she dried her hair, she could only think of one thing: even if she had all the time in the world, she didn't think she'd ever be truly ready for Professor Sex.

She had just enough time to half dry her hair and toss on a caramel-colored microfiber slip dress that barely supported her breasts before the doorbell rang. Barefoot, she raced downstairs and threw open the door to let Kane in. For a moment she could only stand there, staring at him in amazement. Kane was just too good-looking for words. He didn't have his glasses on, enabling her to easily see the intense glint in his midnight eyes. The black cashmere sweater molded to the definition in his shoulders and arms, but the hem couldn't conceal the erection straining at the zipper of his pants. His dark hair fell over his forehead like a raven's wing, making him look downright devilish.

Finally she found her voice. "Hi."

"Hi, yourself." His expression heated as he backed her over the threshold and closed the door. She reached for him, his name a thick, needy breath on her lips.

"Not yet," he said, his voice a bite. "If you touch me right now, as badly as I want you, it'll be game over and dinner will be ruined."

That's when she noticed he had a canvas shopping bag in one hand and a small leather duffel in the other. She backed away, giving him room to pass her and head to the gourmet kitchen. As she followed him, she wondered if she was the only woman in town who'd mistakenly thought that Kaname Sullivan was a harmless, mild-mannered man. She'd never been more glad to be so wrong.

"What are we having?" she asked, hoping to break the sexual tension building inside her. Telling her not to touch him only made her want to caress him all the more.

"I noticed yesterday that you had a grill attachment," he answered, nodding at her multi-burner stove as he emptied the contents of the grocery bag into the fridge. "So I bought vegetables and swordfish steaks to grill. But first, I need an appetizer."

"Sure. I keep a fully stocked fridge. I'm sure I can whip something together. What do you have a taste for?"

"You." He turned to her, holding out a hand. "Come here."

The soft words were completely at odds with the hunger in his gaze. Mesmerized, she moved forward, body and mind focused on Kane and everything he offered.

As soon as she slipped her hand into his, he lifted it to his mouth, pressing a soft, lingering kiss to the back of her hand, then another to her palm. "In *The Perfumed Garden*, Sheik Nafzawi talks about a woman's pleasure and how important it is for the man to see to her needs in order to satisfy his own."

"He-he does?" she managed to ask, watching breathlessly as Kane kissed his way from her wrist to her elbow, leaving fire in his wake. She'd read *The Perfumed Garden* cover to cover, yet she couldn't recall a word of it at that moment.

"Absolutely." He lingered at the soft skin of her inner elbow, nibbling and licking. Nadia would have never believed the spot would be an erogenous zone for her, but Kane's expert touch caused her nipples to pearl and moisture to gather between her thighs.

He continued, punctuating each phrase with kisses as he continued up her arm. "'You will excite her by kissing her cheeks, sucking her lips, and nibbling at her breasts. Lavish kisses on her navel and thighs, and titillate the lower parts. Bite at her arms and neglect no part of her body.'"

"I think I like this sheik," she gasped as Kane nipped at her earlobe.

"I think I like this area right here," he answered, his lips grazing her collarbone, her throat, then her chin. "You taste like the sweetest spices, Nadia Spiceland. I want to take my time exploring you, neglecting no part of your beautiful body."

He claimed her lips.

Finally. Nadia twined her arms around Kane's neck, kissing back with equal fervor. At his silent urging she parted her lips, allowing his tongue to sweep inside. She groaned, he groaned, they both groaned, animalistic grunts of need and demand.

His hand slid down her backbone to cup her ass, bringing her core against the hard ridge of his arousal. She pressed against him with a whimper of pleasure, butterflies dancing in her stomach, wanting to get as close to him as she could possibly get. He trailed kisses from her mouth to her throat, turning her until her back pressed against the end of the island. His hands swept up her arms to her shoulders then back down, pushing aside the straps of her dress. The smooth fabric slid down her body, stopping only when the straps caught the bend of her elbows, exposing her breasts.

He looked at her in silent fascination, as if he'd never seen breasts before. Tension ramped up inside her, tightening her nipples to bullet points. Slowly he raised his hands, reaching up to cup both. A jolt of electricity shot through her, making her gasp, a gasp that fell into a long moan when his thumbs slowly and lightly brushed over the nut-hard peaks of her nipples.

He rolled both her nipples between thumbs and forefingers. She reached back to grip the countertop before she embarrassed herself by melting into a puddle of need on the floor. "Your mouth," she said, the gravelly sound of her voice loud and unfamiliar. She lurched forward, thrusting her breasts into his hands. "I want your mouth on me. Please, Kane."

"How can I refuse a request like that? But I want to see you. All of you." He dragged the dress straps all the way down her arms and she let go of the counter long enough to slip her wrists free. The lightweight dress glided down her body and pooled at her feet, leaving her bare to his gaze.

He stepped back to give her a long, slow perusal. She lifted her chin, bearing his scrutiny despite burning with the need to cross her arms over her body. Every woman had that moment of uncertainty, of overthinking a man's reaction to seeing her nude. Sure, she'd been naked with him last night, but they'd been so desperate to come together that there hadn't been a moment like this, this sensual examination.

Her breasts weren't as large and perky as Siobhan's, but she could make eye-catching cleavage when she put her mind to it. As for the rest of her body, well, she'd lost weight during the stress of her television days, eating pills instead of meals, her stay in rehab, and the long hours of blood, sweat, and tears getting the café up and running. She was still in the process of getting back to a decent weight, but she didn't have much more to go before she actually got her hips and butt back.

"Nadia," he said, and her name sounded like a prayer or a plea on his lips. His eyes lit up with the heat of his appreciative grin. "Everything about you is beautiful."

"E-everything?"

"Everything." He stepped closer to kiss her throat again, his teeth lingering on her collarbone. "Your smile, your sweet and spicy scent, your arousal. The sound of your breath catching in your throat, your moans and whimpers, the curve of your ear, your nipples and belly button and right toe. It's all beautiful to me."

She wanted to laugh, to lighten the intensity and relieve her sudden onslaught of nerves, but the truth she heard in his tone stole her breath. Gripping her waist, he lifted her onto the counter. The shock of the cool granite juxtaposed with the warmth of his hands and the fire in her blood. He caressed her breasts again, his touch almost reverent and going a long way to easing her nerves and firing her senses. She leaned forward, her breasts heavy and aching for his mouth.

She parted her lips to repeat her demand but he leaned forward to lick her right nipple then gently blew on it. Before she could process that sensation, his mouth closed over her nipple. She moaned loud with appreciation, clutching his sleek head closer. When he sucked on it she felt the pull all the way to her womb. Then he bit down with the perfect combination of pleasure and pain.

She cried out, her hips bucking against him. "Oh God, yes! More of that."

"As the lady desires," he said with a laugh, then repeated the lick, suck, bite maneuver on her left nipple. Moisture gathered at her entrance, threatening to dampen her thighs and the counter beneath her, but she didn't care. Instead, she wrapped her legs around him, dragging him closer, needing him closer.

He started up the leisurely kissing expedition again, feasting on her exposed skin, making her belly flutter and clench as he kissed and licked and nipped his way down her abdomen. Drunk on the headiness of his caresses, she leaned back on her elbows, watching as he explored her body with lips and teeth and tongue.

She whimpered a protest when he bypassed the most obvious target, instead nibbling his way down her inner thighs to her knees, her calves, her ankles and toes. True to his word, or the sheik's suggestion, he neglected no part of her body. By the time he returned to her center she was quivering and panting, almost mindless with want.

"This part of you is beautiful too," Kane told her, cupping her mound. "Beautiful and wet. I bet it's needy too."

"Yes," she breathed out.

"What do you need, Nadia? Tell me."

She'd never been shy about asking for what she wanted, or taking what she needed in the bedroom. She saw no reason to be different now. "I want your mouth on me, Kane. The same way you did my breasts."

He lightly traced the folds framing her opening with a sweep of his thumb, his expression drawn tight with desire. She wrapped her legs around him again, aching for him, ready to beg for him to give her what she wanted, what she needed.

"As the lady desires," he said again, leaning forward. He slid his hands beneath her knees, folding her legs toward her chest, opening her up. Nadia was so primed for him she doubted it would take more than one stroke for her to blast off.

A keening moan of pleasure broke free from her at the first long caress. She felt a shudder pass through him, then his hands slipped down to frame her slit, opening her farther for his questing tongue. The pleasure spiked like electric shocks, prickling along the surface of her skin. She sent her hands scrambling across the countertop, seeking a way to anchor herself, finally thrusting her fingers into his hair.

Passion rose hard in her and she tugged on his hair, wishing he'd hurry. He bit the inside of her thigh. She gasped, a rush of heat sweeping through her as he brought her to the edge—close, so very close—only to bring her back down, sensually torturing her with lips and tongue and teeth, with licks and suckles and bites. He feasted on her with expert enthusiasm, driving her crazy, reducing her world to just her pussy and his beautiful, glorious, amazing mouth.

Her thighs quivered with the need to come, to relieve the passion and pressure flooding her body, stretching her skin, filling her lungs. She moaned his name repeatedly, begging him for release. Just when she thought she couldn't handle it anymore, couldn't take another tongue lash, he sucked on her clit.

She came screaming, feet pressing on his shoulders as her hips arched off the countertop. The orgasm continued, bowing her body with the muscle-clenching force of a seizure, catapulting her right out of her mind.

"Nadia? Are you okay?" Kane's voice sounded far away.

She stared up at the pendant lights hanging above her. "Yeah." The word came out slurred and three syllables too long.

"Can you sit up?"

"No."

"Let me help." His arms curved beneath her, lifting her to a sitting position.

She wrapped her arms around his neck, giving him a drunken, ferocious openmouthed kiss, tasting her excitement on his lips. "You need to fuck me now."

"Dammit, Nadia." His gaze ignited as his arms tightened around her. "You make a joke of my self-control. I want nothing more than to be inside you. But I can't be slow and sweet right now."

"Good, because I need it hard and fast." Her fingers dug into his shoulders. "Please, Kaname."

"God, Nadia." With quick movements, he produced a condom out of his pocket, dropped his pants, and tore open the packet. He rolled the condom on as she watched.

She licked her lips. "I can't wait to suck you off the way you did me. You should know what this feels like."

"I think I'm about to find out." He cupped her buttocks in his palms. "Guide me home, sweetheart."

She reached down between them, fitting the blunt head of his cock to her passion-slick opening. He slammed forward with a grunt, impaling her. Their simultaneous groans filled the air as she wrapped her legs securely about his waist. The sensation of him inside her, hot and hard and thick, made her whimper with relief.

"Fuck, Nadia." He rested his forehead against hers, his breath shuddering out of him. "You're like liquid fire and I'm willingly burning alive."

He partially withdrew then thrust home again, again, again. "Don't know how long I can last."

"We've got all night for round two," she reminded him. "We need this, just like this, right now." She clamped her inner muscles down on him.

It was like tossing alcohol on a flame. With a growl he began to fuck her in earnest, his muscular body slamming into her like a battering ram. Nadia could only hold on for dear sweet life as he set his teeth to the curve of flesh between ear and shoulder, holding her in place for his sensual onslaught. The friction of her bare skin against the fabric of his sweater combined with the hard edge of the counter beneath her and the silken steel of his cock inside her to set her nerve endings alive.

As hard and as long as she'd come before, she shouldn't have had another go in her. But Kane had lowered her inhibitions and elevated her desire, and her body once again tightened with the need to come. She reached between them, splaying her fingers around his surging cock, using her thumb to stroke her clit.

"Yes, baby, yes," he uttered against her throat. "Come for me, sweetheart. Let me feel you clamp down on me again."

Unbelievably her body answered his demand as an orgasm not quite as violent as the previous one rocked her to her core. Her nails dug into his shoulders as she bucked against him, her channel spasming around his cock.

"Fuck." Kane drove into her so brutally it was a wonder he didn't uproot the island. Then he tossed his head back, his features strained as he came with a loud, guttural groan before sagging against her, his head resting on her shoulder.

SEVEN

"Oh my God." Nadia slumped against him, her soft body pliant. "We just had sex on my kitchen island."

"Hell yeah, we did," Kane replied, warm with pleasure and satisfaction. He licked her throat, the taste of her addictive. "I hope this proves to you that last night wasn't a fluke."

"I have never been so thoroughly convinced in my life." She straightened, groaning when he withdrew from her. "But this is my kitchen counter. I roll dough out on this granite!"

He removed the condom, snagging a paper towel to wrap it in. Not wanting to be too far from her, he cleaned up at the kitchen sink then righted his clothing. "I'll help you scour it clean," he told her, helping her down and keeping her steady as she regained her footing. "Just tell me where the cleaning supplies are. And the garbage can."

"Under the kitchen sink. But you can't scour granite. It's granite!"

He'd been in the process of returning to the kitchen sink, but turned back to her. It sounded like she was freaking out, but why? "Nadia?"

She clung to him, looking up at him with cognac-colored eyes, panic pushing away sated passion. "I think I'm freaking out."

He cupped her cheek. After only twenty-four hours of intimacy he couldn't be near her without touching her. He was out of his mind with wanting her, and he didn't care. What he did care about was her having doubts. He didn't like it. "Are you freaking out because of the sex, or because the sex was on the countertop that you roll dough on?"

She was still naked, her dress a pool of fabric on the floor. Her balance of soft curves and hard angles was poetic perfection, which told him just how sex-addled she'd made him. She sucked her bottom lip between her teeth, and damn if he didn't feel his cock stirring again. "Uhm, would you feel bad if I said both?" she asked as she reached for her dress, stepped back into it.

"I feel bad that you feel bad." Deciding to give her a bit of space, he rummaged beneath her kitchen sink for the supplies she needed. Realizing what he had in his hands, he straightened, his eyebrows raised. "Wait. You clean your countertops with vodka?"

She reached for the giant plastic bottle of alcohol. "This stuff really isn't fit to be called vodka. At least no Russian worth her salt would put it to her lips. Nana Spiceland had me cleaning her kitchen with the rotgut stuff since I was five and helping her and my father Victor cook."

She handed the bottle back to him, then pulled a thick white cloth out of a drawer. "But I cut my vodka with castile soap and rosemary oil. It cleans without streaking, without damaging my granite, and I like the smell of rosemary. Just pour it on."

He did as ordered, then watched her use both hands to push and pull the thick cloth across the counter, her arm muscles flexing with the pressure she used. She had a strong grip, he knew, but he wondered if the pressure she exerted now was her usual strength from making pastries all day long or a manifestation of her nerves. "Do you want to tell me why you freaked out?"

She sighed as she leaned against the counter, giving him an excellent view of her cleavage. "I know I asked for this loud and clear. And I like it. I really like it. I guess, well, I guess I wasn't expecting it to be so damn good. I mean, I know you're used to it, but I've been out of the dating and sex scenes for more than three years. I'm rusty."

What the hell? He wrapped his hand around her wrist to get her attention. "What is it that you think I'm used to?"

"This." She waved a hand between them, sending the scent of rosemary wafting through the air. "You've done this a lot, I know, and I've had my fair share of partners too, but this sort of intensity is a new experience for me."

"Would it help you to know that this intensity is new to me as well?"

"Is it?" Disbelief colored her tone.

"Nadia." He tapped the back of her hand to get her to look at him. "I've had lots of sex. Most of it was good and some of it was great because it's important to me that my partner and I get what we want and need out of it. If you want, we can sit down and discuss our sexual histories and share our medical records. What I want is to make sure you feel like you can trust me."

"I trust you, Kane." She paused, blinking as if surprised by her words. "I do trust you. I'm just a little skittish."

More than a little, and it was enough to make him wonder if she had trust issues from a previous relationship. "I understand. I have to admit, I wasn't prepared for how visceral my reaction to you would be either. It's all right to be cautious. I want you to feel safe with me."

"I do."

He shook his head. "If you did, you wouldn't have freaked out."

A flush crept across her cheeks as she dropped her gaze. "Kane . . ."

"It's okay, Nadia." He reached out, lifted her chin. "It's my responsibility to make sure you trust me to keep you safe so that you're able to let go and truly enjoy yourself, whether that's reenacting scenes from *The Perfumed Garden* or something else. I don't take that responsibility lightly. Do you believe me?"

She searched his expression. He hoped his sincerity came through. Finally the uncertainty cleared from her eyes. "I believe you."

He released a breath. "Do you trust me to keep you safe while maximizing your pleasure?"

She folded her bottom lip between her teeth. "Maximizing?"

So fascinated was he by the way she worried her full bottom lip that it took him a moment to process her question. "You mentioned other things besides the *Garden*."

"True." Thoughts moved behind her expressive gaze. "Maybe I should have some sort of safe word," she suggested. "That way I can explore, you can push me, but we'll both know when I'm really at my limit."

She scrunched her shoulders. "I mean, I'm not into pain or anything. I guess you could say that I've seen enough and read enough to be kink-curious. Everyone's into something in Los Angeles, you know?"

Kane smiled. He'd been about to suggest something similar. A frank discussion about hard limits might be unsexy, but establishing ground rules up front meant a better time could be had by all later. Nadia was sensual and passionate by nature, he could see that clearly. That passion made her daring. He wanted to be the one to help her explore, to push her boundaries. He wanted to be the one to awaken her full sensuality.

"I think that's an excellent idea," he told her. "Any idea what you'd like your safe word to be, or do you want to think about it for a while?"

"I already have an idea of what I'd like to use." Her teasing smile lit her eyes. "Sticky buns."

He ran his forefinger down her cheek to her chin, tilting her face up. She hadn't bothered with makeup, but the remnants of afterglow still flushed her cheeks and shone in her eyes, making her beautiful. "I think that's a perfect choice."

"I think so too." She caressed his shoulders. "Sorry for the freak-out."

"Don't ever apologize to me for that. You felt what you felt, we talked it out and now we're good. And your countertop is drunk." He gave her a quick, hard kiss. "Are you ready for dinner?"

He clearly heard her stomach rumble, causing them both to laugh. "Apparently I've worked up an appetite. Give me a moment to clean up and I'll come back to help."

"Sure thing." He released her, watching with admiration and appreciation as she strolled out of the kitchen then up the stairs to the second level. Grinning like the village idiot, he finished cleaning up, put her cleaning supplies away, and began rummaging through the well-stocked professional kitchen as he began the prep work for dinner.

Relief filled him. He could understand Nadia being uneasy with the explosiveness of their connection, considering that she hadn't been in a relationship in a while. It had taken him by surprise too. She'd caught his attention and held it from the first day he'd seen her in the café. She was sugar, she was spice, she was the answer to a question he hadn't even known he was asking.

He needed someone like her, he realized. Someone who could make him forget the pressure of his job, the bleak evil of his consulting work. Someone willing to explore all the pleasures that human sexuality had to offer without thinking they were dirty or depraved.

Nadia could do that, ease his hunger for more when it came to sex. Though he had to admit, sex with Nadia was plenty damn hot without enhancements. He doubted he'd be able to look at her kitchen island or sofa without remembering how she'd come for him.

As he worked, he took a long perusal of the main level of her home. He'd been rightfully occupied the night before and hadn't paid much attention to his surroundings. The main floor was completely open, save for a small room she used as an office just off the foyer opposite the coat closet and half bathroom. The living area boasted furniture designed for lounging and relaxing, microsuede pieces in rich browns, copper and pear green accented with brightly patterned pillows and knitted throws that made him wonder if they'd been handed down from her grandmother. A dark wood entertainment console sat on one wall, filled with the obligatory flatscreen TV and other components, including the surprising addition of a gaming system.

Then again, Nadia probably had her friends over frequently and loved entertaining. He didn't know of any other single woman her age with a rustic trestle table with seating for eight that stood in the open dining area in front of the kitchen. Though she probably worked some hellaciously early hours running the bakery, he had a feeling that her friends were important to her and they gathered together often.

The oversized windows on the far wall framed French doors that opened onto a balcony that presented a view of the gentrified business district that made Crimson Bay a tourist destination for people looking to get away from big SoCal cities for the weekend. Although night had fallen he was sure bright natural light spilled into the room during the day, emphasizing the openness without making it seem cold or sterile. Overall, the place was bright, warm, and comfortably sexy without trying, quite like its owner.

Nadia returned a few minutes later, brimming with energy and smiles, her earlier uncertainty gone. He nodded at the stack of index cards in her hand. "What are those for?"

"I thought I'd write down each of the sundry positions mentioned in chapter six," she answered. She dropped the cards and a couple of pens on the breakfast bar before joining him in the kitchen. After a quick survey of his preparations so far she pulled out a package of metal skewers for the vegetables he'd cubed. "That way we can randomly choose one when we get together."

"Good idea." He gestured toward the satchel he'd left over by the coffee table. "I have a couple of different copies of the book. Feel free to pick whichever version you want. Oh, and write down a few wild cards too."

"Wild cards?"

He began to thread the vegetables as she retrieved his bag. "If you draw a wild card, it means that person can choose whatever they want to do, from the book or otherwise."

A speculative gleam lit her gaze as she settled onto a barstool. "Whatever we want, huh?"

"Within reason. You may have some hard limits that will have you using your safe word."

She nodded as she mulled that over. "What about you? Do you have a safe word, or hard limits?"

He brushed a balsamic marinade over the vegetable kebabs. "I'm not into blood play, so no needles or knives. As for a safe word, why don't I use yours? That'll make it easy for both of us."

"Okay."

He glanced at her as he turned on the gas to the grill attachment. The wickedness that danced in her eyes flipped his switch, making him hard again. "Do I even want to know the ideas spinning in your head?"

She gave him a cheeky grin. "Probably not."

"Considering our first date, I'll just have to hope that you draw a wild card sooner rather than later." He transferred the swordfish steaks to the grill. "I hope you don't mind me making myself at home in your awesome kitchen."

"Surprisingly, no." She flipped open the Burton translation, then drew the stack of cards closer. "But that's probably because you screwed me into acceptance. Though I must say, I think having a man who's not my father cook me dinner is very sexy."

"Noted. I look forward to impressing and arousing you with my culinary skills."

"Go easy on me," she said, laughing as she began to make notations. "Thanks to you, I've gone from zero to two hundred in the sex department. Not that I'm complaining, but I still need to be able to function. I do have a café to run, you know."

He did know, and he wanted to make sure he didn't have a negative impact on her and her schedule. "What are your hours at the café? I'm assuming your day starts really early."

"It does," she answered with a nod. "We open at seven. I'm usually downstairs by four to start the breakfast pastries that I prep the afternoon before. I have an assistant who comes in about an hour after I do. After the breakfast goods we bake our designer cupcakes and pastries and whatever breads Siobhan needs for her lunch menu. Since we're in the business district, our business dies off at two, and we close by three. We do a limited menu on Saturdays with breakfast items from nine to eleven and lunch from eleven to one. Sunday is my sleep late day since we're closed, though for me that's usually somewhere around seven, and I'm usually doing planning and prep work for the start of the week."

He filed away the information. "What made you decide on a bakery and café instead of a restaurant?"

"Restaurants have a higher fail rate than cafés, which aren't much better. Besides, Siobhan and I know our limitations. The last thing either one of us needed was the stress and long hours of trying to get a restaurant up and running. The café lets us indulge our love of cooking and baking and trying out new recipes, and not having to handle a dinner crowd means we don't have to overextend ourselves and we can still have lives. Mostly."

"Can I ask why you didn't try for another cooking show or writing cookbooks after you got out of rehab? For some of those Hollywood types, being in rehab is almost a fashion accessory."

A shadow crossed her expressive features as she slid off the barstool. "For some it is. Rehab might even boost their careers, giving them a weird sort of street cred. But for some of us it's impossible to recover from and the only option is to burn the bridges and leave town."

He remained silent as he watched her pull a bottle of red out of her wine fridge, then uncork it to breathe. "You think you wouldn't have recovered your career."

She placed a set of wineglasses on the counter, her moments measured. "Honestly?"

"Always."

"I didn't try. I saw the writing on the wall. Even if I hadn't, I didn't think I'd be able to hack it. It was a grueling life and I got caught up in it and lost myself in the process. I didn't want to face that sort of stress or temptation again."

He gave her a considering look as he tested the doneness of the fish. Nadia was a survivor. He knew that by the matter-of-fact way that she admitted her shortcomings and took responsibility for her actions. Beneath her passion was a core of steel. Once she learned from a mistake, he doubted she'd let herself get trapped again.

"You didn't think you could handle Hollywood, so you decided to become a small business owner instead. Sounds like you can handle more than you give yourself credit for."

The smile she gave him lit the room. "Thank you for that. But it helps to have a solid network of support. I doubt Siobhan and I could have been as successful as we are if it weren't for our friends and chosen family."

"So no expansion plans outside of the business district?" he asked as he plated their food.

"God, no," she replied with a laugh, taking their wine, glasses, and silverware over to the dining table. "We like our little place, like being part of the community and knowing our regulars. If we do any expansion, it'll be to open for a longer stint on Saturdays, but that's about it. We're making a decent enough amount of money to support the café and ourselves, and we're happy with the way it is. I've had enough of letting ambition drive my life and make my decisions. Now the decisions are based on what's right for me and Siobhan, what can we handle. It's worked pretty darn well for us for the last handful of years."

"Sounds like it." He shut off the grill then followed her with their plates. "If you hate it, you won't hurt my feelings. Much."

Nadia snorted. "Somehow I doubt your ego is that fragile, Professor Sullivan."

"You're right," he said as they settled at the table. "It comes from being confident in knowing what I'm capable of."

"What are you capable of?"

He gave her a long look. "Whatever I put my mind to."

She saluted him with the wine bottle and a lopsided grin before pouring. "Here's to discovering everything we're capable of."

"I'll drink to that."

EIGHT

"So what made you go into the field of human sexuality, when you could have so easily been a chef?" Nadia asked as she dug into the delicious meal. "It's not like people wake up one morning and go, 'Hey, I want to study how people think about sex.' I didn't even know it was something you could study for a degree program."

"True, and thank you," he said as he watched her eat. His focus should have made her self-conscious but he seemed pleased that she enjoyed the food he'd prepared for her. "You'll be happy to know that there's no great tragedy in my past that led me to my chosen field. Not really."

"Not really?" She munched on a skewer of vegetables, cupping her hand to catch the juice that squirted when she bit into a tomato. "What does *not really* mean?"

"My parents and I lived all over the world before we settled in Seattle when I was thirteen. So I got exposed to a lot of different cultures and people. Some places are more sexually repressed than America, but many aren't. There are some that recognized a third gender, for example. It was halfway through my freshman year in college when I had an epiphany. It might have been the copious amounts of alcohol and the lively discussion on men and women and dating and sex and what was acceptable that inspired me. Anyway, I realized that sexual education—real education, not just lip service—would go a long way to encourage sexual acceptance in society as a whole. Especially if we could all agree that consenting adults are sovereign in their own bedrooms."

"Or kitchens," she added with a sly smile.

He winked at her. "Or their own kitchens."

"Okay, so you got a degree in sexual psychology and became a professor. But you do more than teach, right? You write too."

"Actually, I did some writing and counseling before I became a professor," he replied, pausing to finish off his vegetables. "I got on with a think tank in D.C., published some more, and then got noticed by Dean Campbell at Herscher. She invited me to join the newly created Center for Human Studies here. Then the Red Light Rapist case happened."

She nodded. "I remember a little about that. Every thin blonde woman between eighteen and thirty thought she was a target. How did you get involved?"

He fiddled with his wineglass, looking sheepish. "Well, I had the temerity to tell the FBI their profile was wrong. Things went downhill from there."

She stared at him in disbelief. "Taking on the FBI? Is that what got you on all the national news channels?"

He grimaced. "Yeah, it was apparently a slow news week.

Anyway, the publicity led to more speaking engagements, a book deal, and a rush to get the department ramped up. After all, Dr. Kaname Sullivan, Professor of Human Sexuality, Center for Human Studies, Herscher College, sounds awfully impressive to the media. It made it seem like I actually knew what I was talking about."

"You did know what you were talking about."

"True." He said it matter-of-factly, as if he had no reason to be modest when it came to his career. Truth be told, he didn't. "The net result was record enrollment in our program, which made everyone at Herscher happy."

She took a sip of her wine. "It might have been a slow news week, but I'm sure the fact that you're drop-dead gorgeous didn't hurt."

"You just called me gorgeous. I'll have to remember that."

"Don't let it go to your head, Professor. I'm surrounded by gorgeous people."

"But not drop-dead gorgeous ones," he replied with a grin. "I'm sure my genes had a lot to do with my popularity, but I'm lucky in that I have a brain to back up my looks. The book deal followed, and like I said, we're bursting at the seams as far as enrollment is concerned. I'm hoping that will translate into tenure pretty soon, since I really do enjoy teaching."

"Maybe it's my imagination, but I thought I heard a *but* in there. Am I wrong?"

"No." He took her hand, kissed her fingers. "The downside is that I have to deal with ambitious colleagues and young coeds with stars in their eyes, not to mention overactive imaginations."

"The nickname."

"Yes, the nickname," he agreed. "Not only that, but the road to tenure is always a rocky one. I have options though. I'll survive."

"Goodness, Kane. Coworkers and students?" Her muscles trembled with the need to hug him, offer him comfort. Other than the first day he'd come into the café, she'd never seen him upset. He was always cool, almost detached, even though she knew now he was anything but. She had no idea what he faced daily in his job.

"And with that, I'm done talking about myself. I'd much rather talk about you."

"Me?" She waved her free hand with a laugh. "We've already talked about me."

"I'd like to get to know you better, Nadia."

"There's nothing much to talk about. My life's pretty boring now."

He snorted. "With the company you run and the friends you keep, I seriously doubt your life is boring."

"Okay, maybe not boring," she conceded. "But it's nothing like it was before."

He kept a hold on her fingers, and she enjoyed the warmth, the easy comfort. The realization that she trusted him had surprised her. Trust wasn't an easy thing for her anymore, not after her experiences in her former life. There was something about Kane, though, something about his quiet, commanding air and ability to smoothly take control that told her that she could trust him. She believed that he would push her while making sure she was safe. Surely sharing bits and pieces of her life was a small price to pay for that?

"Do you miss it? Your former life?"

She dropped her gaze. "Sometimes," she admitted softly. "It was cool being the 'it' girl for a while. Being young and pretty and

thin with a slightly bent personality didn't hurt either. I had the show and cookbooks, and outside of the show I got requests to do birthday and wedding and party cakes for a lot of musicians and young Hollywood types, which meant I got into a lot of parties. At parties you get exposed to things, sometimes without even realizing it. Partying and shooting the show took a lot of energy, and I leaned on my manager more than I should have. The problem with burning the candle at both ends with a flamethrower chaser is that you burn out way too fast. Which is exactly what I did. Then reality hit me in the face for good measure, and I paid the price."

"Do you want to talk about it?" he asked, rubbing his thumb lightly over the back of her hand.

Her shoulders tightened. She wanted to draw her hand away. She wanted to hold on forever. "No, I don't. Not to you."

A muscle in his cheek flinched. She knew she'd hurt his feelings when he released his grip. "Okay."

"Kane." She blew out a breath, wrapping her fingers around his hand and bringing it to her chest. "The Los Angeles me was completely different from the Crimson Bay me. I like that you don't know that other version of me. That you only know this Nadia, the café owner. The reality show me wasn't very nice at the end, and I'd rather that you not know too much about her because I don't want you to look at the current version of me differently. Does that make sense?"

"It does."

She squeezed his fingers. Even though she held his hand against her chest, she still felt the same warm tingles resonating throughout her body whenever he touched her. "I like this current version of me. I think this is the real me, the way I was before I went to Hollywood. I also really like the way you look at me now."

It seemed to take an effort for him to tear his gaze away from where his hand lay folded against her cleavage. "What way is that?"

"Like you could eat me up."

"I can. You're a smorgasbord of pleasure, Nadia, and I want to take my time with you." He lifted her hand to his mouth. "Spend the weekend with me."

The request punched her low in the gut. She wanted to say yes immediately, and that alone made her pause. "Spend the weekend with you? At your place?"

He nodded, confirming she hadn't misheard him. "If you can't do Friday night because of working the café Saturday morning, then spend Saturday afternoon and all day Sunday with me. I promise not to keep you up too far beyond your bedtime. But if I do, I'll make sure you're so exhausted you'll fall asleep immediately."

"Kane . . ." His name was half whine, half plea from her throat.

"Do you not want to spend the weekend with me?"

"Are you kidding? My lady parts are still jumping for you and are all *heck yeah*. But the rest of me is thinking there's no way I can keep this up. I think I'm going to have to change my multivitamin to an oyster blend or something."

He laughed. "I'm pretty sure that's only alleged to work on the male of the species, but it'll be interesting to see the results."

He nibbled at her fingertips, making her moan. "I don't know if you noticed or not, but I didn't mention the words *sex*, *garden*, or *orgasm* in my invitation. In fact, it's entirely possible that I simply want to show you my kitchen. My mother has a ramen recipe that will make you cry tears of joy, and I'm not talking about the stuff that's fifty for a dollar and in every college student's pantry."

Cooking with Kane. The idea was certainly tempting. If he

approached the culinary arts with the same dedication with which he approached sexual pleasure, cooking with him was sure to be a decadent, fulfilling experience. The man knew how to appeal to her most basic needs. Still, "Somehow I doubt that we can be in the same room alone for more than half an hour and not end up having sex."

He sucked her forefinger into the warmth of his mouth and she nearly slid off her chair. "You may be right. Or we could challenge ourselves and go for a whole hour before having sex. So does that mean yes?"

She closed her eyes, the only way she could manage the sensations churning inside her. "It means I wish I could, but I already have plans."

"Oh." Disappointment filled his voice.

A twinge of guilt spiked through her. Or was that her own disappointment? "If you recall, you and I just started a couple of days ago."

"That's true." He pressed a kiss to her wrist, leaving thrills in his wake. "I suppose I'm being greedy, but I haven't finished my very thorough exploration of you yet."

"One Friday a month Club Tatas hosts the Crimson Bay Bombshells. They're a burlesque troupe, and Sugar is one of the performers. The show's this Friday. I'd like it if you would join us."

His brows lowered in confusion. "I thought Club Tatas was a drag joint?"

She snorted. "I should be surprised that you know that, but for some reason I'm not. Yes, Club Tatas is mostly a drag revue. But on the second Friday, they add a burlesque show. Sugar performs in that."

"You mentioned Sugar before. Which of your friends is Sugar? Siobhan?"

"Bingo. Sugar Malloy is Siobhan's stage name. She's really good." She traced his eyebrows with her free hand. She hadn't realized how pleasurable the simple act of touching another person could be. Then again, she hadn't had an overwhelming need to touch someone like she felt with Kane. "Will you come? We get dressed up in costumes and just hang out. Even Vanessa comes, and it's not usually her type of scene. The core—that's me, Audie, and Jas, my assistant baker—sit with Vanessa because we tend to not drink when we're out, so she has a safe buffer around her."

Those fathoms-deep eyes watched her as he digested that information. "Does Vanessa need that buffer because she's still in recovery for alcohol?" When she nodded, he added, "Will she mind that you told me?"

"I don't think so. If you're going to hang out with me, you'd eventually end up hanging with my friends. You'll need to know what you should and shouldn't do around them, like ordering a round of tequila shots for our table."

"Makes sense." His expression remained thoughtful. "Is she the only one?"

"All of us are recovering from one thing or another. It's part of why we stick together and have one another's backs. But we also like the hell out of one another."

She paused, wondering if he was having second thoughts. Equal parts relief and disappointment welled inside her. She wanted to keep seeing Kane. And, she realized with surprise, she wanted to be with him outside of a bedroom. She liked talking to him. Would Kane want to interact with her and her friends in a social setting, though? She and her friends had issues they were in various stages of managing, and some were managing better than others. Some-times things went great and sometimes they got messy.

"None of us are perfect, and we try our best to accept people as they are, without judgment, since we're all works in progress. Do you think you can handle that? It's no big deal if you think it's too much trouble. It can be a bit much at times for outsiders to take on."

"I can handle it." He gave her a quick kiss. "Thanks for inviting me. I know exposing your circle of friends to me, to us, has got to be a big deal for you."

How the hell did he know that? "Have you been talking to Siobhan?"

"Why would I be talking to Siobhan?"

"You're being very accommodating," she noted, narrowing her eyes at him.

"Of course." He kissed her shoulder, then her collarbone, then her throat. "You're not too much trouble. Even if you were, you're worth it. Besides, I have the best incentive to be accommodating."

She laughed. "I appreciate that. I do have the early shift at the café this Saturday, and prep work to do on Sunday. But I trade out with Jas, and he'll work next weekend."

"Are you telling me that you're free next weekend?"

"Yep, that's exactly what I'm telling you."

He rose to his feet, gathering their plates. "Great. Why don't I clean up while you finish making the cards? Then you can have the honors of the inaugural draw."

"All right." She took her wine then returned to the breakfast bar to finish writing out the notes, conscious of Kane moving around her kitchen with casual assurance. It should have bothered her, the easy way he had, but instead it gave her a sense of calm. His confidence relaxed her. He wasn't trying to prove anything. He simply was what he was.

He held out a canvas shopping bag to her. "I found this under the sink. Will it work to hold the notecards?"

"Perfect."

She scooped up all the folded cards and dropped them into the bag. He shook it, tumbled the cards together, then held the open bag out to her. "Ready?"

With her nerves dancing with excitement, she reached in, pulled out a card. Kane leaned in close as she unfolded the card. *"El keurchi,"* she murmured, sure she'd butchered the pronunciation. "The fifteenth manner."

"Belly to Belly." Kane pulled her to her feet. "'The man and the woman are standing upright, face-to-face; she opens her thighs; the man then brings his feet forward between those of the woman, who also advances hers a little.'"

With his hands to her hips, he subtly guided her into the proper stance. "'In this position the man must have one of his feet somewhat in advance of the other. Each of the two has the arms round the other's hips; the man introduces his verge, and the two move thus intertwined.'"

Nadia's breath stuttered in her chest as she settled her hands on his hips. "This might be a little difficult to do, since I'm a few inches shorter than you."

"Then you need to make sure you're wearing heels," he murmured, his lips grazing hers. "When I see you on Friday."

He stepped away. It wasn't until he replaced the books in his satchel that his words registered. "Friday? But today's Wednesday!"

"I have a late class tomorrow, and since you have to get up before the roosters do, I won't come by tomorrow." He cupped her cheek before kissing her again. "I don't want your work to suffer. I take my responsibilities seriously. Besides, you're my sole supplier of sticky buns."

His concern touched her, even if it didn't make her happy. She could go a couple of days with little sleep, but she knew she was at her best with at least six hours of rest. "I appreciate the concern, but we don't have to go—"

"Oh, and no masturbation without my permission."

"What?"

Sternness hardened his features. "If you need self-gratification, you have to call me first. Though your reward will be greater if you wait until Friday."

"But . . ." Two whole days? He'd ended her sexual drought with a thunderstorm of pleasure and now he wanted her to abstain for two whole days?

She opened her mouth to protest again, but he cupped the back of her neck with one hand, drew her closer. "You promised your orgasms to me, Nadia. Can I trust you?"

She stared up at him, one hand on his chest. She hadn't expected that he needed to trust her just as much as she needed to trust him. Trust had to go both ways, didn't it? "Does that mean you won't masturbate either?"

"It does. We're in this together."

Well, as long as she didn't have to suffer alone. "All right then. Until Friday."

She just hoped she could last until then.

NINE

Nadia and her friends made their way into the show level of Club Tatas on Bay Street, aiming for the left side of the stage. A sizeable crowd already clogged the floor, waiting for the Crimson Bay Bombshells to take the stage.

Siobhan had joined the group about a year and a half ago. Her vivacious personality, dangerous curves, and beautiful blonde-haired, blue-eyed looks made her a hit with the crowd. Why she didn't capitalize on the adulation and indulge in a steady stream of lovers was a continual topic of discussion in their Bitch Talk sessions. Nadia knew her friend still bore scars from her ruined marriage and estranged relationship with her daughter, but she didn't like that Siobhan thought she still had to do penance for that. Hopefully Nadia's affair with Kane would inspire her friend to move forward.

If Nadia didn't kill Kane first.

It had been the longest two days of her life. Thursday morning, the repercussions of her sexual acrobatics had come back to haunt her with long-unused muscles lodging a protest as she went about her duties at the café. Thursday night she'd indulged in a long soak in the tub, then distracted herself with a touch-base phone call with her fathers and entries in her recovery journal. While she did talk to Kane, their conversation had been brief, with neither taking the other up on the request to self-gratify. By the time she'd gotten dressed and met up with her friends, Nadia was spoiling for a fight and the need to come.

"I thought you were coming with the professor," Jas, gorgeous in a black patent leather bustier and blue-black wig, said as Nadia slipped into one of the chairs that had been commandeered for their group. His girlfriend Tracy, wearing a black suit, smiled a welcome.

"She was," Audie quipped. "Several times from what I heard."

"That's what you get for hanging around outside my door," Nadia snarked before turning back to their laughing friends. "Kane had some last-minute stuff he had to do. He's going to meet us here later."

"You did let him know what kind of club Tatas is, right?" Jas asked. "I'm surprised you're not standing at the door waiting to claim him as soon as he walks in."

"He's a grown man, he can take care of himself." Nadia looked around for a waiter, wanting to dodge the questions she knew were on the way. "Besides, I don't need to stake a claim. It's not like that."

"So you're saying you're not exclusive?" Audie wondered, her eyebrows shooting skyward in surprise. "That doesn't seem like the kind of relationship you would go for."

"Kane and I are sexually exclusive," Nadia explained, trying to capture a waiter's attention. "That's about as relationship as this thing is going to get."

She could tell herself that while sitting here with her friends. She could tell herself that at work or when she was alone. When she was with Kane, when they were breathing the same air, her brain seemed to short-circuit. All she could think about was having more of him as soon as possible. Even now she could feel the desire rising up in her, a craving that overrode everything else. Just like—

No. She shook her head. Craving Kane was nothing like craving a drug-induced high. She wasn't hurting anyone by having sex with Kane. Her eyes were wide open, she knew what she was doing. And what she was doing was having the best sex of her life with a man who wasn't going to try to break her to make her more dependent on him. Who wasn't going to complicate things. The moment it became more than that, she'd walk away. She'd have to.

"It's just sex."

"Okay," Vanessa said, her tone soothing. "It's just sex, not a relationship. At least the professor is living up to his nickname."

Nadia pressed her thighs together. "He most definitely is."

Audie leaned close. "Have y'all done anything kinky yet?"

"Audie!" Nadia turned. "Where is the waiter for this section?"

"Don't try to deflect the conversation!" the redhead exclaimed. "You know I had to ask you about that. The professor wouldn't have the nickname he does just from the missionary position."

"I'm not giving you guys any more details," Nadia insisted, looking around to avoid eye contact with her friends. They talked, they shared, they bullshitted each other, but she wasn't feeling it at the moment. Probably not ever, not about Kane. It was one thing to talk about having sex, but the details, the other . . . it was too intense, too everything to share it. "Screw the waiter, I'm headed to the bar. Anybody want anything?"

Audie ordered two tequila shots. Vanessa gave Nadia a sympathetic smile before ordering a bottle of water. As a recovering alcoholic, Vanessa was the de facto designated driver. Nadia usually stayed sober with her, if only so she could cock-block for Audie to help her with her mission to limit her one-night stands.

Nadia made her way to the bar, holding down her flouncy skirt along the way. Everyone dressed up for the burlesque shows, the costumes ranging from saloon girls to steampunk to fifties rockabilly and mobsters. She'd chosen an imperial red corset with a cherry blossom pattern atop a black ruffled miniskirt that was more petticoat than skirt. Thigh-high red and black striped stockings, platform Mary Janes and a red and black fascinator completed her look. She hoped Kane would swallow his tongue when he saw her. She hoped he'd show up. She hoped he'd regret not coming over after his class ended.

Not wanting to examine her thoughts on the matter too closely—*keep it light, keep it light, girl*—she caught the bartender's attention and placed her order. Kane filled her mind, and only a few of her thoughts were charitable.

He'd sent her a text saying he'd meet her at Tatas. He hadn't mentioned a time and she hadn't wanted to ask. That wasn't what keeping things casual was about. She wanted to be cool and collected and prove that she wasn't sitting around waiting for him even if that was exactly what she was doing.

"Heh. I sure would like to steam her punk."

Nadia rolled her eyes at the large brown-haired man laughing with one of his friends. How unoriginal. She inhaled, torn between ignoring the guy and offering a pithy comeback, when another voice said, "That's not how you pick up a lady."

"Kane." Nadia's heart did one heavy thud as she turned around, then promptly forgot her anger as she caught sight of him sitting on a barstool.

He'd dressed to the theme of the night. Wine-red shirt beneath a black pinstriped vest complete with pocket watch and chain. Loose-fitting black trousers, shiny black shoes, and a black Fedora with a red satin band completed his look. Oh yeah, she'd be his gun moll any day.

Not that he needed to know that. Yet. "How would you pick me up?" she asked, ignoring the frat guy and his friend.

"I'd appeal to your sense of daring while offering a better alternative than steaming your punk."

He lightly grasped her fingers, his licorice-dark eyes glinting with appreciation and mischief as he pressed a kiss to the back of her hand. "'The languishing eye puts in connection soul with soul, and the tender kiss takes the message from member to vulva.'"

Poetry and descriptions that she'd laughed over in college provoked a different response when Kane spoke them. Her blood heated, her sex growing damp and heavy with the need to be filled.

"You win." She forgot about her erstwhile suitor as the heat in Kane's dark gaze captivated her, lured her in.

"I always try to." He passed several bills to the bartender, then settled his hand on her back, his fingers lightly tracing her corset lacing. "Especially when the prize is as worth it as you are."

Nadia sighed, fighting to keep her eyes from sliding closed as Kane's fingers worked their magic on her bare skin. Some people were pure swagger and false bravado with nothing to back it up. There was nothing fake about Kane. His natural assurance was sexy because he knew who he was, what he wanted, and what he was capable of. "Have you been here the entire time?"

"Not long." He tugged on her laces, and she swallowed a moan. "What are you thinking, Nadia?"

"That you're dangerous."

He leaned closer, his lips brushing her cheek. "You think you aren't?" His hand tightened on her laces again. "Especially wearing this?"

His hold and his voice caused a slow roll of lust low in her belly. "I hope you like what you see."

"*Like* doesn't come close to describing what I think about you in this corset." His index finger stroked her spine. "How long is the performance tonight?"

"N-ninety minutes."

"Ninety minutes to be on our best behavior. I don't know whether to weep or applaud. This is definitely going to be a test."

"What do you mean?"

"You'll see soon enough." He gathered half her drinks. "Let's go join your friends."

Nadia led the way back to their group, only to discover that all but one of the chairs had been filled. "Thanks for savings us seats, guys."

Audie gave her an apologetic smile as she gestured to the guy occupying one of the seats. "I hope you don't mind. Jack—"

"Jace," the stranger corrected, his gaze fixed on Audie's ample cleavage.

"—Jace is here alone, so I said he could sit with us."

"We're short a seat," Nadia pointed out. When it came to bagging guys Audie operated with single-minded focus, damn the consequences, and sometimes, her friends.

Kane solved the problem by putting down the drinks, sliding into the chair, and patting his lap. "Sit here."

Nadia hesitated. She knew how the night would go. Audie wouldn't last half the performance before making out with the new guy, if she didn't disappear with him outright. What could Nadia say though, without looking like a bitch?

Truthfully, Nadia wasn't sure she could survive an hour and a half sitting on Kane's lap. She'd been on a low simmer for the last forty-eight hours and she desperately needed relief. She didn't know if Audie's need for sex was mental more than physical, but if the redhead felt anything close to what Nadia had endured for the last two days, Nadia could almost understand why Audie was continually on the hunt.

Kane curled his fingers into the lacing across her back, snagging her attention. She saw the command in his expression but also concern and silent support. She immediately relaxed. She was there to have fun with her friends and watch Siobhan perform. Audie was grown and her choices were her own. She didn't need Nadia to play babysitter.

Nadia sank onto Kane's lap. Her short skirt and thong provided zero coverage, her bare buttocks sliding across the smooth fabric of his pants as she settled into place. His erection pressed against the back of her thighs, the heat of him branding her through the fabric.

She darted a glance at him. "A test for both of us, as I said." The velvet of his voice slid over her senses, pebbling her skin. "Ninety minutes until *el keurchi*. Now introduce me to your friends."

She belatedly made introductions, heat staining her cheeks as she noted the knowing glances from her extended circle of friends. With another fifteen minutes until show time, Nadia expected Kane to be bombarded with questions. He was, but he handled it well, engaging Vanessa in college talk and asking Jas about his cupcake-decorating technique, posing for photos. All the while, he would take sips of his icy drink, then trace his chilled fingertips over her spine, keeping her desire on a slow simmer. But if she thought that would be the extent of her torture, she was mistaken.

When the house lights dimmed and the mistress of ceremonies took the stage, Kane shifted his left hand. Nadia held her breath, tension filling her as she tracked his movement from her knee to her thigh, then to the hem of her skirt. He wouldn't, would he?

The first act took the stage, a ribald flasher skit that got the crowd roaring with laughter. Kane's hand slipped under her skirt and between her thighs. Nadia froze, biting her lip against a gasp of pleasure as his forefinger unerringly found her clit.

"Kane?"

He pressed a kiss to her bare shoulder. "I said you couldn't self-gratify," he said, his voice for her alone. "I never said I wouldn't pleasure you. Open your legs."

She couldn't. She shouldn't, not with her friends here, not with the crowd, the performers. But . . . it was dark enough, the table tall enough, her friends distracted enough.

Kane pinched the inside of her thigh. Nadia jumped, unable to hold back a *squee* of surprise. "Are you all right, Nadia?" Vanessa asked from the opposite side of the table.

"Y-yes," she answered, shifting to the position Kane demanded. "I just got hit with a draft of cold air."

Vanessa smiled. "Kane needs to do a better job of keeping you warm."

"I'll try harder, ma'am," the man in question said, his expert fingers finding their way beneath the flimsy barrier of the thong. He brushed his lips against her shoulder again. "If you want me to stop, you know what you have to say."

Her safe word, or rather, her safe phrase. If she said *sticky buns*, Kane would stop. She didn't want him to. Maybe she was too aroused, more bent than she realized, but the thought of this man stroking her to a climax in the middle of the club made her body tighten with anticipation. She wanted this. She wanted him.

She held back the words, twisting enough to kiss him instead. He took the opportunity to push his forefinger into her slick channel, his mouth devouring her moan of pleasure. "You're beautifully wet for me, sweetheart," he whispered with approval. "I think you like this more than you care to admit."

"I can admit it," she managed to say. "To you. I can also admit I like what you do to me."

"I'll be sure to keep up the good work. Oh, and Nadia?"

"Yes?"

"You still don't have permission to come."

The other performances passed in a blur as Kane stroked her to the edge repeatedly, only to bring her back down. It was ninety minutes of the most exquisite torture she'd ever experienced. She hadn't known her body was capable of holding out for so long. By the time the emcee announced Siobhan, Nadia was ready to explode.

The track for "When You're Good to Mama" from the musical *Chicago* rolled through the sound system. A spotlight appeared on the curtain, which parted to reveal Siobhan dressed as a very sexy prison guard with a crop instead of a police baton. The crowd, full of regulars, applauded as she strutted the stage, belting out the song in a clear, strong alto as she peeled off layers of the uniform. As the song reached its crescendo, Sugar took off the last piece to reveal bright pink glitter pasties and a black thong, the standard reveal for Club Tatas.

Nadia leapt to her feet, clapping and cheering as Sugar blew kisses while leaving the stage. She turned to Kane. "Isn't she fantastic?"

"She is." He snagged her around the waist, dragged her back down to his lap. "She's got a beautiful voice."

"Right." She snorted in disbelief. When she and Siobhan were side by side, Nadia knew everyone's eyes weren't on her. Compared to Siobhan's voluptuousness, Nadia was virtually flat-chested. It wasn't something she envied about her partner; it was a fact of life. For Kane to be so ambivalent about Siobhan's striptease when every other hetero male had his tongue dragging on the ground was suspect. "Is that the only thing you noticed?"

He pierced her with a glance. "I was finger-deep in a hot woman's pussy. Forgive me for being distracted."

"Ah . . . oh." His blunt response took the wind right out of her sails. "Well. Okay then. I'm sorry."

The harshness left his features. "You'll make it up to me." He glanced at his watch. "In fifteen minutes."

It was the longest fifteen minutes of her life. The emcee closed out the show and the house lights rose. Nadia noticed the empty chairs beside them. "Looks like Audie bailed," she said to no one in particular, unable to squelch the pang of regret.

"That's Audie being Audie," Vanessa said, rising to her feet. "I'm going to bail too. That's me being me, tired after a long day of work. Kane, you don't mind taking Nadia home, do you?"

"Of course not." His hand was warm on her back as he guided her to her feet. "It was nice to officially meet you."

"You too, Professor."

"Hey, do you guys want to come dancing with us at Down Below?" Tracy asked.

"I've got the breakfast shift tomorrow," Nadia answered, not wanting to give her assistant and his girlfriend the brush-off, but not in the mood for Club Tatas' basement dance club. "Next time for sure."

"Do you need to say good-bye to Siobhan before we leave?" Kane asked.

"She's usually in high demand after the show, taking pictures and signing autographs. She's got a serious local fan club. I'll just send her a text and tell her that I'm headed home."

"Do it. I've got ten minutes to get you out of here."

She pulled her phone out of her tiny crossbody purse then sent the text. That done, Kane led her out of the club and across the street to the premium parking deck. "How much longer?" she asked as they made their way to his car.

"Seven minutes." He handed her inside.

She waited until he joined her, then said, "I'd better get my apology out of the way."

Before he could stop her, she reached over, unzipped his pants, then reached her hand inside to find him still hard. She stroked him, pushing the foreskin back, then leaned over and did what she'd fantasized about for the past two days: took him into her mouth.

"Christ, Nadia!" His hips surged up, the head of his cock bumping the back of her throat as his hand tangled into her hair.

She came up for air. "Hold on. I'm still apologizing."

He started the car as she continued her delectable exploration, discovering the feel of him in her mouth, learning his taste as he drove. The sounds of his harsh breathing filled the car, giving her a thrill of pleasure.

"You like pushing me, don't you?" he ground out. "Almost as much as I like pushing you."

She hummed in agreement, running her tongue along his length before swirling around the head again. She liked knowing she could drive him to lose control, to push him to the same edge she balanced on, a heartbeat from letting go. Moisture had soaked through her panties long ago and she shimmied out of them, needing something, anything to ease the need that hadn't let her go from the moment she'd seen Kane in the club.

"Dammit." Kane pulled her free as he jerked the car to a stop, slammed it into park, then killed the engine. "Come on."

She got out of the car without waiting for Kane's assistance, ready to run for the elevator. She took a step then stopped as soon as she noticed the unfamiliar surroundings. "This isn't my place."

"I know. We're still in the parking deck." He draped a jacket over her shoulders then tugged her into the shadows around the corner from a stairwell, pressing her back against the wall.

Nadia gasped as she realized his intent. "Right here?"

"You dare to blow me in the car but balk at doing *el keurchi* here?" Reaching beneath her skirt, he easily thrust two fingers inside her, readying her even more. "Be daring, Nadia. Want me as much as I want you."

Be daring. She'd told him that's what she wanted. She had to live up to her own expectations, her own wants. At that moment, she wanted him inside her more than she wanted her next breath.

Uncertainty vanished as she reached for him, wrapping her hand around his thickness. He hadn't bothered tucking himself back into his pants, a sure indication that she'd pushed him to his limit. He grunted in approval as she guided his cock to her entrance, rubbing the tip along her slit to coat him in her juices and tease them both.

"Nadia . . ." Kane's voice was a low growl of warning. He threw his hips forward, surging through her fingers, embedding himself inside her.

"Hands on my hips, sweetheart," he ordered as he shifted his weight, his hands gripping her ass beneath her skirt. "*El keurchi*. Belly to belly, face to face, lips to lips. Squeeze me, babe. Squeeze me with that sweet pussy of yours."

Her inner muscles clamped down on him as he rocked forward. Fire erupted in her veins as desire steamrolled her. The man, the intensity, the risk of discovery all combined into a heady aphrodisiac. They moved together, a frantic, jerky dance of need that led to only one outcome.

Much too soon she could feel it, feel the orgasm rushing up from her toes. "Kane," she gasped, then shattered.

His mouth slammed down on hers, swallowing her cry as she came. His fingers dug deep into her buttocks, each wild thrust bumping her shoulders against the concrete wall. With a hoarse groan he buried himself to the hilt, spasms shaking his body as he poured deep inside her.

After a long moment, he pulled away from her. "Are you all right?"

"I'm better than all right." She reached out, cupped his cheek. "Are you?"

"I forgot a condom." He tucked himself in, straightened his clothes. "I forgot a fucking condom."

"We saw each other's records," she reminded him. "We're both clean, and I get birth control injections. We're good."

"Yeah. We're good together." He blew out a breath, then guided her back to the car. "You have an uncanny ability to make me lose multiple levels of control, Nadia Spiceland."

She forced a laugh. "You make it sound as if that's a bad thing."

"I don't know." He started the car. "Right now, I'm too damn satisfied to care."

TEN

"Dads!"

Surprised but pleased, Nadia stepped back to allow both her fathers to step over the threshold. Victor Spiceland immediately grabbed her up in one of his huge bear hugs, spinning her around until she was dizzy and giggling. "I can't believe you guys are here. You weren't due to come down for a visit until next month!"

"We had some free time," Nicholas Spiceland explained as he took his turn for a hug, dropping a kiss to her forehead.

"We were in the neighborhood," Victor answered at the same time.

Nadia took a step back, settling her hands on her hips. "Just in the neighborhood with time on your hands, huh? I may be a baker and not an engineer, but I do know that San Francisco is a hundred miles away and therefore not in the neighborhood."

"What, we can't come visit our favorite daughter?" Victor asked, maple brown eyes twinkling.

"I'm your only daughter," she reminded him, torn between exasperation, affection, and amusement. "What's up?"

"We weren't able to be here for your birthday," Nicholas explained in his quiet tone that had always managed to soothe her and keep her in line. He shed his coat, then took Victor's as Nadia closed and locked the door. "So we rearranged some things and started the family tour early."

She watched him hang their coats in the coat closet, her heart brimming. Her dads—actually, the entire Spiceland family—were her collective rock. They had walked the rocky road of recovery with her, from the moment she'd regained consciousness in the hospital after the accident to the day she'd left the rehabilitation facility somewhat better equipped to take control of her life and her choices. They'd helped her find a Narcotics Anonymous group that suited her and attended counseling sessions with her.

As thrilled as they'd been when she decided to leave Los Angeles after she left rehab and started her recovery, they'd been worried about her decision to start over somewhere new instead of returning home to San Francisco. It had taken them more than a year to accept her move to Crimson Bay, but they'd finally realized the small town had done wonders for her and Siobhan. The fact that they were less than two hours away by car helped. What helped more was each day she lived without popping pills, each day that took her further away from the person she had been, a person on a steep trajectory to self-destruction. She was in a good place now, and they knew it.

"It's okay, Dad," she said, giving him another hug as they made their way toward the kitchen, as everyone who visited her did. "We talked on the phone."

"He worries," Daddy Vic said, giving his spouse's shoulder an affectionate pat. They'd been together since their college days, and though she'd rolled her eyes at their public displays of affection as a kid, she loved and admired their easy way with each other. "He had to see for himself."

"I worry," Nicholas agreed. "Vic frets. He wouldn't relax until we were on the highway headed here."

Nadia stared at the two men she loved most in the world. Nicholas Spiceland had always been the quieter of her dads, as tall and silent as a redwood and just as permanently there with his unwavering support. His sternness and strict nature were a perfect foil for Victor, who was a head shorter but broader in the shoulders and had always worn his emotions on his sleeve. To Nadia, Victor was a walking, talking teddy bear, always ready to dispense a hug or a word of encouragement to his children.

Victor was the one she'd turned to for every scraped knee and broken heart, but Nicholas was the one she'd been terrified of disappointing. He hadn't wanted her to enter the reality show cooking competition but had supported her through it, ending up her most boisterous supporter when she'd won and got her own show. The only time she'd ever seen Nicholas cry was when she'd awakened in the hospital after the car accident that had killed her manager and nearly killed her. Seeing her stoic father break had riddled her with guilt she was still trying to overcome. She never again wanted to be the cause of that sort of pain for her fathers again.

"I'm okay. And I have the girls here. We support and encourage each other."

"How are the girls?" Victor asked as he inspected the contents of her fridge. He was always of the opinion that there wasn't anything that a good meal couldn't cure, especially a meal shared with friends and family. It was his enthusiasm as well as days spent in the kitchen with him and Nana Spiceland that made the decision to start a café a no-brainer.

"They're good. I'm assuming you're planning on staying over?"

"Only if we're not intruding," Nicholas said.

"Of course we're staying," Victor chimed in.

Nadia shook her head with a laugh. "I think you do that on purpose, just to keep us kids on our toes. Did you leave your bags in the hallway?"

"In the car," Nicholas said. "We can probably get a room at the B and B on Bay Street if you have plans."

"Just finished working out, then I planned to start on a few things for next week's menu." An image of Kane immediately came to mind. Saturday afternoons were spent taking care of personal errands while Sundays were about café business, but she'd been waffling on the idea of calling Kane to take him up on his offer to spend the remainder of the weekend together. Though they'd parted well enough the night before, something about Kane's after-sex reaction in the parking deck didn't sit well with her. She wanted to make sure they were still good.

"What're you thinking, princess?" Victor asked. "Are we interrupting something?"

Both men looked at her expectantly. Butterflies began to stomp grapes in her stomach. There was no way she was ready to tell her fathers about Kane. What in the world could she tell them anyway? "Hey, there's this great guy who's a customer at the café who I've been banging every chance I get"? Yeah, that would go over well. Not.

"No, just café business, like I said. Maybe I can invite everyone over tonight for an impromptu dinner party."

"It would be great to see the girls," Victor said. "Maybe we can even take you all out to your favorite party place."

"Oh no," Nadia said, shaking her head for emphasis. "There's no way I'm going to a drag bar with my dads."

Victor grinned at her discomfiture. "Why not? It will be fun. We could use a night out on the town."

"If anyone deserves one, it would be you guys," she agreed, "but not with your kid. You guys can take yourselves to the show."

"You can ride in with us and then we can go our separate ways at the door," Victor argued. "Far be it from us to keep our favorite daughter from trawling for hot guys."

"First, I'm your only daughter," she automatically retorted. "Second, I don't need to trawl for guys. Third, if you're serious about going to Tatas, I need to call the police chief and give him a head's-up that my dads are in town and encouraging my friends to be on their worst behavior."

"Vic, I thought we were planning a date, not playing chaperone," Nicholas said. "You know how the girls are. They'll be incorrigible just because we're there."

"Of course. That's part of the fun!"

The feeling was mutual, Nadia knew. Her fathers had taken her friends under their collective wing. Her friends were just as gaga over her fathers as they were about their "extra daughters," and Nadia didn't mind a bit. She knew how awesome her dads were, and considering that Siobhan's father had passed years ago, Audie didn't know hers, and Vanessa had a strained relationship with hers, she was glad her fathers wanted to be a paternal presence in her friends' lives.

"How's Audie doing?" Nicholas asked. Of all her recovering friends, Audie was the one who concerned Nicholas the most, and as the youngest, the one he felt most paternal toward.

"I honestly don't know, Dad," Nadia replied with a sigh. "She seems fine, but . . . I worry about her. I don't think she's hit her bottom yet."

Nicholas frowned. "I figured you and Siobhan would be enough of a steadying influence on her by now."

"I know," she replied, pleased that he'd consider her a steadying influence of any type. "I'm not at a good enough place to be a sponsor to anyone, and her issues are completely different from mine, but I'd hoped Siobhan and I could be living examples for her and anyone else in our group."

"That's all you can do, pumpkin," Victor said, giving her a one-armed hug. "That, and be ready to give her help when she asks for it. You can't force her."

"You're right." Audie had shown up at the café just before noon looking none the worse for wear, so Nadia had to accept that Audie knew how to take care of herself.

She blew her bangs out of her face, seeking to lighten the mood. "Speaking of people with issues, you said you were on a family tour. So I guess after me, you're going to San Diego to see Sergey?"

"Yes." Victor shook his head, his smile dimming. "I don't think he's doing as well as he wants us to think."

Her oldest brother had just watched his marriage to his high-school sweetheart implode without warning. Despite his best efforts, he hadn't been able to convince his wife to save their relationship.

"Poor Sergey." She realized with a flash of guilt that she hadn't talked to him in more than a week. "Is he in a bad way?"

"Jane moved her things out last week," Nicholas said. "I think he was holding out hope that she would change her mind as long as her belongings were still there, even if she wasn't. He's taking it pretty hard."

"It's still hard to believe that she'd leave him after all the years they've had together. Almost twenty years. She has to know he doesn't blame her for the miscarriages." Sergey and his wife had tried for years to have children, only to meet with repeated heartache. She'd thought they were going to adopt or try surrogacy, but the disappointments must have taken a toll, and their marriage had paid the ultimate price.

"I know," Nicholas said. "I suppose the grief and the guilt finally outweighed the love. Now the guilt and grief is all on Sergey's shoulders. We're hoping to convince him that a change of scenery would do him good."

"Maybe he should come here. This town is great for helping people heal from whatever ails them. I'll call him and ask him to come for a visit."

Sergey had been there for her when her life had disintegrated. Even though he was on the San Diego police force, he hadn't turned his back on her when her drug problem came to light.

"He'll probably appreciate that, but don't push him, okay?"

"I won't." Much. She didn't like anyone she knew to hurt, especially not those she considered family. Whatever she could do for her brother, she'd do.

"I guess Anton is still being Anton, right?"

Victor snorted. "You mean, is he still falling out of skyscrapers and perfectly working airplanes? Yes."

Anton was an in-demand Hollywood stuntman, and when he

wasn't on a set he liked to go skydiving and hang gliding to rest and relax. A true adrenaline junkie, his favorite motto was "I'll rest when I'm dead." Since he was always on the move, trying to catch him for a conversation was a perpetual game of tag.

"And now we come back to you, darling daughter." Victor eyed her as he ransacked her kitchen for dinner ingredients. "Are you seeing anyone yet?"

She fumbled the bottle of wine she'd just extracted from the wine fridge. "What?"

Nicholas rescued the bottle. "I think that's a yes. Don't think I didn't hear you declare that you don't need to trawl for guys anymore."

"You should have been a detective, not an architectural engineer," Nadia complained. "I can totally see where Sergey gets it from."

Victor raised a brow. "Is he wrong?"

Nadia sighed, knowing she was about to open the door to a third degree she hadn't endured in years. "No, he isn't wrong."

Nicholas focused on opening the wine bottle as Victor leaned against the counter, pinning her with a curious glance. They had the nice-dad, mean-dad routine down pat, Nadia knew, perfected over nearly four decades of raising her and her two older brothers. Victor would initiate the questioning while Nicholas would stand in silence, not overtly trying to intimidate but doing a good job of it nonetheless.

Somehow the combination of the two of them created some kind of dad energy field that had she and her siblings confessing to things they swore they'd never divulge to their parents. Yes, she'd kicked Billy Robertson in the shins, but he'd deserved it. Yes, she'd tried a cigarette but had thrown up after the first inhale. Yes, she was an addict.

She looked at both of them in turn. They'd known from their first date that they'd be together, or so they said, buying a home together right out of college. They'd used the same surrogate for her and her brothers. Sergey was the spitting image of Nicholas, from the height to the same golden brown hair and eyes and analytical mind. Middle kid Anton seemed like a bridge between the two men, with Victor's gregarious personality and Nicholas's build. Anyone who looked at Nadia knew that she was Victor's little girl from hair to toes.

"Okay," Victor said into the silence. "You've had time to get your story straight in your head. Are you ready to share?"

"No, but I know you guys won't leave me alone until I do. Maybe we should have a just us dinner instead. No witnesses while you interrogate me."

"Since when is catching up with our favorite daughter considered interrogation?"

She accepted a half glass of red from Nicholas and managed not to roll her eyes. She knew he'd poured her a half serving on purpose, especially since he and Victor had full glasses and there was still wine left in the bottle. Alcohol had never been her problem; she appreciated the buzz, but not the lack of control that followed over-imbibing. That he still worried about her and her drug consumption touched and irked her.

"Dad, you should be more worried about my caffeine and carb intake than my alcohol consumption," she complained, trying to keep her voice light. "A glass a day is my limit, and I usually only drink when I have people over."

"I am worried about your caffeine and carb intake," Nicholas answered, his dark eyes warm as he gazed at her. "I also worry about your cholesterol, your high blood pressure, and whether you're eating or sleeping enough. I'm also concerned about why you're evading a simple question. You're not seeing someone who's already married, are you?"

"No." She held his stare until he nodded, satisfied. "It's just that there's nothing much to tell. It's only been a week."

Victor assembled a mix of foodstuffs on the counter. "You know the drill," he said easily as he surveyed his gastric experiment in waiting. "Name, rank, serial number, when, where, and how."

"I'll tell you everything you need to know after I shower and change into something more appropriate for an interrogation." She eyed the counter. "But we are not having turkey tetrazzini surprise for dinner."

"You love my turkey tetrazzini surprise." Victor grabbed a pot and a sauté pan from the pot rack hanging over the island.

"I did. When I was ten. And then I found out what the surprise was." She turned to Nicholas. "How about Uncle Foo's instead?"

Her father's smile transformed his face from stern to warm. "I like that idea. They've got some of the best spring rolls this side of Chinatown."

"Hey." Victor turned to face them. "There's nothing wrong with my tetrazzini."

"Of course not," Nicholas told his spouse, his expression warming further. "But since it's only going to be the three of us, we should leave making dinner for another time."

"Maybe you're right," Victor said, resigned. Then he brightened. "But I bet you I can get the tetrazzini together before Uncle Foo's delivers."

"I'll take that bet," Nadia said, opening the menu drawer next to the fridge. "Everybody want their usual?"

"I'll place the order," Nicholas said, taking the menu from her. "Why don't you go get changed?"

Nadia knew better than to argue. "Be back in a jiff."

She headed for the stairs, relieved that she hadn't followed through on the urge to call Kane. As certain as she was that she wasn't ready to talk about Kane to her parents, she definitely wasn't ready for him to meet them. She didn't think her sanity would survive the experience.

ELEVEN

Kane knocked on Nadia's door, wondering if he was doing more harm than good by showing up unannounced. He hadn't heard from her since he'd bid her good night the night before, and while he knew she'd had to be in the café that morning, he wanted to see her. Hell, he needed to see her. In the shortest possible time she had become a fever in his blood, a need that crawled through his guts and refused to let go.

She made him lose control. He'd been honest with her when he said he didn't like it. He'd built his life and his career through hard work and willpower, controlling every aspect of his personal and private life. Although he had a penchant for adventurous women, the sensual game was still played by his rules and ended on his terms. Stomping through a parking deck with his dick out because he was too damn horny to make it home went against his nature, but damn, it had been good.

Something about Nadia shredded his control, and he couldn't

figure out what that something was. Her sexual adventurousness, her accepting nature, her skill, her brains, her beauty—all wrapped around a core of strength she didn't believe she had. In his opinion, anyone who could come through what she'd experienced during her time in Hollywood and be the better for it had to have a backbone of steel. He admired her. He hungered for her.

Laughter sounded on the other side of the door, deep and masculine. What the hell? While they hadn't officially had the exclusivity talk, he'd understood that she hadn't been seeing other people and neither had he. When had that changed, and why hadn't she informed him? A guy liked to know who his competition was, if only so he could study him and determine how to eliminate his opponent.

Mentally gearing up, he rang the doorbell. The door opened a moment later. His "opponent" was a tall, older man with brown hair turning to gray, dark brown eyes, and a taciturn expression that immediately put Kane on guard. He cupped a glass of red wine in his hand, displaying a casual familiarity that grated.

"Who's at the door?" Nadia called. "Is it the backup dinner?"

"I don't know yet." The man turned back to Kane. "Who are you?"

"Kane Sullivan." Kane stuck out his hand. "And you are?"

"Nicholas Spiceland." The older man switched his wineglass to his left, then gripped Kane's hand. "Nadia's father."

Nadia skidded to a halt in the doorway. "Oh, Kane!" She blushed to the roots of her hair as she gasped for air. She must have run down the stairs. "I wasn't expecting to see you today."

"I was nearby," he replied. It wasn't a lie. *Nearby* in a small college town was relative. "I should have brought wine, or at least called ahead."

"Wine is always welcome." A second male appeared behind Nadia. Shorter and bulkier than the first man, he had hair as mink dark as Nadia's, though his eyes held more gold than hers. "So are friends of Nadia's."

Okay. The first man, Nicholas, had introduced himself as Nadia's father, but she looked more like the second one than the first. "Hello, you must be Victor. I'm Kane."

"Kane." Curiosity ripened the other man's voice. "You have us at a disadvantage. You know about us, but we haven't heard anything about you."

"That's because I like to be interrogated on a full stomach." Nadia leaned against the door. "Kane, these are my parents, Nicholas and Victor Spiceland. Dads, this is Kane Sullivan, the man I've been seeing."

Well, that wasn't bad as far as introductions went, but they all heard her discomfort. Considering the way both men turned laser-like focus back to him, Kane could understand her quandary. It wasn't as if she could tell them the truth, that he and Nadia were only on their third date but several pages into reenacting an Arabic sex manual. "It's a pleasure to meet you both. I'm sorry to intrude on your time with your daughter. Nadia, I'll see you some other time."

"Not so fast, young man." Victor grabbed Kane's arm before he could turn to leave. "We surprised Nadia with our visit too. You should come in, even if only for a proper welcome and farewell. Though we were just attempting dinner. You should stay and judge our efforts. Nick's nowhere near impartial."

"I'm not sure how impartial I can be either," Kane said as he stepped over the threshold. "I have a thing for Nadia's buns."

Victor laughed, Nicholas frowned, and Nadia flushed tomato

red. Kane realized the suggestiveness of what he'd said and hastened to explain. "That's how we met. The first time I went to the bakery I had one of her sticky buns. Cleared my bad mood right up. I'm addicted now."

Christ, that was a stupid thing to say too. He pushed a hand through his hair. "I suppose I've just trashed any chance to make a good first impression."

"I think we can give you the benefit of the doubt," Nicholas said as he closed and locked the door. "For now."

"Way to make him feel welcome, Dad," Nadia hissed. She turned back to Kane, plastering on a smile. "It's good to see you."

Somehow he doubted it. "Something smells good. What are you having?"

"My version of turkey tetrazzini," Victor said, heading back across the open living room to the kitchen. "It's the bomb."

"Or Chinese from Uncle Foo's," Nadia said, then turned to Kane. "Victor has a habit of taking his food experiments to the extreme. Sometimes his meals are literal gastric bombs."

"How bad can it be, if you learned to cook from him?"

"Brownie points to the boyfriend!" Victor called, just before turning on a blender.

Kane caught Nadia's wide-eyed expression, and wondered if she was on the verge of bolting from her own home.

Nicholas Spiceland chose that moment to step between them. "Wine, Sullivan?"

"Some of that red would be nice. Thank you, sir."

Nicholas raised an eyebrow. "Manners and compliments. How refreshing." He headed for the kitchen.

"I'm sorry," Kane said as he turned to Nadia. She wore jeans and a clingy green top that deepened her eyes, and had her hair pulled up in a clip. She could have passed for one of his students. "I should have called—"

"You wouldn't have reached me anyway. I apparently was so addled last night that I forgot to charge my phone when I got in." She blew out a breath then gave him a true smile. "It really is okay. I just wasn't ready for this. We'd just gotten to the point in the surprise visit where the dads were pumping me for information about my dating life, and I happened to mention that I had one. So fair warning—the longer you stay, the more they'll grill you. They've always been overprotective since I'm the only girl, but after my . . . troubles, they kicked it up a notch. I think they still view me as a six-year-old in pigtails and ratty jeans."

He touched her shoulder, having to satisfy himself with that when he really wanted to hold her hand, kiss her, wrap her in his arms—everything he wouldn't dare do with her parents surreptitiously watching from the kitchen. "I just came over to see how you were doing and to apologize for the way I left things in the parking deck. I was thrown off-balance."

"You like being in control. I like you being in control too." She leaned forward to whisper in his ear. "I also like when you lose it. I still have the imprint of your fingers on my ass."

"Nadia." Fuck. He was not going to get hard in front of her parents. "Maybe I should leave while the scales are still in my favor."

"No." She glanced toward the kitchen, then back to him. Very deliberately she reached up to cover his hand, her fingers tightening around his. Her syrupy-brown eyes gleamed with worry and what he hoped was genuine welcome for him. "I like having you here. I'm glad you get to meet my dads, who are the most awesome men I know. Meeting my parents and my friends in the same twenty-four-hour span—even I know that's way too early in the relationship game. I'm just, I'm just apologizing in advance."

"There's nothing to apologize about. We're not even a week into this. I haven't mentioned us to my parents either. Speaking of parents, it sounds like Victor is debating the culinary merits of hot dogs. Is that the secret ingredient of his tetrazzini?"

"Turkey hot dogs," she admitted. "Processed in a blender with pearl onions."

"Oh." Kane's stomach involuntarily clenched. "I don't think I'm going to be able to improve my first impression by attempting to eat that."

Nadia laughed. "Yeah. Dinner was always an adventure growing up. I developed my cast-iron stomach early, and learned to cook in self-defense. Nicholas ordered a bunch of stuff from Uncle Foo's, and it should be here any time now. If it gets here before Victor finishes, it means we win, and Victor will forget all about his main course experiment."

The doorbell rang. "Looks like we're saved," Nicholas said dryly, handing Kane a glass of wine as he headed to the door. "Why don't you kids set the table?"

Victor accepted his defeat with grace, helping to arrange the food family style on the table. Nicholas grabbed another bottle of wine, and they gathered around the table to dig into the meal.

Or rather, dig into Kane.

"So, Sullivan," Victor said, as he dropped a spring roll onto his plate. "You said you met Nadia in the café. Are you one of her vendors?"

"No. I'm actually a professor of human sexuality at Herscher."

"What does that entail exactly?"

"A lot of discussion and reading through atrocious term papers, mostly," Kane said, taking a sip of his wine. "But our department offers a variety of courses that can lead to professions such as counseling, sexual therapy, social work, and public policy work, among other things."

"Sounds like admirable work," Nicholas replied. "But that's not all that you do, is it, Professor?"

"Dad." Nadia rolled her eyes in a perfect imitation of a sixteen-year-old that utterly captivated Kane. "If you're going to interrogate the man, can we at least let him get to the bottom of a glass of wine first? Or would you rather he leave now so you can be saved the trouble of running him off later?"

Victor hid a smile behind a spoonful of hot and sour soup. Nicholas frowned at Nadia. "I think it's a very valid observation."

"Of course it is." Kane held Nicholas Spiceland's gaze, knowing he was the one who would be more difficult to win over. "In addition to teaching, I've written a couple of books. I've also assisted law enforcement in profiling sexual predators."

Cool brown eyes swept over him. "You made a name for yourself with that Red Light Rapist case."

Nadia stiffened beside him. "I wouldn't call it making a name for myself so much as capitalizing on the unwanted media attention to publicize the necessity of a better understanding of what is and isn't deviant sexual behavior. The publicity benefitted the program at Herscher, and for that I'm glad."

Nicholas regarded him over the rim of his wineglass. "Do you know what Nadia went through?"

"Dad!" Nadia blushed to the roots of her hair. "Seriously, you just met him—and I'm not a teenager headed to prom with the bad boy!"

"It's okay, Nadia." Kane gave her a brief smile before turning back to Nicholas Spiceland. "Nadia told me about her drug addiction and rehab on our first date. All I knew up to that point was that she made the most amazing desserts and had a smile for everyone who came into her café. She remembers her regulars, and has an amazing ability to match a pastry to the person. She and her partner have made their café a must-stop destination and I've never seen anyone leave angry or unsatisfied. She's pure magic."

"Kane." Nadia leaned over and kissed him. "That was wonderful. Thank you."

Tension slipped away as he stared down at her. "It's the truth."

Victor raised his glass. "I'd say a good first impression has been achieved."

"I'll drink to that," Nadia said, lifting her glass. "Now that the interview is over, can we get to the lighter topics of the conversation, like politics and religion?"

TWELVE

"It's your turn to draw."

Nadia held the bag out to Kane, anticipation tightening inside her. Two weeks into Sexapalooza and it was still as intense and satisfying as the first few days. Kane had arrived early with a rustic pizza and a twinkle in his eye that had kept her aware of him on some kind of energy sublevel.

Watching him interact with her fathers the weekend before had been a nerve-wracking but surprisingly pleasant experience. He'd handled their questions with far more grace and calm than she would have been capable of had the situation been reversed. Victor had given her a thumbs-up before they'd finished dinner, while Nicholas had waited until breakfast the following morning to deliver a gruff "He'll do."

And Kane did. Very well, in fact. So well that Nadia's body readied itself for his skillful mastery as soon as she saw him. She was having the best sex of her life and learning more about herself, and her wants and desires in the process. All she had to do was keep things light and fun. Kane was as deep into her life as she could allow him to go, and as long as he didn't ask for more than she could give, they would be okay.

Kane reached into the bag and pulled out one of the folded index cards. A smile spread like sunrise across his face. "I think I'm going to hold this one in reserve for the weekend. Why don't you pick instead?"

"What did you draw?" she asked, reaching for the card.

"Not going to tell you," he retorted, holding the card out of reach. "It's a surprise."

She folded her arms with an almost-mock pout. "I'm not all that keen on surprises or being made to wait."

"Too bad." He slapped her lightly on the ass. "Good things come to those who wait. I promise the surprise will be in keeping with everything you've asked for, and I'm more than happy to oblige."

Nadia licked her lips and barely refrained from rubbing her stinging buttocks. The slap had startled and stung, but she didn't mind. As aroused as she was, it only amplified her need. She was sure she'd soaked her panties and her shorts sometime during dinner, just as she was sure her arousal was obvious to Kane. Yet he'd made no move to provide relief, and though it left her frustrated, she didn't dare attempt to ease the ache herself. She'd sworn her orgasms to him and he'd already proven expert at making them worth the wait.

She liked ceding control to him. Every other aspect of her life she kept tightly leashed—running the café, planning and creating her pastries, staying clean. Controlling those areas was necessary and beneficial. Exercising that control kept her life orderly, showed her parents that she was capable, and telegraphed a big *fuck you* to all the naysayers she'd left behind in Hollywood.

"Nadia." Another stinging slap redirected her focus. He ran his palm over her butt cheek, soothing the burn into something far more pleasant. "You're not paying attention. Does that mean we're done for the night?"

"No!" End the night without sex? No way in hell was she letting him leave without coming once or twice. "I'm sorry."

"Are you?" He reached out to cup her mound, his middle finger pressing the fabric of her shorts and panties against her slit. "It doesn't feel like you're sorry. Far from it."

"I can't help it," she groused as she pressed against his hand. "You made me this way."

"Me?" A devilish twinkle lit the depths of his eyes. "All I did was feed you."

"I had to keep my hands behind my back," she reminded him. "While sitting on your lap. And you kept kissing the tomato sauce from my mouth after every bite."

"Yet you didn't complain once." Kane moved his hand from between her thighs. She couldn't suppress a whimper of disappointment. "I enjoyed you enjoying your food. Almost as much as I enjoyed watching your nipples get hard while I fed you. And this."

He pulled her shorts and panties down before cupping her again. "I really enjoyed this, knowing I made you like this."

"Kane . . ." His name was part plea, part curse as he pushed two fingers inside her. She gripped his shoulders, her eyes sliding closed as waves of sensation washed over her, flooding her with desire, with need for this man.

"We're going to have to arrange some mirrors," he murmured, the tenor of his voice hypnotic as he stroked into her core. "You need to see how beautifully flushed you get when you're aroused. Your eyes get misty, your lips plump up. As the sheik said, 'If you desire coition, place the woman on the ground, cling closely to her bosom, with her lips close to yours; then clasp her to you, suck her breath, bite her; kiss her breasts, her stomach, her flanks, press her close in your arms, so as to make her faint with pleasure.' That is what I intend with you, Nadia. Are you faint with pleasure yet?"

"Not yet." Nadia gritted her teeth as he stroked her. "Maybe . . . maybe I need you to get with the licking and biting and kissing."

He pulled his hand away again. She uttered a short, pithy curse in Russian as he brought his fingers to his lips to lap up her taste. His answering laughter sent frustrated desire zipping through her sex. "It might be good to mention at this point that I understand some Russian, even if I don't speak it. It would take some doing, but I could do what you just suggested. I thought you wanted me to bite you though."

She almost cursed again, but swallowed it down. Of course Kane would know the Russian equivalent of *go fuck yourself.* He probably could say it in every language known to man, including Klingon. He—

Her thoughts scattered as he dipped his head and nipped her just below her navel. Her knees unhinged, and he guided her down until she straddled his thighs. She settled onto his lap then placed her hands on his shoulders. Though she was naked from the waist down, Kane was not. She was almost close enough to feel the ridge of his erection against the fly of his jeans. Maybe if she shifted just a little, she could get close enough to ease the pressure. . . .

She yelped when Kane pinched her ass. "Don't even think about it," he reprimanded her. "Your orgasms belong to me, remember?"

She growled. What the hell had made her agree to that? A moment of insanity fueled by lust and curiosity. Oh yeah—and the mind-blowing, body-tingling orgasms he delivered. "I remember," she managed to answer, lust thick in her throat. "I just need—"

"We're following the sheik's rules," he told her, his voice hard, as if he needed the reminder as much as she did. "A thorough exploration, complete with bites and kisses, until you're begging to be fucked."

She gasped. "I don't think he put it quite like that."

"That's my interpretation." He raised one perfect eyebrow as he stared at her. "Do you disagree? I can always stop."

She remained silent, though her hands fisted on his shoulders. His low chuckle vibrated along her senses as he gathered her hands, kissing her knuckles. "Let's get you out of this top."

She obligingly lifted her arms as he skated his hands up her sides, pulling her tank top up and off. Knowing he was coming over tonight, she hadn't bothered with a bra after her shower. The fabric of the tank top and Kane's heated glances and sensual touches had kept her nipples at attention most of the night. There was something supremely carnal about sitting on his lap like this, completely bared to his gaze while he remained fully clothed.

"I can see your thoughts in your eyes," Kane said softly, his hands low on her waist, almost cupping her buttocks. "Care to share?"

"I was just thinking how decadent this is, straddling you like this." She ran her hands down the front of his shirt. "Like I'm some sort of harem girl at your service."

He grabbed her wrists, stopping her foray toward his zipper. "Hands on my shoulders," he ordered, suiting action to words. "You move them, I stop. Understood?"

She dipped her head to hide her smile. Kane was obviously nearly as worked up as she was, and the thought gave her pleasure and evened their play. "Understood, sir."

He sucked in a breath. "You like the idea of that, don't you? Being my harem girl?" His fingers dug into her skin, lightly parting her buttocks. "You don't have to answer. You're so aroused your clit's standing at attention."

He blew a cool breath down the front of her, causing her to gasp as the flow of air tightened her nipples almost to the point of pain. "Kane! I'm going to ruin your jeans."

"I don't care." How could he sound so collected when she was ready to shatter? "It's proof that you want me, that you want what I can do to you and for you. It pleases me. You please me."

The praise warmed her insides. She held on to him, certain she'd slide into a puddle of need on the floor if not for his hold. "Thank you."

"Look at that," he murmured, his breath warm against her breasts. He reached up, his fingertips tracing around her areolas, making her nipples pucker even more. "Your nipples are begging to be kissed. Is that what you want, Nadia? Do you want me to kiss you here?"

"Y-yes, please." Tremors swept through her as she vibrated with pent-up lust, desperate for an outlet. Lips, tongue, teeth—at that moment she didn't care. Anything he did short of stopping would ease the ache. She braced herself for the sensation of his mouth on her skin.

He drew the moment out, closing the distance between them a millimeter at a time. Her breath caught in her lungs, her heart stopped, the world disappeared as she focused on the parting of his lips, the peek of his tongue, and finally, finally, the touch of the tip to her nipple.

She gasped at the electric contact, then cried out as he set his teeth to her. Pleasure-pain spiked through her, arching her back, robbing her of air. Once started he didn't stop, drawing the nipple deep into his mouth as he rolled the other between thumb and forefinger, then switching his attentions. The dual sensations ricocheted through her like lightning strikes, the pull of his mouth and the pinch of his fingers creating a direct connection between her breasts and her womb, fueling her hunger, building the pressure, stoking her need.

"Please, Kane." She clutched at his shoulders, fighting against the urge to grind against him. "I need to be fucked. I need you to fuck me."

His gaze bored into hers as he reached for the bag at the end of the sofa then held it out to her. "Pull a card, Nadia."

She did. "The eighteenth manner."

"Yes. *El kebachi*, after the fashion of the ram. Do you remember the details?"

She shook her head. "I'm guessing doing it ram style means rear entry?"

He smiled, and heat stained her cheeks as her thoughts went to her slapped and pinched and supersensitive butt. She'd agreed to anal sex once, years ago. The experience had been painful and unfulfilling. She had a feeling that Kane would make it good for her, make it something she wanted, something she'd even beg him for.

"Down on your knees, sweetheart."

She immediately obeyed, sliding off his lap and to her knees on the thick rug in front of the couch. Clasping her hands in her lap, she looked up at him, waiting, wanting.

His gaze roamed over her slowly, taking her in as he rose to his feet. "So beautiful. And so ready for me, I think. On your elbows now, so I can see how ready you are."

Nadia turned sideways between the couch and the coffee table, slowly sinking down to her elbows, laying her hands flat on the floor. The position tilted her ass up in the air, thrusting her empty and aching pussy back and out. A tremble went through her, not one of fear or cold, but one of pure, blind need. She needed him to fuck her. Not make love, not have sex, but a hard, animalistic pounding that was about nothing but getting off fast and furiously.

Her position meant she couldn't see Kane, but she heard him move. Her breath caught at the sound of his zipper. Her awareness fanned out, wanting to sense him. She enjoyed watching him undress, watching him strip away the university professor and reveal the man beneath the jackets. She loved seeing the change come over him as social filters fell away and he allowed the hunger and need and dominance to take control.

Without her sight to aid her she was left with her imagination, imagining him stepping out of shoes and socks, removing his jeans and tossing them over the back of the sofa. In the silence she pictured him carefully unbuttoning his shirt before slipping it off and laying it next to his jeans. Next came his underwear, his boxer briefs sliding down his thighs to reveal the beautiful length of his cock, the thick head already shiny with pre-come. Her mouth watered as her mind filled with the gorgeous, breathtaking image of a naked and aroused Kane.

"Are you imagining me naked yet, Nadia?" he asked, his voice low and amused in the silence.

"Yes." Anticipation stretched her nerves whisper-thin when he knelt behind her. Her skin prickled, her desire hitting the breaking point as she waited for the first touch.

She still jumped when his hands settled on her buttocks, his thumbs dipping into the crease, opening her up to his gaze. "I can see how wet you are, Nadia," he told her. "Like spilled honey on your thighs, begging to be tasted."

She should have been embarrassed with how much she wanted his touch, his tongue, his cock, but she was beyond that. "Taste me, Kane," she half begged, half demanded. "I need your tongue on me."

He set his teeth to her left cheek, bit down. She cried out, her pussy flooding with desire. He soothed the sting with a gentle lap of his tongue, then continued licking over her heated skin. He held her open as he licked in the crease of her buttocks, circled his tongue over her perineum. She shuddered, her brain momentarily forgetting how to form words.

"You like that, don't you?" he asked, brushing his thumb over the puckered opening. "Have you had anal sex, Nadia?"

"Once," she admitted, her breathing short and choppy. "Didn't like it."

"I can make it good for you." His thumb gently pressed against her, and damn if she didn't want him to breach her there. "I can make you want it."

"Believe you," she managed to say, pushing back against him. "Need you. Please, Kane."

He sucked in a breath. "Love the way you beg for it." He dipped his fingers into her drenched slit. "Love how ready you are."

One moment she was empty and aching, the next shockingly full as Kane buried himself in one powerful thrust. With a guttural groan he began to power into her, a steady rhythmic ride that made her spine tingle with each slap of his balls against her. Matching his rhythm she rocked back against him, tilting her hips to drive him deep, deeper, so deep.

His hand tangled in her hair to hold her in place. The other, fingers slick with her juices, teased her back opening. "Yes, yes—oh!"

His thumb penetrated her and the world went white-hot. She came with a short, sharp scream, her inner muscles clamping down on his cock and his thumb as she rode the ecstasy he gave her.

Dimly she heard him curse, and he shifted his grip to her hips as his pace actually increased, the force of his thrusts scooting them across the carpet. Passion coiled inside her again, spiraling higher while her inner core clenched around him in time to his strokes. Just when she thought she couldn't hold off, couldn't wait for him, he slammed against her, a hoarse shout tearing from his throat as he jetted inside her.

The feel of his orgasm triggered her own. She collapsed, taking him with her. His weight felt good against her, covering her, his hips still moving as if he couldn't help himself.

She released a bone-deep sigh of contentment. "Kane," she whispered, because his name said everything she needed it to.

He pulled away from her slowly. "I'm going to make it my mission to have sex with you in a bed."

She rolled over with a laugh. "Beds are overrated."

"You say that now." He kissed her, slow and stirring. "Wait until you feel the rug burn on your knees."

"It was worth it. So worth it."

Somehow they made it upstairs and into the master bath. In the shower he lathered her body with soothing strokes, mindful of the carpet scrapes on her arms and knees. He always took care of her afterwards, as if doing so gave him as much pleasure as foreplay did.

After toweling dry, he guided her to bed and tucked her in, a move so tender it brought surprised tears to her eyes. "What's wrong?"

"I'm good, I just . . . I don't want you to go. Will you stay?"

The smile he gave her made her belly flip-flop. "I'd like that."

He joined her beneath the sheets, cradled her against his chest. It had been years since she'd slept next to a lover, but this felt . . . nice. Better than nice.

Like something she could come to crave.

THIRTEEN

Tuesday rolled around, as it had a tendency to do. After the morning press and the lunchtime rush, the café quieted down. With all the baking and cooking done for the day and their part-timer manning the register, Nadia and Siobhan joined Vanessa and Audie for their informal Tuesday recovery-group meeting, affectionately known as Bitch Talk.

Jas had coined the term, and it suited them perfectly. Sometimes they gathered to bitch and moan then get on with their lives. Other times, one of them was in sore need of a verbal bitch slap, which the others were more than happy to deliver. Still other times, others from the community dropped in, or came for the formal group meeting that Jas ran on Sunday afternoons with the help of some psychology advisers from Herscher.

Nadia was more than happy to lend their space to the community, and she knew Siobhan felt the same. Letting various groups meet at the café was just part of their core value of giving back, as much as donating leftover food to the food bank or running extended hours in the week leading up to finals. The one thing that had almost made them change their mind about putting down roots in Crimson Bay was the discovery that the town didn't have a group for those in narcotics recovery, nor did it have one for alcoholic recovery. Even Herscher College hadn't had anything open to the public and very scant opportunities for students outside of one-on-ones with school counselors. Since sharing and support were integral parts of the road to recovery, Nadia and Siobhan had established their group in the café. Though the numbers ebbed and flowed, the four of them were always the center of the group, and Siobhan as the eldest was its leader.

Nadia looked at each woman at the table. They were her friends, her sisters of the heart, and she loved them like family. "Would anyone like to start?"

"I can." Vanessa nodded, staring down at her tea. Her hand shook as she lifted the mug to her lips then set it back down without taking a sip. "I was in the parking lot at Murphy's last night."

Nadia suppressed a groan of dismay. Murphy's was the local bottle shop. Its stock in trade were beer kegs for the local college kids, but it also offered plenty of wine and hard liquor.

"Vanessa." This time they all leaned toward her, but no one gripped her hand. Not yet. That wasn't how Bitch Talk worked.

Vanessa sighed, her hand trembling as she gripped her mug. Of the four of them, she was the outsider—all class, culture, and discipline with an impeccable and fashionable wardrobe and not a hair out of place. Outwardly, not as much of a mess as the rest of them were. Vanessa was always perfectly put together, her dark shoulder-length waves usually pulled back in a graceful chignon, smartly arched eyebrows and makeup expertly applied to her smooth bronze skin. Somehow she didn't even leave lipstick prints on her mugs. Her posture was always ramrod straight as if she'd spent years at Catholic school. She was, by all appearances, perfect.

That perfection came at a price, Nadia knew. The pressure Vanessa Longfellow's family put on her to achieve and have the perfect life had led her to alcohol when she was a teenager. For years she'd hid her dependency, smiling on the outside while slowly dying on the inside.

"I sat there, staring at the door," Vanessa said, her voice smooth, calm. "I imagined myself walking up to the entrance and stepping inside. The bell would tinkle overhead, and the clerk would greet me with a smile as soon as he realized I wasn't a college kid. He'd tell me about the wine tastings they were having the following weekend, and I'd ask him about the latest shipments from my favorite winery up north. Then I'd slowly walk down the row of wine, taking my time, looking at all the pretty bottles. Then the hard liquor. So many pretty bottles."

She laughed, a bitter sound out of place in the cheery café. "Next thing I knew I was at the checkout, and I had a cart—a *cart*—with six bottles of wine, a bottle of Midori, a box of Chambord, and a cheap bottle of vodka. It was the bottle of vodka that made me stop. Do you know why? Because it's the kind Nadia uses to clean her countertops at home."

"God, what happened?" Audie asked, her usual vibrancy muted.

"I lied and said that I forgot my wallet, then ran out," Vanessa confessed. "Then I drove home and snorted up a pint of ice cream."

"I think she means what happened to set you off," Siobhan clarified.

"And why you didn't call one of us while you sat in the parking lot," Nadia added, one eyebrow arched.

Vanessa pursed her lips slightly, spinning the mug of tea in her hands. "Mother called me," she said, then stopped. For a long moment she sat silent, her mouth working silently. "About my sister."

This time Nadia did reach out, wrapping her fingers around Vanessa's free hand. While Nadia didn't know Vanessa's mother or sister personally, what she did know of them was unpleasant. "What did she do?"

"You mean Katherine? What hasn't she done?" Vanessa replied, bitterness filling her tone. "She's exceeded every one of my parents' high expectations. The best college, the best grades, the best degree. Charity work with my mother. And now she's engaged to the president of Caldwell Investment Services."

"Isn't that guy like, fifty?" Siobhan asked. "And your sister's twenty-six?"

"Yes, but it doesn't matter. All my mother cares about is how well his pedigree will elevate the Longfellows. She said, 'I thought you'd like to know that while you're wasting away in that little California backwater, your younger sister is engaged to be married to the man who endowed the Caldwell chair at MIT.' Then she proceeded to ask me if I'd bought a cat yet, since she despaired of me ever giving her grandchildren worthy of being Longfellows."

"Ouch," Siobhan said with a wince. "That's pretty damn harsh."

"It's par for the course with Madeline Longfellow." Vanessa grimaced. "I know I shouldn't let that woman get to me. I know I should let it go. She's just doing what Father tells her to do, what she sees as her motherly duty to unleash fine upstanding citizens onto society. It infuriates them that they gave birth to such a flawed child."

"Stop it!" Nadia cut in as she leaned over the table. "Don't you dare talk about yourself like that. You know good and damn well that you aren't flawed!"

"Aren't I?"

"No!" all three of them shouted in unison.

"She then dropped the little gem that they'd done a genetic test, seeking to prove that the hospital where I was born had made a mistake," Vanessa told them, her voice again pleasant and even. Apparently showing emotion wasn't to be done if one was a Longfellow. "They've been arguing about whose family tree may have rot in the roots."

Nadia listened to her friend with horrified dismay. Vanessa was a sweet young woman, beautiful, and at twenty-eight, still had plenty of life left to live. It wasn't her fault that she was born into a family that valued the appearance of perfection more than love.

"You don't need them," Nadia said vehemently. "They may be your born family, but we're your chosen family. We're your sisters. We have your back, and to hell with anyone who doesn't think you're awesome just the way you are!"

"Damn right," Siobhan agreed.

"Fuck yeah," Audie said in her blunt way.

"I'm still mad at you for not calling one of us," Nadia continued. "What's up with that? I know I'm not your sponsor, but I am your friend. I would have come right over."

"Well . . ." This time Vanessa's smile was genuine. "I actually figured that you'd be busy. And naked. Very busily naked."

"Ah . . . oh." A blush burned up Nadia's neck to the roots of her hair. "I, ah, I probably was. I still would have come."

"Enough about me," Vanessa said, once again the picture of

composure. "I managed to come to my senses and live to be sober yet another day. Personally, I'd much rather live vicariously through Nadia. It's been a full two weeks of you and the naughty professor. I'm assuming he got all the cobwebs out of your Tunnel of Lurve?"

"Vanessa!" Nadia gasped. Vanessa so rarely relaxed enough to get blue that it was shocking when it happened. It was a sign that they were finally rubbing off on the woman. Nadia personally thought she'd be much happier if she lowered her inhibitions a lot more, but her parents had shoved the stick so far up her behind that Nadia doubted they would ever be able to extract it. That didn't mean they wouldn't try though.

"So?" Audie prodded. "Are you going to fill us in or what?"

"I'm afraid to," Nadia admitted. "We probably come off as boring compared to what you're used to."

"Hey," Audie protested, bumping her shoulder into Nadia's. "Aren't you guys supposed to be living examples of what constitutes normal? How am I supposed to know what plain old everyday sex is supposed to be if you guys don't demonstrate it for me?"

"I'm not demonstrating jack shit to you, beyotch."

Audie batted her lashes at Nadia's teasing. "Or maybe you guys should come to a swing club with me one night so I could do a live demonstration for you. Or you could invite me to join you. Then we can compare notes or something."

"Or nothing." Vanessa took a sip of her tea, her composure once more firmly in hand. "I think my ears need bleaching."

"*So* not going to happen either way, Audie," Nadia retorted, unsure if the redhead was joking or not. She knew Audie often spent her weekends partying in one sex club or another. While she wished Audie didn't go alone, Nadia would rather have Audie in the relative safety of a swinger's club than trawling bars.

"How are you doing, Nadia?" Siobhan asked, giving everyone verbal whiplash with the abrupt change of subject.

"I'm good." She couldn't hold back her smile. "We're good. He's good. I don't think I've ever been this good before."

"Oh, that's awesome!" Siobhan said, her happiness obvious. "I thought your parents would have scared him off."

"Oh trust me—the third degree they put him through was not pretty." Nadia shook her head. "The game of 'let's embarrass Nadia's date' that happened at the club wasn't all that cute either."

"Whatever." Audie waved her hand dismissively. "He had fun, and you're obviously still together, so it's all good, isn't it?"

"Of course it is."

"Do I hear a *but* in there?" Vanessa wondered.

"Not really. I'm more than likely borrowing trouble where there's none to be had. I should really just keep my eyes wide open and enjoy it for what it is."

"What is it?"

"The best sex of my life." She sighed.

Siobhan leaned an elbow on the table. "That doesn't sound like a good sigh. What's going on?"

"Nothing." Nadia chewed her bottom lip. "He stayed over last night for the first time."

Audie huffed. "Seriously? You've been boning the guy for two weeks and that's the first time he's had to use your toothbrush?"

"Audie!" Vanessa and Siobhan reprimanded in unison.

"So he stayed over. What's the big deal?"

"He stayed because I asked him to." She'd thought about it all morning after he'd left. "I asked him to stay, and he gave me this smile like I'd given him a birthday cake or something."

"Maybe you did," Siobhan said. "Maybe he's happy that you finally trusted him that far."

"Far enough for what?"

"To have a real relationship with him, and not just a sexual one."

Nadia blinked in surprise. Did Kane want a real relationship with her? She wouldn't have thought so. His career kept him busy just as hers did. "I don't know if he wants something like that. His schedule's pretty demanding, and I wake up before God does almost every day. How would it work?"

"Exactly the way it's working now," Vanessa pointed out.

Siobhan regarded her, blue eyes serious. "Do you want a relationship with him? Beyond the sex?"

Nadia hunched her shoulders. "I don't know. When I'm with him, when I'm thinking about him and what I want, everything's so clear. It's early days yet, but we seem to get along well even when he's not making me scream or beg for more."

"He's that good?"

"He's better than good. Sometimes we'll do something out of the book and sometimes we won't. Either way, it's all *damn* and *whoa*. Whatever you heard about his reputation—aside from the rumor that he dates his students, which he totally doesn't—multiply it by a thousand. The man knows his way around the bedroom. And the living room. And the kitchen."

"Woo hoo!" The catcalls and clapping echoed in the mostly empty café. Rosie looked up from her textbook, shook her head with a grin, then went back to studying.

"Sounds like you've got it going on!"

"It's working right now," Nadia said with a nod. "Because it's not like work. He knows my schedule is hella early, and he teaches one night a week. Plus I think he's still doing consulting work. So it's not like we have much of an opportunity to do anything that real couples do. I think I'm okay with it. I mean, I just want the sex, not the baggage. Been there, shredded the T-shirt."

None of them had won blue ribbons in the relationship department. It took a strong person to stand with an addict in the midst of recovery, a level of patience that a lot of people simply didn't have. It took a lot for the addict to find their inner strength and get their shit together, and they had to do it because they wanted to for themselves and not for anyone else.

"I actually think I'm jealous," Audie piped up.

"Jealous of what?"

"Our girl Nadia. Her words may be saying no to a relationship, but the rest of her is all 'sign me up!'"

The table broke into laughter. "I'm not that bad or that obvious, am I?" Nadia asked, the tips of her ears burning with embarrassment.

"Only to those of us who know you," Audie answered. "Sounds like you and the professor are doing so well, it almost makes me want to give up my footloose and fancy-free ways and try that whole moon-and-stars steady boyfriend thing. You know, monogamy." She shuddered. "Don't know if it's for me, but it sure seems to agree with Nadia. Before you know it, we're going to be left behind, choking on her dust while she rides off into the sunset with Professor Sex."

"I wouldn't do that!" Nadia protested. "I need you guys. You know that, right?"

"Of course we know it." Vanessa reached out and clasped Nadia's hand. "We're here for each other. I'm pretty sure the professor knows that too. He certainly seemed to get it when he saw all of us together at the club."

"He said he did." Nadia managed a weak smile. "He called us the sisterhood of the crazy pants, but he was laughing when he said it."

"He's got us pegged," Siobhan said. "And he's got you pegged. In a good way."

"Aw, crap." Audie glanced at her watch, then stood. "I've got an appointment in fifteen minutes. I gotta go. I'll catch up later." She blew kisses at them all, gathered her stuff, then flew out the door.

Siobhan frowned. So did Vanessa. "Something's going on with her."

Guilt kicked Nadia in the heart. "Maybe I should talk to her."

"Give her a little breathing space," Siobhan suggested. "She'll come around. She always does."

It was true. Audie, at twenty-five, was the youngest of their group and felt closer to Nadia than she did to either estranged mother Siobhan or outwardly perfect Vanessa. All her life she'd been made to feel unwanted, and so she expected those she became close with to reject her. Nadia knew it was difficult for Audie to trust anyone, but they'd made major headway in the two years since Audie had come to a recovery-group meeting in one of many attempts to get her sex addiction under control. Though Audie made her want to scream in frustration sometimes—she was a beautiful girl who needed to love herself first and best—she would continue to be there for Audie, just as she'd be there for the others in their little recovering family.

"When you talk to her," Vanessa said after finishing her tea, "remind her that she promised she wouldn't take stuff out on us. And that we owe her a couple of bitch slaps."

The bitch slaps were mostly verbal, though they'd been known to slap each other's shoulders to emphasize a point. When they'd first formed their group, they'd all sworn to be real with each other. Sometimes that realness turned ugly, but whoever thought recovery was pretty had never been through it.

After Vanessa took her leave, Siobhan and Nadia began the process to close down the café. Nadia couldn't help thinking about Audie's reaction. Did Audie have a problem with Nadia and Kane being together? Why would she?

"Don't let what Audie said get to you," Siobhan said, as if reading Nadia's mind. "You know her issues. She's just worried about losing your friendship."

"I know." Nadia sighed, then went back to cleaning tables. "I don't know what to do about it. I can tell her that's not going to happen until I'm blue in the face, but she still won't believe it."

"You prove it by doing it. Eventually she'll get it through that gorgeous red head of hers."

"You know I'm not going to choose between you guys and Kane, right?" Nadia asked, her stomach churning with worry. "That there isn't a choice?"

Siobhan paused her sweeping. "You need to have a balanced life, Nadia. We all do. I've got the burlesque troupe. Vanessa has an art critique meet up or something. Kane gives you an outlet you desperately needed. If it grows into something more, I for one think it's a good thing. And about damn time."

Nadia bit her lip. "But what if it becomes too much? If I spend too much time with him? What if it begins to affect our friendship? Or, God forbid, our business?"

"Seems to me that the professor is doing everything he can to fit into your life as it is," Siobhan observed. "Has he asked you to change your schedule?"

"No."

"Has he asked you to not go out with us?"

"No."

"Has he asked you to choose between us and him?"

"No."

Siobhan arched a pale brow. Finally Nadia laughed. "How do you do that?"

"Do what?"

"Give me a bitch slap without me realizing it?"

Siobhan shrugged. "It's a talent. Seriously though, I understand that you're concerned. This is all new and exciting and unlike anything you've experienced before. You have good reason to be cautious. But you also have good reason to embrace this for the good thing that it is. Let yourself enjoy it."

Nadia took a deep breath. "One day at a time, one step at a time."

One of their many mantras that got them through their tough spots. "Exactly."

"You know," Nadia began, "maybe you need to take a walk through *The Perfumed Garden*. Make your own declaration of sexual independence and hook up with a hot college student."

"A student?" Siobhan laughed. "What, I don't rate a professor?"

"There's only one Professor Sex at Herscher, and he's claimed." Nadia grinned. "There are tons of gorgeous college seniors who could use the influence of an experienced woman. I know I saw a few at the club the other night who definitely wanted to capture the attention of Sugar Malloy."

Siobhan forced a laugh. "I'm thirty-five, Nadia. I've got nothing in common with a bunch of frat boys. I certainly don't want anyone looking for a surrogate mother. We both know my maternal record is shitty."

"You make it sound like you're an old maid or something, ready to sign up for AARP," Nadia chided. "You've got your whole life ahead of you just like the rest of us."

"I know that," Siobhan replied with excessive calm. Strange how she sounded like Vanessa in that moment. "I also know that I broke my high-school sweetheart's heart and I have an eighteen-year-old daughter who can't stand the sight of me and won't take my calls because I chose prescription drugs over family. Why would I want to inflict that drama on some poor guy?"

"I want you to have this feeling." Nadia gave her partner an impulsive hug. "I want you to be happy."

"Then it's a good thing I am happy, isn't it?" The entrance bell chimed and Siobhan broke into a smile. "Speaking of happy . . ."

Kane entered, a shopping bag in his hand. Nadia hurried over to him. "Hey."

"Hey yourself." Snaking an arm around her waist, he dropped a kiss on her that made her forget she stood in the center of the café, in front of the windows, in front of everybody. She shoved her arms beneath his jacket and kissed him back with enthusiasm.

He laughed as they broke apart. "If I'd known that was the reaction I'd get, I'd have brought you presents before now."

"Presents?" She snatched the bag from his grasp. "What sort of presents?"

"For Saturday night." His voice did that low and sexy dip that went straight to her clit. "For my wild card, and your fantasy."

"M-my fantasy?" She could barely get the words out.

"Yes." He brushed her cheek with the back of his hand. "I decided to torture you with an early sneak peek. Don't open it here unless you want Siobhan and your staff to know our Saturday night plans."

"Kane." She clutched the bag to her chest. Whatever was in it had a little weight to it, but not much. Maybe it was a corset. The thought made her nipples tighten in anticipation. "You do realize how far away Saturday is, right?"

"Fully aware, beautiful. I'm torturing myself too."

"What am I going to do with you?"

"Whatever the lady desires." He kissed her again. "Talk to you soon."

FOURTEEN

Kane lived in a sleek, four-story condo on Bay View Road that offered every resident a premium view of the bay and the spectacular sunsets that gave the town its name. Knowing the price of her two-story downtown condo made Nadia realize that Kane must have made a better living from his side jobs than she'd guessed.

She shivered in her long, lightweight coat, balancing on a thin edge between excitement and nervousness as she knocked on his door. Beneath the coat, she wore the present he'd given her on Tuesday, the present that was the key to the fantasy weekend. She reminded herself that she'd asked for this, that she'd wanted to surrender on her terms, wanted to be pushed by someone strong enough, capable enough to take the gift she offered and treasure it.

The door opened, and Nadia's breath caught in her throat. Kane looked gorgeous as usual, but there was a feral rawness to his features that made her pussy clench. He wore loose-fitting black pants with a red sash tied around his waist. His chest and feet were bare and for some reason, that really turned her on. He had a swimmer's build, a broad chest and shoulders built for powering through water, a tapered waist, deliciously defined arms and legs. His dark hair tumbled over his forehead in a careless style that was incredibly sexy, and his black eyes gleamed at her with hunger, with possession and satisfaction.

"Are you my new harem girl?"

Want surged to life inside her. They were just words but they served as a checkpoint, an acknowledgment that once she crossed that threshold, she'd leave her comfortable world behind. "I am," she replied softly. "Are you my master?"

Approval lit the depth of his eyes. "I am," he said, his voice a low purr. "Come."

She stepped through the doorway, conscious that she was entering predator territory. The condo seemed large and open, with oversized windows and glass doors dominating the far wall. Gauzy white curtains stained orange with the afternoon sunlight didn't block the view of a wide, private balcony and its sun-drenched view of the bay.

She barely noticed that the décor was a stylish and masculine mix of Zen and Old World style that suited the man who lived there. Barely registered the low-slung furniture of rich dark wood and equally dark leather standing in strategic points about the large room, broken only by golden candlelight and pops of scarlet here and there: a gigantic abstract painting that looked like a woman's sex after it had been thoroughly pleasured, a couple of throw pillows for sitting on the floor. Didn't give more than a passing thought to the seductive, rhythmic music pouring from a meticulously carved cabinet that took up another wall, its doors open to reveal a large flatscreen and other entertainment electronics. No, her entire focus fixated on the center of the room and what awaited her there.

A black metal contraption stood on a plush white rug. It looked like a cross between gymnastic bars and a sex swing. Beside it lay a pile of bright red rope.

Her confidence wavered. She turned to him as he shut and locked the door, her heart pounding against her chest. "Kane?"

"You're mine, Nadia," he told her, his voice firm. "Mine to pleasure, mine to treasure. This weekend you've given yourself over to my care in every way, so we both get what we want. You know I won't hurt you. You know what to say to stop anything at any time."

He stepped closer to her, concern and lust and magnetism shining in his gaze. "Last chance to change your mind. Will you surrender yourself completely to me this weekend? Will you trust yourself with me?"

"Yes," she whispered. "Yes, master."

"Good." His smile spread like sunshine through her, making her feel ridiculously pleased for having pleased him. "Now let me see you."

He reached for the belt at her waist, untying it. Her mouth went dry when he went to work on her buttons, taking his time opening her nearly ankle-length coat as if she were a present and he wanted to savor unwrapping her.

She felt like a present, a very scantily wrapped present. When she'd seen the outfit he'd bought her for the first time, she'd been excited, aroused, and touched. Her fantasy, come to life. Then she'd seen his note: *Your master expects you to arrive, dressed and ready, at three. Do not be late.*

Driving to his place wearing nothing but the costume and her coat had been a sweet, nerve-wracking thrill. Kane was giving her the fantasy she'd mentioned in passing. An almost throwaway statement that he'd noted and gone to great lengths to make happen. That he would do this for her stunned and delighted her. The least she could do was completely surrender to the sensual game and make sure he enjoyed himself as much as she intended to.

He loosened the last button then pushed the coat from her shoulders, tossing it over a nearby chair. The cool air hit the wide gold coin collar that draped from her throat to the top of her bared breasts. A matching belt hung low on her hips, with two pieces of gossamer fabric the color of fire acting as flimsy excuses for modesty panels. Bracelets lined her forearms, and clinking coin earrings cascaded from her ears. With her coat gone, she felt like a harem girl in truth, come to see to her master's pleasure, whatever that would be.

Kane sucked in a breath as he stepped back to survey her, a long perusal that budded her nipples. "I bought a harem girl but I am delivered a fire goddess."

The soft, reverent words nearly undid her. Need filled her, the need to please him. "What does my master desire of his harem girl?"

"Everything." Raw desire roughened his voice, made his features seem harsh as he gestured to her barely there outfit. "Though I must say, while seeing you in your finery is stunning, I now have an overwhelming desire to see you in my ropes."

Nadia's heart hammered so hard in her chest she was certain Kane could hear it. Her gaze was once again drawn to the metal stand and the pile of ropes as Kane walked over, retrieved a smaller coil from the stack, then crossed back to her.

He traced her skin with the tip of the rope, the end at once soft and stiff. "The fully restored and translated version of *The Perfumed Garden* has two manners attributed to India that involve the use of rope. Their names are *el zedjadja*, piercing with the lance, and *el hedouh*, hanging."

Her eyes widened as she looked at the stand, then back at him. "H-hanging?"

"*Suspension* might be a more accurate description. As the sheik said, 'The man brings the woman's hands and feet together in the direction of her neck, so that her vulva is standing out like a dome, and then raises her up by means of a pulley which is fixed in the ceiling. Then he stretches himself out below her, holding in his hand the other end of the cord, by means of which he can lower her down upon himself, and so is able to penetrate into her. He thus causes her alternately to rise and descend upon his tool until the ejaculation takes place.'"

He paused, as if waiting for her response. "That sounds very intense, master. I'm not sure I could enjoy myself enough to please you while I'm hog-tied to a pulley like that, no matter how magnificent you are. Perhaps the other one?"

He guided the rope down the valley between her breasts. "Piercing with the lance would have you suspended from the ceiling by means of four ropes tied to your wrists and ankles. A fifth rope would be around your waist, binding you in such a way that it wouldn't hurt your back of course."

"Of course. Sir."

He raised an eyebrow, then lightly slapped her left nipple with the end of the rope. The sting shot a sharp burst of need straight to her clit. "Don't be cheeky, harem girl," he admonished her. "Your pleasure pleases me, but I will withhold it if I have to."

"I apologize, sir." Stopping this delightful interlude was the last thing she wanted to happen.

"After you're properly and safely suspended, I'd stand in front of you, fill that gorgeous pussy of yours, then give you a gentle push."

He gripped her hips, pushing her away then bringing her back to him. "You'd fuck me by the motion of your swings," he told her. "The same as if we used a sex chair."

Nadia licked her lips, desire so thick in her system she found it difficult to form words. "Which . . . which manner will you introduce your poor harem girl to, sir?"

The grin he gave her fueled her desire into a blaze. "Both."

"B-both?"

"Yes. I drew a wild card the other night, which inspired me to create this weekend for you, and to introduce you to *Kinbaku*. That's a Japanese form of binding."

"*Kinbaku*," she repeated, trying out the word. *Kaname's Kinbaku.*

"Your nipples just got harder," he said, his voice low and husky. "I think someone really likes the idea of being tied up in my ropes."

"Yes," she tried to say, but the word wouldn't escape the want thickening in her throat. She swallowed, moistened her lips, tried again. "Yes . . . sir."

"Right answer." He trailed the end of the rope down her rib cage, over her belly. Goose bumps broke out over her skin, her breath coming in short gasps as he stroked the end of the rope over her navel. "When I first started exploring human sexuality, I began with my mother's native country and quickly became fascinated with the binding art. *Kinbaku* can be a show, an art exhibit, a punishment, a power exchange. It depends on the intent between the rigger and the living canvas. For many, it's all about the art, the grace and beauty of the human canvas combined with the artful placement of the rope. For others it's about dominance and submission, or the meditative effect of being bundled up and the grace of surrendering. And some people use it as a prelude to sex."

His gaze pinned her in place as he slid the braided cord over her swollen clit. "It will be all of that for us, and more. Spread your legs."

With her heart suddenly doing a tap dance in her chest, she did as he ordered. He reached up, his movements almost formal as he removed the heavy coin collar from her neck. Next he removed the matching earrings, then the bracelets and finally the belt. He stripped her in silence, and as he did so he stripped away everything that had held her back—every bit of uncertainty, worry, and past specters. Everything fell away, everything else was unnecessary except for this moment, her, him, and the rope.

The first coil of rope he wound just above the rise of her breasts, then added another. As she'd thought, the cording was supple yet lightly rough, a weird balance that dug into her skin and made it easy for him to knot. As he coiled and knotted the rope above and below her breasts he kept up a low monologue, telling her how beautiful she was, how wonderful the rope looked on her skin, how much pleasure he got from seeing her in his ropes.

He wove the ropes into a diamond pattern on her skin, but she could feel a knot strategically placed against her anus with another knotted just above her throbbing clit. Rope parted her labia, holding her open. Each tightening of the knots sent waves of sensation through her body that were at once soothing and sexually stimulating. She fell under his spell, succumbing to the joy of pleasing him, the security of being tied, the comfort and relief of giving herself over to him and his care. In that moment, that perfect place of bliss, she felt as if she truly belonged to him. Nothing and no one could tear them apart when they had these ties to hold on to. The more he worked, the more pliant she became, surrendering as she did, the only sounds their combined breathing and the slide of the rope over her flesh.

He then guided her hands behind her back and used another length of rope to bind her at the bend of her elbows then again at her wrists, secure but not tight enough to hurt. A sense of helplessness swept over her, a sharp moment when she had to decide to fight or surrender, decide whether being bound like this was too much or exactly what she needed.

Kane stepped back in front of her and she could see the question in his eyes. That he knew her so well, knew the indecision swirling inside her, made the decision easy. She smiled and nodded, letting her acceptance show in her eyes. "I feel beautiful."

"You are beautiful." He cupped her cheek for just a moment, a smile of approval bowing his lips. Warmth spread through her and she sank beneath it, sank into experiencing the weight of the ropes, the soft but scratchy pressure across her skin, losing focus as Kane's hands and the ropes became her entire world.

Her eyes slid closed as she slipped under, into a place in her head she'd thought only a pill could deliver her to. This was better, so much more everything, because Kane had control.

She didn't know how long the binding took or even how he did them as he added more ropes to her waist and legs, molding and shaping her body as he saw fit. But she came partially back to herself when he gripped her shoulders, the rope, tilting her horizontal then lifting her off the ground. A length of rope led from a knot between her shoulder blades up to a large hook on the upper bar and as she watched Kane added more ties until she was suspended entirely along her right side, her left leg stretched toward the floor, her right leg bent and suspended. Then he stepped back, leaving her alone.

For a moment her heart hammered in her throat, the fear of falling overriding everything else. Then she breathed deep, realizing the ropes held her, supported her. Her eyes slid closed as she surrendered, relaxing completely, her head lolling, hair falling into her face. She felt secure in her immobilization, cradled and comforted even though her position and the placement of her bonds left her completely open and vulnerable.

She had no idea how long she'd hung there, moments, minutes, mental hours. Suddenly the silence became too much. She opened her eyes but couldn't see anything with her hair falling into her face, obscuring her vision, the darkness of the room burned the color of fire by the fading sunset and low candlelight.

Yet as much as she enjoyed the ropes, it was the process of being bound by him, of going under because of him, of being connected to him that she truly craved. Suspended there, blinded by her hair, deaf to everything but the pounding of her heart, she couldn't feel him, couldn't sense him in the silence. A feeling of abandonment flared to life inside her, burning away the contentment. He wouldn't leave her. Not like this. He wouldn't. She trusted him.

Panic boiled up her throat, threatening a scream. Just as her muscles tensed with the urge to escape, he touched her. The curve of his hand on her cheek, brushing her hair back from her eyes, made her sob in relief. She went limp again, sagging in her bonds, craving his touch, his nearness, his heat. Craving everything he could give her.

"Do you remember your words, Nadia?" he asked, moving so that she could see him. He'd removed his clothes and stood before her beautifully, heartbreakingly, gloriously naked, his cock so hard and ready it pointed up like a beacon.

She blinked back to full awareness. Staring up into the depths of his eyes, she felt as if he saw straight through her, through the old pain and fear and bullshit to the vulnerable soul beneath. "Yes . . . sir."

"Do you need to say them?"

His touch soothed her fragile nerves. "No, sir. Having you touch me makes it better."

He used both hands to touch her, his fingers stroking over every inch of exposed skin, teasing her, cupping her, filling her. Each touch brought him back to her, her to him, reconnecting until his presence filled her senses. She sighed as contentment returned again.

"Do you like this, Nadia?" he asked after another long silence, his nimble fingers plucking on her already-hardened nipples. "Do you like being bound like this, suspended like this?"

"Love it," she answered after a long moment, her words slurred. Desire stirred, rising through her blood like a leviathan from the deep, sweeping away her trancelike state.

"Perhaps I'll tie you in something every day, so that while you're working and baking and chatting with your friends you'll feel my ropes and think of me."

A low moan of pure lust pushed out of her. A spicy little secret that no one would know about heated her blood and liquefied her core. "Think about you all the time already, sir."

"I'm glad." Positioning her so that she could still see him, he stepped between her outstretched thighs, her raised leg resting high on his waist. He ran his hands over each cord, tracing a path down to her thighs until his thumb rested against the knot at her clit. A jolt of want shot through her. "Whose is this?"

"Y-yours."

His free hand stroked over his penis, pushing the hood back, revealing the engorged head already shiny with a bead of pre-come. "And this?"

"Mine," she answered, surprising them both with the growl in her voice, the possessiveness. "That's mine."

"Yours." With his gaze never leaving hers, he curled his left hand into the ropes around her waist, using them for leverage as he entered her, a slow, measured progression that she felt every moment of. "Mine."

When he bottomed out he held still, hot and hard inside her, filling her completely. A possessive light blazed in his eyes as he stared at her, then at the spot where they joined. "Ours."

Emotion welled inside her, threatening to choke her. "Kaname."

"You need to let go, Nadia," he ordered, his soft voice at odds with his hard body as he pulled out of her. "Let go, and trust that I'll catch you."

She stopped breathing as he filled her again in one long, slow, toe-curling glide. He threw back his head, the tendons of his neck standing out, his body rigid as her slick sheath welcomed him anew. "God, Nadia," he groaned. "Good, so damn good."

He began to move, long, slow strokes all the way out then all the way back in. She couldn't hold him, couldn't reach for him, could only accept the pleasure he gave her. Accept him she did, keeping her gaze locked to his, her inner muscles clamping down on him, her clit bumped by the knot and the root of his cock each time he buried himself deep.

Desire ignited an inferno inside her as she danced between being restrained and being unchained, between holding on and letting go. The ropes around her torso abraded her skin in a sweet pleasure-torture-pain-bliss that sent tingles shooting throughout her body. She surrendered to it, surrendered to Kane, to his mastery and his skill and his care, knowing that he'd catch her when she fell.

Her orgasm ambushed her a heartbeat later. She came with a keening cry, caught up in a white-hot ecstasy that rocketed her up and out into a sea of transcendental delight. As if her orgasm had given him permission he quickened his pace, the deep strokes coming faster and faster as her body hung suspended for him and his sensual onslaught. His hand settled on her mound, stroking and squeezing her clit, drawing her pleasure out stroke by sinful stroke. She tried to hold back, tried to delay her second climax, but she was too open, too needy, too ready for him.

The orgasm struck like a lightning bolt, hot and powerful and blinding. This time she screamed, body rigid, pleasure short-circuiting her senses. Kane grabbed her ropes with both hands as he went wild, growling as he drove into her, taking her with an intensity that was almost brutal. He came with a shout, clutching her close as he flooded her womb.

Warmth enveloped her. She opened her eyes to find herself in Kane's arms in the shower, the ropes gone. The diamond pattern marking her skin was the only reminder that she'd been bound. "Did I pass out?"

He kissed her as he helped her stand. "You went deep, sweetheart. Almost too deep."

"You gave me permission to let go. I knew you'd be there to catch me."

"I always will," he promised. "Always."

In that perfect moment, she believed him.

FIFTEEN

The dance beat that signaled Audie's ringtone jerked Nadia out of a sound sleep. She fumbled for the phone on the nightstand, conscious of Kane's warm bulk behind her. "Hello?"

"Nadia."

"Audie? What time is it?"

"I don't know." Audie's muffled voice wavered, thinned out. "I'm sorry, I shouldn't have called you."

"Wait." Nadia sat up, rubbing away sleep. "You sound weird. What's wrong? Did something bad happen?"

"Yeah." Audie choked back a sob. "I messed up, Nadia. I messed up so bad. Can you come?"

"Of course I can." Audie had been acting strange for the last couple of days, but refused to talk to Nadia about whatever was bothering her despite Nadia's repeated attempts to get her to talk. In the short time that she'd known the younger woman, Nadia had never seen Audie cry, though she knew the redhead had plenty of reason to. She knew Audie's gleeful fuck-em-all attitude—literally and figuratively—was a weapon in the arsenal she used to keep people at bay, to protect the scared little girl she kept hidden away. For that armor, so ingrained, to crack now meant that something truly horrible had happened.

Nadia slid out of bed as Kane stirred. "Are you at home?"

"Yeah," Audie said. "My neighbor called the police. I don't want to talk to them without you here."

Police? Dread gripped her as she searched for her clothes, only to remember that she'd been in harem girl mode all weekend, which meant no clothes. She juggled the phone as she found and opened her overnight bag, pulling out a sweater and a pair of jeans. What the hell had happened at Audie's that the police needed to be called? "Audie, I'm on the way. But if the police get there before I do, you have to let them in, okay? You don't want them to break the door down or anything dangerous."

"Okay." Another sob. "Don't call Sugar or Vanessa. Please."

God. "All right, Audie. I won't call them. I'll be there in a few minutes. I promise."

She disconnected, tossing the phone on the bed before hopping into the jeans, followed by her bra and the sweater. She turned to find Kane out of bed, already getting dressed. "It's Audie. Something's happened."

"So I gathered." He pulled his jeans on, carefully tucking himself in. "Do you know what's going on?"

"No, but it must be bad. Audie never asks for help. And she never cries." She grabbed her phone, headed for the hall. "I have to go."

"Of course. I'm going with you."

She turned to face him. "You don't have to do that."

"I know." He nudged her hip to propel her back into motion. "I'm going anyway."

"It might not be a good idea," she argued, heading for the door. She didn't think Audie would appreciate her bringing Kane along, and, if she was being completely honest, she wasn't sure she wanted Kane to see the messier aspects of her life and her friends' lives. Though Audie was a part of their recovery group, Nadia and the others all knew Audie hadn't hit her rock bottom yet. If this moment was it, it was going to be messy, ugly, and extremely painful.

She wrenched open the coat closet door and pulled out her coat, then shoved her feet into her ballet flats. "Audie sounds like she's in a bad way, Kane. She said her neighbor called the police."

"Then we'd better hurry." He slipped his own jacket on, then pulled out his keys.

Why was he being so insistent about this? "Kane, seriously—"

"No arguments, Nadia," he said as he ushered her out the door and into the hall. "What the hell kind of man would I be if I let my woman go out at two in the morning and drive alone and upset to wherever her friend lives?"

She blinked at him. Oh my God, did he just say *my woman*? Her brain couldn't begin to process the implications of his use of those words, not when she needed to get to Audie. Something had happened, something bad, and she needed to be there. "Okay."

Out of sorts, she allowed Kane to guide her out to the parking garage. Kane was right, she wouldn't have been worth crap driving through town to Audie's apartment complex on the southeastern side of the city. She gave Kane Audie's address, watching as he plugged it into the car's GPS. His calm, assured demeanor wrapped around her, dampening her panic for Audie. She focused on the fact that Audie was alive and had been well enough to call her. That she'd called for help—and her neighbor had called the police—worried Nadia more than she'd cared to admit to Kane.

He saw her worry anyway. Wordlessly, he reached over, giving her hand a reassuring squeeze. She returned the squeeze, suddenly grateful that he'd chosen to accompany her. She could have Audie's back, knowing that Kane would have hers.

Flashing lights and curious neighbors led the way to Audie's second-floor apartment in a complex filled with singles and college students. Nadia waited until Kane killed the engine before leaping out of the car and running up the stairs. She pushed through the onlookers and into Audie's busted door, before pushing her way inside, then jerked to a stop.

It wasn't as bad as she'd feared.

It was worse.

"Audie!"

Audie sat in the only unbroken chair at her kitchen table. Her bottom lip was busted, her left eye swollen shut, the turquoise beaded top she wore ripped and stained with blood. "Oh, Audie."

"Should see the other guy," Audie mumbled. She managed to open her left eye, then groaned. "You brought the professor with you? Great, like I needed more witnesses to my stupidity."

Nadia blinked back hot tears spurred by the sudden fury burning through her. She knelt beside Audie, mindful of the paramedic working on her. "Who the hell did this to you?"

"My date," Audie mumbled, wincing as the paramedic dabbed something on the laceration above her right eye. "He didn't want to take no for an answer."

God. Bile rose in Nadia's throat. "Did he . . . ?"

"He tried." Audie glanced at her before her gaze shifted away. "Threw me down, ripped my shirt. I went for his nuts. He hit me, I hit him back, and world war three started. Jane pounded on the wall and said she'd called the cops. He took off."

"You told the cops who he was, right?"

When Audie remained silent, Nadia leaned forward. "You do know what his name is, right?"

Audie glared. "I might not be able to bag a professor, but I have some standards."

Nadia bit back a retort. They both knew obtaining last names wasn't high on the list of priorities when Audie went out bagging and tagging. "Audie, if you remember his name you need to file a police report so you can press charges when he's found. Whatever happened up to the point you said no doesn't matter. What he's done to you isn't right. He attacked you. Who knows what would have happened if your neighbor hadn't been home?"

Audie closed her eyes. "I met him tonight at Miller's Bar. His name is Brian. I think his last name is Peacock or Peabody. Something like that. He said he's a regular there."

Miller's was a known meat market for the college-aged crowd. People went there looking for a good time with their preferred poison, whether that poison was drugs, alcohol, sex, or a combination thereof. It wasn't a place Nadia would go within ten feet of, not even in her former life.

The police officer stepped forward. "Did you go there with anyone else?"

"No." Audie pulled her lips back in a grimace. "It's not the sort of place my friends would be caught dead in."

"Audie." That hurt, even though Nadia had just thought the

same thing. Kane squeezed her shoulder, and that brief touch of support comforted her as she regained her feet.

"Can you provide a description of your attacker, miss?"

Audie sighed then winced in obvious pain. Nadia reached out, but the paramedic stopped her. She understood why, but the urge to protect her friend prickled across her skin. She needed to do something.

Audie gave the officer a description of her erstwhile date and his car as the paramedic finished tending to her. As soon as the officer indicated he had enough information, Nadia turned to the paramedic. "Are you taking her to the hospital?"

"No! No hospital. This is embarrassing enough without being carted out of here on a gurney in front of all my neighbors!"

"Ma'am." The medic looked up at Audie, his eyes dark and sympathetic in his olive-toned face. "I know this isn't easy, but it's my job to take care of you. You're alert now, but you were fuzzy earlier, do you remember?"

Audie frowned, winced, then frowned again. "Not a ma'am."

Concern clenched Nadia's stomach muscles. That wasn't a good sign, was it? Audie could have a head injury, internal bleeding, and the people that were supposed to take care of her were sitting around like it was just another day at the office.

"Audie." The paramedic spoke again, his voice soft yet commanding. "Do you remember me?"

Nadia watched Audie focus on the man kneeling in front of her. "You're Jose, Jose with the kind eyes."

"That's right." He smiled, and it was like looking into the face of an angel. "Do you remember what I told you?"

"You promised to help me. Most people always make promises they don't keep though."

Nadia clamped a hand over her mouth to hold back an automatic denial. Before she could lodge a protest, the paramedic spoke again. "Then it's a good thing I'm not like most people. Everyone here wants to help you. That means letting me do my job, letting all of us do our jobs. We need to make sure you're okay, that there are no internal injuries. And you need to give the police all the information and evidence you can."

"Nadia can pack a bag for you," Kane said, the calm in his voice soothing Nadia's worry. "I called a friend of mine. Her name is Sally Jensen and she's an advocate and a counselor. She'll meet us at the hospital and help you through the next part."

Nadia held her breath, but Audie nodded. "All right."

The two men were able to convince Audie where Nadia could not. In that moment, she didn't care if it meant that Audie would get the help she desperately needed. The paramedics bundled Audie into the ambulance while Nadia quickly packed a bag and followed with Kane.

The wait at the hospital was interminable. She wanted to be with Audie, but when she asked if she could, the nurse who'd gone to check didn't return. She paced the waiting room, too keyed up to sit, to drink the coffee Kane had gotten for her.

"I should call the others. Should I call the others?"

"Having them here would be good for you," he answered. "But you said Audie asked you not to call them. You don't want to do anything to upset her further."

"You're right. I know you're right." She stopped pacing, biting down on her thumbnail instead. "What's taking so long?"

Kane crossed to her, wrapped his fingers around her wrist, then gently pulled her hand down. "You want the doctors to be thorough," he told her. "The police also need to finish their report and document every bit of evidence in case Audie decides to press charges."

"In case?" she echoed. "What do you mean? Of course Audie's going to press charges!"

"I hope she does. That's why I called Sally Jensen. She's very good at what she does. Audie is in good hands."

Nadia wanted to believe him. Through it all Kane was a silent, steadfast presence. She wanted to push him away. She wanted to bury her face in the crook of his neck and just breathe him in. Mostly she wanted to be in his ropes again, free to do nothing but feel the pleasure he gave her.

No. She couldn't think like that, think about that, with Audie in trouble and hurting. Taking a deep breath, she stepped back from him, back from the comfort he offered. "You should probably go."

A hint of a frown creased his forehead. "I will. Once we make sure Audie is okay and you're home."

She couldn't let him do it, couldn't let him get more involved in her life and the lives of her friends. He was already in deep enough that even this moment of trying to push him out ripped at her, ripped her deep. She had to do it, and she had to do it now before she fell even further.

"That's not necessary, Kane," she told him, wrapping her arms about herself. "You've had a long day, and I can't ask you to do anything else for us."

"You had the same long day, Nadia," he reminded her, his tone so gentle and understanding it almost broke her. "You don't have to ask, because I want to help. Besides, your car's at my place. If the doctors release Audie, I'll drive both of you back to your place and drop your car off tomorrow."

He closed the distance between them again by hooking his hand into the band of her jeans. Wrapping his fingers around her wrists, he gently pried her arms open, then cradled her against his chest. "Stop trying to push me away," he said against her hair. "It's not going to happen."

Surrendering, Nadia closed her eyes and held on to him as tightly as she dared. She knew in that moment that Kane meant what he said. She also knew it was a promise he wouldn't be able to keep.

SIXTEEN

A long while later, Nadia helped Audie into her condo. Audie had refused to stay overnight for observation at the hospital, and Nadia had volunteered to monitor her until morning. She hadn't said much since she'd been released, just a quiet thank-you to Kane when he'd dropped them off out front. Nadia could almost envy her friend's numb detachment if not for the price Audie had paid.

"Why didn't you want me to call Siobhan or Vanessa?" Nadia asked as they slowly mounted the stairs to the bedroom.

Audie sighed. "Come on, Nadia. You know why."

"I guess it's because you don't want them to know what happened to you. But come on, Audie, they're going to see you. They're going to find out. I won't lie to our friends. That's not how Bitch Talk works."

Audie straightened with an effort, away from Nadia's support. "I don't need to be bitched at, and I sure as hell don't need to see their pity. I'm the fuckup of the group and we all know it. Well, Vanessa and I were running neck and neck there for a second but tonight is the icing on the cake. Yay me. Can I have a judgment-free pass as my prize?"

"None of us judge you," Nadia denied as she opened the door to her guest bedroom, wondering what Audie meant with her comment about Vanessa, then deciding not to worry about it. At least the room was clean and the bed made. With her dads within an easy drive and friends who liked to crash, Nadia always kept it ready.

"Yeah, right." Audie shuffled toward the bed. "The only reason they tolerate me is because of you."

The accusation stung. "You know that isn't true!"

"Ask them if you don't believe me. You'll see." Audie stopped before she reached the bed, teetering. "God, I need a shower."

"Of course." Grateful for the change of subject, Nadia dropped Audie's oversized tote bag down on the queen-sized bed, then forced a cheery tone into her voice. "I packed you a sleep shirt, a change of clothes, and some underwear. Do you need help?"

Audie stiffened. "No."

The dismissive tone slapped at Nadia. "Okay then. Towels and washcloths are in the linen closet next to the bathroom, and so is the stash of extra toothbrushes. I'll go make you something to eat while you get cleaned up."

She retreated to her kitchen, her mind reeling. Surely Audie didn't believe half of what she'd said. Audie had to be mentally and physically exhausted after her ordeal, dealing with the police and her hospital visit. After food and rest, Audie would be good as new, and hopefully ready to make changes in her life.

Nadia loaded a tray with soup, crackers, a sandwich, and fruit then returned to the bedroom. Audie was already there, a bottle of pills in her hand, looking young and vulnerable with her auburn hair pulled back in a damp ponytail, her bruises standing out in stark relief on her pale skin.

"I didn't know how hungry you were, so I brought different things," she said, placing the tray on the nightstand. "The soup's just a vegetable broth if that's all you can stomach right now. And the fruit is melon, so it hopefully won't be too much trouble for your lip."

"You didn't have to go through so much trouble." Audie slid beneath the sheets. "I appreciate it."

"It's not any trouble." Nadia added pillows to support Audie as she leaned against the headboard, then settled the tray across her lap before settling in a side chair.

Audie lifted the soup to her mouth, careful of her busted lip. "Was your professor upset that you had to stop your sexy-times for me?"

Heat suffused Nadia's cheeks. "We were asleep, and no, he wasn't upset. He wanted to help."

"Of course." Audie's smile managed to look sad and condescending. "You're so nice, Nadia. You're more of a sister to me than my sisters ever were. Maybe that's the problem."

Confusion and concern swamped Nadia. Audie wasn't acting like herself, not really. She was always snarky, but this . . . this had an edge to it, and Nadia was the one receiving the cuts. "What's going on with you? Why in the world would you go to Miller's by yourself? You know what kind of place that is."

"Of course I know what kind of place Miller's is. That's why I went."

"Audie . . ."

"Don't you 'Audie' me." She put the empty soup mug down. "We can't all be perfect like you, Nadia, with the perfect career, the perfect life, the perfect boyfriend."

Nadia shook her head in disbelief or denial, she wasn't sure which. "I'm not perfect, Audie. Far from it. You know that."

"Yes, you are," the redhead insisted. "You stopped using drugs. You got clean. You opened your own business. You're in a real, live relationship with the most eligible bachelor in town, who's so into you he can't see anybody else, even if it's because you're not giving him the real you. You're getting your shit together. I'm still wallowing in mine."

"I'm still a work in progress, Audie," Nadia said with a calm she didn't feel. "We all are. I've come a long way from my rock bottom, but I'm not done putting myself back together. I think what happened tonight is your rock bottom, or at least you should let it be."

"Why should I? Maybe I like where I am. Maybe I like my shitty life just the way it is. Have you ever considered that?"

"If you did, I don't think you would have accepted Sally Jensen's help at the hospital. She can help you, Audie. You just have to want the help."

"I don't need you to preach to me, Nadia. Just because you're in a perfect place doesn't mean you get to be all high and mighty."

Nadia sucked in a wavering breath. "You . . . you can't mean what you're saying. The drugs they gave you . . ." Except she knew firsthand the drugs didn't change you, they just made it easier for you to be what you really were.

"Oh, I mean it all right. I'm so fucking jealous of you that it hurts." Audie smiled bitterly. "And I hate it that I'm jealous of you. It almost makes me hate you. But I don't. Do you know why? Because I can't figure out why a professor like Sullivan is taking a risk by being with you. Maybe it's because you've got him fooled. Maybe you haven't told him everything that happened when you were an addict. But it doesn't matter. One day you're going to crash and burn again. Every addict does. Siobhan's been through twice. Vanessa's probably on her way. When the professor discovers the real you he'll take off and then you'll be right back down here in the filth with me with nothing and no one."

Nadia shot to her feet, anger and hurt battling for territory inside her. "That's not fair, Audie."

"So what? Life's not fair. If it was, then all those years that I towed the line and tried to be a good daughter despite my genes would have paid off for me. They didn't. So why should I bother? Why should I change my ways? It's not going to make a damn bit of difference."

"Of course it's going to make a difference," Nadia insisted, the throat tightening. "It already has. You were in the process of getting your life on track, Audie. We all know that. We've seen it and we've been behind you a thousand percent. Even when you falter."

She folded her arms across her chest, tears threatening to choke her. "But it's hard, Audie. It's hard for us to watch how little you care about yourself when we love you and want the best for you."

"Words. They're so easy for you to say because of where you are right now." Audie moved the tray off her legs. "Maybe the best thing for me is to not have to try living up to an impossible goal just because you want me to be acceptable. I really, really hope that you can keep living the good life, even though we both know that you and I are good-time girls, not long-term women. I hope your business keeps going and I hope the professor keeps forgetting that you're an addict. I hope you enjoy where you are and who you're with while you can. Most of all, I hope you never ever end up down in the shit with me."

"Audie," Nadia whispered, her chest so tight with pain she couldn't breathe. She reached out, but Audie rolled over, turning her back.

Shell-shocked, Nadia picked up the tray and left Audie's room on unstable legs. She made her way back downstairs and to the kitchen, her hands trembling so violently that she had to fight to keep the tray balanced. White noise filled her mind as she cleaned up on autopilot, the routine of restoring her kitchen to order failing to soothe her.

Weary but too heartsick to go to bed, she crossed to her living room and threw herself down on the sofa as the white noise erupted into blinding pain. She rubbed at her chest, but that did nothing to ease her pain and disbelief. How could Audie have said such horrible things to her? Did she actually believe the things she'd said, or were they a product of her embarrassment or the drugs she'd been given?

She leaned back against the pillows, staring up at the ceiling. No, painkillers didn't invent new emotions. They just amplified what was already there by lowering your inhibitions and numbing the emotional and social filters that made you care about the consequences of your words and actions.

So Audie was jealous of her. Had that jealousy driven her to go to Miller's looking for yet another random hookup as a substitute for having a real relationship? If that was what jealousy did, what would hatred make her do?

Yet despite everything, Nadia still cared. She still cared about what happened to Audie. As much as she was sad for her friend, she fervently hoped this was the wake-up call Audie needed to get her life back on track. She didn't want to think about what could happen if Audie pushed herself even further into dangerous territory.

Knowing all of that did nothing to ease her hurt. Audie had deliberately said those things to wound her, to wound their friendship. Now she had the luxury of sleeping away the after-effects of her harsh words thanks to a little pill while Nadia had to feel all of it.

She closed her eyes and curled her hands into fists as the old need rose, the need to be numb, the need to forget, to put off facing everything and everyone for a few hours of insensate bliss. To put four or five or eight pills on her tongue for that first bitter taste before she chugged them down with a generous cup of vodka and waited for the sweet nothing. Audie wouldn't even know some of her pills were missing. . . .

No. Her eyes flew open as she cast about for something to keep her anchored, to keep her from sneaking upstairs and pilfering one her friend's pills. Her gaze fell to her phone lying on the coffee table. She snatched it up, then hesitated. She'd promised she wouldn't call Siobhan or Vanessa, but Siobhan was the reason she'd made it through rehab. Siobhan would help her right her keel, but she'd also be furious with Audie. Nadia couldn't handle another emotional outburst at that moment.

She could call Kane.

Indecision raked her. She'd tried to push Kane away earlier, but he'd refused to go. Did she dare expose him further to the sudden mess her life had become? He'd already seen plenty, and she still hadn't shared everything with him yet. Was Audie right, and Kane would cut and run if he knew everything about her life as an addict?

No, she didn't believe that. She wouldn't believe that. He'd been protective and supportive from the moment Audie had called. He'd contacted a counselor. He wouldn't do all that then turn around and abandon her. He wouldn't.

Hope and dread mixed inside her as she sent a tentative text to Kane, not expecting him to respond. **Hey.**

Hey yourself. How's Audie doing?

Thank God. Nadia clutched the phone to her chest for a moment, so relieved that he was still awake and willing to reach out to her. She wanted to call him, but she wasn't sure she'd be able to get more than a couple of words out without crumbling into an emotional heap. **She's asleep right now. Don't know what morning will bring.**

Morning brings another day, another chance to do the right thing, and that's what's important. How are you?

Not good, she answered honestly.

Do you need me?

Maybe she didn't want to need him, but that didn't make the need go away. She didn't want to be by herself, not when she was feeling so alone. Kane could at least banish that abandoned feeling, and perhaps the other need would slide back into the dark recesses where it belonged. **Yes.**

A brief pause, then: **I'll be there in five minutes.**

Her hands shook anew. Five minutes? If he was that close, that meant he hadn't gone home. It took five minutes to get to her door from the parking deck.

With her lungs threatening to burst as they searched for air, Nadia dropped the phone on the couch then surged to her feet. Her body seemed unwilling to help her cross the long distance, unwilling to fumble open the locks. She flung open the door, then stopped.

Kane stood in the hallway, still wearing the clothes he'd worn earlier, rumpled and tired but so beautiful to her starving spirit. She drank in the sight of him, her heart thudding into hard action once more, her lungs finally able to draw air again.

"Kaname," she breathed. "You're here. You're really here."

She saw concern wash over his face a split second before he opened his arms, scooping her up. She fell against the warm wall of his chest, a sob fracturing her control. Feeling his arms around her, smelling the spice of his scent, hearing his low voice offering words of comfort, pushed her over the emotional edge. Burying her face into the side of his neck, she breathed him in once, twice, then broke, muffling her sobs against his skin.

Dimly she was aware of him kicking the door closed, striding over to the couch, then sitting down, all the while holding her close. "I'm here, sweetheart," he crooned, rocking her gently as he stroked her back. "I'm here."

She had no idea how long the tears had her in their grip, how long she clung to Kane like a rock in a fast-moving emotional stream that threatened to sweep her away. Finally she pushed back, gulping down a huge breath of air. "I'm sorry."

"You don't ever have to apologize to me." He cradled her face in his warm, capable hands, his thumbs lightly brushing at her tears. "Can I get you something? Water, coffee, tea? Wine? Tissue?"

She managed a weak smile at his attempt to lighten her mood, then slid off his lap, drained. "We're at my place. I'm supposed to be asking you that."

"You were crying. I'm supposed to fix things so you don't cry anymore."

Remembering Audie's words had her heart lurching in her chest again. "I don't know if you can fix this, Kane."

He kissed her forehead. "Then let me start with something small. Can I get you something to drink? Or do you want something to eat?"

She leaned against him, appreciating his presence more than she could put into words. "Tea would be good. Chamomile or the jasmine. It's in the—"

"I know." He kissed her again, then rose. "I'll get it. You take a moment."

"All right." She stood as he crossed to the kitchen. "I need to go splash my face. I think I snotted all over your shoulder."

"The neat thing about clothes is that they can be cleaned." He pulled down two mugs then opened her caffeine cabinet where she stored all her coffees and teas. He'd learned his way around her kitchen with an effortless grace, just as he'd become an integral part of her life. At that moment, she didn't mind. She didn't mind at all.

"Kaname."

"Hmm?" He looked up, the dim light reflecting off his glasses before revealing his night-dark eyes.

"Thank you for being here." She curled her toes into the throw rug, hugging herself. "For coming back, or rather, for not leaving in the first place. For knowing that I might need you, even if I didn't know it. I-I appreciate it."

His smile lit up his entire face, the tenderness in it pushing away the last of her sorrow. "You're very welcome, Nadia. Always."

His words were a welcome, but his tone was an invitation, an offer for so much more than a demonstration of antiquated sexual treatises. At least, that's what it sounded like to her wrung-out mind. Touched, she made her way to the half bath, turning the taps on so that she could splash her face. One look in the mirror had her groaning aloud. She was a wreck, her hair spiked up at odd angles, her skin blotchy from crying, her eyes red and swollen and devastated.

She hadn't bawled like that in years. In fact, she'd taken great pains in her recovery to make sure she wouldn't have to experience any emotional upheavals. Feeling pain led to wanting to do anything to numb the pain, leading her down a slippery slope she never wanted to traverse again.

"One day at a time, one step at a time," she told her reflection, repeating the mantra that had been a part of her life for the last few years. When things became overwhelming, it helped to turn away from the big picture, to focus on little, manageable things. Like splashing cold water on her hot mess of a face, pulling herself together piece by tiny piece.

Somewhat composed, she returned to the living room to find Kane waiting for her on the couch, two mugs of tea on the table in front of him. As always, he'd kicked off his shoes and left them by the door. He'd also taken his sweater off, leaving him in just his jeans.

Nadia groaned. "I did ruin your sweater," she said as she flopped onto the couch beside him. "I hate ugly crying."

"It's just a sweater." He handed her a mug of tea. "Chamomile. Thought you'd appreciate the calming effect."

"I do." She took a tentative sip, mindful of the heat seeping into her fingers. "I appreciate everything you've done."

"You've said that already." He pushed her hair back from her face, tucking the longer strands behind her ear. "And I've said you're welcome. This is just one of those things I do for my girl when she needs me."

My girl. The words should have sent a shaft of panic zinging through her, but at that moment, they were exactly what she needed to hear.

"Now, tell me what happened."

"You know what happened," she answered, unwilling to expose him to the toxic conversation she'd had with Audie.

"I know what happened with Audie was emotionally traumatic for you, but that's not the only thing all these tears are for." He brushed at her cheeks again. "You were crying as if someone broke your heart. Did Audie say or do something that upset you?"

"You could say that." She returned her mug to the table, then turned to face him. Haltingly, she gave him an edited version of her conversation with Audie. The longer she spoke, the tighter his jaw became until she was certain he was going to explode.

"Please don't be angry at her, Kane," she said, reaching out to clutch his forearms. "She's in a really bad place right now, and I don't think the painkillers were helping her think clearly."

"You still don't say crap like that to someone who's your friend," he said, his voice tight with repressed fury. "Especially after that friend rushes to your side in the middle of the night to take care of you and give you a place to stay."

185

"I know," she whispered. Tears burned in her throat, and she tried to swallow them down, swallow down the pain, the hurt, and, God help her, the anger. "I know, but I don't want to give up on her. I can't give up on her. We're her family. Where would I be if my family had given up on me?"

"Ah, sweetheart." His fury dissipated as he pulled her into his arms again, just as she'd hoped he would. She went, needing the comfort he offered, the connection. "I'm sorry you had to go through that."

"She thinks she's going to lose me. To you." Nadia hiccupped. "She said that before."

He stiffened. "I wouldn't make you choose between me and your friends, Nadia."

"Siobhan said the same thing."

"Siobhan is pretty smart." He tilted her chin up. "You believe us, don't you?"

"Yes." Somehow she knew he wouldn't make her make that kind of choice. What she didn't know was if she'd do it to herself. She'd done it once before, and was still living with the fallout all these years later.

He stroked her hair, calming her, and maybe himself. After a while he spoke. "Do you mind if I put on my counselor hat for a moment?"

"Go ahead."

"I don't know anything about Audie or about her past, but I have worked with enough people to know that there must be a past trauma that has bearing on what she's doing to herself now. Audie's self-worth is tied in to people wanting her. She measures that in her number of sexual partners and also in how far she can push her friends. She thinks anyone interested in her, whether it's for sex or friendship, wants something from her."

"Why would she do that?"

"She's afraid of losing the things that are important to her, but she also thinks she doesn't deserve them. So she keeps picking and picking in an effort to drive you away, which she doesn't want, in order to say that she was right to believe that people just use her for what they can get out of her."

"Oh, God. Audie." She covered her mouth with trembling hands.

"Her choices are not your fault, Nadia," he said gently but firmly. "Even though she didn't make good choices tonight, that doesn't mean she should have been hurt like that. This could be a turning point for her. That's part of the reason why I called Sally Jensen. I'm hoping she'll work with Audie, get her on the right track. Sally can help her help herself. Audie's a good person underneath it all. She just has to believe it herself."

She wanted to believe him. She needed to believe him. If he was wrong it would mean that she'd have to give up on Audie, and that was the last thing she wanted to do. Especially when she knew it wouldn't take much for Audie to give up on herself.

"I guess I'm not as thick-skinned as I used to be." She huffed out a laugh. "A few years out of Los Angeles and my skin has already softened."

"I'm glad you don't have thick skin," he said, hugging her tightly. "You're much more touchable this way."

"Thank you. You say the sweetest things." She yawned.

"You're exhausted. Come on." He stood, helping her to her feet. "I won't stay if you don't want me to, but I want to make sure you get some rest."

"Kaname Sullivan, you're as exhausted as I am. There's no way I'm letting you drive home now." She folded her arms across her chest, biting on her bottom lip. "Besides, I wouldn't mind having you beside me while I fall asleep. It's . . . comforting."

He pulled her close. "I like sleeping beside you too, Nadia Spiceland."

They made their way upstairs to her bedroom, stripped down, then slipped into bed. He reached for her as he usually did post-sex, wrapping her in his arms and tucking her against his chest, her head resting over his heart.

She cupped his cheek, listening to the reassuring rhythm of his heartbeat. "I'm sorry our weekend was interrupted."

"We'll have other weekends. Tying you up and having my way with you won't be a onetime thing if I can help it."

"You won't have to try too hard to convince me." She pressed her lips to his skin. "What you did for me tonight, and for Audie . . . I've never had anyone be there for me like that outside of family and Siobhan. You were my hero tonight."

"Thanks, but I'm not a hero. I'm just a man who wants his woman to realize she doesn't have to go through things alone. I'm here for you as long as you'll let me be."

Nadia closed her eyes against the almost painful warmth that spread through her at his words. She wanted to believe him. Here in his arms, it was easy to believe him. But Audie's words stayed with her long after Kane fell asleep, and though she tried to bury them deep, she knew they'd fester for a long time.

SEVENTEEN

The bell over the café door jangled, signaling a customer. Nadia looked up, hoping it was Audie. They hadn't seen her since the Sunday after her attack nearly two weeks ago. While Audie had slept, Nadia had called Siobhan and Vanessa. Together the three of them had staged an intervention of sorts, except that they hadn't issued ultimatums since those never worked with Audie.

It hadn't been a pretty moment, a highly charged nonconfrontational confrontation in which curses were hurled, tears were shed, apologizes were made. In the end, Audie had agreed to work with the counselor, then Siobhan had offered to take her to get her car so she could make her meeting with the advocate. It had been almost a week without any returned phone calls or text messages, and Nadia worried that Audie had cut her losses and run.

Her heart fluttered as she caught sight of Kane walking toward her. He was sinfully gorgeous in his dark navy suit, crisp white shirt, and multipatterned tie. She recognized a power suit when she saw one, and this was definitely one. It was so unlike his usual style of dress that she instantly suspected something was wrong.

"Kaname." She rounded the corner of the counter, stopping in front of him. "What's wrong?"

"Nadia." The strain in his dark eyes eased slightly as he took her hand. "When you say my name like that, it makes everything all right in my world."

"Now I know something's wrong." She stared at him, wanting to soothe him but hyperaware of her staff and the few customers watching. She guided him to their most secluded table. "What's going on? Why are you dressed for a funeral? Your parents are okay, aren't they?"

"My parents are fine, but something's come up." He squeezed her hand. "I have to go down to Los Angeles for a couple of days."

"For work?"

He nodded. "I've been asked to consult on a case, and they want to meet in person."

It was Thursday. A couple of days meant that their weekend together was in jeopardy. "That makes sense. It must be important, or they wouldn't have asked for your help. Have they told you what they'd like for you to do for them?"

"No." He frowned, rubbing his thumbs over her knuckles as if she was his human worry stone. "It depends on the nature of the case. It could be anything from me reviewing their work and agreeing with and signing off on their conclusions, to working up a full-fledged profile. I'm hoping it will be something simple, but if it was, they wouldn't have called me."

190

She smiled despite her disappointment. "That's because you're good at what you do and they know it."

That brought an answering smile to his lips. "Your faith is a treasure I keep close to my heart."

"Ooh, that's a good one. You should write that one down and use it for the next time I'm all hormonal."

He wiggled his eyebrows. "You seemed to be just fine the last time you were hormonal."

"That's because a certain professor seems to have discovered the perfect cure for cramps." She sobered. "How long will you be gone?"

"Until late tomorrow at the least, but more than likely I won't be back until sometime Saturday. I would ask you to come with me, but I know you can't leave the café."

"Not really." Except that in an emergency, she could get Jas to take over for her. Her assistant could reproduce her recipes as well as she did. To go to Los Angeles though, even to be with Kane . . . she didn't think she could do it. The bad of LA far outweighed the good. "It's just that I haven't been in Los Angeles since I left four years ago."

"I know, sweetheart." He drew their clasped hands up. "It's merely wishful thinking on my part. I don't want you to be there any more than you want to go, even for me. Besides, I'm not sure how much free time I'd have. My goal is to spend every waking moment working so I can get back here to you as soon as I possibly can."

"It seems like there's always something interrupting our weekends," she said wistfully. She didn't want to think of the import of that, didn't want to think there was some deeper meaning in the fact that their efforts to be together for longer than a night at a time were stymied at every turn.

"That just makes the time we do get to spend together that much sweeter." He leaned closer. "I would like nothing more than to walk through the *Garden* with you this weekend, you know that. I find myself living for the moments I get to be inside you, so much so that I'm tempted to drag you upstairs right now."

"Ooh." She bounced in her chair. "Can we? Even a quickie would hit the spot right now."

Reluctance crossed his features. "Dammit, no. Every quickie we've attempted has turned into a marathon. I have to leave like five minutes ago, but I couldn't go without seeing you. You know I'll be thinking of you every moment I'm away from you, right?"

She tried for a joke. "And that's different from any other day how?"

He released a soft gust of laughter. "True. I do think about you more often than is probably healthy, but I don't give a damn. Thoughts of you are infinitely better than the other things I have to think about."

"Like the case you have to consult on."

"Like this case." His lips thinned. "We're going to have our weekend, Nadia. Even if it doesn't start Friday night. If I have to drive all night from Los Angeles, I'll be back on Saturday."

"I'll be here, waiting."

"Will you?" He stared at her, his eyes intense with need, with something else she couldn't name.

She tightened her grip on his hand, then reached up to cup his cheek. "Of course I will. I have a feeling the reunion sex is going to be pretty freaking epic!"

He pressed his cheek against her palm. "I have the feeling I'm going to need it."

Worry crawled through her veins. "Is it that bad?"

Again his smile vanished. "It sounds like it."

She couldn't help it. She got up, sat in his lap, wrapped her arms around his neck and kissed him. It didn't matter who watched them or how much grief she'd catch from her staff later. She'd do anything to erase his stress, to give him something else to think about. Considering how he'd been there for her when she was dealing with Audie, it was the very least she could do.

It wasn't about keeping the relationship scales balanced. Not anymore. Something weighed on Kane, something he probably couldn't talk about for a variety of reasons. Whatever it was, she didn't need to know. All she knew was that he was bothered, and if she could do something to take that bother away, she'd do it even if only for a little while.

His hands tightened on her waist, pulling her even closer as he deepened the kiss, changing it from soothing to sensual. As always she found herself sliding into his sensual web, drugged by his kisses, craving the sensations only he could evoke within her.

He pulled away, reluctance limning his features. "Damn, Nadia," he breathed. "What you do to me should be a federal crime!"

"Does this mean that you're going to detain me, Professor?" she whispered in his ear.

He growled. He actually growled. "If I hadn't already promised I'd be there in a few hours, I'd say to hell with everyone and kidnap you to Lake Tahoe or something."

"You're not a reckless man, Kane," she said, rising to her feet.

"With you, I feel completely, wholly, and most unapologetically reckless." He gave her a rueful smile as he stood. "But thanks for being the voice of reason."

He stepped back from her, straightening his jacket, regaining his composure. "I'll be back as soon as I can."

"Wait a moment." She hurried to the counter and asked Rosie to bag up one of the sticky buns while she made a chai latte to go. Taking the bag from Rosie, she came back around the corner and pressed the bag and cup into his hands. "Here's a care package for the road. I know the buns always put you in a good mood, so at least you'll be good for the plane ride."

"Nadia." He drew in a deep breath, his lips parted as if he wanted to say something. She waited, but all he said was, "I'll call you when I get in and when I'm able to leave. At the very least, I want your voice to be the last thing I hear before I go to sleep tonight. All right?"

"Same here. I don't care how late it is, you call me. Promise?"

"As my lady desires." He pressed his forehead against hers for a moment, then turned and quickly walked out the door.

"Whew." She sagged against the table, her heart aching. Kane had barely been gone a minute and she already missed him. Missed him so keenly that it felt like physical pain.

"Is everything okay?" Siobhan asked as she approached.

"Yeah." Nadia straightened, and gave her partner a shaky smile. "He's been asked to consult on a case, so he's heading down to Los Angeles. He said he'd try to get back early Saturday, but there's a good chance the weekend's toast."

"Oh honey, I'm sorry. I know you were looking forward to spending some quality time with the professor."

"I was, but something always comes up to throw a monkey wrench in our plans. Do you think it's a sign?"

"A sign of what?"

"That I shouldn't be with Kane."

"I think you're creating drama where there is none, hon," Siobhan said. "We all just watched that very public display of affection you two had. You damn near melted the window."

Heat stained Nadia's cheeks. "Well, ah, if we're going to rate this on the sex alone, this relationship thing gets an A-plus."

"And the problem with that is?"

"What about the other stuff?"

"What other stuff?"

"The other stuff that makes a relationship a relationship."

Siobhan cocked her head. "Like what?"

"Like going to the movies, or bowling. Like spending more than an overnight with each other. Every time we've tried to take a full weekend together, something's happened. I mean, that's just weird, isn't it?"

Siobhan settled her hands on her hips. "Are you doing that freak-out thing again?"

"I think so." She folded her arms across her chest. "This thing with Kane . . . I want it to become something and at the same time I don't."

"Because if it becomes something, emotions get involved." Siobhan gave her a knowing look. "And if emotions get involved, you think you're going to screw it up."

"Of course I'm going to screw it up," Nadia retorted. "Have you met me?"

"I have. This you and the old you. I've also met your professor and I know enough about him to know he's got his crap together, and he's not the selfish bastard that Gary was."

"Siobhan!"

"I know, speaking ill of the dead and all that." Siobhan waved her hand in dismissal. "But he was selfish. Wanting to have his cake and eat it too. You may have walked into that mess with your eyes wide open, but he put down the rug over the trapdoor and invited you to walk across it."

Nadia winced, but sometimes the truth hurt. "Kane doesn't know any of that. I haven't told him, and he hasn't looked it up on the Internet."

"Are you sure about that?"

She cut Siobhan a glance. "You think he'd still want me if he knew?"

"That's the real issue, isn't it? It's not about what he makes you feel or being afraid of those feelings. What you're really afraid of is that he'll learn everything about the way you were, and that will be enough to make him not want to be with you the way you are now."

"Give the lady a prize." She'd told Kane about her rehab stint, but he still saw her as that hot bakery lady. Would his opinion change when he found out about Gary?

Siobhan slapped her hands down on Nadia's shoulders. "So here's what I think. I think your emotions are already engaged in this relationship. Yes, you are in a relationship, whether you spent one hour or forty-eight hours together. If you don't believe me, remember how he supported you through the night of Audie's attack. Someone who is just in it for sex wouldn't have done that."

"You're right."

"Of course I'm right. I'm the oldest and the voice of experience.

Maybe it's time to adjust your schedule, give Jas some more responsibility. If the relationship is worth it, if Kane is worth it, then you should bend a little. And for goodness sakes, don't let your fear override your instincts."

Nadia eyed her partner. "You know, I think you need your own talk show. They're doling them out like Halloween candy these days, but you'd actually be good at it."

Siobhan let loose with her throaty laugh. "Like hell. I'm good at failed relationships, trying again, and failing again. And I'll probably go through it yet again beating my head against a very stubborn wall."

Nadia knew Siobhan meant her nonexistent relationship with her daughter. She wrapped her arms around the other woman. "So you've heard from Colleen then?"

"No, which I suppose is answer enough. Still, I'll try again." Siobhan blew out a breath, then gave Nadia a watery smile. "Keep hope alive, right?"

"Right." She hugged the blonde woman again then stepped back. "It looks like my Friday night is open. Want to come over for a low-nutritional value dinner and a superhero movie marathon? Just you and me?"

"You're on. And I won't even be mad at you if you cut out after a phone call from a certain college professor."

EIGHTEEN

Kane walked into his hotel's bar, his need for a drink eclipsed only by his need to hear Nadia's voice. The case he'd been called to consult on was horrific and shaped up to be big in a career making or destroying sort of way. The prosecution wanted to prove that the accused was completely sane and each side had provided experts to support their supposition. It seemed that no one wanted it to go to trial, but there was no way that anyone, especially the victims' loved ones, would let the accused get away without some repercussions. A trial was not going to be easy, and he wasn't sure he wanted to be a part of it.

He spotted his friend Simon Mayhew at the bar and went over to join him. "Hey, Simon. How's it going?"

Simon's dark face split into a huge grin. "Kane, good to see you, man! You know me, things are so good, complaining would be a crime!"

Simon signaled the bartender. "What's your poison?"

Kane ordered an Irish whiskey, neat, then took the barstool next to his friend. As usual, Simon had already become buddies with most of the patrons nearby. It was a gift he had, a gift that made him a top-notch investigative journalist and a regular on the twenty-four-hour news channels. They'd met on the set of one such program, talking about the Red Light case. Their back-and-forth had apparently made for great television, and they'd been invited back together numerous times.

They worked well together, so well that when their mutual agent had suggested that they collaborate on a book, Kane had quickly agreed. One nonfiction crime book had become three, and neither of them had looked back.

"So what brings you down from the bay to the City of Angels?" Simon asked after Kane took a sip of his whiskey.

"I'm consulting on a new case."

"Really." Simon turned to him, and Kane could easily see the wheels turning behind his coffee brown eyes. "Local or federal?"

"Come on, Simon, you know I'm not going to divulge that."

"Now I'm really intrigued. Are you sure I can't convince you to become an unnamed source?"

Kane snorted. "Like it would be hard for anyone to figure out the identity of your source."

"You have a valid point, Professor," Simon said with a sage nod. "However, I wouldn't be a good journalist if I didn't point out that people can speculate all they want, but I never reveal my sources."

"I know you don't. I still have no comment."

"All right, man. I can respect you being a man of integrity and all." Simon sat back, lifting his glass in a silent request for a refill.

"Want to tell me why you wanted to meet? Not that I don't like seeing that pretty face of yours, but my wife is way hotter."

Kane suppressed a flash of jealousy at the mention of Simon's wife. Simon and Caroline Mayhew had been married for nearly twenty years, right out of high school. Although he had managed to dodge all of Caroline's attempts to fix him up with one of her seemingly endless supply of single friends, Kane wanted what they had. He wanted what his parents had.

An image of Nadia came unbidden to his mind. Not naked and spread for him but standing in front of him in her Sugar and Spice T-shirt and those jeans that hugged her curves, concern and care lighting the depths of her eyes as she'd sent him off with a cup of tea and a bag of pastries. That Nadia was the treasure, the one she rarely allowed to the surface even though the care she felt for those close to her was intrinsic to her nature. He wasn't going to push her, but that didn't mean he couldn't lean a little.

"Hey, are you all right?"

Kane polished off his whiskey then asked for another on the rocks. "Yes. I wanted to talk to you about a new business opportunity."

Simon's alert gaze sharpened. "What sort of business opportunity?"

"We've made a name for ourselves with our nonfiction work," Kane reminded him. "What do you think about trying our hand at writing fiction? I'm thinking thrillers, police procedurals, that sort of thing."

Simon stared at him for a charged moment, leaving Kane to wonder if his friend thought he'd popped his mental clutch. Then Simon burst into loud laughter that drew the attention of everyone in the bar.

"I say it's about damn time we do something like that!" he exclaimed, thumping Kane on the back. "We already do a good job writing and researching the nonfiction stuff. It shouldn't be that hard for us to switch to fiction, come up with a compelling main character or investigative team and the unusual cases they encounter."

"That's what I thought too," Kane said, warming to the idea. This was the best part about working with Simon—they fed off each other's ideas like piranhas at a buffet. He pulled out his smartphone and began taking notes as he and Simon tossed ideas, characters, and potential plots around. The more they talked, the more the thought of writing fiction grabbed him. They could do this.

"My schedule's tight right now, but we really need to jump on this. We need to call Stewart and sound him out about it."

"He's probably got some contacts he can feel out. Will you have some free time tomorrow? We can meet in my office and call him."

Kane shook his head. "My schedule is slammed tomorrow, and I want to be back home tomorrow night if I can help it."

"Oh yeah?" Simon raised an eyebrow. "Any particular reason you're in a hurry to get back to small-town Crimson Bay when the bright lights of LA are waiting for you?"

"Fuck off, man."

Simon broke into booming laughter. "There's definitely a particular reason. What's her name?"

Kane hesitated. Simon wouldn't be satisfied with just a name, and considering that he'd made Los Angeles his base of operations for the last fifteen years, it was more than likely that he'd know all about Nadia and her former life.

"Sorry, Simon, but I'm going to play this one close for a little while longer," he finally said. "It's still new, but so far, so good. As for the project, we can do our usual communication thing—text, e-mail. I'll try to shuffle some things around, see if I can come back down in about a month or so if we need to do a face-to-face."

"If you do, you should stay with us," Simon told him. "You know Caro would love to have you."

"Meaning, Caro would love to hook me up with a new batch of eligible women." Kane held up his hands. "No thanks."

"The only way Caro's giving up on you is if you give in to the inevitable, my friend," Simon joked. "Surrender to the joy that is domestic bliss."

"I don't have any plans to surrender yet," he replied, trying not to think about a certain curvy brunette who had taken up residence in his mind a few weeks ago and showed no signs of moving out any time soon. "If I do, you'll be the tenth to know."

"Dude, that's harsh." Simon took another sip of his beer, his gaze assessing. "Everything all right at Herscher?"

"You act like you're an investigative reporter or something." Simon was just too damn good at his job.

"Seems to me that's a smoke signal right there. What's going on?"

"Nothing but the usual drama that ensues when contracts are up and tenure is on the line." He shrugged. "It doesn't hurt to keep my options open. Who knows? Maybe we can get this series off the ground and then remaining an assistant professor won't be that much of a big deal."

"Either way, we need to make this happen." Simon stood, reached for his wallet.

Kane stopped him. "I'll just put it on my room tab. Thanks for coming out."

"Are you kidding me? I'm all over this project. Definitely worth the drive." They clasped hands then did the straight guy half-hug thing. "Good seeing you, Kane."

"You too, Simon. I'll flesh out our notes then send you a copy. Give my love to Caro."

"Nobody gives Caro love but me. I'll tell her you said hello, though."

Simon left. Kane settled the bill then headed for the elevator, his phone still in his hand. He wanted to call Nadia, but it was after nine and she had to get up at four. It would be selfish of him to call her just so he could hear her voice.

But he wanted to, He really wanted to.

Back in his room, he quickly stripped then showered, pulling on a pair of boxers before climbing into bed with his phone and his laptop to flesh out his notes. The meeting with Simon had gone much better than he'd hoped. Optimism surged in his veins, optimism that had been in short supply earlier in the day. Trying to get inside the mind of a perpetrator was never an easy thing, especially when one had to wall off one's own moral code and assume the cold mantle of objectivity.

He didn't have to like the case to sign on, but he did have to believe in the cause. He had to believe his input helped, or there wasn't any point in doing it.

The new collaboration with Simon Mayhew gave him the positive energy he needed to get through the next day of meetings. So did the promise of Nadia waiting for him at home.

Sweet yearning filled him, just from thinking of her. She was important to him, more important than he could let her know as of yet. Despite nearly two months of intimacy, he could sense that she didn't fully trust him. She trusted him with her body, but despite agreeing to give a relationship a try, she wasn't ready to trust him with her emotions yet, with her hopes and fears. She was still skittish and he understood that. She probably had good reason to be cautious, given the fallout from her drug addiction past.

Still, he wanted her to know that he wanted more than reenactments of *The Perfumed Garden*, the *Kama Sutra*, and the other sex manuals. He hoped he'd shown that, by supporting her as she'd dealt with Audie. He needed her to know, in gestures grand and small, that he was in to her for far longer than it would take them to complete the book. By the time she realized it, he would be a necessary part of her life.

His phone buzzed. Expecting it to be Simon asking for their notes, he was surprised to find a message from Nadia. She'd snapped a photo of herself lying on her side in her bed, a piece of paper with his name written on it balanced on the pillow beside her. **Missing you**, the accompanying text said.

He was already calling her before the action registered, hoping that it wasn't a delayed text, that she was still awake.

She answered immediately. "Kaname."

He slid down in the bed, laptop forgotten, work a distant memory as the sound of her voice saying his name wrapped around him. "I'm sorry I didn't call, sweetheart," he said. "It's late and I didn't want to wake you up. I know how early you have to get up to open the café."

"Jas is going to take care of it," she answered, her voice soft. "And I took a nap earlier this afternoon so that I could be awake for you tonight."

Warmth that had nothing to do with the two shots of whiskey he'd consumed earlier spread through his chest. "Thank you," he managed to say past the sudden lump in his throat. He coughed to clear it. "And thanks for the picture."

"You know you're welcome." A rustling sound as if she'd turned over in bed. "I do miss you, Kane."

"Will you do me a favor, Nadia?"

"Sure. What do you need?"

You. "Whenever you can remember to do it, I'd love it if you would call me Kaname."

"Oh. Of course I can do that." She gave a light laugh that rippled through him. "It's weird how sometimes it feels right to call you Kane, and other times it feels right to call you Kaname."

"I know." He'd noticed. When she felt comfortable and secure in their intimate moments, she lowered her guard and called him by his full name. When she did, she paired it with a sexy, breathy tone that never failed to harden his cock. As it did now.

He reached into his boxers to adjust himself, thought better of it, then took himself in hand instead. That felt much better, though not as good as it would be if it were her hand gripping him.

"How was your day? You don't sound right."

He didn't want to talk about his day, especially not the part spent examining photos and talking motives and psychological impacts. The fact that she could tell that he'd been bothered by the case told him she was more tuned to him than he'd hoped. "I'll be all right. The day was longer than I would have liked, but hearing from you is a definite improvement."

"I'm glad I could help make it better. You sure you don't want to unload on me? I've learned to be a pretty good listener, and I don't judge."

"I appreciate the offer, babe, but I'll be okay. I did take some time this evening to meet with a friend of mine, Simon Mayhew."

"Oh yeah. He cowrote some books with you, didn't he?"

"He did," Kane answered, ridiculously pleased that she knew that. "We're talking about diving into fiction, writing a thriller series together." He gave her the highlight reel of his brainstorming session with Simon.

"That's a great idea! And it sounds like you're really excited about it."

"I am. We're still in the preliminary stages, but Simon's just as into it as I am. I'm going to try to arrange things so I can get back down here soon for a proper planning meeting."

"Good." She paused, and when she spoke again her voice was barely a whisper. "Maybe I can go with you next time."

The offer wasn't made lightly, Kane knew. Nadia had put LA in her rearview and hadn't looked back. The import of her making the offer now, to return with him, wasn't lost on him. "I'd like that."

He heard her blow out a breath, as if clearing out the emotional weight of her statement. "When do you think you're going to be home?"

"It depends on how late the meetings run tomorrow," he told her. "If I can, I'll be on the last flight out. But it will more than likely be Saturday morning."

"If you can come home tomorrow night, you need to come by and get me," she ordered.

He hesitated, torn between wanting to do exactly that, and needing time to clear the remnants of the consult from his mind before seeing her. "It'll be late, and I'll probably be in a shitty mood."

"Which is exactly why you should come get me, or just come here and stay the night, then we'll go to your place Saturday morning. I mean it, Kaname. Even if it's just sleeping, we need to be in bed together tomorrow night."

He closed his eyes for a moment. She had no idea what she did to him, how deeply she had burrowed beneath his skin. "Are you sure I wouldn't be interrupting another thrilling Girls Night Out?"

"It's a Girls Night In, and no, you won't be interrupting," she answered. "Siobhan's going to come over. We're going to talk a little business then drink a little, eat a lot, and ogle some superhero movie man-candy. By the way, she very graciously gave me permission to kick her to the curb and head out immediately if you come home tomorrow night."

"Well, if Siobhan gives her blessing . . ."

"That's right, mister," she teased. "So you'd better come get me."

"As my lady desires."

"Speaking of which, there is something else I desire."

"Oh?" He settled back into the pillows. "What's that?"

Huskiness threaded through her voice. "I desire . . . to know what you're wearing."

He smiled at the teasing note in her voice. "A sheet."

"Only the sheet?"

"The sheet and blanket," he clarified. "And my boxers."

"Are you hard, Kaname?"

The soft question made him instantly, undeniably hard. "I am now."

"Good," she purred. "Push the bedclothes down."

Intrigued, he did as she demanded, kicking the covers aside. "Okay."

"What color are your boxers?" she wanted to know.

"Red."

"Nice." He heard her take a deep breath. "I'm imagining you lying there in your boxers," she whispered. "Imagining you sliding your hand down your chest then beneath your waistband, gripping your waiting cock. Can you do that for me?"

"Done," he said, adding a hiss of pleasure as he firmed his grip on his shaft.

"Stroke it," she breathed. "Stroke it like I'm stroking myself right now."

"You are?" His breath caught as he fell under the spell her words wove.

"Yes," she confessed. "It's why I called you, so we can give each other permission to come."

"What do you think of to get worked up?"

"We're in bed together," she said softly. "I've got my back against the headboard, and you're sitting up near the end of the bed. You have your cock in your hand and I've got my fingers on my clit. We're matching each other stroke for stroke."

She released a sigh ripe with unfulfilled desire. "I think watching each other stroke off would be extremely hot."

"God, Nadia!" He had to pinch off to suppress the urge to come. They should have had phone sex long before now. "What other fantasies do you have?"

"I'm on my back on the bed, looking up at you," she said after a moment, her words breathy. "I love watching your face. I love how the pleasure takes you over. Your eyes light up with an inner fire, and your lips part when you're close to coming. You're watching me touch my breasts and stroke myself while you're slowly and deeply taking my ass."

"Fuck." His hips were moving now, lifting off the bed, pushing his cock through his fist, making him wish it were Nadia's tight sheath gripping him. "You want that?" he ground out. "You want me to take you like that?"

"I want to try," she admitted breathlessly. "A cock is different than a finger."

"Damn, Nadia—you've got me on the edge of coming!"

"I am too. I'm wishing that your cock was inside me, stroking so deep and fast when we're right there, right at the moment, and then you fill me up—"

She broke off with the signature moan that let him know she was coming. A few more rapid strokes and he joined her, spurting into his boxers like a horny teen, her name a deep groan on his lips.

A long while later he heard her voice calling him from far away. "Kaname?"

He fumbled for his phone, lifted it back to his ear. "Do you realize how incredibly sexy you are?"

Her laughter, rich and a little shaky, filled his ear. "So are you, Professor. I wanted to provide enough incentive to make sure you come over as soon as you get back."

He got up to head to the bathroom to clean up. "If I have to rent a car and drive, I'm coming for you tomorrow night."

"Excellent." She yawned. "Then my job here is done. I'm going to sleep well tonight, that's for sure. Sweet dreams, Kaname."

"They will be now. Good night, Nadia."

He put down the phone then braced himself against the sink,

his mind unable to focus on anything other than Nadia. She was exactly what he'd needed, exactly when he'd needed it. Her laughter, her smile, her sweet body shredded every bit of stress, every clump of darkness. Being with her for the last few weeks had caused a fundamental shift in his universe, a change in direction from where he thought he needed to be to where he wanted to be.

Finally, he mustered enough energy to clean up, pull on fresh underwear, then fall back into bed. With his heartbeat back to normal and sleep embracing him, a simple truth came to him: Nadia Spiceland was quickly becoming the most important thing in his life.

NINETEEN

"You need to start dating."

Nadia placed a tray with dessert and two steeping teapots—one of chrysanthemum tea for Siobhan, and a Sencha green for herself—on the coffee table. The remnants of their margherita pizza had been put away, and the second superhero movie rumbled away in the background.

"I'm not taking your bait," Siobhan said evenly, snagging a plate of double-dutch chocolate pie from the tray. "One would think you'd be bored by now and stop trying."

"I'm not trying to bait you. Much," Nadia replied, settling in on the other end of the couch. "I refuse to believe you don't have any prospects, not with the fan club your alter ego has."

"Oh no, you don't," Siobhan laughed. "That's so not going to happen."

"Yes, it is." Nadia poured a serving of her tea, added a dollop of honey. "We just need to narrow the list to the best candidates for the job. What possible reason could you have to not want to have some sexy-times of your own? And if the word *age* comes out of your mouth, I'm taking your dessert."

Siobhan directed a scowl her way. "You're a right beyotch when you're getting it on the regular, you know."

Nadia laughed, ignoring Siobhan's sour tone. "Which is why you need to jump on one of your fanboys like yesterday." She took a sip of her tea, then added another measure of honey. Kane would probably flip over the way she was destroying the flavor of a good Japanese tea, and she smiled to herself at the thought.

"Why are you smiling at my misery?" Siobhan demanded, her scowl deepening.

"Eat your chocolate, and I'll tell you." She waited until her partner took the first mouthful of the double-dutch chocolate pie which had nothing Dutch in it. "Your misery is self-inflicted. Why would you deny yourself the opportunity to have a basic human need met?"

"You know why." Siobhan returned her half-eaten dessert to the coffee table.

"Colleen." Nadia sat back with a sigh. Siobhan's daughter was the epitome of a difficult child, wrapped in an eighteen-year-old's body. Colleen only showed up when she wanted something from her mother, preying on Siobhan's guilt and dangling the carrot of reconciliation. Then she'd fly into a rage over some perceived slight and stomp off again, leaving Nadia to patch Siobhan's heart back together afterwards.

In fact, the only time she and Siobhan had come close to a knock-down, drag-out fight was a year ago when Siobhan had wanted to hire Colleen to work in the café for the summer. Nadia had seen the trouble brewing in Colleen's eyes and had refused. Her refusal hadn't gone over well. Siobhan had overridden her, and when Jas had caught Colleen stealing from the register, Colleen had blamed Siobhan, Nadia had blown up, and their partnership had teetered on the edge of dissolution.

"Siobhan," Nadia said slowly, choosing her words with care. "Are you saying that you don't even want to try dating because things are still unsettled with Colleen?"

Siobhan's shoulders stiffened. "There's always a chance things will work out with her."

"I know. I certainly hope so." Nadia injected every bit of sincerity she could into her words. "I want you to come to some sort of resolution with your daughter, if only so you can move forward."

"I am moving forward," Siobhan insisted. "Every day I'm not reaching for a bottle of pills is a move forward."

"Siobhan." Nadia stopped, her throat closing off with the threat of tears. "You can't put your life on hold waiting for Colleen to straighten out hers."

"I know that!"

"Do you?" she pressed. "You think being by yourself is your way of doing penance for leaving your daughter and husband because of drugs. When are you going to stop punishing yourself, Siobhan? When are you going to realize that you have to live life now?"

"I am living my life now." Tension squeezed every bit of inflection from Siobhan's voice. "I have the café. I have my burlesque shows. And I have my friends who seem to relish giving me a hard time."

"Bitch Talk doesn't only happen on Tuesdays, you know," Nadia reminded her. "You perform once a month. The café takes up enough of your time, which is why we've been talking about interviewing for a manager to free up some of your time in the office. I think we should move up that timetable. As for your friends, you know we're behind you, giving you all the emotional support we can. We can't give you everything though, and you know that. You need more. We all need more. We can't emotionally starve ourselves because we might get hurt or hurt others. That's not living."

"Dammit, Nadia." Siobhan wiped at her eyes. "Where did you learn all this touchy-feely self-help crap?"

"From a certain blonde bombshell who decided she was going to be my friend even though I didn't want one."

"You wanted one, you just didn't want to admit it."

"You saw right through me. Saw me true. And just recently you told me that I had my whole life ahead of me and I couldn't spend it elbow-deep in pastry dough."

"Me and my big mouth," Siobhan groused. "If I promise to think about acquiring a living, breathing sex toy, will you quit bitching at me?"

"For a little while," Nadia promised, relieved. "Just let me point out that there's nothing wrong with having a fling. A woman's got needs, darn it."

"Speaking of a woman's needs, when is the professor coming home?"

Nadia's good humor dissolved. "He's supposed to come home tonight, but it's possible he might not be back until tomorrow."

"Is whatever he's working on in Los Angeles not going well?"

"I don't know. He doesn't want to talk about it, which to me means it's very, very bad." She reached for her phone. She hadn't heard from Kane in hours, and it worried her. Not that he hadn't contacted her, but that he was probably dealing with something unpleasant that required his complete concentration, and it was that something that worried her. He'd seemed so subdued yesterday, so unlike the man she'd come to know and appreciate. His energy had quickly changed thanks to a little phone sex, and she was glad to have been able to do that for him. She had the feeling it was going to take something a little more live and in person to ease his burden this time.

She thumbed her phone out of sleep mode, then sent him a text. Hi! Are you going to make it back to the Bay tonight?

It was a long while before he responded. I'm on the last plane out. Boarding soon.

Something about the phrasing of his text bothered her. This one didn't feel as teasing as most of his other exchanges with her. It made her wonder again what sort of consult he was doing in Los Angeles. Her overactive imagination provided all sorts of details for what sort of heinous crime he'd been asked to offer his expertise on. She knew a good bit about the grime that lay beneath the glitter that made up Tinseltown. What must it be like to have to see the results of that day in, day out for a living? How did Kane handle it? How did anyone?

It was ridiculous trying to interpret the emotional tone of a text message, but Nadia did it anyway. Those few simple words told her that the day hadn't gone as well as the previous one, which she already knew hadn't been stellar.

She showed Siobhan the text message. "Am I being paranoid, or is that not a good sign?"

Worry crossed her friend's face. "It might be nothing, but I think you need to ask him directly to know for sure."

She hesitated before sending him another text, not wanting to bother him but needing to know how he was doing. Are you still coming here when you land?

She waited, clutching the phone, her heart pounding. The longer it took him to respond, the more worried she became. What the hell was going on in LA?

No.

She stared at her screen, surprised at the bright shaft of pain that speared her. Kane wasn't coming to get her. He didn't want to see her.

Before she could clear away the crushing disappointment enough to think of a proper response, a chime signaled another incoming text. Sorry. Exhausted, sweetheart. Heading straight home when I land. Will see you tomorrow.

The tightness in her chest eased. It wasn't as if he was breaking up with her. He simply didn't want to see her tonight.

Siobhan took the phone from her hand then scanned the last of the conversation. "Son of a bitch. At least he realized how fucking harsh that one-word answer was, even though his explanation is lame." She glanced at Nadia. "Are you okay?"

"No." She shook her head for emphasis. "And neither is he. Something's not right, and I need to find out what it is."

"What are you going to do?"

Whatever was happening with Kane, it wasn't good. She wished she could have screwed up her courage and gone with him, even if she couldn't have been by his side every moment of his day. She could have been waiting for him in his hotel room when he returned, waiting to hug him and kiss him and take him away from the pressures of the world for a while. Waiting to be there for him as he'd been there for her with Audie.

The answer was simple. "I'm going to wait for him at his condo."

Siobhan frowned at her, uncertain. "Are you sure that's a good idea?"

"No, but if I accept that text at face value, I'll end up sitting here for the rest of the night wondering and worrying about what's going on with him."

"Waiting had never been your style."

"Exactly. I have to see for myself that he's okay."

"Good for you. Way to grab the bull by the horns."

"Or the Kane by the balls." She stood, gathering the remnants of their tea and dessert. "Either way, he's dealing with me tonight."

They quickly cleaned up, then Nadia grabbed her already-packed overnight bag and followed Siobhan down to the parking deck. Siobhan slid into her fire-engine red Falcon convertible in the guest spot. The vintage car suited Siobhan and her burlesque personality, and she often did car shows in full sixties costume.

"Are you sure you're going to be okay?" the blonde asked as she started her engine.

"As sure as I can be about anything," Nadia answered, opening the passenger door on her MINI Cooper and tossing her bag inside. Every instinct told her that Kane's place was where she needed to be, but what if her instincts were wrong?

"Call me if you need me," Siobhan demanded. "Otherwise I'll assume the reunion went as planned."

"Will do. Thanks, Siobhan."

"You're welcome," her best friend said. "Good luck."

Nadia climbed into her car and started the engine. Drawing a fortifying breath, she pulled out of her space and headed for Kane's. Something told her she'd need much more than luck tonight.

In no time at all she completed the short drive to Kane's, punched in the gate code, and made her way to guest parking. Still questioning herself, Nadia made her way to his door, dropped her bag onto the floor, then tucked her skirt around her legs before sliding to the ground beside it. She figured she had another half hour to wait until he came home. Hopefully her fingernails would survive.

What had happened? All sorts of scenarios ran through her mind. She hadn't known Kane all that long, but she knew him to be an even-keeled sort of guy. What was he dealing with that would impact him like this? Knowing the serial rapist case that had made him a household name, she could only imagine the horrific images he'd been confronted with. If that was the reason he'd withdrawn from her—and that's what she felt like, no matter his intent—then in her mind that was even more reason to see him.

Yet as the minutes ticked by, more doubts kicked in as she began to question herself. If he'd had as bad a day as she imagined, would he want to see her on his doorstep? What if the last thing he wanted to deal with was an obnoxious girlfriend who couldn't handle rejection?

Girlfriend. She almost laughed aloud at the way she'd labelled herself. She and Kane had agreed they were in a relationship, but what they were to each other, what she felt toward him, was way more than the term *girlfriend* could contain. He'd seen her ugly cry and hadn't run screaming. He knew she was a recovering addict, and hadn't blinked at that either. Maybe he didn't truly understand all that being a drug addict who didn't do drugs entailed, but he was supportive and treated her normally, both acts which were worth their weight in gold.

Kane had gone above and beyond for her, had been there when the last thing she thought she'd wanted was for him to witness her meltdown. The very least she could do was do the same for him. More than that, though, was the realization that the thought of him being sad or hurt, hurt her. It hurt just as much as Siobhan's pain hurt her, just as much as Audie's pain had hurt. Maybe even more. If she were wrong, if she ended up being the fool, she'd be all right with that because she'd rather have come over and been proven wrong, than stayed at home and been proven right.

TWENTY

"Nadia?"

She looked up, then quickly scrambled to her feet. Kane stood in the hallway, a wheeled suitcase behind him, his clothes rumpled and his hair in disarray as if he'd repeatedly run his hands through it. Fatigue weighed down his shoulders, his features, but she'd never been so glad to see him. "Hi."

"What are you doing here?"

The blunt question stopped her forward motion, her opened arms falling limply to her sides. He didn't look happy to see her. He looked annoyed, which meant she was wrong after all. He didn't want to see her tonight. Maybe he didn't want to see her tomorrow, either.

"I'm sorry." She hugged her arms about herself, fighting a swell of embarrassment as she mentally bailed on her earlier plan. "I wanted to see for myself that you were all right," she said, trying for a breezy tone and failing miserably. "Now that I have, I'll get out of your hair so you can get some rest."

Clutching the strap of her bag, she lowered her head and moved past him. His hand shot out, clamped around her wrist, spun her. Her back made contact with the corridor wall, hard. She gasped as he caged her in, his palms flat against the wall on either side of her head, his big body trapping hers. She stood frozen as he leaned in, feeling a little apprehensive and a little turned on.

"I'm really angry with you right now," he said against her cheek.

Flares of hurt and anger ignited deep inside her. "Angry with me? Why? Did I ruin your Friday night plans? Were you blowing me off so you could be with someone else?"

God damn it, that last part sounded pathetic. She shoved at his chest, but he easily caught her by the wrists, pulling her hands above her head. The only way she could free herself was by kneeing him in the nuts. As angry as she was, she wasn't that angry. "Let me go, Kane. I'll let you get back to whatever you'd rather do than be with me tonight."

"No." He shoved a knee between hers, her short skirt a flimsy barrier. His breath sawed in and out as if he'd just completed a marathon, his eyes burning with an intensity she hadn't seen from him before.

"I wanted to see you," he said as if she hadn't spoken, his voice scraped raw. He pressed closer. "I needed to see you. That's why I went by your house."

"You did?"

She felt him nod, felt the tension in his muscles as he held himself in check. "I went by, but you weren't there. At first I thought you were avoiding me because you didn't answer my last text. I realized that I'd more than likely pissed away my chances with you."

He shuddered. "You have no idea what that did to me. I was angry that I felt that loss on top of everything else I've dealt with today, and I'm angry that I had to feel it longer than necessary. I'm angry that I thought I was going to have to call all your friends and try to track you down tonight just for the hope of hearing you say my name. Then I come home and find you here. Why are you here, Nadia?"

"Because I want to be," she answered, recognizing the truth of it deep in her bones. "Because you need me to be."

With a pained groan, he crashed his mouth against hers in an action much too brutal to be called a kiss. Maybe he meant it as a punishment, but she could feel his anger, the edge of desperation in it, his need for her. Instead of pushing back she surrendered, softening against the hard lines of his body, offering whatever he needed from her.

The kiss softened as his anger seeped away. His grip on her wrists lessened, then he slid his hands up to thread his fingers into hers. There was only one thing he wanted. "Say my name."

"Kaname," she whispered against his lips, too overwhelmed to speak louder. "I'm here, Kaname. I'm with you, and I'm not going anywhere."

He drew another shuddering breath then released her. Without another word, he unlocked his door, disabled the alarm, then gestured her inside before retrieving their bags.

"Will you talk to me?" she asked when the silence began to weigh on her. "Tell me what happened so I can help."

He made his way across the condo to the master bedroom. She followed him. "I'm not having my best day," he finally said, his voice tight as he undressed. "It's nowhere near close to a good day. I couldn't get out of Los Angeles fast enough, but sometimes stuff sticks with you. Having you here is helping."

"Then allow me to help you. Do you want a shower or a soak in the tub?" Though Kane's kitchen was almost as nice as hers, his master bath made her go green-eyed with envy, thanks to the over-sized tiled shower with multidirectional shower heads and a soaker tub sized for two.

"Shower. As much as I'd like to relax in the tub with you, I want to wash the grime off."

Needing to help him in some small way, she moved into the master bath and started the shower. Kane wasn't grimy, not that she could see, but she understood the need to get clean. She'd taken to using showers as a form of therapy, washing away her old life, old sins, old ways of thinking. Maybe Kane needed something like that too.

He strode into the room, his mood hanging over him like a thundercloud, entering the shower without a word. He stood beneath the overhead spray, head down, eyes closed, hands hanging limply at his sides. He looked . . . defeated.

No way in hell was she going to leave him like that. He'd let her in, an unspoken request for help. She could do no less than deliver on that request. It was about soothing him, offering him comfort. She wasn't sure if she could, but she knew she had to try. Kane needed her; she felt that in her bones. He didn't need her to help with his cases, or transcribing notes, or offering a woman's perspective. No, he needed her to pull him back from whatever dark place he had to go to in order to do his consultation work.

She quickly undressed then joined him in the shower, adjusting the multidirectional panels to cover them both. Then she reached into one of the tiled alcoves and retrieved his shampoo, pouring some into her palm. Stepping behind him, she began to lather up his hair, sinking her fingers into the thick strands so that she could massage his scalp. He groaned, his head dropping back, shoulders slumping as some of the weight of his mental burden slid away.

She took her time, enjoying touching him, knowing the luxurious sensation of having someone shampoo her hair and wanting to prolong it for him. After rinsing his hair, she grabbed his soap, a spicy scent that she'd forever connect to him. She ran her lathered hands over his skin, injecting as much care and comfort into each touch that she could.

She started at the nape of his neck and his shoulders, massaging at the tightened muscles, humming a nonsensical tune as she went. Taking care of him like this, serving him like this, sent sparks of pleasure through her. Making others happy made her happy. It was why she'd chosen baking, because desserts made everyone happy. If shampooing Kane's hair and massaging his tension away could give him a respite and ease his mood, she'd do it happily.

Down his left arm then up his right, she loosened his muscles from shoulders to hands, even massaging his palms and fingers. Next, she directed her attention to his back, using the heels of her hands to work at the tight muscles there. Down each bump of his spine, along his ribs, back down to his tailbone, she continued the soapy massage.

He did move then, leaning forward, bracing his hands against the opposite wall as he widened his stance. She re-lathered her hands before sinking to her to knees, massaging her soapy hands over his buttocks and thighs, the crease between his cheeks. She took her time, giving attention to every inch of his skin down to his toes.

The silence stretched but the tone of it changed, becoming lighter as more tension left his body. Moving around to face him, she soaped her way up his calves to his thighs. He'd told her that he swam every other day, taking advantage of the condo's communal facilities, and it showed. He had a swimmer's body, powerful shoulders, tapered waist, strong legs and she knew just how fine a machine it was.

Next she cupped and soaped his balls, keeping her touch light and gentle. He straightened as she tended his resting cock next, and though he hissed as soon as she took him in hand, that was his only reaction.

"I'm sorry, Nadia," he said into the damp silence. "I just don't have it in me tonight."

"Good thing I don't need it in me tonight," she told him, pushing her wet hair out of her face and sitting back on her heels so that she could look up at him. "That's not what this is about."

The haunted look had receded from his eyes, and the deep lines around his mouth were faded. He wasn't all the way back yet, but he was getting there. "What is this all about?"

"You," she said simply. "It's about you and what you need."

"Nadia," he whispered, his eyes sliding closed. "Thank you."

Moved, she continued her upward trajectory, spreading lather over his groin, his abdomen, his chest. Rising to her feet, she ran her hands over his heart, his collarbone, and his throat. Then she stepped back, letting him scrub his face while she quickly lathered and rinsed off.

He shut off the water, and they stepped out of the shower. Using towels from the heated rack, they toweled themselves dry. Kane blew out a breath then smiled at her, his first true smile that reached his eyes and chased the last of the shadows away.

"There he is," she said softly, ridiculously overjoyed at seeing his good mood return. "Or is it because my mascara is making me look like a half-drowned raccoon?"

"You're beautiful," he said simply. "Inside and out."

"Kane." She stepped up to him, wrapping her arms about his waist, molding her body to his, hugging him with her arms, body, and heart. He returned her embrace, his arms encircling her shoulders. They stood like that for a long time, reconnecting, reaffirming.

Finally they went to bed, Nadia tucked under his shoulder with her head resting on his chest. As the night settled around them, Kane cupped her cheek. "I'm sorry I said I wasn't coming over to get you tonight."

"It hurt," she was able to admit. "It felt like you'd rejected me."

"That's something I never want to do, even unintentionally." His thumb lightly brushed her cheek. "It was hard to let go of the case I'm consulting on. Sometimes you see things. You see things you can't stop seeing no matter what you do. You get filled with rage or despair, or if you're lucky, determination. It was hard today. A girl, not even a teen. It's bad enough that I have to see it, study it, get into the mind of the person who did that. I don't . . . I need you to not be exposed to it. It's hard to unsee it. It's hard to accept."

A sudden flash of insight had her asking, "So, other women you've been with, they couldn't handle that part of what you do?"

"No." He dropped his hands away from her. "They didn't understand it, since consulting actually isn't my job. I can say no, refuse the request for help. I don't need to do that, and others didn't understand why I would continue to do something that can leave its mark on me like it does. They couldn't deal, so they left. Can't say that I blamed them. Or you, for that matter, if you decide it's too much to deal with."

Her heart broke for him, for this man who had come to mean so much to her in so short a time. "Oh no, Professor, you don't get to push me away." She turned fully onto her side, her arm draped across his waist. "I haven't asked you to stop doing something that's obviously very important to you, and I won't. I wouldn't. Did you forget? I'm not like most women?"

He blew out a breath. "You're not like any woman I've met before. Thank God."

He turned onto his side, wrapped his arms around her, and just held her. It felt like he was holding on, the grip of someone in search of comfort. She hugged him, lifting her upper leg so that it rested high on his outer thigh, cradling him against her breasts, pressing soft kisses to his forehead, his nose, his lips. He shuddered, his grip tightening, but remained silent. She let him have it, knowing he knew she was there, would be there, when he was ready.

He took over the kissing as he usually did, just the way she loved. The kisses changed, intensifying, his grip on her softening, becoming the opening forays to pleasure. Sandwiched together as they were, with her mound poised and ready, she knew the instant he hardened with need.

"Looks like someone's got it in them after all," she joked.

He laughed, and it was wonderful to hear. "Not yet," he said, "but she will. If you can forgo the drawing of a card, I think this is a good time for one of the sheik's side-by-side positions, the twenty-first manner."

She mentally ran through the sundry positions mentioned in *The Perfumed Garden*. That's the one called *love's fusion*, right?"

"A poetic name, but it's a very intimate position. Basically what we're doing right now without the fireworks."

"I personally see fireworks every time we're together."

"Then let's see if we can keep the streak alive." He hooked his hand under her knee, guiding her upper leg until it rested high along his flank. Then he thrust his upper leg between her thighs, positioning his cock at her entrance. He slid his hand between their bodies, his questing fingers stroking over her clit before sinking into her waiting sheath.

She stuttered out a sigh of pleasure against his mouth, nipping at his bottom lip as he tested her readiness to take him. The hour she'd waited for him to return home after saying he wasn't going to see her had been pure torture, making her unsure of where she stood with him. This, right here, right now, told her more than words could that he did want her, did need her. It righted her world, put her back on secure footing, made her want him even more.

He gave her what she needed, rubbing the head of his erection along the moist opening of her slit before slowly and surely pushing his way inside. She felt every inch of his sensual invasion, her breath catching as ripples of pleasure rolled through her.

They paused when he was as deep as he could go, their bodies adjusting to the sensation of being bared to each other. This moment, this intimate interaction was different from everything that had come before. She knew it, and knew Kane realized it too. This time it wasn't just about hitting the peak. It was much more than that. They'd reached a new level of intimacy physically and emotionally, and the position Kane had chosen was the perfect expression of that.

She entwined her arms about his neck, opening herself to him fully. He swept his tongue inside her mouth as they began to move together, advancing, retreating, advancing again, their tongues mimicking their actions below. Kane didn't seem to be in a mood to hurry and neither was she, savoring the feel of their bodies gliding together.

"Nadia," he whispered against her lips, his strokes still slow and deep, the root of his cock bumping her clit with every thrust. "You knew exactly what I needed, and you gave it to me. Thank you for pulling me back. Thank you for not taking no for an answer."

"Thank you for letting me in," she answered, tears pricking her eyes as the emotion of the moment began to overwhelm her. "Thank you for giving me what I needed."

There was no talking after that, just the meeting of mouths and bodies. Kane slid his hands down her back, his fingers delving into the cleft of her buttocks, teasing at her rear entrance. Remembering how she'd confided her fantasy of him taking her there made her even slicker for him, Before the weekend ended, she would realize that fantasy. She knew Kane would see to it.

"Kaname." Her breath quickened as the urge to come rose within her, stirred by his finger at her puckered opening, the root of his cock bumping her slit, his length hitting all the right spots inside her, the kisses that always made her light-headed. Her inner muscles quaked around him, heightening the passion. Like bodysurfing, she allowed the wave of pleasure to sweep her up and carry her away.

She broke with a low moan against his open mouth, arms and legs and body tightening around him. He groaned as her inner muscles milked his orgasm from him, grinding against her, fingers digging deep as he flooded her sheath. The sensation, so wonderful, so intimate, surprised another smaller orgasm from her.

She sighed as the perfection of the moment washed over her. Kane continued to hold her close, sharing soft kisses with her, apparently not ready to pull away. That was perfectly all right with her. In fact, everything was perfectly all right, as long as Kane was with her.

With a soft smile curving her lips and Kane still joined with her, Nadia fell into a worry-free sleep.

———

Kane awakened to the scent and softness of his woman draped across him, sound asleep. He breathed in deeply then released it, the last of the tension of LA leaving his system.

Nadia didn't realize what a gift she was to him. Seeing her outside his door after the shitty weekend in Los Angeles, after going to her house and not finding her there, had filled him with relief so strong it had nearly buckled him. She'd sent him reeling through a landslide of emotions—relief, anger, lust, and a bone-deep need— that ripped at his control and shook him to his core. Then she'd opened her arms, her body and, he wanted to believe, her heart to him, and it had been like seeing sunshine after days of darkness.

He wanted more. More of her warmth, her sunshine, her body and her surrender. More of her laughter, her sighs, her moans of completion. He wanted more than drawing names of sexual positions out of a bag, more than exploration for exploration's sake. He wanted everything, but something told him that Nadia held something back.

He knew it had something to do with her time in Los Angeles, something that made her reluctant to return to the city. Something that had to do with her drug addiction and recovery. She'd told him that he could find out everything he wanted to know with a good online search, but that wasn't the way he wanted to learn Nadia's secrets. He wanted her to trust him enough, trust them enough, to share them.

Maybe he could help things along by researching drug addiction and recovery. Surely Narcotics Anonymous had information for partners and loved ones. He thought briefly about asking Siobhan or Nadia's parents, but didn't want to overstep, didn't want to do anything that would make Nadia take two steps back when he wanted to move their relationship forward.

He reached for his phone to check the time, and found a sticky note stuck to the front. Squinting, he made out Nadia's handwriting. *Something else for you to look at.*

Curious, he thumbed the phone to active. His background image had been changed to an image of Nadia smiling softly, wearing one of his shirts. Something tightened in his chest as he navigated to the gallery. There he found a slew of new photos, all of them of Nadia, all of them taken the night before. Blowing him a kiss. Looking over her shoulder. The shirt sliding off one breast. Making funny faces. Soft and seductive. And then one of her lying next to him as he slept.

His hand shook as the returned the phone to the nightstand. She'd done this for him, in response to the horrors he'd seen in his consultant case. Images infinitely better to look at, images that soothed his soul and lightened his heart. That was the moment that he realized that he was in love with Nadia Spiceland. And maybe she was falling for him too.

TWENTY-ONE

"What do you want to do today?" Kane asked.

Nadia leaned back against him, settling deep into the steaming water. "I'm doing it," she said. "This soaking tub is absolutely decadent."

"I agree, especially since mine comes with my own personal water nymph." He drizzled water across her shoulders with a natural sponge. "I'm pretty sure there are hazards to soaking in water all day though, considering we don't want to become human stew."

"There is that. I thought you'd have the weekend all planned out."

"I have some suggestions." He cupped her breasts. "Beginning with christening every room and horizontal surface in this condo."

"I hope that means that you have vitamins and extra tea on hand, so I can keep up with you."

"I'll be sure to schedule plenty of rest breaks for you." He stood, stepping out of the tub before turning and helping her out. "I do have to go shopping for the ingredients to make the ramen."

"Ooh!" She bounced with excitement as she dried herself off. "You're making the ramen this weekend? Can you share the process with me or has your mother made you swear to never share her recipe?"

"Tomorrow." He eyed her as she toweled dry. "And you can certainly help me make it. But if you keep moving like that, we won't make it out of the house, and we'll be forced to order pizza or something."

She tucked the towel around herself. "I'll be good."

"I know you will," he said, following her into the bedroom. He'd cleared out a drawer for her in the low-slung dresser, but when she veered toward it, he took her hand and led her over to his walk-in closet. "You won't need any clothes while we're inside," he told her. "I have a better idea for you. Lose the towel."

The obvious command in his tone made her perfectly aware that the dynamic had shifted with the rising of the sun. Conscious of his hungry gaze, she stepped back, then reached for the end of the large bath sheet tucked into her cleavage. She loosened the knot then let the towel billow to her feet. Naked, bared completely, she stood before him, shoulders back, hands on hips, secure in her skin because she could see the approval in his eyes.

"You're so beautiful," he whispered, his tone reverent and intense. "And you're mine."

The sheer possessiveness of his words sent a shiver through her. This was a man. Everyone before him had been a boy, inexperienced in discovering what a woman wanted, uncovering what a woman needed. Not Kane. She wanted to be possessed by him. Not owned, but claimed in a soul-deep way that left no doubt, no hesitation, only unadulterated pleasure.

"Kaname," she whispered, the longing clear in her tone.

"While you're here, I want you to wear this." He reached into the closet and drew out a beautiful robe of burgundy silk embroidered with gold and white lotus flowers and gilded cranes.

"Oh, Kaname," she whispered as he helped her put it on but didn't tie the sash. "It's beautiful. You should take some pictures of me in this. That way, if staring at work photos gets too bad, you can flip through your phone and look at my pictures instead."

He stared at her, his expression unreadable. "You already gave me a few of those, wearing my shirt."

"I know, but a couple more of me wearing this or the harem girl outfit wouldn't be bad."

"You would let me do that?"

She nodded. "If it makes you happy, that would make me happy too. Just password-protect your phone. And for the love of all things sexy, don't send them to anyone else."

"I won't." Possessiveness lit his eyes. "No one gets to look at you like that but me. Now hold your hand out."

When she did, he reached into his pants pocket, pulled out a glittering length of gold chain. At each end dangled an intricate-looking clamp. He dropped the chain into her palm, and her breath stuttered as she took in the rubberized tips and realized what they were for. Her nipples pebbled instantly, without him having to touch them. But she knew that he would.

"I love your breasts, how sensitive they are," he murmured to her. "I love how your nipples get hard when you're thinking about me, thinking about sex. You're thinking about it right now, aren't you? Thinking about my hands cupping your breasts, my mouth sucking on your nipples. Thinking about how it will feel when I put this on you."

"Yes," she gasped, light-headed with lust as moisture gathered between her thighs. "Yes, please."

He parted her robe then cupped her breasts, thumbs stroking over the distended tips, causing her to moan softly. "I have more presents I want to give you," he murmured, his voice soothing and exciting her at the same time. "You'll get them little by little, after we see how you handle these. I don't want to overwhelm you."

"I'm not!" she gasped out, squeezing her thighs together. "I won't be overwhelmed."

He gave her an indulgent smile. "We'll see. Because you'll wear these for the rest of the day."

Then he leaned down, taking one of her nipples into the warmth of his mouth. She groaned loudly, gripping his shoulders to prevent herself from falling over. The man had a talented mouth. Talented hands. Hell, he was talented, period. Nadia had never had a lover pay attention to her reactions with such a single-minded purpose as Kane did. It made her feel special, important. As if her pleasure was more important than his own. It made her even more determined to give him pleasure in return.

When his teeth lightly closed down on her, she yipped. He immediately soothed the sting with his tongue but when he would have moved away, she clamped her fingers into his hair. "It didn't hurt," she assured him. "Not in a bad way."

"Good." He straightened. "Are you ready for your gift?"

It took her a moment to catch her breath "Yes."

Caught in a sensual daze, Nadia watched Kane's nimble fingers glide over her nipple, plumping it to near-painful stiffness before taking the chain from her hand and gently attaching and tightening the tweezerlike clamp. Her automatic hiss slid down into a moan as the pain quickly became pleasure. He looped the filigree chain about her neck before draping it down to her other breast and repeating the process. Enough length remained in the chain to drape between her breasts, making her wonder what it would feel like if he tugged on it.

He stepped back. Only then did she remember to breathe, the deep inhale lifting her breasts. Appreciation lit the dark depths of his gaze. "What do you think, sweet Nadia? Be honest."

She had to struggle to remember how to form words. "I think . . . I think I'm wet."

He cocked his head. "You think? You aren't sure?"

She shook her head, licking her lips. "Maybe you should check," she suggested. "See if I'm fibbing or not."

He immediately stepped forward again, his long fingers cupping her mound. She bit back a moan even as she thrust her hips forward, wanting his hand, needing his fingers inside her. He obliged her silent entreaty, two fingers easily sliding into her core.

"Damn, Nadia," he breathed against her mouth. "That's the look I want a picture of in my phone."

"What look is that?"

"Your desire. Looking at the way your eyes go all hazy with lust and your skin flushes makes me wish I could paint. Though I seriously doubt I'd ever be able to fully capture your passion with something so mundane as oil or watercolors."

She could get drunk on his words alone, so heady did he make her feel. She nipped at his bottom lip, groaning as her clamped nipples brushed against the soft material of her robe. She could feel her orgasm stirring, rising up from deep inside her, sensations buffeting her in a sensual storm.

As if sensing how close she was, Kane pulled his fingers away.

"Not yet," he admonished, then nearly undid her by licking his fingers. "You're not on the edge yet. You still have a ways to go."

"How do you know?"

"You're not begging."

She arched a brow at him. "You think you can make me beg?"

He smiled down at her, such a masculine smile that her pussy clenched in response. "Yes."

"Do you . . ." She licked her lips. "You said you want me to wear these all day?"

"Just about," he said again. He hooked his index finger onto the chain dangling between her breasts, giving it a slight tug. She gasped. "I'll adjust them so that they're not too tight. I want you to be aware of them when we go out."

"Ah . . ." Lust clogged her throat. "Out?"

"Yes." Another tug. "You'll wear this and that pretty sundress when we go shopping later. And shoes of course, but that's it."

No bra, no panties. Her mouth dried. Somehow she'd have to go out with Kane and attempt to act natural while nearly naked and continuously aroused. She was so hot for it, for him, that the lust made her drunk. His intent of having sex all weekend suddenly seemed deliciously possible.

She looked down, noticing the tenting in the towel draped low on Kane's hips. "Is that one of my presents?"

"Do you want it to be?"

"Oh yes," she breathed. "I want to have you in my mouth."

The towel twitched as he hardened more. "For all of the detailed advice the sheik provides in *The Perfumed Garden*, he makes no mention of the joys to be had from oral or anal sex. Those aren't the only things he was mistaken about, but they are the worst, in my opinion."

"I agree with you," she said, her voice soft as she gazed up at him, her nipples hard and tight between the clamps, her sex empty and aching. "It's amazingly intimate and requires huge amounts of trust. But it's also a power exchange because one partner is focused on giving physical pleasure to the other, but there's also power in being able to control another's pleasure like that."

"Is that what you want to do, Nadia?" he asked as he stared at her. "Do you want to control my pleasure?"

Oh God, yes. She could feel her clit throbbing painfully between her legs. "Yes, please."

He walked over to the edge of the platform bed, stopping beside two black floor cushions. "Kneel," he commanded softly.

She dropped to her knees on the thick pillow as he stood in front of her, stance wide, feet planted on the smooth hardwood floor. She could see his erection bulging against the front of his towel. Her mouth watered with the need to take him, to suck him down as deeply as she could, to feel his seed spill down her throat. It was a power exchange as she knelt before him, gazing up at him submissively, yet knowing she could control his pleasure, make him come hard this way, made her feel invincible.

"May I?" she whispered.

When he nodded, she reached up, loosening the towel. She pulled the edges apart slowly, savoring the motion, the action of undressing him. Teasing them both. She sat back on her heels to better savor the sight of Kaname Sullivan is all his masculine glory. The light scattering of hair across his chest blended into a kissable trail down to his groin, framing his cock and balls so beautifully her breath caught. Unable to help herself, she rubbed her cheek against him, relishing his hardness, drawing out the moment before she'd have him in her hands.

His cock was beautiful, standing out proudly from his body, so hard it was a smooth rod of masculine virility. Uncircumcised, the head peeked out at her, glistening with pre-come. Kane was as caught up as she was, as horny as she was, as ready as she was.

Reaching out with her tongue, she lapped at the pre-come that seeped from the head. He shuddered in response. Once again she rubbed her cheek along his length, enjoying the feel of his heat and hardness against her skin. Her hand came up to cup his balls, gently massaging them as she began to press kisses along his shaft. He groaned his approval, hips shifting forward, needing more contact with her.

She wrapped her right hand around his thickness, stroking the head of his penis free of the foreskin. Looking up at him, she could see the approval, his pleasure in his eyes. It warmed her, slicked her insides, knowing she could please him this way. Knowing he'd reward her with pleasure in kind.

Once more she kissed up his shaft, then held his gaze as she opened her mouth and took him in.

"Yes, Nadia, babe. Just like that," he whispered in encouragement as she sucked his length into the warmth of her mouth. "Christ, you feel so good."

A slow withdrawal and then another slow suckle and she began to take him in earnest, hollowing her cheeks to give him the pressure and suction he loved. He continued to praise her in his soft, erotic voice, weaving a sensual spell she couldn't help getting lost in.

She slipped her left hand between her legs, thrusting her fingers into her soaking pussy. Her hips bucked in response to the intense pleasure. Yet as much as she wanted to linger, her desire wasn't her purpose.

Pulling her hand free, she brought her fingers up to the soft patch of skin behind his balls, searching for his puckered opening. While they hadn't explicitly talked about this before, she had a feeling that Kaname wouldn't have a problem with her teasing him there.

He didn't. His hips rocked in silent assent, and she pressed her forefinger against his anus, teasing him until he relaxed enough for her to push through.

He thrust his fingers into her hair, holding her in place as he wanted her before he surged into her mouth. She took him deep, relaxing her throat until her nose pressed against his groin. He held her there, withdrawing just as she became desperate for air.

"Nadia."

She looked up into his face, seeing the strain in his features, the fire of lust and need for her burning in his eyes. "I'm going to fuck your mouth now. I need you to fuck yourself with your fingers. Tell me when you're close."

She nodded, slipping her right hand between her thighs. She relaxed her throat again, a trick she'd learned during her pill-popping days. Kane cradled her face in his hands, then began to slowly and thoroughly fuck her mouth, working it just the way he worked her pussy, drawing all the way out then pushing all the way back in. His movements rocked his cock into her mouth and drove her finger over his prostate. Over and over he fucked her mouth and she timed the thrusting of her fingers with the movement of his hips, riding the hard edge that led to a hard-won orgasm. She wanted to come, needed to come, but she needed him to come too. When she felt it rising, sweeping through her and about to break free, she hummed around his cock.

"Nadia." His pace increased, his hands cradling her head, his rhythm losing its smoothness as she chased his orgasm. "Come for me, sweetheart. I'm there, I'm there. Ah, God."

He clenched down on her finger a second before his cock pulsed in her mouth. At the first splash of semen on her tongue, her orgasm crashed into her. She moaned around his cock, eyes sliding shut in pure ecstasy as she rode her fingers and swallowed his come.

Kane pulled free of her, breathing hard, legs shaky. She'd pushed him to the edge of his control; now it was time to return the favor. He lifted her to her feet, the robe billowing about her. Keeping his gaze on hers, he pulled the sash free, then pushed the robe from her shoulders. "Give me your wrists, sweetheart."

She immediately offered them to him, and he made quick work of binding her wrists with the sash. Her breathing deepened, her eyes going wide and dark at the passion riding her. He helped her back on the bed, positioning her with her hands above her head and a pillow supporting the small of her back. Even though he'd just come hard in her mouth, the sight of her stretched out on his bed—hands bound, nipples clamped and tight, thighs spread, her expression one of complete surrender—sent blood rushing south, filling his cock and hardening him again.

Kneeling in front of her, he spread her folds with his hands. "So beautiful, like a lotus flower," he said against her, breathing in the spicy scent of her arousal. "And you got it ready for me just the way I like it."

He lifted her legs, his hands catching her behind her knees to hold her open. Then he set his tongue to her, licking from the rosette of her ass to the top of her clit. She cried out his name, the sound sweet to his ears. Kane continued the sensual onslaught, licking at her delicate oversensitive folds, teasing her clit. He circled the engorged nub with his tongue, then lightly sucked it into his mouth. Again she cried out, lifting her hips, desperate to get more of his mouth on her.

Setting her feet on his shoulders, he pushed two fingers inside her, he began to stroke her, driving her higher with lips and teeth and tongue and fingers. "I'm going to give you the pleasure you gave me, sweetheart," he whispered against her passion-slick folds. "I'm going to get you ready then I'm going to fulfill that fantasy of yours."

He pulled his fingers free of her drenched pussy, then found the entrance to her rear opening. She was so wet the moisture had traced a path for him, easing his way. He lapped at her pussy while pressing against her back entrance with a steady pressure, slowly pushing his index finger all the way inside her. She groaned deeply, the tight opening clamping down on him. Then she rocked her hips upward in a silent entreaty for more.

Kane expertly stoked her passion, ramping up her desire until he could push two fingers into her tight opening. Her breath came in short, loud bursts as he fucked her with tongue and fingers, her hips thrusting up against his mouth and down onto his hand.

"Kaname," she gasped. A tremble swept through her body. "Kaname, I need you!"

Damn, he liked the sound of his name on her lips. "You have me, sweetheart."

"I need you inside me!" she sobbed. "I want to come around you. Please."

"You will," he assured her. "On the third time. After coming this time on my tongue."

Then he sucked her clit into his mouth as his fingers thrust deep. The orgasm hit her like a thunderclap. She came on a loud groan, her back bowing off the bed as she rode the intense wave of sensation.

Nadia floated back to awareness when she felt the cool slick slide of gel at her rear entrance, his fingers preparing her for his thick cock. Need swept through her, making her pant, hungry for more, hungry for anything and everything he offered. Finally he leaned over her, claiming her mouth in a toe-curling kiss that obliterated everything but her passion for him. Wrapping his hand around his erection, he fit the head against her relaxed opening. She tensed even though she knew she shouldn't.

"Look at me, sweet Nadia," he said, his voice barely above a groan. "Watch the pleasure you give me."

She did, and he pushed the head of his cock inside her. She knew it was just the head, but damn if it didn't feel like his fist. She gasped, then forced herself to breathe. Kane tugged on the clamp on her nipple, redirecting her focus back to him. "You feel so good, sweetheart, clenched tight around me. Better than anything I've felt before."

He captured her lips again as he sank into her in slow degrees, keeping the sharp bite of penetration wrapped in waves of pleasure. She wrapped her legs high around his waist, wishing she could touch him, but instead keeping her bound hands where he'd positioned them above her head. Then she felt his balls against her and knew he had at last gone as far as he could.

"Are you all right?" Kane asked, his voice tight with the strain of remaining still. She could feel his entire body vibrating, sending subtle shocks of pleasure rolling through her.

"Yes." She flexed her hips, impaling herself on his thick erection. "Very much yes!"

He rose to his knees, bracing his hands on either side of her head as he began to thrust into her, slowly withdraw, then thrust in again. "Touch yourself, sweetheart," he ordered, a growl in his voice. "Touch yourself as you told me you would on the phone the other night."

Nadia slid her bound hands over her breasts, the silky fabric contrasting with the bite of metal to supersensitize her nipples. She gasped at the pleasure of it, and Kane's expression tightened with approval and desire. Her hands skated down her belly to her mound. A sob tore from her at the first quick pass of her fingers over her swollen clit, but she didn't stop. Couldn't stop.

"Christ, Nadia," Kane ground out as he moved inside her, his way easing as she completely accepted him. "You are so fucking hot. So damn beautiful. Can't get enough. Never get enough."

His pace increased as they locked eyes with each other, each feeding off the other's desire. Wild, unfettered, he drove into her, hooking her knees on his shoulders to open her up even more. She continued stroking herself, amazed that she could feel the storm of another orgasm approaching. Over and over she leveraged herself up, lifting her hips to slam against him, just as wild as he was, just as needy as he was. Her fingers circled her clit, her nipples tight to the point of pain as she fought to hold on, to stay with him, to go with him when he went.

But when he balanced on one hand and tugged at the chain between her breasts with the other, he slammed a hammer down. She broke, mouth stretching wide in a scream of pleasure so intense, so overwhelming she couldn't draw in air. Kane shouted her name as he slammed against her one final time, spurting deep inside her rear channel, his features stretched in the agony of ecstasy. Sublime orgasmic joy swept her up and carried her away to a blissful place where nothing existed but her and Kaname and the pleasure they shared.

TWENTY-TWO

Nadia awakened to a view of the sky lightening beyond the shades, and realized she'd overslept. She probably would have slept longer, had it not been for a delicious aroma filling the bedroom.

She quickly handled her business in the bathroom, donned her robe, then went in search of Kane. She found him in the kitchen, standing in front of his gas cooktop, stirring an oversized stockpot. Dressed in a white T-shirt and navy lounge pants with his thick, dark hair tousled and hanging over his forehead, he looked much more relaxed than he had the day before.

"Hey," she said, stepping up behind him to wrap her arms around his waist and rest her cheek against the middle of his back. "How long have you been up? You shouldn't have let me sleep so late."

He gave her hands a light squeeze, then returned to stirring the pot. "I haven't been up long, and it's not too much past your normal weekend wake-up time. You obviously needed the rest, especially when you consider how I tired you out yesterday."

Yesterday had been one of the best days of her life. Their shopping trip had included a drive along the coast with a stopover in San Francisco, though Nadia had demurred on stopping by her parents' place. She was not going to try to spend time with her fathers while wearing nipple clamps and no underwear. They'd done the tourist thing instead, taken loads of pictures on their phones, raided a tea shop, ate lunch on the wharf, then returned home to have foreplay on the kitchen island and sex on the private balcony as they watched the sun drop into the bay.

"That's the best way to get tired, so don't you get apologetic about that." She reached up to kiss the back of his neck. "What's in the pot, doc?"

He turned in her embrace, his eyes clear and warm behind his glasses. "I've started the broth for the ramen."

"Ooh, yum!" He side-stepped so she could wave her hand over the steaming pot, cupping the aroma to her nose. "Chicken broth?"

"Yeah. It's still in the early stages though, still have to add some seasoning. Want some coffee or tea?"

"The strongest tea you've got," she answered, then grinned when he turned on the gas beneath the kettle already in place. "You know me so well."

"I'm learning," he clarified, a satisfied grin curving his most-kissable lips. "You have more layers than a lotus flower."

Heat flared in her cheeks. "You described me as a lotus flower before. Down there."

He did laugh outright then. "Why are you being shy and demure now, when you spent most of yesterday in a kimono and nipple clamps?"

She felt the heat spread to the tips of her ears. "It seems kinda disrespectful, talking dirty in front of your mom's ramen recipe."

He kissed her on the nose. "You're cute when you're embarrassed. I promise, following my mother's ramen recipe does not create some psychic connection between their house and mine. You can be all outwardly sweet as you want. I like knowing you save your spicy side for me. I like you when you're sweet, like Friday night, and I like you when you spice it up, like you did yesterday." He held her gaze. "I just like you, Nadia Spiceland."

Butterflies fluttered in her stomach, but it was a pleasant sensation. "I like you too, Kaname Sullivan."

"Good to know, since I'm slaving over a hot stove for you. Would you like to know more about ramen, or would you prefer I save the lecture and just tell you when it's ready?"

"I want to know everything you're willing to tell me. I want to learn."

He grinned. "You realize you just gave this professor permission to drone on for hours about the history of ramen?"

"If you start to drone, I'll just have to dig into my bag of spicy tricks for a proper distraction. What can I do to help you with the soup?"

He pointed to an assortment of vegetables on the kitchen island. "If you could slice those leeks and the scallions, that will be great."

After washing her hands, she moved the cutting board closer to her end of the island, chose a knife and began slicing the leeks into inch-wide pieces. Kane strained the stockpot then reset it with fresh cold water, the chicken bones and assorted parts, and a large white onion cut in half. She watched as he added her leeks, cloves of garlic, and some mushrooms to the pot. "How do you want the scallions?"

"We'll use slices of the green parts to top our soup later," he said, adding sliced ginger before stirring his concoction together. "We need the white to go into the soup now."

"Have I mentioned how sexy it is to see a man slaving over a hot stove?" she asked, as she made quick work of the scallions.

"You have, and I took note of it, which is why you're getting ramen today. It's part of my full-court press to win your affections."

"You already have my affections." She handed him the white scallions.

He smiled at her, but it wasn't his usual confident grin. Did he really doubt that she cared for him, or was he talking about something more, something she wasn't sure she could fairly offer him?

She decided not to think about it. Today was their last day together before they returned to the craziness of their work schedules and she didn't want to be at odds with him on their day of relaxation. "I'm ready for my ramen lesson, Professor."

"Remember that you asked for it," he said with a grin. "Ramen is a balance of all the ingredients in subtle but perfect harmony. There can be as many different types of noodles are there are Italian pasta shapes because each ramen restaurant likes their own. While the noodle is an integral part, it's nothing without the broth."

"Have I mentioned how wonderful it smells?"

"That you did. Some people will do a seafood-based broth, some areas are known for their pork-based soup. My mother has always done the Tokyo-style ramen, which uses chicken broth, soy sauce flavoring, and a thin wavy noodle." He handed her the package of fresh noodles they had picked up during their trip the day before.

She examined the package. The noodles were made out of flour, water, salt, and something called *kansui*. "What's *kansui*?"

"It's an alkaline water that gives the noodles their yellow color.

Because we're doing the chicken broth, we're using that kind of noodle. Some of the other styles will use a thicker noodle."

"Thin broth, thin noodle?"

"Exactly. Mom told me to start with the traditional Tokyo style before introducing you to some variations because she didn't want me to throw too much at you. I told her that you could handle it."

"You told her mother about me?" she asked, her voice coming out as a squeak. Pleasure and panic danced in her chest. "When? What did you say? What did she say?"

"I mentioned you to my mother and father. I told them I'd been seeing a beautiful American girl who owns a café, makes the most delicious pastries, and knows the importance of a good cup of tea."

"You did?" she asked, aware she grinned like a loon but not caring. Sure, Kane had accidentally met her parents way early in their relationship, but she hadn't expected that he'd mentioned her to his parents yet, even though she felt more emotionally close to him than she would have thought possible.

"I did. I also sent them a photo of you—one of the ones we took together when we were in San Francisco yesterday," he added, as if he'd seen her about to panic at the thought of his parents seeing her intimate poses. "They agree with me that you're a gorgeous woman."

It wasn't the heat of the tea that made her feel flushed. He complimented her so easily they almost seemed like practiced lines. She could hear the sincerity in his voice though, see it in his eyes. He believed the words he used to describe her, leaving her no choice but to believe them herself. "Did you tell your parents about my . . . issues?"

He ran his thumb across her lower lip, making her aware that she'd pulled it between her teeth. "You mean, did I tell them that you spent some time in rehab?"

When she nodded, his expression turned quizzical. "Would you want me to?"

"Yes. No. I don't know." She shifted her weight, nervous about Kane's parents knowing about her. "I don't want them to be worried about the woman you're spending time with."

"We're dating, not spending time," he said, his tone a gentle reprimand. "As for my mother, she worries more when I'm not dating, no matter how many times I tell her I'm being as choosy as she wants me to be. My dad, on the other hand, is more laid back with his pressure. He's ready to be a granddad though. The fact that I told them I'm seeing someone and provided them with proof was a cause for celebration up in Seattle. I'm sure my dad will be calling tomorrow with a list of baby names, especially since I'm making Mom's ramen for you."

He grinned at her, but she wasn't so sure he was joking. Kane was a successful man deep in his thirties. His parents probably had certain expectations of their only child. Expectations she didn't think she could meet. "Do you think they'll like me?"

"How could they not?"

She frowned up at him. "Two words: drug addict."

He frowned back. "Three words: recovering drug addict. You're a beautiful woman, Nadia Spiceland, and your inside matches your outside. You make me happy. My parents can tell that already, and one look at you, they'll understand why."

She worried at her lip again, torn between wanting his parents' approval and calling herself crazy for even considering needing that approval. What if they couldn't get over her past? What if they didn't think she was good enough for their only child?

What the hell was she doing, thinking about this already?

"Hey." He ran his palms down her arms from her shoulders to her hands. "We're having a stress-free Sunday, remember? We're not thinking about anything that will get us down. We're going to relax, have some wall-shaking sex, relax some more, have the most amazing ramen you will ever have in your life, relax some more, have more sex, then go to bed wrapped around each other. All right?"

She smiled; she couldn't help it. "As my professor desires."

The kettle began to sing. He turned it off after adding the scallions to the broth, then stood back so Nadia could steep her tea as she wanted. "The broth is going to take the better part of eight hours," he said as she added loose-leaf tea to the tea strainer then poured hot water over it. "Would you like some breakfast? I have cereal, oatmeal, and the makings for omelets."

"Uhm, I don't know—whatever you want to have. I usually don't eat breakfast."

"Nadia. Breakfast is the most important meal of the day."

"I know that, Dad, which is why I'm in the café at four a.m. making it for everybody else."

"You can't save yourself for ramen." He crossed the fridge, brought out eggs, cheese, and a container of cut fruit. "I'll make eggs and toast. You take your tea to the living room. Find something on television for us to watch. I like documentaries, old movies, anything but reality show crap."

He froze. "Well hell, I just served myself my own foot for an appetizer."

She burst into laughter as she took a seat at the dining room table. "Oh, man, the look on your face is priceless! Don't worry, babe. I'm not offended. It *is* crap, even my own show. Both of them."

He cleared his throat, then returned to his breakfast preparations. His discomfort was cute, but she wouldn't tell him that, not when he offered to make her breakfast. "You enjoyed them while you were shooting them, didn't you?"

She busied herself with straining her tea into a mug. She'd promised herself that there would be nothing else between them, and that included her past. She owed it to Kaname to answer any questions he wanted to know. "It's hard to answer that. The competition one was very stressful—you had to deal with the producers, the other contestants, the judges. There was always someone after you, and you had still had to be creative and hope you connected with the audience. I was lucky."

"And talented, and engaging and camera-friendly."

"All of that too." She cradled her mug between her palms. "And driven and blind and stressed and naive and trusting. In a word: *stupid*."

God, she had been. That was the worst part, that she thought she'd known it all, that she'd had everything under control once she won and got her own show. She should have known that it simply meant she was at her highest point and everything after that was a slow glide to her inevitable fall.

"Nadia?"

She looked up as Kane placed a plate of cheesy scrambled eggs, fresh-cut fruit, and wheat toast in front of her. He took the spot next to her with a matching plate. "Sorry, I must have zoned out. This looks terrific!"

"I would have asked you how you preferred your eggs, but since you only know them as an ingredient in your pastries, I figured I'd take a chance and present you with the crowd-favorite: scrambled."

"Very funny. You're lucky you're so good in bed." She scooped a forkful of egg onto the corner of her toast and took a bite. "Uhm, delicious. Wow, this breakfast concept is a winner!"

She attacked the food, partly because it was that good and partly because she wanted to deflect further questions about her former life. Once they cleaned their plates, she gathered the dishes and took them into the kitchen to place in the dishwasher. "Is the ramen broth okay?"

"It will be fine for a while. It needs to simmer. I'll make sure it doesn't boil down too far and in a couple of hours I'll need to make the *char siu*. That's the pork that tops a bowl of Tokyo ramen, but it's pretty tasty with rice too. It can be made with pork belly, but our family prefers pork loin."

"How do you cook the pork?"

"You brown it like you normally would, but then you simmer it in a pot of water mixed with soy sauce, sugar, and garlic for about an hour, thirty minutes each side."

"What kind of spices do you use to flavor it?"

"Flavor is different from seasoning," he explained. "The soups are either a salt flavor, a soy sauce flavor—not the red top kind you find in Chinese restaurants—miso, or a pork flavor, which really is more a style. As for condiments, it depends on your taste buds. Some spices are married to the bowl when the soup is created, and some spices can be added like a condiment at the table."

He filled a glass with ice and water. "I could go on and on about ramen but I think I'll stop while I'm ahead. It was always our go-to comfort meal. No matter what was going on, no matter how bad, it was always better when we got to the bottom of a bowl of ramen."

"I like hearing about it. A day you learn something new is a good day."

"I can agree with that."

He led her into the living room, where they settled together on the couch. She flipped through the channels until she found a history documentary they agreed on, then settled back against him. "You've told me all about ramen and your mother's recipe, but didn't you mention that your father's Irish? Did you grow up eating any traditional Irish meals?"

"We had a few in the rotation," he said, cradling her in his arms. "Shepherd's pie was always a favorite, and so was stew. And I can't forget Irish soda bread."

"I make that every St. Patrick's Day for the café," she said. "Actually, we celebrate for the entire week. Siobhan does a stew and shepherd's pie and a corned beef sandwich. Not a shamrock or green pastry in sight. Maybe I can make the soda bread for you one day soon and you can tell me whether I do a good job or not."

"I'll tell you a secret." He kissed the top of her head. "Give my dad homemade soda bread and he'll be putty in your hands."

"Good to know," she said, making a mental note. "What about the son? Will he be putty in my hands too?"

"He already is."

He had an amazing ability to say the right thing to make her heart flutter in her chest, make her slide one step closer to full-blown love. The thought no longer frightened her, she realized. In fact, she welcomed it.

"You can be putty, but I like it much better when you're hard. Think we can christen the coffee table before you have to check the soup?"

The slow grin he gave her warmed her blood. "As my lady desires."

TWENTY-THREE

Nadia fell back against the pillows, giggling. Kane fell to the pillows beside her. "You'd better not be laughing at me."

"No, no," she said, gasping for air between giggles. "With you. Definitely laughing with you, I swear. What in the world was that position called again? *X marks the spot*?"

He chuckled. "I believe the sheik gave it the most colorful name of *the bend of the rainbow*."

"Well you definitely have to be bent to do it. Let's not and say we did, okay? I don't want to hear either of our bodies make noises like that ever again."

He worked to catch his breath. "Works for me."

She snorted, covered her face, then snorted again. It was kind of adorable, even if she was laughing at him, and not with him at all.

Kane looked down, then grimaced. "I think I just lost my enthusiasm."

"Oh Kane, I'm sorry." She tried to smother her laughter, which, while admirable, was obviously a lost cause. "I still want to have sex, I just need to—I can't seem to stop giggling! Give me a moment, okay?"

"That's my cue to go answer nature's other call. I'll give you time to recover." He kissed her to show there were no hard feelings, then got up to head to the adjoining bathroom. Truth be told, he actually enjoyed her laughter. It meant she was comfortable with him, and he wanted that.

There were moments when it seemed like she was throwing up mental roadblocks, speed bumps to halt the forward motion of their relationship. Most of the time, though, she didn't overthink what they were doing or how fast they were doing it, she just relaxed and enjoyed their time together. Those moments were golden, and he did everything he could to make sure they happened often. Even if that meant she laughed at him. Or with him.

When he returned to the bedroom it was to find Nadia on her side facing him, her earlier laughter gone, a renewed passion brewing in her eyes. She'd put on the nipple jewelry, the gold clamps plumping the dark beads to stiff peaks. "Kaname."

Did she have any idea what it did to him when she used his full name like that? She probably did, since there was no hiding his reviving enthusiasm. "What chased your laughter away?"

"You did. Or rather, your fine behind as you walked away." She smiled. "And the view coming back. You are such a gorgeous man, Kaname Sullivan. Do you realize that?"

"When you look at me like that, I kind of get the feeling."

"I can do more than look," she said throatily. "Come here."

"As my lady desires." When she spoke like that, he had no choice but to follow through. He climbed back into bed beside her, leaning over to capture her mouth. As he did, her hand skimmed down his chest and past his abs to take him in hand.

"The sheik dispenses knowledge on a wide variety of sexual subjects," she told him when they parted. "He was also an authority on proper manhood size. What was it that he said?"

She stroked him, fingers curled snugly around him. "Oh yes. 'The virile member, to please women, must have at most a length of the breadth of twelve fingers, or three handbreadths, and at least six fingers, or a hand and a half breadth.'"

Sitting upright, she wrapped both hands around him, her right thumb teasing the head. "I happen to think you're very virile."

He tilted his head back, enjoying the sensation of her hands on him. "I happen to think you inspire me."

She stroked him again. "I treated you badly, laughing like that. I'd like to make up for it."

"You're doing a damn good job."

"I can do better." She kissed him, so slow and deep he reached for her. She slipped out of his grasp, then kissed her way down his throat, wet, nipping kisses that hardened his cock painfully. He hissed as she gently closed her teeth on his nipples, enjoying the sensation of her mouth on his skin, her hand still working his erection.

"Nadia . . ." Anticipation stung him, tensing his stomach muscles.

"Hmm?" Her lips grazed his abdomen, her tongue dipping into his navel.

"Urgh." All rational thought fled as his hindbrain growled, *Fuck yeah.*

She laughed softly, her breath a warm puff of air over his cock.

"That's what I thought." She ran her tongue around his engorged head as she expertly pushed his foreskin back. The same wet nipping kisses were employed again as she kissed her way down the underside of his cock to his balls, laving them with her tongue. Then her mouth closed over him.

He threw his head back with a loud groan, pressing into the pillows as she began to draw on him. Willing his eyes to stay open, he stared down, watching as she worked him with mouth and hand. It was the most erotic thing he'd ever seen, the sweet sensations hardening him even more.

Caught, helpless, he thrust his hands into her hair, lifting his hips in an age-old rhythm. Thankfully she allowed him to set the pace, her hands cupping his balls, squeezing him gently as she suckled him. His breath caught in his throat as she turned her head enough to fix her gaze to his, watching his pleasure as he watched her please him. He felt her stare like a physical caress, as if she'd gathered him in a full body hug. Their connection snapped into place, sure and strong and undeniable as she demanded that he give her his orgasm, called for it with mouth and hand and gaze.

He could feel it, sooner than he wanted, sooner than he'd hoped, boiling up from his toes, threatening to consume him. "Nadia," he ground out, the only warning he could give her as he struggled to contain his need to come.

She ignored him. Or rather, she insisted that he come for her with a long suckling draw that made his eyes roll back as he surrendered. An electric zap raced down his spine to his balls as he came hard and long, her name half curse, half praise as it tore from his throat.

It wasn't enough. It was never enough. As she released him and moved to sit up, he caught her about the waist and lifted her to straddle him. With a sharp jerk of his hips he thrust his still-hard cock into her wet and wanting sheath. *"Screw of Archimedes."*

Her gasp of surprise descended into a deep groan of pleasure. She settled onto him, her inner muscles rippling to accommodate him. Passion lit the depths of her molasses-dark gaze as she leaned forward to place her hands on either side of his chest, rocking her hips as she began to ride him.

Wanting to give her every bit of the ecstasy she'd given him, he cupped her breasts in his hands, gently tugging on the clamps gripping her nipples. She moaned and tightened around him in response, a deep, vibrating sound of pleasure he felt down to his balls.

"Kaname," she whispered, her voice thick with desire as she increased her pace, their bodies slapping together. "Make me come, Kaname."

"As my lady desires," he managed to grind out, left breathless by the vision of Nadia, his Nadia, looking like a goddess as she rocked above him, taking her pleasure. He dropped his right hand down to the sweet spot where they joined together, gently pinching her slit tight around his cock before releasing it. Tight then release, tight then release. She moaned again, and he could easily sense her need for more.

Raising his knees, he planted his feet on the bed for leverage so he could lunge up as she plunged down, her sweet heat making him as hard and as needy as if he hadn't come like a freight train just minutes before. He turned his wrist, his thumb stroking over her clit. She moaned again, the sweetest sound he'd ever heard, leaning back against his upraised knees as her movements became jerky, almost frantic.

"Kaname," she panted, her eyes fastened to his. "Kaname . . ."

He knew what she wanted, what she pleaded for. He circled her clit with his thumb, ramming upwards with his hips to impale her completely. "Come for me, Nadia," he demanded. "Come for us."

She threw her head back, coming with a keening cry. The sight of her in the throes of her pleasure, the sensation of her muscles clamping down on him threw him over the brink again, lifting his hips clear of the bed, coming deep inside her like coming home.

After a quick trip to the bathroom, Nadia joined Kane back in bed, limp-limbed and completely sated. He turned off the bedside lamp then pulled her close as he loved to do, one hand low on her belly, the other just below her breasts, the front of his body fused to the back of hers. It was a possessive hold, and she found it didn't bother her in the least. "This has been the best weekend ever," she said, almost drunk with contentment. "The company, the gifts you gave me, the road trip, and that incredible ramen. Five stars all around!"

"I couldn't agree more," he said, his hand spread over her abdomen. "By the way, I added a key to your keychain."

"You did?"

"Uhm-hmm." He murmured against her shoulder. "Condo key."

She froze. "Are you serious?"

"Very. I don't want you waiting outside for me ever again."

"Oh." She entwined her fingers with his hand on her belly, giving them a squeeze. "Thank you. That means a lot to me."

"You're welcome. There's something I'd like to ask you, though."

She yawned, then snuggled in. "Hmm?"

"We're having a department dinner two Fridays from now at

the conference hotel near campus. Faculty and staff mostly, but there will also be a few alumni and potential donors in attendance. I'd love it if you would be my date for the evening."

She remained silent, trying not to tense up, but she did anyway. This was the first time that Kane had invited her to accompany him to a college event, and she couldn't help wondering what it meant.

"Are you sure you want me to go with you?"

This time he tensed. "I asked you. Pretty sure that means I want you to come with me."

"I know you did, but you know me. I don't exactly fit in with a highbrow environment." She turned in his arms, curling her hand into a fist on his chest. "I think Vanessa would be a better choice to go with you, especially if you need to be in fund-raising mode. She has lots of experience with this sort of thing."

He loosened his hold on her and she immediately missed the contact. Then the lamp snapped on. She blinked against the brightness that clearly illuminated the irritation sparking in Kane's eyes.

"This party is for faculty and their significant others," he explained. "I appreciate you wanting to rent out your friends and I'm sure Vanessa is a lovely woman, but are you seriously suggesting that she take your place? Are you honestly telling me that you want me to go with someone else—someone other than the woman I'm dating?"

"Kane." She pressed against him, wanting to make sure he understood what she meant. "I'm a washed-up former reality television star and recovering drug addict. You shouldn't forget that."

"How can I forget when you mention it every time we're together?" He sat up, irritation blossoming into anger. "Is that how you think I see you? Or is that how you want me to see you?"

"Not all the time, but you can't pretend that it isn't true." She pushed herself upright, sitting up against the headboard. "It's what I am. I'm not being self-deprecating just for the fun of it, Kane. I am what I am. Part of my ongoing recovery is accepting that I'm an addict. I'm always going to be an addict. I'm just an addict who doesn't use anymore."

He didn't like her talking about herself like that, she could tell by the way he frowned at her. She knew it sounded negative, as if she were constantly putting herself down. While she knew she had some hard-won good qualities, being fully aware of her limitations kept her feet firmly grounded in reality, and not the fake television kind.

Finally he shoved his fingers through his hair with a deep sigh. "I know it's a part of you, Nadia, and I think I understand why you describe yourself that way. I may not like it, but I'll accept it."

She blew out a relieved breath. "Thank you."

"That's just one aspect of you, though. That's not the only thing you are. Remember, you're layered like a lotus flower. I want you to know the way I see you." He clasped her hand in his. "I see a smart, successful businesswoman with an open, warm heart and a generous nature who is fiercely loyal to her friends and is taking steps to continue living her life as her best self. I should also mention that you're beautiful, sexy, creative, adventurous, and slightly bent."

"Oh, Kaname." Tears flooded her eyes. "Is that really how you see me?"

"It's how I've always seen you."

Overcome, she threw her arms around his neck, hanging on to him as if she'd been lost at sea and he her lifeline. She'd been seen as many things over her life: a dutiful daughter, a bratty sister, a meal ticket. A drugged-out failure. No one had ever described her the way Kane had described her, not even the man she'd thought had loved her. "Kane, the way you see me . . . I'll treasure that. Always."

He ran a hand down her bare back. "Does this mean you'll go to the dinner party with me?"

She drew back, and she could see the worry in his eyes along with the desire that was always there. But she also saw a pure, sweet longing that made her wonder if it was her own longing reflected back. "What's the dress code?"

"Not formal," he assured her. "What's that style called? Not all the way to the floor, sort of dressy but not like you're in the office?"

She had to smile at his description. "You mean cocktail dress?"

"Yes, that's it! You could wear that blue dress you wore on our first date." His eyes glazed over. "I really loved that dress."

She laughed. "You mean you loved what was underneath."

"Absolutely. So it's a yes, you'll come with me?"

How could she refuse him? She nodded. "Yes, I'll go with you."

"Good." The obvious relief that swept through him brought on a keen guilt that she hid by closing her eyes and lying back against the pillows. Kane hardly requested anything of her, so she had no problem agreeing to go to the faculty dinner with him. She knew, however, that it was an important event for him and his career at the college. She just hoped that her presence wouldn't be too much of a detriment for him, and he didn't end up regretting asking her to attend with him.

TWENTY-FOUR

"Thanks for coming shopping with me, guys," Nadia said as she entered yet another dressing room. "I think I would have given up two shops ago!"

"Any excuse to come boutique shopping in San Francisco is a good excuse," Vanessa said. "Helping out a sister from a different mister is even better."

"You're the one helping her out," Siobhan said, settling on a bench. "I'm just here for moral support. And the shoes!"

"Why can't I find anything I like?" Nadia mourned. "I'm acting like I'm seventeen and this is prom!"

"Why are you so nervous?" Vanessa wanted to know. "You and Kane have gone out plenty of times by now."

"I know." Nadia looked through the selection of dresses that Siobhan and Vanessa had helped her gather, wishing that Audie were with them. Audie could always defuse their tension with a raunchy joke or a snarky comment. "We've gone out to dinner, to the club, and we had that day-trip up here last weekend. This will be the first time that we've gone to an event associated with the college and his colleagues."

Siobhan picked out a black tea-length number with a scooped neck and cap sleeves. "Well, this one won't work. You need to wear something special since Kane is basically outing you as a couple to his coworkers."

"Yeah." Dizziness welled inside Nadia. "I think I need to sit down."

"You're really worried about this, aren't you?"

"I can't help it. I really want to make a good impression. He won't talk about it much, but I know he's under pressure at Herscher. He doesn't need anything to detract from his goal of getting a full professorship. Or anyone."

Siobhan settled her hands on her hips. "Are you thinking you're not good enough for the crowd at Herscher?"

"It's not about that. Not really. I just wanted Kane to be prepared in case there's someone there who remembers the old me. He hasn't had to deal with any negativity associated with my past so far, and I'd like to keep it that way." She gave her friends a rueful smile. "I even suggested that he take you instead, Nessa. You've got more experience dealing with that type of crowd."

Siobhan snorted. "I bet that went over real well."

"Kane didn't like the idea. At all. No offense, Nessa."

"None taken." Vanessa smiled at her. "I wouldn't have gone even if Kane had agreed to your crazy idea. Why wouldn't he want to take the woman he's dating to a faculty and spouse event?"

"That's what he said." Nadia blew out a breath. "I brought up the whole drugs thing and we had a minor argument which he won by telling me how he sees me."

Both her friends looked at her, matching expressions of eager curiosity on their faces. "And?"

"And the man has a way with words," she admitted, flushing. "I couldn't refuse him. So here we are, a week out and with me panicking in a dressing room hoping I don't embarrass my boyfriend."

Vanessa and Siobhan looked at each other, then burst into laughter. "What the hell is so funny?" Nadia demanded.

"You said the *B* word," Vanessa said, gasping.

"And you didn't break into hives either," Siobhan added.

"What *B* word? *Bitch*? Because I'm about to break that one out!"

"Boyfriend!" they said in unison.

"I . . . uhm . . . oh." Heat crawled up her throat to her ears. "I, ah, I guess I did."

"You're really into him, aren't you?" Vanessa asked, her smile indulgent.

"Guys." Nadia sank onto the bench between her friends. "He's awesome. I think about him and I get all fluffy inside. We had the most amazing weekend together last week—it was so deep and fun and sexy and comfortable. His kitchen is as nice as mine, and you should see that master bathroom!"

"Most women would be talking about the million-dollar views you get on Bay View Road and how much a certain professor is worth to be able to afford a condo like that," Vanessa pointed out. "You, on the other hand, care about his kitchen."

"It's a great kitchen," she insisted. "And an even better bathroom. That soaking tub is to die for!"

Vanessa leaned close. "Sounds like you're more than into the professor."

"Hush, Nessa," Siobhan admonished. "You'll freak her out, and she's already dancing on the edge as it is!"

"Oops. My bad."

"I'm okay," Nadia insisted. "I'm pretty sure. He told his parents about me. I want to tell my dads that Kane and I are *dating* dating when we meet them for dinner later, but maybe I should hold off. I just need to get through the faculty thing. If there are no issues there, I think everything will be okay."

She hoped so. Ever since Kane had asked her to accompany him to the event, her stomach had been in knots. Her argument with Audie had resurfaced to dominate her thoughts, which was just stupid because she knew Kane. She knew what they'd shared over the last few weeks. Every time he'd taken control, every time she'd surrendered, he'd made it worth it, with tenderness and care and trust. Everything was going right with them, and she held the security of that close to her heart.

Vanessa stood, flipped through the swath of dresses hanging on the rack. "Try this one," she said, handing Nadia a hunter green silk sheath with an overlay of beaded black mesh adding sparkle to the top layer.

"Are you sure about this?" Nadia asked, holding up the dress.

"Trust me," Vanessa said, pushing her into the dressing room. "I've got a certain eye for these things. It's why you called me, isn't it?"

Nadia entered a dressing room to change, hoping that this dress would do the trick. She was tired of the stress of finding the right dress, of worrying about being the right date for Kane, of presenting the right face to the world. She was tired of worrying about Audie, about Siobhan, and Vanessa, whose serene smiles hid an inner turmoil. She was tired of the stress of feeling guilty that her relationship with Kane was going as well as it was even as she waited for the other shoe to drop, whatever the hell that meant.

She smoothed the knee-skimming skirt down, then took a look at herself in the mirror. "Vanessa, you are a genius!"

Her friend laughed in obvious delight. "Come on out so we can prove it to Siobhan."

She opened the dressing room door then stepped out, walking toward the three-way mirror. "Vanessa, you're good," Siobhan said as she and Vanessa circled Nadia. "That's the perfect dress for her."

Nadia had to agree. The deep green color complemented her skin tone and deepened the color of her eyes. The dress itself hugged her breasts and created a smooth flat line from her ribs to her knees, emphasizing the length of her legs. The cut and color suited her dramatic, fun-and-flirty side while giving her an air of class and sophistication she hadn't been sure she possessed.

Nadia threw her arms around Vanessa. "Thank you, it's perfect! I owe you big-time!"

"You're welcome," the other woman said with a smile. "I can come over and do your hair and makeup for you too, if you like. You need a burgundy lip to bring out that sexy pout, and we'll make your eyes dark and mysterious without looking like you're auditioning for a drag show. Some emerald studs are all you'll need to go with it. Oh and sexy lingerie. Lingerie always gives me that extra bit of confidence I need."

"We'll make a party out of it," Siobhan suggested. "Make sure you don't have any last-minute jitters."

Nadia was sure she'd have them regardless, but appreciated the gesture. "Thanks. You guys are the best friends ever!" She sobered. "I wish Audie was here."

An uncomfortable silence fell. Nadia hadn't heard from Audie in several weeks, and it bothered her. All she'd gotten in response to her repeated texts and phone calls was an apologetic text and assurances that Audie would be fine and that she was getting help.

"Nadia." Siobhan patted her shoulder. "Audie's getting help. She'll be back when she can."

"I hope so." Though Audie's problems weren't fueled by drugs or alcohol, she did have an addictive personality. Nadia just hoped that Audie would take the help to heart and come back to them soon.

A week later, Nadia was primped, waxed, trimmed, and coifed to within an inch of her life. She'd even indulged in a manicure. At the very least she knew she wouldn't be a visual detriment to Kane. She just wasn't sure about the rest.

Wanting to make a decent impression on Kane's behalf, she tapped into that part of her she'd hoped she wouldn't have to visit again, the part of her that had pretended she was an LA party girl. That version of herself had known how to lie to her producers as she insisted she was fine, had known how to smile at those she'd rather slap, to talk to those she'd rather avoid. If she could channel enough of the reality star Nadia and pretend the other guests were Los Angeles people, she would be able to make it through.

With that in mind, she was able to open her door and greet Kane with a smile. He wasn't wearing his glasses, leaving his eyes clear. He wore a black power suit with a crisp white dress shirt that provided the background for a bright red tie patterned with gold embroidered cranes and medallions. She knew without asking that it was a lucky tie. "Well hello, you gorgeous, sexy professor man you."

"Hello yourself." He took her hand, and she spun in a slow circle for him. She'd leaned on her girls for help for the evening, and her friends had come through in spades, helping her with her hair and makeup, finding the perfect accessories to match the dress she'd bought the week before. A black velvet wrap, a beaded clutch purse, and black strappy stilettos completed the look.

"You're beautiful," he murmured, appreciation lighting his eyes. "I'm the luckiest man in Crimson Bay tonight."

"Kaname," she whispered, need welling inside her.

"Are you wearing panties?"

She nodded, her mouth suddenly dry. "A thong."

"Is it like the one from our first date, with a special surprise inside?"

"Ah." Her lips parted. God, she should have thought of that. It would have been a perfect distraction for both of them. "Unfortunately, no."

"Take them off."

She stared at him, trying to decide if he was serious or not. From the gleam in his eyes, he seemed extremely serious. "If you want them off, you'll have to help me," she told him. "I don't want to break my neck trying to pull them off over my shoes."

"We definitely don't want that," he said, guiding her over to the barstools at the kitchen counter, then kneeling at her feet. "Lift your skirt, sweetheart."

She complied, putting on a show with a slow teasing glide up her thighs. He reached up, hooking his fingers in the straps of her burgundy lace thong, then pulled it down her thighs, past her knees to her ankles.

He stopped, staring at her mound for a charged moment, then stared up at her, dark eyes blazing. "You shaved."

"Special occasions call for special measures."

"I think your special measure is entirely appropriate." He reached into his jacket pocket, extracted a gleaming piece of gold. "This is the second part of that present I gave you two weeks ago."

He held it up, and she noticed a gold clip with a red jewel dangling from the center. Two other gold chains with red gems dangled below it.

Nadia found it difficult to draw enough air to speak. "Is that what I think it is?"

"If you think it's clitoral jewelry, then yes, it is what you think it is." He leaned forward, his thumb stroking over her outer lips. Her body heated as her blood rose, swelling the bundle of nerves at the center of her pleasure. A gasp tore from her throat as his tongue stroked over the sensitized flesh, spiking her desire with a bolt of sensual electricity.

"Kaname!"

He brushed his thumb over her again, then slid the clip over her now-distended clitoris. She immediately felt the slight pressure of it framing her clit, but what was worse—or so much better—was the way the crystals bumped over her tingling flesh with every movement. She'd be in a perpetual state of horniness the entire night.

Heat burned her ears, swept down her throat to her nipples then on to the object of ornamentation. "Kane," she protested, "I can't go to your party wearing this and no panties!"

He sat back, his gazed fastened to her newly decorated flesh. "Why not?"

"Why not?" she repeated. "You know how wet I get. If I go

without panties, I'm in danger of dripping. I can't be in there with your colleagues with . . . with my pussy leaking!"

"Even though I would volunteer to take care of that for you, you're probably right." He pulled her thong back up, patted it into place.

She arched a brow at him. "You weren't planning on me going thong-less at all, were you?"

He gave her a cheeky grin. "Sweetheart, I know your body. This is our secret, no one else's, a secret that will provide a much-needed distraction."

Realization dawned. "You did this so I wouldn't be nervous about going to your party, didn't you?"

"Guilty as charged." He rose to his feet, licking his lips. "Are you ready?"

"To be fucked? Yes."

"That makes two of us." He offered her his arm. "Let's get to the party. The sooner we get there, the sooner we can leave."

"This is a pretty important event, isn't it?" she asked after they made it to his car.

"It's a cocktail party. There will be drinks, appetizers, and conversation. Lots and lots of conversation. People will jockey for position as they usually do when they're out with their bosses and coworkers. It will probably bore you to tears. It would bore me too if I didn't get to look at you and know what you're wearing for me."

"Thank you, but you're avoiding the question," she said, fighting the urge to squirm. The thong wasn't doing enough to keep the crystals from teasing her clit. "How important is tonight for you?"

"My contract will be up soon," he answered as he left the parking deck and turned the car toward College Street. "I need a renewal or a grant of tenure to a full professorship. The people who can make that happen will be in the room tonight."

Acid flooded her stomach, driving desire away. "Is your career on the line?"

"No." He reached over to take her hand. "If my tenure isn't secured, I can still teach as long as they renew my contract. Given the amount of money I've brought into the college over the last few years, I don't think they can afford to let me go. But if they totally screw me over, I have other options to fall back on, like the writing and consulting work, doing research, or joining a think tank again."

Her heart sank. "You don't like the consulting work enough to do it full time," she pointed out, remembering the case that had taken him to Los Angeles a couple of weeks ago. Remembered how his psyche had taken a hit, and how much he'd needed her afterwards.

"It's not that I don't like it. I like helping people. I like educating others on the difference between healthy and unhealthy sexual predilections, and doing my small part to stop those who take it too far. Sometimes that means walking through darkness in order to understand that darkness. Sometimes it's hard to shake it off completely."

He turned to her briefly, but she felt the weight of his gaze. "I have you to come back to now. You to look at. Just the thought of you makes it bearable."

A lump formed in her throat, impossible to ignore. She was glad that she could help him like this, glad that she could be a welcome distraction. Kane meant too much to her for her to allow him to stress out alone.

She hugged the knowledge to herself. Over the past few weeks, since the confrontation with Audie and his return from Los Angeles, Nadia's relationship with Kane had changed, deepened. She was emotionally attached to him, no matter how she'd tried to convince herself otherwise. He had become an integral part of her life, and his happiness was important to her. The nights she spent in his arms, whether for sex or not, had become as necessary to her as breathing. She'd do anything for him.

The feeling was as exhilarating as it was scary. It felt too close to obsession and that worried her. She'd also been obsessed with Gary, her manager. He'd taken advantage of her and her trust, made promises he had no intention of delivering on, and had driven her to the point that her life had imploded.

Kane was nothing like Gary. He was driven, yes, but only for himself. She felt safe with Kane, safe in a way she hadn't felt since she'd left home. She trusted him completely, and even thought herself in love with him, and that knowledge spread through her like sunlight. She'd tell him so tonight, after the party was over. Wrapped in the comfort of his arms, she'd tell him that last part of her painful past, and hope that he'd be as accepting as he'd been about the first.

"Nadia?"

She blinked at the soft sound of Kane's voice, then took a look out her window. "Oh, we're here. Already."

She reached for the door handle, but he stopped her. "What's bothering you, sweetheart?"

"What makes you think something's bothering me?"

He raised a brow. "The fact that you're dodging the question is a clue. So is the way that you've got my hand in a death grip right now."

"God." She loosened her grip, then tried to extricate her hand from his. He wouldn't let her.

"Nadia."

"I'm sorry." Her shoulders slumped. "I think I'm working myself up to a full-fledged anxiety attack." She hadn't felt this kind of pressure to perform since her cooking-competition days. The only recent time had been during the grand opening week for Sugar and Spice, when she'd sat for interviews with the local and college newspapers.

"Maybe we should leave," Kane said, his expression one of concern.

"No." She blew out a breath, focused on her breathing, trying to find her calm, find her center. In. Out. Repeat. "Tonight is important to you and that makes it important to me. Think of me as your designated cheerleader for the evening."

"Just for the evening?" he asked softly.

"Of course not. I'm going to be there for you in the same way you've been there for me."

"You have been there for me, and words cannot express how much that means to me. Tonight is significant, but so are you. If you're not comfortable in any way, we can leave right now, no regrets."

Her stomach clenched. She didn't want Kane to make sacrifices on her behalf, especially if it cost something dear to him, like the chance at a full professorship. Tonight wasn't rocket science. All she had to do was be the best version of her current self that she could possibly be.

"We're going to stay. You're going to network, I'm going to have a good time, and when we get home, you're going to properly reward me for my good behavior."

The smile he gave her pushed all anxiety from her mind, leaving behind nothing but thoughts of Kane and the promises inherent in the sexy curve of his lips. "Thinking of ways to reward you will definitely be the highlight of the next couple of hours," he said, his voice low and thick with intensity. "I promise we won't stay one moment longer than necessary."

"I'll hold you to that promise, Professor Sullivan."

"As my lady desires."

TWENTY-FIVE

N adia glanced about the crowded room, feeling less intelligent with every passing moment. Faculty parties seemed to be on the same level as political events. Lots of politicking, lots of jockeying for position, with fake smiles and compliments as a thin veneer over a whiff of desperation.

Still, she managed to keep her LA smile in place. She posed for photos with Kane and others, some faculty, some alumni and other boosters. As she nursed a single glass of cabernet, she made small talk, charmed a group of potential donors, talked desserts with a few people she recognized as regulars at her café. She felt relatively confident enough that she wandered away from Kane to give him the opportunity to network as he needed to without having to worry about her.

Kane had been right about one important thing. Her new accessory was doing a stellar job of keeping her mind off her social discomfort. Instead, she was acutely aware of her physical discomfort. She had to do something to take the edge off. Kane probably wouldn't like it, but she was sure he'd find a creative way to make her pay.

She made her way to the ladies' room and into a stall, grateful for the paper seat covers and the floor-to-ceiling doors that provided complete privacy. As soon as she got herself settled, the outer door opened again and a group of women entered. They immediately got to the point. "Did you see the woman Professor Sullivan brought with him?"

"Pretty dark-haired thing?" one of the other women asked. "I haven't seen her on campus before. Does anyone know who she is?"

"I heard that she runs that café down on Main," one of the gossipers said. "Sugar and Spice, I think it's called. But there's more to her than that."

The salacious tone had Nadia curling her hands into fists. She shouldn't be sitting there listening to a bunch of ancient rejects from the mean girls club, but she couldn't move. She needed to know her enemy.

"What? What did you hear?"

"I hear he's using her for his research work just like he's used all the other ones. Some new paper he's working on."

"Don't be catty, Lorraine. Green isn't your best color."

The other women laughed. "I'm telling the truth," Lorraine insisted. "It's for some new paper he's writing. Supposedly she's got some special experience that's the focus point for his paper."

Ice filled Nadia's veins. No. She couldn't believe it. She wouldn't believe it. Kane wouldn't use her like that.

"What sort of experience?" someone asked.

"Do you really have to ask? For Professor Sex?"

The women laughed again, and that was almost enough for

Nadia to barge out of the stall and give them all a piece of her mind. They weren't done, however.

"That's not all," the salacious one said. "I hear that she used to have a cooking show. I heard she got fired from it because she was high all the time."

"She's a *drug user*?" someone asked in a shocked whisper.

"Well, I don't know if she still is, but she definitely was when she got canned by the network. Apparently they don't keep killers on the payroll."

"She *killed* someone?"

"There was no proof, and she didn't go to jail. But that poor man did die, and she was with him when it happened. She probably paid people off. You know how those Hollywood types are."

Nadia bit down on her hand to keep from screaming. She had been cleared of any wrongdoing in criminal and civil court, but who cared about facts? Truth was, she had been strung out on sedatives before the accident that ended her television career and killed Gary. Even without the accident, she'd been on a countdown clock to termination anyway.

Someone sniffed in obvious disapproval. "Why would Sullivan bring someone like that to an event like this? The man is supposed to know better."

"Exactly. How does he expect to impress donors with a date like that?"

"He has to impress the board as well," Miss Disapproval added. "His contract is up for renewal in a couple of months. I hope for his sake that she is the subject of his research paper and not anything more. He certainly can't assume he'll get a full professorship if he's in a real relationship with her."

"A professor and a drug user?" Someone tittered with laughter. "That won't fly. Not even for Professor Sex. Not even at Herscher."

Nadia bent over double in the privacy of the stall as the women left, fighting to get enough air in her lungs. Pain ruptured in her chest like a broken blister, poisoning her thoughts, her emotions, her hopes, everything.

She had to think, had to focus, but it was hard to move beyond the agony that stung her eyes and scoured her heart. The women and their cruel words ripped at her, tearing at her defenses, reinforcing her belief that coming to the event with Kane had been a bad idea from the start.

Were they right? If they were, what were they right about? That Kane didn't have a future at Herscher if she stayed with him, or the idea that the only reason he was with her was for some sort of sexual research?

She swallowed down another whimper of pain. Either idea hurt. She didn't want to be a detriment to Kane, but she knew that what was acceptable in Hollywood didn't necessarily track on the outside. People still looked askance at drug addicts even if they were in recovery. A stint in rehab was almost a fashion accessory in Los Angeles. Here in Crimson Bay, for all of its progressiveness, addiction was frowned upon, the people suffering from it, shunned. She well remembered how the city had been bereft of support groups before she and Siobhan had arrived, and how they had to take it upon themselves to launch one.

Nadia shook her head. If Kane wanted a future and a full professorship at Herscher—and she knew that he did—he wouldn't be able to have it as long as he wanted a relationship with her.

Surely he was aware of that. Not only was he smart, he was

focused, driven, strategic. Controlled. He had to have known what the reaction among his colleagues would be, having someone like her on his arm at this high-profile event. He'd probably weighed the pros and cons and decided to make a calculated risk, knowing he'd have plenty of data to collect for later use.

Despair weighed down her shoulders. It made a twisted sort of sense. Kane hadn't batted an eye when she'd told him she was in recovery. He'd observed her in her café before he had approached her. That she'd wanted to explore *The Perfumed Garden* had been pure bonus. He'd pushed her sexual boundaries, coaxing her to wear nipple clamps while grocery shopping and clitoral jewelry to his networking event. . . .

The last curling edge of desire faded, leaving her cold and mortified. All the things he'd said to her, all the things he'd done to her and for her—had they all been calculated acts designed to yield data for his research? She hadn't even bothered to ask him details about his work at Herscher. She'd assumed that he was teaching out of a textbook, not writing the curriculum himself.

Of course he was. She could imagine the title: *Sexual Habits among the Addicted*. He'd document everything they'd done together, every sordid detail. Everything he'd done had led to this. Testing her, pushing her buttons. Putting nipple clamps on her then taking her out in public. The jeweled clip that was on her clitoris even now. He'd had it already, she just knew it. It matched the clamps he'd given her earlier. So why didn't he use them before? Why wait until the night of the faculty event to put the clip on her, making her walk around his event horny and desperate for him while he worked the room.

It was the ultimate power trip, and she was his clueless pawn.

She couldn't breathe through the pain that threatened to crush her. She thought he'd wanted *her*, her, not just any woman's body. She'd been falling in love with him, surrendering to him, believing she could be safe with him, and all the while he'd only been using her.

She'd been through that before. She couldn't do it again. Never again.

Nadia turned on her heel and walked away with her head held high, fighting to keep her anger under control. Damn those women. Damn Kane, for bringing her here. It was time to get a taxi home and leave all this drama behind.

TWENTY-SIX

It didn't take Kane long to realize he'd made a monumental blunder bringing Nadia to the party. She'd handled the attention from the curious and the schemers well at first, making him proud. Then he'd noticed that her usual warm smile had an edge to it, her good mood sharper, her tone of voice too bright. It had bothered him that she wasn't enjoying herself at an event that was important to him, a situation she would find herself in again if she stayed with him. Then he realized that she'd fallen back on her Hollywood social skills, using them as defensive armor to protect herself from the sharks trawling the class ocean.

They were sharks. How he hadn't considered that some of his colleagues would have watched reality shows and the cooking network five years ago was a serious error on his part. Crimson Bay was a small college town, but it wasn't a backwater. More than one person had recognized her from the cooking competition show; others recognized her from her own cooking and lifestyle show. Recognition had led to speculation as people pulled out their smartphones and ran a search on Nadia, completely overlooking the fact that she was now an upstanding member of the business community.

He began to make his way toward the ballroom exit, knowing Nadia had gone to the ladies' room. He had to get her out of there. It had been a mistake to bring her, a mistake to expose her to his status-hungry colleagues. He also had to apologize to her. She'd tried to warm him and he'd ignored it. Now he wondered what price he'd have to pay for his cluelessness.

"Cheeky move, Sullivan, even for you," Darrell Connors said as he joined Kane.

Kane suppressed a flash of irritation. The adjunct professor was as ambitious as they came. If he couldn't advance on his own merits, he'd rip at someone else's. There was a reason Connors was still an adjunct and not an assistant professor.

"What are you going on about now?" Kane demanded, craning his neck to catch sight of Nadia. How long did a ladies' room visit take anyway?

"Bringing your pet project to the faculty party," Connors said, giving him a look that had Kane clenching his hands into fists. "I'm still trying to decide if that was sheer brilliance or a career-limiting move."

Connors looked around the ballroom, waving at the assistant dean, who ignored him. "Our fellow faculty members seem split down the middle as far as their opinions go."

Fuck. Kane took a sip of his drink to hide his burgeoning anger. His fellow faculty members could eat shit for all he cared. "Pet project?"

Connors laughed, and Kane had to fight to keep his Irish in check, before he gave in to the urge to punch the other man so hard he'd have to shit to find his teeth. "Come on, Sullivan—you don't really expect us to believe that you're dating that woman with any degree of seriousness, do you? I know she's a looker, but even good looks can't erase all the baggage that one comes with. That won't fly with Herscher's board. So you must be using her for research. Is she worth it?"

Kane could easily imagine letting his Irish off the chain. One solid punch to the jaw would send the other man flying and would telegraph to all the fucking vultures in this room that his woman was not a fucking project.

He wasn't going to do it. Wasn't going to give his colleagues the satisfaction of watching him lose his shit. He also wasn't going to just stand there and let an adjunct insult Nadia.

"Ah, the board." Kane stared at Connors, then smiled. The smile must not have been as bland as he'd intended because Connors took a hurried step backward. "Perhaps you and I should approach the board members together, Professor. I suddenly find myself curious to know what they would think of a certain slimy, status-hungry adjunct professor with a predilection for coeds' literal dirty laundry. Shall we find out?"

Kane watched in satisfaction as blood drained from the adjunct professor's face. "Uhm, ah, no. I don't think that's necessary, Sullivan. Oh, look there's Professor Long. I need to have a word with her."

"Don't let me keep you." *Or catch you walking alone in the parking lot, you rat bastard.*

Connors backed away, then spun and plunged into the crowd. Done with the event, his colleagues, and quite possibly his career at Herscher, Kane finished his whiskey, handed off the glass to a waiter, and searched for Nadia among the speculative faces staring at him from the crowd. He caught sight of her near the ballroom entrance, head down, making her way toward the exit.

He sliced through the crowd, which gave him a wide berth. Making a beeline for the door, he ignored everyone and everything else, focusing on one thing, the only person that mattered in that moment.

"Nadia, wait."

She stopped, but didn't turn around. He gripped her wrist. "Were you leaving?"

"Yes," she said, her voice hollow. "This was a mistake."

"I know, but don't worry. You won't have to deal with this again."

She flinched, then averted her gaze. "Looks like Audie was right after all."

"Audie? Right about what?"

"You. Us. This."

He tightened his grip on her wrist. "Please tell me you are not going to take relationship advice from fucking Audie!"

She did wrench her hand free then, folding her arms across her chest. "I know you're not talking badly about my friends!"

He could feel a headache brewing between his eyes. With so much anger boiling inside him, the last thing he wanted to do was get into an argument with Nadia. Not here, and certainly not about her friends when there were so many other things they needed to talk about. "I didn't say anything negative about your friends. I'm just saying Audie should be the last person you take relationship advice from."

She drew back. "Oh, and I suppose you think I should take it from you?"

His eyes narrowed. "Since I'm the other half of this relationship, I'd like to think my opinion matters more than anyone else's besides yours."

"What my friends think is important to me."

"I'm not saying it shouldn't be," he retorted, his ears heating as he struggled to hold on to his temper. "But Audie doesn't know shit about relationships. If you want her advice on picking up stray sex partners and fucking their brains out, she's your girl. But there's a difference between *Dear Abby* and *Dear Penthouse*."

"Oh my God!" She stalked away from him, her hands fisted at her sides. "How can you talk so horribly about her like that?"

Dammit. He could face a room full of academic fucktards and stay calm, but two seconds with Nadia and his control frayed like an old rope. "Do you want me to lie? It won't change the facts."

"You're not being fair to her."

"Fair? Was she being fair to you when she said all that crap to you that night you went to help her?"

He blew out a breath. "Audie's views on relationships and what denotes a healthy one are horribly skewed and her interpersonal skills are sorely lacking. She needs serious and intensive therapy to uncover whatever her underlying issues are with love and intimate interactions, and I hope like hell that that's where she is right now. If she doesn't get help, she'll continue to spiral down until she self-destructs. And you are going to let her take you down with her."

Nadia's expression hardened. "Spoken like a psychologist."

"That's what I am! I've never lied to you about what I am or what I want with you. Isn't lying against the principles of recovery?"

She froze. "What did you say?"

"About what?"

"The principles of recovery. I never told you about those. We've never talked about the steps, the program. How do you know?"

"I did some research on recovery from drug addiction. I wanted to have the information in case I needed to help you with anything."

"Oh my God." Horror spread across her features. "So it's true?"

"Is what true?"

She shook her head, hurt tarnishing her beautiful eyes. "I didn't want to believe it. Even when they said it, I didn't want to believe it, but it makes sense."

"Nadia, for the love of God, stop." He shoved his hands through his hair. "Why the hell are we arguing like this? What's going on?"

"Nothing."

"Like hell it was nothing! You didn't even act like this the day after Audie got hurt. What's going on with you, Nadia?"

"Are you using me, Kane?"

He stepped back, shock blanking his features. "What did you say?"

"You know what? I don't want to talk about it." She turned away. "I just want to go home and forget this night ever happened."

He snagged her arm again. "Not yet."

"Let go of me, Kane," she hissed. "You're causing a scene."

"Like I give a damn." He led her to a darkened alcove, found an unlocked door, then nudged her inside. "We need to talk about this, Nadia. I want to know everything everyone said to you tonight."

She sighed, and the defeat in her tone, in her posture spiked his fury again. "It doesn't matter who said what, it was all the same. People either thought you were slumming or they thought you were using me as the subject of your next book or paper."

"What?" His vision flashed red. Connors's use of the phrase *pet project* suddenly made sense. Someone actually said that to Nadia's face?

"Am I just a chapter in your next paper, Kane?" She looked at him, the disbelief cutting him deep. "What's the title anyway? 'How to Love a Drug Addict'? 'The Sexual Needs of the Addicted'? Is that why you're with me?"

"Of course not! Do you seriously think I've been using you as the focus of a research paper all this time?"

"What else am I supposed to think?" she retorted. "You volunteer to act out positions from *The Perfumed Garden* with me. You don't blink an eye when I tell you about my addiction issues—"

"That's because it's in the past," he ground out.

"It's not in the past!" she shot back. "That's what I've been trying to tell you. You think those people out there would really give a damn if my drug abuse hadn't happened? I tried to tell you this, but you brushed it off, and it leaves me to wonder why."

"Why what?"

"Why someone with your intelligence, credentials, your career, and your media standing would want to be with me. Why would you stick around after dealing with my friends and my family so soon? Why would you stick around after my confrontation with Audie? Why would you be with me? I couldn't come up with a good reason—until your coworkers gave me one."

"A professor needs to publish or perish. That's the rule for tenure, and yes, I want tenure. We're a research institution. We do studies of all kinds all year. Sometimes I will lead studies, gathering data from volunteers. I've interviewed hundreds of subjects for my thesis, my articles, and my books. Men and women, young and not so young. But I do not fuck any of my subjects. I have never put personal information into any of my published material, and I don't intend to start. Give me some credit for having some ethics if nothing else. My colleagues gave you crap."

"Did they?" she asked, her voice quavering. "Every single one? The women in the bathroom seemed to think I was research, as if they couldn't imagine Professor Kaname Sullivan dating me. Maybe all of this has been one gigantic real-life study for you. The nipple clamps, the clit jewelry—you put them on me then parade me out in public so you can document my reaction."

"You started that game, Nadia, on our very first date. I took it to the next logical step, so don't put that on me."

She shook her head as if what he said didn't matter, or she didn't care. "You want me to believe this isn't some grand study, when everyone else thinks it is?"

Slowly he placed his hands on her shoulders, turned her so that she could see his eyes. "For the last time, this isn't about fucking research!"

"What is it about then?"

"What it's always been about. This!"

He crushed his mouth to hers, desperation and anger and need roaring through him. He would prove to her that what they had was too raw, too strong, too fucking real to be research.

She responded immediately, thrusting her hands into his hair. She kissed him just as hard and demanding as he kissed her, biting down on his bottom lip to draw blood.

Something inside of him snapped. He yanked up her skirt, wrapped his hands around the string of her thong, and pulled. She gasped as the fabric easily gave way. He cupped her mound, feeling the hard edge of the clamp framing her clitoris, the heat of her core, the liquid fire of her need. Heedless of his burning lip, he continued to kiss her as he stroked her clit with his thumb, two fingers sliding into her moist heat.

"I want you," he growled against her mouth. "You want me. That's what this is about. That's what this has always been about."

With his left hand, he fumbled for his zipper, freeing his erection. Backing her against the nearest surface, he pulled his hand free of her heat to cup her buttocks, lifting her just enough to shove himself home.

She hissed and he mentally cursed himself. It was a rough invasion, rougher than he'd ever entered her before. Part of him silently cursed himself for hurting her, for pushing her, for reinforcing her doubts about him. The other part of him needed her to know that she was his, that they belonged together.

He tried to slow his thrusts, ease back on his kisses, but she tugged on his hair, her inner muscles gripping him. Fucking him in a storage closet at a stuffy faculty party, one moan from being discovered—it obviously turned her on considering the way her pussy massaged his cock in rippling waves, the way her breath caught in the back of her throat, the way her hands gripped his shoulders.

"Nadia." He groaned, still hard inside her. "You drive me crazy and you shred every ounce of control I possess. You're under my skin, in my blood and I can't get enough."

"Kane . . ."

"No." He rolled his hips as he thrust into her, drawing a moan from her. "Say my name."

"Kaname," she breathed.

"Do you want this?" He drew all the way out, then drove back home again. And again. And again.

"Yes."

"Yes, what?"

"Yes, Kaname."

"Do you want what I can give you?" he demanded. "Do you want to come?"

"Y-yes, Kaname," she gasped.

He drove into her again, his palms cupping her buttocks, fingers digging into the crease of her ass as he sped into her warm channel. If he could just give her pleasure, if he could just make her come, make her understand where she belonged, he could erase every doubt, every bad memory of the night.

"Do you want me, Nadia?" he asked, his voice scraped raw. "Do you want all this, knowing that it's coming from me?"

Tears spilled down her cheeks. "Yes, Kaname. Yes."

There was no holding back then. Burying his face into the side of her throat, he rammed into her wildly, desperate to give her pleasure on top of pleasure. He slipped his left hand between their heaving bodies, unerringly finding her distended clit, framed perfectly by the clamp. He stroked over her sensitive flesh as he stroked into her, urging her to come. Biting his throat to keep from screaming, she came, her body clenching down on his as if it would never let go.

"Fuck yeah, baby. Mark me as yours." His hips slammed into her once, twice, a third rough time. He groaned, burying his face in the curve of her neck as he came.

After a minute or ten he managed to command his muscles enough to loosen his grip on her, allowing her feet to slide to the floor. He stepped back. Nadia looked as if she'd been thoroughly used, her hair and makeup mussed, lips swollen, tears in her eyes.

"Fuck," he said again, a cold knot forming in the pit of his stomach. "Nadia, I . . ." His voice faded. He didn't know what he could have said, he didn't know if there was anything he could say. He'd lost control of the evening and himself.

She didn't look at him as she straightened her skirt. She bent down, picked up the ruined thong. Her breath shook as she breathed deep, and for a blistering moment he thought she was going to break down.

It would have been better if she had. Instead, she reached beneath her skirt, pulled off the clip, then folded the jewelry in the fabric before tucking it into her miniscule purse. "I'd like to go home now."

"Nadia—"

"I can't do this now," she whispered. "I just want to get out of here, please."

Guilt choked him as his heart sank. He'd wanted to prove to Nadia that he wasn't using her, and instead he'd dragged her into a supply closet for a quick, dirty fuck. He'd failed to convince Nadia that he was with her for no other reason than that he wanted to be with her. In fact, he had a sinking feeling that he'd made everything worse.

TWENTY-SEVEN

T hings had changed between them, and she didn't know what to do about it.

Nadia sat in the passenger seat of Kane's car, fighting a rising panic. He'd withdrawn as they'd straightened their clothing and made a surreptitious exit out of the hotel. In fact, he hadn't said a word since she'd asked him to take her home. It was much the same way he'd been when he'd come home from his trip to Los Angeles—angry, depressed, heartsick. Defeated.

Had he finally faced the truth of what she'd been trying to tell him all along? Being with her in any sort of long-term way was a liability. He never would have lost control if not for her. He never would have experienced that level of censure from his colleagues if he hadn't chosen her as his date. He certainly wouldn't have had an argument and then angry sex in a storage closet if it weren't for her.

Misery swamped her as she watched the streetlights pass by her window. The censure would happen again, she knew. People looked at her differently, treated her differently when they found out about her past drug abuse. Drug abusers didn't have the marginal social acceptance that those who abused alcohol did. You could be falling down drunk at a party as long as you weren't mean or didn't attempt to drive yourself home, but only God would help you if you popped Oxy or Percocet to numb the pain.

She still hadn't told him everything. The rest of her story hung between them as thick as the heavy air of distance he'd erected. Perhaps it didn't matter now whether she told him or not. She had the feeling there was nothing she'd be able to do or say that would change the night's outcome.

The thought gave her heart palpitations. She didn't want to be without Kane. Despite everything that had happened, she still wanted to surrender to him sexually, still wanted to care for him and be cared for by him. The idea that she would no longer be with Kane, no longer be able to experience the keen edge of passion at his hands, left her twitchy. Sweat dampened her palms and her stomach cramped with stress and fear. She wasn't sure she could be without him, even if it was the best thing for them.

He slowed in front of the café, and for a moment she thought he intended to drop her off at the curb. Instead he went around to resident parking, parked, then made the journey with her to her front door. He didn't try to touch her, didn't try to kiss her good night, simply stood in the center of the hallway with his hands shoved into his pockets, wearing an expression that suggested he wanted to be anywhere else, any place other than with her. He might as well have been a stranger standing there, so cold and remote.

She unlocked her door then disabled the alarm. Kane made no move to follow her inside. Dread stretched cold fingers around her heart. Even though she knew things had to end, she didn't want them to end like this. "You're not going to come in?"

He flicked a glance at her. "Do you think that's a good idea after everything that's happened tonight?"

Her heart sank. "Don't we need to talk this out at the very least?" she asked with more courage than she felt. "Since we had angry sex in a supply closet, don't we owe it to ourselves to have apology sex in a bed?"

She didn't want their last time together to be the supply closet in a hotel surrounded by people who didn't like them. No, their last time together should be a safe and sensual exploration full of the apology she needed to give and receive.

"I need you to answer one question for me," he said, his voice careful, so very careful. He spoke that way around his colleagues, around strangers. He'd never spoken in the controlled, distant tone with her before, even when they'd first met. That he did so now chilled her to her core.

"What question is that?" Somehow she'd managed to sound almost calm when she was actually screaming inside.

"Do you think I'm using you? Do you actually believe that ballroom full of strangers who would step over my burning carcass if it meant they could climb up the tenure ladder more than you believe the man you've been sleeping with for the last couple of months?"

"No," she said, holding his gaze. "I don't think you're using me."

"God." Kane's mask slipped, the agony and relief stark on his face. "Nadia."

"It's going to be all right." Taking his hand, she led him inside and then upstairs. He needed the make-up sex as much as she did, even if they both knew it would be breakup sex. Even if he didn't know it then, he would realize it soon enough. Because maybe his colleagues were wrong about him using her, but they were right that she was a detriment to him. If enough of his fellow academics thought that, then the powers that be probably thought the same thing. Kane loved his job at the university and as he vowed he wouldn't make her choose between him and her friends, she wouldn't make him choose between her and his career.

Once in her bedroom they undressed in silence, their gazes locked together, heating, stirring the passion that always simmered between them. She drank her fill of the sight of him, this beautiful, handsome man who had so much power over her, power she'd given to him. Power she now had to take back.

"The fifteenth manner," she murmured as she climbed onto the bed. "From the second set of sundry positions."

More of the remoteness left his eyes. "Called the *pounding on the spot*, or more accurately, *sitting sex*."

"That's right," she said, giving him a true smile. She held out her hand to him. "Will you walk through *The Perfumed Garden* with me, Kaname?"

He only hesitated a moment before taking her hand. "Walking through the *Garden* with you is always a pleasure, Nadia."

He sat on the bed, shifting to the center with his legs stretched out in front of him. She straddled him, looping her arms around his neck and crossing her legs behind his back. Slowly, softly, she covered him with kisses, starting at his forehead, then his nose, to his cheeks, and finally brushing his lips. Sweet kisses, apologetic kisses, good-bye kisses.

His hands splayed across her back as he returned her kisses, just as soft, just as sweet. Taking his time, just as she took hers. Hot licking kisses along her jaw, her throat, her collarbone as he bent her backward so that he could kiss-lick his way down to the rise of her breasts. She sighed when his mouth closed over one nipple, sucking it deep into the warm recess of his mouth while he teased the other to a hard, sensitive peak.

Her hands slid down his shoulders, over the muscles of his arms to the hard planes of his abdomen. She wrapped her fingers around his erection, standing hot and proud between them. He groaned around her nipple as she stroked him with firm pressure, fingers sliding down then up to the head to gather the moisture already there, slicking it onto her fingers before she glided them back down then repeated the action.

He took her other nipple into his mouth, lightly biting down with a delicious amount of pressure that flooded her core and made her restless with want. She wanted to take her time, wanted to savor these sensations, the way that Kane had become an expert on her body so quickly and thoroughly. Need rose within her like a leviathan breaching the waves, making her powerless to everything but the desire.

At his silent urging, she gripped his shoulders, lifting up enough for him to fit the tip of his erection against her entrance. She sank down on him, taking her time, wanting to savor every moment of the heated possession. With every inch of him inside her she sat still, breathing through the fullness, breathing him in, accepting his invasion into every part of her, body, mind, and heart.

He claimed her mouth again as he began to flex against her, short, shallow strokes that sent bright punches of pleasure arcing along her nerves. She undulated against him in return, her nipples brushing against his chest hair, sensitizing them both.

Emotion slammed into her, shattering the fragile dam of her control. Tears welled in her eyes, spilled over as she rocked against him, the sensation sweet-sharp like the thinnest blade slicing into her.

"Kaname," she whispered against his mouth, not wanting to break the spell that draped them but needing more, needing him. Needing to surrender to him, needing him to claim her one more time. One last time. "More, Kaname."

He immediately folded his legs then pitched forward, sending her to her back on the bed. Still deep inside her, he threaded his fingers with hers, lifting them over her head. She wrapped her legs high around his waist, settling him even deeper than before.

The first rolling thrust in this new position scraped against her inner walls, sending waves of sensation crashing through her body. She wanted to close her eyes, but she couldn't. His gaze held hers, demanding she not turn away. It enabled her to clearly see the pleasure in his eyes, but she could also see his pain, his anger, his bewilderment. Lying atop it all was another emotion, something that outshone everything else, something that humbled her and scared her.

That emotion remained uppermost in his eyes as he moved in her, a slow glide out and even slower glide back in, then a rapid motion that left her breathless one moment and wanting to scream the next when he withdrew completely.

She knew what he was doing, staking claim to her body, to her, branding every part of her with every part of him. She surrendered to it, to him, because she couldn't do anything else. Didn't want anything else. Kaname was it for her. She knew it to the depths of her bruised and battered soul.

So she threw her whole self into this moment, into being with him, into pleasing him. Offering up everything she could, every-thing she had, allowing him to take what he wanted because she knew she wasn't going to offer it to anyone else.

She knew he saw the moment she surrendered. A shudder swept through him, and he had to close his eyes for a brief moment. When he opened them again, that emotion she didn't dare name burned brighter than before, obliterating everything else. He kissed her tears away, kissed her doubts away, kissed her fears away. Showed her the perfection of them together, moving in pleasure together.

It swept her up, higher than she'd gone before, higher than she thought it was possible to reach. Higher than she could contain. He launched her right into the stratosphere and she went, eyes wide and mouth open in a scream of pleasure she couldn't vocalize, her body seizing with the overwhelming ecstasy that ripped through her.

His fingers tightened on hers a second before he threw his head back and thrust deep one final time. A deep guttural groan shook him as he spilled inside her deep, so very deep that it felt like a per-manent brand.

"Kaname." She buried her face in the crook of his neck as he released her hands, then curled arms and legs around him as if holding him close would keep her from falling apart again.

"I'm here." He braced himself on his elbows, his hips still circling against her as if he couldn't help the movement. He didn't seem to be in any hurry to move away, and she appreciated it. Doing anything other than holding him was beyond her. All she could do was feel. She tried to push away the fear, push away the uncertainty, to enjoy the moment while she could even though she knew every problem would still be there, naked and exposed in the morning light.

Nadia awakened a handful of hours later, sitting up out of a dead sleep, her heart pounding frantically. Kane sat in the window seat on the far side of the room, a dark shadow against the ambient light filtering through the curtains.

She turned on her bedside lamp to its lowest setting. Soft golden light spread through the room. "Kane. What are you doing, just sitting there in the dark?"

"Watching you sleep and questioning my sanity."

"Why?"

"Seemed like the appropriate thing to do at three in the morning."

The bleak anger had returned, wiping out the sensual bliss they'd reached before. She could see it in the stillness with which he sat, the precision of his words. Her heart thumped like an old engine trying to turn over. Looking at her alarm clock, she noted it was nearly five. He'd sat watching her for nearly two hours. Watching and wondering.

She licked her lips. "Did you find any answers?"

"Just more questions."

His tone made her stomach clench. "I was hoping that we could talk. I could make some coffee, and I have some of those buns you like."

"Talk." He huffed out a laugh. "Talk about what? How my girlfriend believed, despite everything I have said and done that proves it to the contrary, that I'm using her for some sexual experiment? Talk about how my colleagues brought out their verbal pitchforks last night as if they'd been invited to go on a monster hunt? Or maybe we should talk about how, as far as you're concerned, the sex we just had was good-bye sex."

She hung her head. It was ending. "It doesn't have to be good-bye, Kane," she said. "Can't we go back to what we started out with? A no-pressure reenactment of *The Perfumed Garden*? Wasn't it better before we tried to make this into a relationship?"

"There's no going back, Nadia. I love you. I can't recork that bottle."

She gasped, pulling the sheet closer around her and shrinking away. Kane loved her. He loved her, and even though he said it, it sounded like he wished he hadn't.

"I . . . I don't know what to say."

"There's nothing to say." He barked out a bitter laugh. "You would be the perfect relationship for most men. A hot woman who doesn't want anything more from a man than a steady supply of spicy sex. But I'm not most men, Nadia. I want more than that. I need more than that."

She opened her mouth, but words wouldn't come. "I can't—I need time, Kane. I need you to know everything before you can say that to me again. I need to tell you what happened to me—"

He slashed his hand through the air, cutting her off. "If this has anything to do with your past drug abuse, I don't want to hear it."

She shrank back from the harshness in his words. "Why?" she managed to ask.

"How many times do I have to say it? It doesn't matter. That's in the past. Do I need to give you a play-by-play of everyone I've slept with? Hand you my entire curriculum vitae since my first kiss? We shared our tests so you know I'm clean, the rest is immaterial, like your drug abuse. It's in the past so it's not important to me."

Her heart sank. His offhanded dismissal of that pivotal point in her life stabbed at her. So did his steadfast refusal to let her talk about it. Why couldn't he see that rejecting that part of her past was akin to rejecting her? "It was important last night."

"Nadia, dammit." He sighed. "Do you really think I give a damn about what anyone at Herscher thinks about who I'm dating? Do you really think that little of me?"

"No! I didn't mean it like that."

"How did you mean it?"

She breathed out harshly, then back in, drawing air into her lungs. One breath at a time, one step at a time, one day at a time. She tried to explain, willing him to understand. "It's an important part of me. Who I was and who I am. If you can't see that . . ." A sudden tightness in her throat threatened to choke her. If he couldn't see that, if he couldn't understand that, then it didn't matter if he loved her or not.

He shot to his feet. "What I can't see is why you're using something that's over and done with as a crutch to keep me at bay. It's a bullshit excuse, and you know it. It's not the truth."

That hurt. She slid off the bed, wrapping the sheet around herself. "You think I'm using my past as a crutch? Like I need or want that sort of attention?"

"Then why do you keep bringing it up?"

"Because other people do! No one at that dinner last night wanted to talk about sticky buns or cookies or soda bread. All they wanted to know was why did Professor Sex hook up with a druggie? It's going to always come up. It's going to always matter."

"That's absurd."

"What's absurd is you thinking I need to use my past as a crutch against you. There are easier ways to keep you at bay. I could have just said no on day one."

"But you didn't." He folded his arms across his chest. "You wanted someone to care for you, care about you and burn for you the way you wanted to do. Now that you've found that, it scares the shit out of you. Do you know why?"

"I'm sure the professor is going to educate me."

He didn't blink at her sarcastic barb. "You're afraid of losing control, of being controlled by your emotions. It's okay to be sexually controlled in the bedroom but you'll be damned if you're going to give anyone control over your heart. You're afraid of giving everything."

"That isn't true!"

"Isn't it?"

She wanted to pull her hair out. "I've given you everything I've got. Why isn't that enough?"

He released a pale imitation of a laugh. "You haven't given me everything and you know it."

"I surrendered my body to you. We've explored sexually. You know I care. What else do you want?"

"I want you, dammit! I want all of you, including your heart. I want you to fall for me as hard and permanently as I've fallen for you. I tell you that I love you and you practically have a panic attack."

Said panic attack reared up again, her heart threatening to hammer its way out of her chest. "I can't do this," she blurted out. "I won't be addicted to you, Kane!"

He stopped mid-rant. "Addicted?"

"That's what this feels like." She wrapped her arms around herself in a search for warmth. "I can't think straight when I'm with you. All I can think about is how much I need the pleasure, of what I can do to please you, to see you smile, to make you give me more. I lose myself with you, and that scares me. I lost myself like that once before, and I don't want to go there again."

"I'm a person, Nadia. I'm a human being. Not drugs." His dark gaze pinned her in place. "You said you trusted me. Do you think you're not safe with me?"

"I feel safe with you, Kane. But you can feel safe and still be lost. You can think you're safe when you're actually far from it."

"That's fucking great." He threw up his hands. "I say I love you, and you tell me you don't know if you're safe or not when you're with me. I say love and you say addiction. Why, out of all the women I could have fallen for, did I have to fall for an addict?"

A bright slash of pain struck her, stopping her heart. "I think . . ." She stopped, drew a shaky breath, then tried again. "I think you should leave now."

"God damn it! Nadia, I'm sorry, I didn't mean—"

"Yes, you did, and it's okay." It wasn't. Not when her insides were crumbling. "We need time and distance to sort through all of this. It's obvious that trying to make this more than it was meant to be wasn't a good idea."

"I get it. It wasn't a relationship for you. I was just a substitute addiction, something to get you off, a quick hit to get you through your day."

She flinched. "Kaname, I'm sorry—"

"So am I." He hesitated, his hand on the doorknob. "You accused me of using you. But who was really using who here, Nadia? Think about that."

He walked out. He didn't look back.

TWENTY-EIGHT

Going through rehab had been a horrible experience.

Going through a breakup? Pure hell.

Kane stopped coming to the café. While she understood, it still hurt. The pain . . . she was right likening it to withdrawal. She couldn't eat, couldn't focus. Sleep was a distant memory as she obsessively replayed every moment, good and bad, that she'd spent with Kane.

The only thing that helped was working in the café. Baking, making a mess while crafting a confectionary masterpiece, and then restoring cleanliness and order afterwards. The precise measurements of ingredients engaged her mind, rolling and cutting dough enabled her to pound out her frustrations, and restoring her kitchen to clean order gave her a measure of control. On the inside, she felt as if she were treading water. She went to work, chatted with customers, interacted with the staff, and deflected every attempt Siobhan made to get her to talk.

She didn't want to talk. Talking would pick at the wound she desperately needed to scab over. She didn't want to think. She didn't want to feel. She didn't want to face the fact that she might have forever ruined the best thing that had ever happened to her.

She tried to avoid it, and for the most part she succeeded. During the day, it was easy to keep herself busy with the daily operations that running a successful bakery and café entailed. Verifying inventory, placing orders, planning menus. In the afternoon she retreated to her condo and spent time experimenting with new recipes, creating a bakery bible for Jas.

The nights were the worst, the nights and the first weekend. At night the silence pressed down on her, making her more aware of what she was missing, more aware of the emptiness beside her in bed. More aware of the pain that echoed through her whenever she thought of Kane, wondering where he was and what he was doing.

Somehow she made it through the first week. She couldn't call it a success, but the fact that she didn't die from her broken heart made her think she would actually be able to survive without Kane. If she kept telling herself that like her recovery mantra, she might actually believe it in three or four years.

Into the second week without Kane she retreated to the office once Siobhan arrived to prepare for lunch. She'd attempted to help her partner with the lunch menu, but after she'd broken into tears over a pot of chicken stock Siobhan had banned her from helping. Now she spent her spare time making plans to overhaul the café's website. It wasn't her forte, but she'd keep at it. Anything that would keep her mind engaged and not thinking about Kane.

"Hi, Nadia."

She glanced up to see Audie standing in the doorway. Audie

looked . . . healthy, and Nadia realized that it had been several weeks since she'd seen her friend. No signs of her assault remained. In fact, she looked open and relaxed, though caution shaded her green eyes as she regarded Nadia.

"I don't know whether to hug you or hurt you," Nadia said, rising to her feet.

"I think I deserve both."

Nadia stepped around the corner of the desk and hugged her friend, pounding Audie on the back a little harder than necessary. "Where have you been? What have you been doing? When did you get back?"

"Slow down, *chica*," Audie said, taking a seat at the small round table tucked in the corner. Their office was small by design so they could maximize the space for the kitchen and dining area. Still, they managed to pack in two computers on a modular desk and a four-top table they could use for samples, brainstorming, and eating.

"I was at a wellness retreat in the foothills. I worked with the counselor in person and online and she's going to do some life coaching sessions with me as well. I'm basically broke now, but I think I've got a handle on myself and my life, though I still have to deal with the trial."

"Oh, Audie, I'm so happy for you," Nadia said, hugging her friend again. And she was. She'd been so worried about Audie after she'd disappeared. It relieved her to know that Audie had in fact gotten her life turned around. At least someone had some forward motion going in their life. The irony that Audie had gotten her life together while hers had fallen apart wasn't lost on Nadia.

"As for when I got back . . ." Audie gave her a sheepish smile. "I just got in. Siobhan told me what happened between you and the professor."

Nadia stiffened. "Of course. You wouldn't want to give up your ringside seat to the implosion of my life, now would you?"

Audie winced. "I deserved that," she said softly. "I deserve a lot more. But no, I'm not here to gloat. I'm here to help."

"Help with what?"

On cue, Siobhan entered the office, bearing a plate of cookies and several tall, frosty glasses of milk. Vanessa entered behind her. "You still look like crap," Siobhan observed as she placed the tray on the table.

"Considering that you've actually seen me at my worst, I guess I'm not doing as well as I could be with the whole breakup thing. What's this?"

"I thought it was time to stage an intervention."

"An intervention of what?"

"You. To make sure you either shit or get off the pot."

Audie laughed. "I've missed your mouth, Siobhan. No one expects the mouth of a sailor is hiding behind that peaches and cream façade."

Nadia grabbed a macadamia nut cookie and a glass of milk before settling back behind the desk. She told herself it wasn't a defensive move, having the desk between herself and her friends. "I appreciate you guys coming over and crowding up the office, but an intervention isn't necessary."

Siobhan took the chair closest to her as Vanessa also sat. "We know this isn't the usual intervention," Vanessa said. "You do need to talk about the professor and your relationship, though. It's not fair to either of you to be in limbo like this."

"It's not in limbo," Nadia admitted. "It's over, and I'm still in detox. It's better than denial, but painful as hell. Being without him hurts. I can't eat, I can't sleep. And I'm irritable all the time."

She looked down at her cookie. "All I can think about is him, and when I'm not thinking about him, I'm thinking about the pain. I'm thinking that maybe if I took something, just a little something to help me sleep, I'd be all right. Just until I get over the breakup."

"You know that's not how it works, Nadia." Siobhan squeezed her hand. "You're four years clean. You can't slide now."

"Wrong. I substituted Kane for the drugs. I was addicted to Kaname Sullivan. I still am."

She should have recognized the signs. The need that caused her hands to shake, her body to tremble until she could have him inside her again. The pain that cramped her sex when she'd gone too many hours without coming around him. The sweat in her pits and the burn in her chest when she didn't know how long it would be until she could see him, smell him, touch him. The need that consumed her, a need stronger than hunger, more vicious than thirst. And finally, finally, the bliss when he gave her what she needed, what she craved, the intensity of orgasm rolling through her blood, her synapses, overtaking her and sending her straight to nirvana.

"Are you sure what you're feeling is addiction? Not something else?"

"I don't know what else it could be." She rubbed her arms in a half-hearted attempt to warm herself. "You don't forget the hunger for it. The desperate craving. And then I realize this desperation is the same thing I feel—felt—with Kane. I crave him. I need him so much it hurts. I'm addicted to him, and if I'm addicted, it can't be a good thing. Not for me. Right?"

Siobhan squeezed her hand. "I've got to show you something. Grab my tablet out of the bottom drawer, will you?"

Nadia opened the bottom desk drawer and pulled out Siobhan's tablet computer. She handed it over, waiting while the blonde thumbed through her settings.

"You remember this, don't you?" She slid her tablet across the tabletop. Nadia picked it up, realizing it displayed a publicity shot from *Spice of Life*, her old cooking and lifestyle show. Not of her in her chef's whites, but in an amber-colored party dress for one of her on-the-town segments. The dress accentuated her curves, her dark hair falling past her shoulders in soft waves, makeup that rivalled any beauty queen's. She'd been glamorous and outgoing and sexy, a combination that had made her show a popular one.

She'd also been a bitch and high as hell.

Nadia studied the publicity shot critically and with perfect hindsight. Her smile was too sharp, her eyes were dazed and bright, almost maniacal, but she could clearly see the plea for help in her gaze.

It took her several tries to speak. "Yeah, I remember this. I don't know how many pills I was up to then, but I was a walking narcotics lab." She put the tablet down. "I can't forget that, even if I wanted to."

Siobhan thumbed through the tablet's gallery until she found another picture she wanted. "Take a look at this one."

Nadia glanced at the image. Her hands immediately began to tremble. It was a picture of her and Kane caught unawares, the people around them blurred out as they moved out of the camera's focus. She wore a bloodred Asian-influenced corset and a short black skirt. He wore a matching red shirt beneath a black striped vest, and she suddenly remembered where they'd been. They'd attended one of Siobhan's burlesque performances and someone had caught them smiling at each other. She couldn't remember what they'd been talking about, but it was something that had made her laugh and flush with pleasure.

Nadia shook her head. "You see how I'm looking at him? Like I worship the ground he walks on. Like I'm completely addicted to him."

"And how is he looking at you?"

She blinked, holding the photo closer. "He looks . . ." She drew a sharp breath. "Like I'm the most important thing in the world, the only thing in the world. Like he's addicted to me."

"That's not addiction, Nadia," Siobhan said quietly. "That's love. You love him, and you're in love with him. Seeing the expression on his face, I'd bet my half of the café that he feels the same way about you."

Nadia stared at the two pictures. The differences were startling, almost as if the woman in the photographs were two different people.

"On the night of my assault, I told you that the professor was so into you that he couldn't see anyone else," Audie said. "I meant it. Any woman would want a man she's into to look at her like that, to want her like that."

"Remember, we've seen in person how he is with you," Vanessa added. "He's protective, not domineering. He's concerned about you without trying to do everything for you."

"He's not Gary, Nadia," Siobhan said into the quiet. "Sullivan's not abusive. He cares for you even when you're not aware of it. He loves you. I know that look. I had that look directed at me on my wedding day."

"He told me he loves me," Nadia confessed, her throat tight. "But every time I tried to tell him about Gary so that he'd understand why I was afraid of what I felt for him, he would brush me off. He said that my past wasn't important to him."

"He didn't understand how important it was for you. I tried to explain it to him."

"You did?" Nadia frowned. "When did you talk to him?"

"The Monday after you broke up," Siobhan answered. "He told me what happened and asked me to keep an eye on you, to make sure you'd be okay. A couple of days later he asked me for any information I had on how nonaddicts could help addicts through their recovery."

The room wavered as Nadia forgot how to breathe. "Kane did that?" Even after she'd hurt him with her brush-off?

Siobhan nodded. "I think he realizes he made a mistake by dismissing your past the way he did. I believe he wants to understand what happened with you so he can help you when you need him to."

Nadia sat back in her chair, stunned. Kane had done all of that for her? Was he really trying to understand her better, so that he could be with her, support her? Was that the undeniable proof she needed that he loved her?

"Do you love him, Nadia?" Audie asked.

"I don't know. I'm not sure."

"Think about it. Think about how your fathers feel about each other, how you'd do anything for them and your brothers," Audie said. "Compare that to how you feel about Kane."

Nadia knew she loved her family. She'd do anything for them to make sure they never knew a day of pain—not that she'd tell her brothers that. When she thought about Kane, her heart leapt in her chest as if redlining. The thought of him hurt because of her was an almost physical pain. Some of her happiest moments over the last few weeks were with Kane, whether it was helping him make ramen, shopping in San Francisco, attending shows, or just being snuggled up on the couch watching movie musicals from the fifties and sixties. She wanted more of those.

She wanted him.

"I love him," she said, her voice clear and sure. "It doesn't matter though, does it? Even if we decide we can't live without each other, there's the fact that being with me didn't go over well with his colleagues. What if something like that happens again? Would that be fair to Kane?"

"You know that's not a question we can answer right?" Audie asked. "You're going to have to go to the source for that one."

"The professor's a smart man," Siobhan told her. "He's already taking steps to try to understand you and help you. He's trying. I think if you go to him and ask to talk, he'll be willing to listen. Tell him that you love him. Everything else will flow after that."

For the first time in days, hope sprang to life in her heart. If Kane was trying on the one subject that was most important to her, then she could meet him halfway. She would meet him more than halfway.

She shot to her feet. "I'm going upstairs. I've got to get ready."

"What are you going to do?"

"If the way to a man's heart is through his stomach, I've got some cooking to do. I still have a key to Kane's place. I think it's time I use it."

TWENTY-NINE

"Sullivan!" Simon Mayhew stepped into the room, clapping Kane on the back. "I would say good to see you, but that would be a lie. In fact, you look like shit."

"Thanks. Good to see you too, Simon." He gestured to the wet bar. "Want something to drink?"

Simon looked at him quizzically. "A little early to be hitting the sauce, don't you think?"

"No." Kane knocked back his Scotch, poured another. "Trying not to think actually."

"Who is she?"

"Who is who?"

"Cut the bullshit, Sullivan." Simon crossed to the bar, unscrewed a bottle of water, then began to fill the coffeepot. "The only reason for a man to do something completely out of character for him is when there's a woman involved, if not to blame."

"I don't know." Kane held up his glass, allowing the amber liquid to catch the light. "I think it's my own damn fault."

"So there is a woman?" Mayhew tore open a packet of coffee then started the brew.

"There's a woman." Kane took a seat at the table near the window that gave him a surprisingly clear view of Los Angeles. God, he hated this city. It was too busy, too crowded, too plastic. Nothing like Crimson Bay. He was going to have to find something to like about LA, though. It was a real possibility that he was going to have to move for the sake of his career and his sanity.

"What's her name?" Simon asked quietly, putting a mug of black coffee in front of him.

"Nadia." Kane hesitated, then set the empty Scotch glass aside. Simon was his friend, had been a good friend for years. If he couldn't talk to Mayhew, he wouldn't be able to talk to anyone. "Nadia Spiceland."

Simon's brow wrinkled. "Why does that name sound familiar?"

Kane sighed. "A few years ago she had a cooking show called *Spice of Life*. Now she owns a café up in Crimson Bay. We've been dating the last couple of months."

"This is the relationship you said you were playing close to the vest?" Simon whistled. "You don't go for easy, do you?"

"Easy is boring."

"True, but there's also less chance of easy biting you in the ass." Simon's expression grew thoughtful. "Tragic what happened to her. It's nice to know she's bounced back from all her troubles, especially the scandal."

"Scandal? You mean the addiction to painkillers?"

"Oh, more went on with her than a prescription drug habit."

"What are you talking about?" Kane asked, frowning.

"You don't know?" Simon scrubbed his chin. "I can understand why she wouldn't want to tell you, but that's a major red flag. Especially since it's pretty common knowledge. She had to know you'd find out sooner or later."

"Find out what?"

"She was in a car accident with her manager, who was also her lover. They were both high as kites, and both were ejected from the car. She survived, he didn't."

"That's awful, but that's hardly a scandal," Kane pointed out.

"It is when you consider that her manager was married at the time, and allegedly left his pregnant wife for his young client. Rumor has it that she might have been driving, and they were arguing because he was going to leave her and go back to his wife. If I remember correctly, the accident reports show that the car left the road suddenly. They're saying she may have deliberately driven off the road."

"I don't believe that." He couldn't believe that. It sounded so unlike the Nadia that he knew it had to be completely ridiculous. "Who the hell is 'they' and why would anyone believe that? Just because it's salacious and people latch on to it, doesn't make it true."

"I'm just repeating what was reported at the time," Simon said, raising his hands in surrender. "Of course there was an investigation while she was in the hospital, but it proved inconclusive and she claimed that she couldn't remember what happened. Since it was his car, authorities decided he was driving, so Nadia wasn't charged with anything, and went into a drug treatment facility straight out of the hospital. That didn't stop the widow from suing her when she got out of rehab."

"She was sued?" It just didn't end.

"Wrongful death suit," Simon confirmed. "You know the burden of proof is lighter in those types of circumstances than in a criminal investigation. Still, the results were the same. There was no definite proof that Nadia was liable for her manager's death."

Kane sat back, floored. "I didn't know."

"She didn't tell you," Simon pointed out. "Why do you think that is?"

"Fuck." Realization slapped him in the face. "She tried. She tried several times to tell me everything about her past, but I kept brushing her off. I said it didn't matter."

He shoved his hands into his hair. "I told her that I didn't see her through that lens," he said. "I saw her as someone who came through that and lives on the other side of it. And when she kept pressing on about it, I accused her of using it as a crutch to keep us from growing closer."

"That's probably a good thing," Simon told him. "Some of those stories from back in the day make her out to be a generally unlikeable person. Where's there's smoke, there's usually a fire."

"Everything you're telling me is how she was, not how she is," Kane retorted. "You of all people know the effect drugs can have, considering how you had to deal with your mean drunk of a mother."

"You're right—I do know," Simon said tersely. "I know enough that I never want to deal with it again. How do you know she won't trip and relapse? Do you want to deal with that?"

"I don't know if she'll relapse. I don't know how I'll deal with it if it happens, but I've been reading some material from Narcotics Anonymous, talking to people with firsthand knowledge. All I can tell you is what I do know. I know she's been clean for more than four years. I know she's helping other people in recovery, opening her café to support groups when there weren't any gathering places in town. I know she has a huge support network of family and friends who love her and want her to succeed."

He stared out the window, not seeing the city outside. "More than anything else, I know she has a huge heart. I know her capacity to care, and receiving her compassion was the sweetest experience of my life."

"Sounds like you love her."

"I do." Without thought, he moved to the closet, grabbed his suitcase, and began stuffing his things into it.

"Going somewhere?" Simon asked, his smile all too smug.

"Don't you dare try to take credit for this."

"For what?"

"I'm going to go get my woman."

He caught the first flight back that he could get. Part of him wanted to immediately head to Nadia's place, to pound on her door and demand that she see him. The slightly more rational part of him said he should at least take a shower before trying to convince her to take another chance with him.

The aroma of something baking filled his hallway. The scent immediately reminded him of Nadia, of sugar and spice and how she made everything nice. Need pulled at him. Somehow he'd find a way to convince her that he was more than an addiction, that what they had could be better than good.

Stepping over his threshold he stopped short, blinking in disbelief. The smell of freshly baked sticky buns hit him square in the face. Someone was baking sticky buns in his kitchen? No, not someone.

"Nadia?"

She stepped into view, uncertainty bright in her eyes and a tentative smile on her lips. "Hi."

"You're here. In my house."

The smile faltered. "I wanted to talk to you. And I wanted to make you some sticky buns since you hadn't had any in a while." She wiped her hands on the towel she'd thrown over one shoulder. "I'm beginning to think this wasn't one of my better ideas, so I'll just head out as soon as I— *Oof!*"

He clutched her to him, burying his face into the crook of her neck, breathing in the scent of honey and vanilla and cinnamon that always seemed to cling to her. "Nadia. Nadia, baby, I'm sorry. I'm so sorry."

She clung to him just as fiercely, hot tears splashing on his neck. "I'm sorry too, Kaname."

It took several tries before he could loosen his grip. "I can't believe you're here. I wasn't scheduled to come back until tomorrow."

She scrubbed at her eyes. "You were on a trip?"

"I went to visit my parents, and I told them all about you. I also went to Los Angeles, to finish up my consulting work and sketch out the book series I told you about. I've also heard from a university that wants to expand their online coursework, and they want me to manage the program. I'd be able to work out of my home office. I told them I'd have to discuss it with my family. Then I had a nice heart-to-heart with the department head at Herscher."

"You're leaving?" she asked, dismay clear in her voice. "But your work at Herscher—"

"Isn't as important as you are," he said, cutting her off. "I'll survive without tenure if it comes to that, but I don't think it will. They need me more than I need them, and I let them know that you're going with me to every faculty-plus-one event they make me attend and I don't give a damn who has a problem with it."

"But Kaname . . ."

"I don't want to live without you, Nadia," he insisted, desperate to make her understand. "That night was a mistake from start to finish, because I handled it wrong. You tried to tell me, and I refused to listen. Honestly, I thought everyone would see you the way I see you—see the beautiful, successful woman that I fell in love with."

Nadia heard the words. He said them so easily, she couldn't believe it. Didn't dare believe it.

"I'm prepared to fight for you, Nadia Spiceland," he declared. "To do whatever it takes to convince you that I love you and want to be with you. To prove that what we have is not addiction, not obsession, but something precious and real and right."

Hope threatened to beat its way out of her chest, but she couldn't let it. Not yet. Not until he knew everything. She took his hand, pressed a kiss to his knuckles. "Kaname, I need to talk to you about what happened with me and Gary. Before anything else, you need to know what happened to me."

"You don't have to tell me anything you don't want to."

"I may not want to tell you, but I need to. I don't want anything else between us, okay?"

"Okay."

She guided him over the couch with its beautiful view of the bay. "I told you I wasn't a good person, before. I'm trying to be now, though. Some days are just harder than others." She looked away. "But you deserve to know everything that happened, everything I can remember. I don't want whatever you feel for me to be built on half-truths. It wouldn't be fair to you."

"All right, Nadia." He took her hand again. "You tell me what you want, how you want. I'm listening."

"I was young and stupid and naïve," she began. "I also connived and schemed and manipulated. No one could tell me anything, not even Gary, my manager. He was the one who got me hooked."

"Your manager got you addicted to drugs?"

She nodded. "The drugs Gary gave me only made it easier to be that person because the pills numbed everything else, even my judgment. They also made me more . . . susceptible to him. I did things for him, because of him that I never want to think about again. I was under his spell, a spell he deliberately wove. I thought I loved him. Instead it was an obsession, another addiction, because he was older and worldly and exciting and I needed the feeling I got from being with him. I trusted him, and because of that I gave him control of everything. He abused that trust. He abused me."

"God, Nadia." His hand tightened on hers.

"It was mostly mental, not physical. Not that it made a difference," she continued. "I never told anyone, not even my therapist. Siobhan didn't learn the truth until about two years ago. I dealt with it by taking more drugs to numb the pain of it, hoping to fill the hole that I didn't realize being with him had created inside me. Then one day I looked into the mirror, didn't like what I saw—didn't recognize who I saw—and I said enough."

"Good for you."

"It was the best day and the worst day. I got up the nerve to tell him it was over, that he was fired from my business, my life, my bed. He didn't take it very well. He said I wasn't going to be free of him that easily, then he drove us into a tree."

She heard his sharp intake of breath, felt the tightening of his fingers on hers. She couldn't look at him though. She didn't want to see his pity or his disgust. Or his regret that he'd given her words he wished he could take back.

Finally, he spoke. "Why did you never tell anyone the truth? You could have saved yourself a lot of heartache over the speculation."

"What would have been the point?" She shrugged, then sighed. "He was dead, I wasn't. On top of that, being in the hospital all that time started my detox. I knew it wasn't my fault, but it felt like it. It didn't matter what everybody else thought of me then because it couldn't have been worse than what I thought of myself."

She sat back, drained. "I got a second chance I felt I didn't deserve. Eventually life moved on, I got clean, and left LA to make sure I stayed that way. Another scandal happened as they usually do and people forgot about me. I was able to heal inside and out, and I finally got to the point where I was ready to try again, try being intimate again, and you were kind enough to offer to help."

She smiled at him, then sobered. "I thought if I could keep my emotions out of it, just keep it sexual and focused on the book, I would be able to handle it and not lose myself. I didn't count on you being different, so unlike any man I'd met before. I didn't count on feeling so safe and cared for so quickly. I wanted to tell you what had really happened with Gary so that you'd understand how important what we had was to me. You kept telling me how you saw me, how you thought of me, and I wanted so badly to be that person for you, because of you. A person who wasn't used, who wasn't treated like an object to exploit."

"Until the party." A tremble rolled through his voice as self-disgust crested his features. "Until I did everything you were afraid of."

"I know you didn't intend it to come off that way, but that's how I felt. Any other day, sex in a supply closet would have been hot. I would have gotten off on thumbing our noses at your uppity colleagues who wished they were having sex like that on the regular. But that day?"

She shook her head slowly as tears pricked her eyes. "I was worried about being a deterrent to you. I was worried about how your coworkers would react when they learned about me. And I worried about why you wanted me to go with you to the party. I felt like an ornament instead of your date, a pretty trinket on display doing whatever you wanted. Some women are okay doing that, but I'm not one of them. I felt like my bad choices were coming back to haunt me. I couldn't let that happen, Kaname. I had to do something about it."

"You had to dump me. I didn't understand it then, but I do now."

"Do you?" she asked, hope making her voice crack.

"Not completely, but I'm trying. I've been talking to your parents and to Siobhan." He flashed a rueful smile. "Actually I endured a verbal beat down from Nicholas and had to grovel to Siobhan. She gave me some materials from Narcotics Anonymous to read up on, and I think your dads might actually tolerate me now."

He wrapped both hands around hers, kissing her knuckles. "I'm learning, Nadia, but I need a teacher. There's only one person I want to fill the position."

She swallowed the lump in her throat, wanting to say yes, needing to say yes to this man, this wonderful man who was trying because he wanted her, really wanted her, warts and all. "I know I've got issues, but I want to try, Kaname. I want to try with you, if you'll let me."

"Shh." He loosened his hold on her hand to brush her tears away. "I don't want you to try with me, Nadia," he whispered. "I just want you to be, with me. Say yes, and we'll make it through together."

"Are you sure you want to do this, Kaname?" she asked. "Not out of guilt or some misplaced sense of feeling like you owe me."

He looked down at her, his midnight eyes soft, tender. "I want to do this. Would you like to know why?"

"I-I think so."

"Because I love you, Nadia Spiceland. Not some ideal you that lives in my head, not the Los Angeles you who starred on television. I love the you that you were, the you that you are, and the you that you will be. I love the survivor, the fighter, the beautiful woman with the ugly cries. I want to walk with you through this, and when you're ready, I want us to finish our walk through the *Garden*. No matter what, I want us to be together. I'm not expecting it to be easy, but nothing worth having ever is. As long as I know there's a chance that you'll fall in love with me, I'll be a happy man."

"Then be happy," Nadia said. "But I'd like to add one condition."

"Name it."

"I want your ramen recipe."

He smiled at her. "A lot of love goes into making the family ramen. Do you think you can handle that?"

"I think I'm willing to prove that I have what it takes, including love," she answered, grinning widely. "Especially love for a certain sexy professor. It *is* the spice of life, you know."

"Then it's good that I happen to have a thing for spice."

AUTHOR'S NOTE

The Perfumed Garden of Sensual Delights is an Arabic treatise on sex written by Sheik Nafzawi in the early part of the sixteenth century. It is a combination of tales and instructions on how to get the most from that most intimate of actions. French soldiers translated the short guide in the early part of the nineteenth century, then Sir Richard Burton created a highly embellished version for his Kama Shastra Society in 1886.

ABOUT THE AUTHOR

Seressia Glass is an award-winning author of more than twenty contemporary and paranormal romance and urban fantasy stories. She returns to contemporary romance with the sexy Sugar and Spice series. She lives north of Atlanta with her guitar-wielding husband and two attack poodles. When not writing, she spends her free time people-watching, belly dancing, watching anime, and feeding her jewelry addiction. Visit her website at seressia.com.